"Rusty and Dusty don't got no mom and I don't got no dad."

Melody took a deep breath. "So, Mom—we could be a family!"

"Oh, no!" Lizbeth gasped. "Melody, baby, you can't just pick up stray people like you do kittens and make them part of your family."

"Why not?" A tear caught in thick lashes, then trickled down a round cheek.

"Well, because...because..." Liz sighed. "Because you can't. And whatever you do, promise me you'll never bring up this subject with Mr. Spencer or his sons."

"But how will they ever think of it on their own? They're *boys* and—"

"*Never*, Melody. Is that understood?"

"O-kay. But will you make enough sandwiches for them? And take the rest of the cupcakes. Please, Mom."

"Melody Lorraine. I can see the wheels turning. You will not lure the Spencers with food. Where on earth are you getting this nonsense? Certainly not from me." Liz threw up her hands. "I want to make sure you know I'm dead serious about this, Mel."

"All right. But jeez!" Melody slid off her pony and plunked down on the porch steps, chin in hand, to wait for the Spencers.

Dear Reader,

Trouble at Lone Spur is a composite of several story ideas that finally jelled into one. I've wanted to set a story in the wide-open spaces of west Texas ever since I discovered that this sometimes harsh, arid land casts a lasting spell. And so do the men who work it! Cowboys—who can resist 'em?

Gil came to me in a flash. A bone-weary rancher who'd inherited a run-down ranch called the Lone Spur. A man left to raise his unruly twin sons alone. I knew those twins; I baby-sat them in another life. Believe me, Gil needed a strong helpmate!

I found Lizbeth in my bottom drawer, along with an article I'd clipped from *Western Horseman* about a female farrier. The article was sketchy, my notes on Lizbeth brief. She was pretty and petite and she was married to a grand national bull-riding champion. A nice guy who was also a good-looking hunk. In my original version of Liz, she and this husband of hers had a sweet young daughter. Wow, talk about problems. Gil needs Lizbeth desperately, and she already has a man in her life! Plus trouble of her own. Stapled to Lizbeth's file were clippings and news stories about children who'd fallen in abandoned wells. More specifically, I'd played around with the idea of what would happen to Lizbeth's marriage if her daughter tumbled into a well while she was off shoeing horses. But I couldn't ask Gil to wait around for her to work through all that. So...I made Liz a widow. Let the trouble at Lone Spur begin!

As you'll see, a finished book rarely ends up the way it starts. For all readers who, over the past few years, have written and asked how I come up with story ideas—I give you *Trouble at Lone Spur*. My secret is out, but I hope that doesn't mean you'll stop writing to me.

Roz Denny Fox

P.O. Box 17480-101
Tucson, Arizona 85701

Roz Denny Fox

TROUBLE AT LONE SPUR

Harlequin Books

TORONTO • NEW YORK • LONDON
AMSTERDAM • PARIS • SYDNEY • HAMBURG
STOCKHOLM • ATHENS • TOKYO • MILAN
MADRID • WARSAW • BUDAPEST • AUCKLAND

ISBN 0-373-70716-9

TROUBLE AT LONE SPUR

Copyright © 1996 by Rosaline Fox.

Printed in U.S.A.

Thanks to my former critique partners in San Angelo, Texas—Ken, Jan, Barbara, Janet and Linda—for helping me fine-tune Gil and Lizbeth's story. Mary, thanks for all the horsey info. Humble thanks to the patient farrier who answered endless questions about shoeing horses. He prefers to remain anonymous—a macho thing, I guess. And finally, thanks to Ken Hoogson for sharing his first-hand experience with mine and well rescues.

CHAPTER ONE

IN THE TWO WEEKS since Lizbeth Robbins had hired on as farrier at Gilman Spencer's ranch, she hadn't laid eyes on the man. The Lone Spur, situated in a sparsely populated corner of Crockett County, Texas, was a quarter-horse operation—and badly in need of her services. But if Spencer's name hadn't appeared on the sign at the entry gate, she might well have believed that her elusive boss was a phantom. Not that Liz cared whether she ever met the Lone Spur's head honcho. She'd already formed her opinions.

From all she'd gleaned listening to Rafe Padilla, the ranch foreman, it sounded as if Spencer was a hard-headed perfectionist who didn't give second chances. She suspected he was ill-mannered, to boot. That notion had come to Liz through personal dealings with his ornery-as-sin nine-year-old twin sons. Last night's debacle cinched it.

While today she could laugh about the incident, it hadn't seemed funny then. She'd been in her grubbiest clothes, hanging stubborn wallpaper in her minuscule bathroom, when all at once, in waltzed this cowboy dandy, a total stranger, claiming he'd come for the candlelit dinner Liz had promised in the note she'd sent him.

Of course, Melody shouldn't have let a stranger in the house. But apparently her six-year-old daughter was dazzled by the Chaps cologne that rose around the cowboy like a cloud. Darned stuff made Liz sneeze. The Lone Spur's biggest Don Juan wasn't happy when she'd ushered him out, suggesting someone had played a trick on him.

Turned out the trick was on her. Liz knew it the moment Rusty and Dusty Spencer tumbled off her porch in sidesplitting giggles. Cowboy Macy Rydell got the message then, too. Even though he should have figured it out from the crudely written note—on wide-ruled tablet paper, no less.

Liz caught the twins and threatened to tell their dad. It didn't faze the little punks. She was normally even-tempered with kids, but this prank had been one too many in a string of antics those miniature con artists had pulled. Obviously trying to run her off the ranch. But Liz needed this job. Gilman Spencer's twins would find out she didn't run easily. No siree-bob!

Liz kicked dirt from her low-heeled Ropers and climbed two rungs up on the corral fence to study the magnificent blood-bay stallion three wranglers had just brought in. She doubted it took three men to handle the animal, but Spencer's hands had been riding in off the range all week to get a look at her. Liz found that amusing. Women must be in short supply on the Lone Spur.

"Aren't you a beauty?" she breathed, her eyes leaving the horse only long enough to locate his name on the clipboard she carried. This was Night Fire, the registered stud Spencer bred with his sand-colored mares to sire the beautiful buckskin quarter horses that made the Lone Spur a power in the breeding industry.

Liz put a check beside the stallion's name. She smiled as her gaze skipped back to admire his long legs and deep chest. "Ah, yes. Night Fire. The name suits you. I'd guess you're a hot lover."

As if concurring with her assessment of his prowess, the horse reared and pawed the air. Liz read the overt challenge in his sable eyes, but she didn't rush to meet it. Instead, she laid the clipboard aside and climbed atop the fence—to let the stallion grow comfortable with her presence and her smell.

She wouldn't actually shoe the stud, only trim his hooves and check for disease. According to the ranch foreman, Night Fire had been favoring his left hind foot—probably an indication that the horn had grown rough and uncomfortable.

Liz snapped off a piece of grass to chew. She loved the way the morning sun caught fire in the stallion's crimson coat. It was easy to see why his offspring were in constant demand.

First day here, she'd heard rumors that her predecessor had been fired over this animal. Liz didn't intend to make mistakes with him—or any of the others. This job was her chance to quit trailing the rodeo from one end of the Southwest to the other. Her chance to provide Melody with roots. Nibbling thoughtfully on the straw, Liz recalled a time when she hadn't minded the rodeo circuit. When love was young and Corbett was alive.

But things changed.

Redirecting her attention to the stallion, Liz tossed the straw aside. It was better not to dwell on the past. It stirred memories of a time when she'd been alone, pregnant, crippled by grief and debt. Thanks to old Hoot Bell, a kindly soul who'd left horseshoeing to follow his lifelong dream of being a rodeo clown, Liz had learned a usable trade. And now, she finally felt strong enough to make a bid for independence—and a permanent home. Working for Gil Spencer meant her child could attend first grade at one school for the entire year. Kindergarten had been a hit-and-miss affair mixed with whatever home schooling Liz could manage between towns.

As she took the first step to coax the wary stallion closer, Liz considered again how nicely things had fallen into place. She knew for a fact that only the biggest outfits could afford to hire a full-time farrier, let alone provide accommodation. Sagging porch and all, the cottage seemed like a castle compared to the tiny camp trailer she and Melody had shared. And the rural school bus already stopped here for the Spencer twins. Yes, life at the Lone Spur was pretty much perfect.

Liz experienced a moment's thrill as the stallion trotted up to sniff her hand. Yup, she'd do whatever it took to please Mister do-it-right-or-get-canned Spencer. She and Melody *needed* the Lone Spur. And if they stayed here, she might be able to conquer another problem, too. These past two weeks she'd had fewer nightmares, fewer bouts with claustrophobia—annoying conditions that had plagued her since Corbett's death.

Liz gave herself a hard mental shake and met Night Fire's liquid gaze. "If you knew us," she murmured, "you'd see the changes in Melody. She's crazy about her teacher and loves having friends. Let's not screw it up, huh, buddy?"

Liz dropped off the fence and slowly made her way back to her pickup to get the tools she'd need to clean and polish Night Fire's hooves. He might have caused her predecessor's downfall, but no mere horse was going to ruin things for Melody. Not if Lizbeth could help it.

The big horse kicked up his heels and circled the enclosure like a frisky colt. Liz eyed him, her thoughts again shifting to his owner. Gil Spencer wanted things done by the book, so that was how she'd do them.

Night Fire whickered, tossed his head and teased her, skittering away. "Easy, boy." Having donned chaps and pliable gloves, she quickly boxed him in and bent to pick up his back hoof. "Oh, oh!" He had extremely dry feet. Someone—the previous farrier, Liz supposed—had rasped too close and destroyed the natural varnish. "Darn. What now?" She climbed out of the pen and reached automatically for her heavy leather apron. She'd have to shoe him, after all, then really soak those feet.

Given the rumors surrounding the horse, Liz checked in the barn to see if Rafe Padilla was available to discuss treatment. He wasn't. Obviously he'd already taken the load of yearlings to market. Liz sighed. She had no choice. And with any other horse, any other owner, she wouldn't have questioned her decision.

Resolute, she fired up her forge. Her thoughts turned once more to the absent Spencer. In observing his sons, she'd formed a mental picture of dear old dad. Not too tall. Stocky. Mid to late forties. The lucky stiff had inherited this gorgeous ranch; so, most likely, would his sons. That fact alone probably contributed to their cockiness. There was no Mrs. Spencer. At least not living on the ranch. Liz had some definite ideas about that, too.

Flame ready at last, she closed the gap between herself and the jumpy stallion. Even though this change in plans put her behind, Liz took time to stroke his neck before she started to work. The horse relaxed ever so slightly and nuzzled the bare flesh below Liz's short dark curls. She hunched her shoulder and laughed as his breath tickled her ear. "Aren't you the charmer," she crooned. "Pity you don't give lessons." Liz was plain peeved to think the twins didn't like her. She'd gotten on well with all the kids who hung out at rodeos. Another strike against Dad—and Ben Jones, the grouchy old ex-cowboy who served as Spencer's houseman. Now, that man was a caution.

Shrugging, she bent to the task at hand. She slid her palm down the horse's leg, then gently bumped his side so that he'd shift his bulk and allow her to lift his foot. "So far," she muttered against Night Fire's side, "the boys tolerate Melody. If I ever see that they don't, I tell you they've swiped the last chocolate-chip cookie from *my* jar."

Keeping up a tranquilizing flow of conversation, Liz slowly and carefully trimmed the stallion's heels. "Whoa, boy." She fitted the cooled shoes, reheated and reshaped them until they were exact. "I guarantee these won't cramp your style with the ladies."

Night Fire whiffled uneasily as she got out her ruler to measure his front feet.

Tailoring shoes took time and was hot tedious work. By the time Liz had molded them to her liking, the only thing on her mind was nailing them home, then breaking for a tall glass of cold lemonade.

Lunch was definitely out. Rafe had said he needed her in the east pasture this afternoon to reshoe three geldings who'd thrown shoes during roundup. Liz doubted she'd finish today, especially since she had to meet Melody's school bus at three-thirty. Pulling old shoes and checking for any sign of hoof disease simply couldn't be rushed. Meticulous as she'd heard Spencer was, Liz was equally so.

Suddenly, when she was almost done, Night Fire began to fight her. "Whoa, fella, what's wrong?" Loosening the tie rope, Liz played it out.

As the powerful horse reared and rose above her, Liz saw the problem. A cowboy—a drifter by the look of him—limped down the lane leading a mare, whose scent was all it took to drive Night Fire wild.

Liz fought back simmering anger. Dolt! Couldn't he see the stallion?

GIL SPENCER'S SIGHTS were set on getting home. About a mile out, Shady Lady had stepped in a prairie-dog hole, thrown a shoe and pulled up lame. It was damned hot out, and Gil's boots weren't made for walking—no *real* cowboy's boots were. Late last night, he'd given the last water in his canteen to the mare. Right now, he was about as dry as a man could be.

And he was mad. For three days he'd been trailing a stock-killing cougar. Today he'd had the cat cornered. All at once the wily animal had escaped into a rock-strewn canyon, to hide in any one of a hundred caves. So he'd been in a foul mood even *before* Shady Lady's accident. Now all that interested Gil was getting shut of the heavy saddle he'd packed a mile and drinking the well dry. That, and showering off several layers of roundup grime. The very last thing Gilman Spencer dreamed he'd see when he hobbled toward the Lone Spur's main barn was some woman wrangling his most expensive stud.

Was she nuts?

Dropping the saddle and Shady Lady's reins, Gil forgot his exhaustion. His thoughts centered on getting the woman out of the corral in one piece and without a lawsuit. Unfortunately Gil also forgot that his bones were thirty-four years old, not nineteen, as he vaulted the fence. Landing much too hard, he fell. His legs buckled and his Stetson flew off, spooking Night Fire.

The stallion screamed and lashed out with the foot nearest Liz. Although his kick was negligible as kicks go, she wasn't expecting it, and she was thrown a good three feet across the corral—sunglasses one way, Liz the other. She landed smack on her backside in the hard-packed dirt.

Gil straightened and froze. His heart pounded, his legs quaked. Was she okay? Lord! Up close she was no bigger than a minute—and Night Fire stood sixteen hands. Gil dug deep for the wherewithal to race to the woman's side.

Too late to matter, Liz connected the man she'd seen in the lane with Night Fire's unprovoked attack. Furious, she leapt to her feet and dusted off her smarting rump. "You may dress like a cowboy," she shouted, "but you lack the brains the Almighty gave a gnat. Hasn't anyone ever told you not to sneak up on a farrier at work? And never, *never* surprise a person working in close quarters with a stallion." Liz shook a small fist under the unkempt offender's nose.

"Is that so?" Gil had heard about enough of the lady's lip.

"Who," he asked icily, "gave you permission to *be* in close quarters with that stud?" Flashing hazel eyes raked every scrawny inch of her before the man snatched up his Stetson and jammed it back on sweaty russet locks that needed a good trim.

"None of your beeswax." Liz didn't like the saddle bum's superior attitude. He wasn't the first man who'd presumed he could give the orders because she tackled what was deemed men's work. She'd met twice his arrogance on the rodeo circuit. But this man had no right taking his error out on her. "Rest assured I'm doing the job I've been hired to do," she snapped.

"Really? Who hired you?"

"God! So, take a hike." Liz stood her ground even though the stranger hovered over her. "Or better yet," she said, wrinkling her nose, "take a bath."

He didn't move. And that was when it dawned on Liz that this saddle tramp might have blown in from Spencer's roundup. Cursing her hot temper, she whirled to check on Night Fire. What if this know-it-all jerk carried tales back to his boss?

"Look, lady—" Gil clamped down on his anger "—I don't know who authorized you to shoe any horse of mine, let alone my prize stud, but I guaran-damn-tee this is your last job on the Lone Spur."

Liz turned back and let her eyes take a leisurely stroll from the top of his crusty Stetson to the tips of his run-down boots. Then she laughed. "*Your* horse? I've seen down-and-out bronc riders at the rodeo where I worked who looked more prosperous than you. I guaran-damn-tee Gilman Spencer'd know his prize stallion's hooves were split, and that without shoes and wet packs those feet will break down."

If her grating laughter hadn't been enough to make Gil see red, her jab about the rodeo definitely did. Nobody, but nobody, mentioned bronc riders in Gil Spencer's presence—not if they wanted to keep their teeth. Half the state of Texas had known before he did that his wife—now ex-wife—Ginger spent her nights in bronc rider Avery Amistad's bed.

The hurt went deeper than mere infidelity. Gil had needed Ginger's support while he worked his butt off pulling the Lone Spur out of the financial mess his father had left it in. But he'd been understanding about her desire to become a number-one barrel racer. So understanding that he'd hired Ben Jones to help care for their infant twins while his dear wife followed the rodeo.

No, Gil didn't like anything about rodeos.

Gil was furious at this woman for reminding him of humiliations he'd managed to suppress. But dammit, he thought, as he took a closer look at Night Fire's hooves, she *was* right about the splits.

As Liz watched the stranger run sure hands down the stallion's leg, a sick feeling began to grow in her stomach. "Rafe Padilla hired me two weeks ago," she stated firmly, assuming—hoping—that would straighten things out.

The woman now seemed subdued, a fact that cooled Gil's temper. Even supposing Rafe had hired her, Gil would never allow anyone connected to the rodeo to stay on his ranch. "If that's true," he sighed, "my beef is with Rafe. But it changes nothing. Stow your gear and be on your way." He glanced away as huge brown eyes blinked up at him, then retreated into blankness again.

Liz's brain stalled. She saw all her hopes, all her dreams for Melody, slipping away.

"I see you still doubt who's giving you your walking papers," the man said harshly. "Here's my driver's license." He pulled a plastic sleeve out of his wallet and sailed it toward her. It plopped at her feet, kicking up a tiny cloud of dust.

Night Fire reared again and pawed the ground. Liz scooped the plastic out of the dirt before climbing through the rails. A terrible crushing weight trapped the air in her lungs as she scanned the picture of a ruggedly handsome clean-shaven man who bore scant resemblance to this scruffy cowpoke. Except for maybe the cool hazel eyes that could freeze a woman's soul. And the name, Gilman Spencer, that leapt off the paper to taunt her.

Liz tried to speak. The words stuck in her throat. Shaking her head, she handed back his license. "I don't understand," she stammered. "The friend who recommended me set it up with Mr. Padilla, but I assumed *you* had hired me." If only she'd asked Hoot more about Spencer. Not that he'd have said anything, closed-mouthed as he was.

Gil jammed his license into his wallet and returned the worn leather case to his back pocket. "*If* I hired women on the Lone Spur, *which I don't* because they distract my wranglers, I most assuredly wouldn't hire a rodeo groupie."

"I beg your pardon." Liz drew herself straight up. Even then the top of her head barely reached his shirt pocket. "Rafe told Hoot Bell—that's my friend—that you were desperate for a good farrier. I *am* that, Mr. Spencer. And for your information, I *am not* a rodeo groupie. I shoe horses as well as any man alive. Better than most."

"Not on the Lone Spur. I'm not that desperate."

"Really?" Liz arched a brow. "Wasn't it a *man* you fired? Padilla probably thought you wanted the shoeing done right this time."

A muscle twitched along Gil's cheek. "Look," he muttered, "I've had a hell of a day—three in a row if you want to get technical. I'm not up to sparring, Miss—"

"*Mrs.*," Liz supplied. "*Mrs.* Corbett Robbins. Lizbeth. You may not believe this, but I usually get along with everyone—" Liz broke off. She'd be darned if she'd grovel. If he had an ounce of decency, he'd have told her up front who he was.

Gil frowned. "Corbett Robbins? The name rings a bell." The frown deepened. "I knew someone once who spouted rodeo stats. Robbins—isn't he national bull-riding champion?''

"Was," she whispered, eyes unexpectedly misting. "Corbett *was* champion. It's been awhile." Spencer's blunt statement hurled memories at Liz, the kind of memories that normally woke her out of a sound sleep. But in the dead of night she had time to conquer her demons, even if she'd never truly forget the horror of watching her husband die in that narrow chute. Some made allowances because she'd been eight months pregnant. Not Liz. She knew that if she'd thrown her jacket, instead of freezing to the bench, she might have distracted the bull and saved Corbett's life.

"I see," Gil sneered. "Old Corbett lost a few purses, so you left him for greener pastures. Well, not on my ranch, sister."

Liz stared vacantly at the man whose bitter accusation broke into her private reverie. Her fingers dug into her thighs as the old pain rocked her heart.

Night Fire whistled and kicked over her shoeing box. The clank of metal jerked Liz fully back to the present. "Corbett was trying to beat his record in Houston—and he drew a rank bull. It was his last ride. Ever. *Not* that my personal life is any of your business, Mr. Spencer. I hired on at the Lone Spur to shoe horses."

"You're quite right about the first part, Mrs. Robbins," Gil said stiffly. Although something in her quiet dignity tweaked his jaded conscience. Not enough to make him relent, but enough to niggle. "I'm, ah, sorry about your husband. I'll give you till, say, three o'clock to vacate the premises?"

He squinted up at the sun as if calculating the time. Indeed Liz saw that he didn't wear a watch. She didn't know why she found such an insignificant fact intriguing, unless it was because she assumed all men who built empires like the Lone Spur were slaves to the ticking of a clock. Especially men like Gil Spencer. Men like her father. The only difference between them was that one raised quarter horses in Texas, the other thoroughbreds in Kentucky. Her attention snapped back to what he was saying.

"... and it'll take me at least that long to make myself human again. Maybe by then Night Fire will have calmed down enough to let me assess any damage you may have done. I think it'd be wise if you're gone by then. I'll deal with Rafe when he gets back."

Liz couldn't remember ever having the desire to hit anyone. Yet she'd have liked nothing better than to smack the arrogance right off this man's face. Instead of acting on that desire, she stripped off her heavy apron. "Three hours won't make you human, Mr. Spencer. But I wouldn't leave by then even if my daughter's school bus had arrived—which it won't. There remains a little matter of two weeks' pay. Not to mention that Padilla promised reimbursement for travel expenses and for the carpet and curtains I put in the cottage."

"Surely you don't expect me to believe Raphael let you shoe my stock for two whole weeks without telling me?"

Liz peeled off one glove and retrieved the clipboard that lay beside the corral. "I don't care what you believe. These," she said coolly, "are the horses I've shoed."

Gil's eyebrows rose to meet a tumble of mahogany curls. "Some of these are the most ill-tempered horses on the ranch."

"Like horse, like owner, I always say." Liz ripped off the second glove.

"Why, you're no bigger than a peanut. Frankly I don't believe you got within spitting distance of some of these corkers."

Liz cut in. "Horseshoeing isn't about size as much as know-how. Funny, I had a feeling I was being tested. Maybe Padilla had second thoughts and figured if one of those nags put me in the hospital, he wouldn't be raked over the coals for giving me a job."

Gil frowned at the list, then at her. "Look, my accountant has the ranch ledgers in town. And the ranch checkbook—for quarterly taxes."

"Things are tough all over, Mr. Spencer."

"I can't go get it this minute. I need some sleep. Besides, regular payday isn't for another two weeks."

"That's your problem." Liz left him standing while she systematically stored equipment in her pickup. The shock of meeting him was beginning to wear off. Suddenly she found despair crowding out the need to have him acknowledge her worth. All she'd wanted out of this job was a chance to give Melody a normal life. But she couldn't expect a man like Gil Spencer to understand.

She shot him a dark glance and was surprised to see he hadn't moved. In fact, he looked as if he'd been hit by a freight train. How had she missed the tired slump of those broad shoulders? Her glance slid away to his drooping black mare. At least she thought the horse still waiting in the lane was black. Her coat was almost too dirty to tell. Covertly Liz's eyes sought Spencer again. Darn, she didn't want to show him an ounce of compassion. He certainly had none when it came to her.

The horse, who stood so obediently, reins touching the ground, shifted to take the weight off a swollen leg in a way that drew Liz's trained eye. "Did the black throw a shoe?'' She sauntered over and ran a hand down the mare's leg before Gil could reply.

The pleasant feminine voice startled Gil from his stupor. He must be getting old. He'd missed sleep plenty of times, but he'd never forgotten to take care of his horse. Finding this woman working on his ranch had rattled him.

"Her leg needs icing,'' Liz said matter-of-factly.

Gil fancied a hint of accusation in her statement as he joined her. "I plan to call my vet.'' He edged her aside and stroked the mare's velvet nose, then picked up the reins and led his injured mount toward the barn.

Darn! Why couldn't she leave well enough alone? Yet no more than a second slipped by before Liz called, "Wait. I'll ice that leg and get a wrap on it while you catch forty winks.'' She caught up to Spencer easily. "Look at you. You're dead on your feet.'' Avoiding his eyes, she murmured, "A vet will shoot her full of cortisone.''

Gil swallowed the refusal that sprang to his lips. Getting by without cortisone would be his preference, too. To find this woman so astute surprised him. Her offer was tempting. So tempting he let her take the reins from his grasp. A light herbal fragrance penetrated the trail dust clogging Gil's nose. He stopped dead, feeling his too-empty stomach tighten. She smiled over her shoulder and the breath left his lungs.

It'd been seven years since Ginger moved out with her cases of powders and paints. With a pang, he wondered if his sons missed the sweet scents of womanhood as much as he did, or if they'd been too young to remember. Gil scowled; he didn't like the path his mind had started to wander. He jogged after the woman and snatched Shady Lady's reins without a word. Back stiff, he entered the dark barn, away from Lizbeth Robbins and the unwanted memories her presence triggered.

Vaguely hurt, she stayed outside. For a minute there, she'd detected a crack in Gil Spencer's tough exterior. A brief softening deep in the green-gold eyes. Perhaps it was worth pursuing. For Melody's sake, Liz didn't want to give up this job without a fight.

Inside, the barn was cool after the heat of the midday sun. She stood a moment to let her eyes adjust and to overcome the sudden choking claustrophobia darkness always brought. Her ears picked up a clank as Spencer heaved the heavy saddle over a rail. Liz gritted her teeth and moved toward the familiar sound.

Gil didn't have to see her to know the Robbins woman had followed him. Ignoring her, he began measuring feed into a trough. "You have unbelievable persistence. And you're wasting my time."

Her hands tightened into fists. To hell with him and his job. No one talked to her like that. "And you, Mr. Spencer, are unbelievably rude. Although I can't fathom why that should surprise me, considering your sons had to get their bad manners from *somewhere.*"

She spun on her low-heeled boots and would have left him had his right hand not shot out to stop her. For what seemed an eternity to Liz, his eyes blazed through the dim light and his fingers cut off the circulation in her upper arm. She would have jerked away if a fleeting something—pain, anxiety, vulnerability, whatever—hadn't crept into his eyes.

She pushed at his hand, anyway, not liking the shiver that wound up her spine.

"What about my sons?" he asked, releasing her the moment she struggled.

"Nothing." Liz truly regretted her childish retaliation. It was just that his arrogance made her so mad. Her temper was a weakness. Hoot always said it would be her downfall one day.

Gil massaged the back of his neck, then closed his eyes and smoothed a hand over gaunt cheeks ragged with a three-day beard. "Does it have anything to do with the meeting their teachers requested? Ben sent a note out to the roundup. I was headed in, but then I picked up the trail of a stock-killing cougar—" He broke off, opened his eyes a slit and sighed. Gil didn't know why he was spilling his guts to a stranger. He should be having this conversation with Benjamin Jones, considering how much he paid the retired cowboy to cook and keep a line on the twins in his absence.

"I shouldn't have said anything," Liz said quickly. "The job is important to me, okay? I was disappointed, that's all. I don't know about any meeting at school." She caught her lower lip between her teeth and glanced away from his tired eyes.

Gil silently observed the emotions crossing her delicate heart-shaped face. Outside, dressed in all that leather, she'd seemed small, but with it off she seemed . . . fragile. Feeling defensive, Gil turned back to the mare. He led her into a large stall with overhead refrigerated plumbing. He'd built it to deal with injuries to ligaments and tendons. As he uncoiled a hose, Gil said gruffly, "Rusty and Dusty don't like school much. Fall is hardest, after they've spent all summer out on the range with me. Going back means they miss roundup. Not that I'm excusing bad manners, mind you. But…out of curiosity, what did they do?"

If she hadn't been occupied inspecting his stall setup, Liz might not have answered with such honesty. She

hunkered down beside where he knelt to lend a hand with
the wrap and spoke without thinking. "You mean besides the snake in my bed? Or emptying my cookie jar on
more than one occasion and then denying it? Or when
they interrupted my work to claim their cat was caught in
a crevice? I went to investigate, got down on all fours
with my nose to the ground, and lo and behold, the furry
ball I reached in and grabbed turned out to be a skunk.
The devious little rats were quite disappointed to find out
I could run so fast. And that's what they pulled the *first*
week I was here."

Disbelieving at first, Gil did nothing while she finished the wrap. Then he reconsidered. "I'm sorry, Mrs.
Robbins. I'll speak with them and withhold their privi-
leges."

Liz secured the loose end and stood, but was thrown
off guard when she saw the troubled shadows lurking in
his eyes. "Hey, look, it's no big deal. Maybe it's because
I'm new and can't always tell them apart," she ventured. "Why don't you go grab some sleep? I really am
capable of keeping an eye on your horse."

Gil rose more slowly, hating to admit her offer held any
appeal. "My sons' behavior is always a big deal to me,
Mrs. Robbins." Dammit, he was disturbed by what she'd
said. Although he supposed there was a chance she was
lying to gain his sympathy. After all, she might have in-
vented these escapades for the sake of keeping her job.
And didn't he just know how deceitful women could be
when it suited their purposes?

"I'll square the Lone Spur's debt to you the minute
Rafe returns. Today. And the mare will be okay until the
boys get home from school. You'll need the time to
pack." Gil touched two fingers to his hat brim and with-

out waiting for a response left the barn through a side door.

Liz curled a hand into the mare's thick mane and gaped after him. Her mistake had been in believing he could be human. Tipping his hat had been out of habit, not courtesy, she decided. For a moment his brusque dismissal hurt more than she cared to acknowledge.

Then the mare nudged her, nibbling at her pocket. Liz got hold of her feelings and went in search of a feed bag. In the half hour it took the animal to eat and drink her fill, Liz rebuilt her defenses. She reminded herself that she had good health, skill in a marketable trade, and Melody. She didn't need anything from the likes of Gil Spencer.

Lizbeth Robbins was a survivor.

CHAPTER TWO

LIZ WASN'T ONE to cry over bad luck, and in her twenty-eight years she'd had plenty—estranged from her family at eighteen, widowed, broke and pregnant at twenty-two. Being tossed off the Lone Spur was a disappointment, but once she got the money she had coming, she and Melody would make do. Without it, they'd be stuck. Liz would be darned, though, if she'd let Gilman Spencer know she only had sixteen dollars to her name.

He said he'd pay her when Padilla returned. She'd watched Rafe load those yearlings, all full of jazz and spirit. The amount Spencer owed her wouldn't make a dent in the profit from Night Fire's offspring.

Liz made her way outside. She reminded herself that she still had to soak the stud's feet. She cast a glance back toward the barn, which she knew contained a stall with the requisite mud floor. But the stallion would tear up the place trying to get to Shady Lady if Liz took him inside. Although the treatment wouldn't be as effective, she'd flood a section of the small corral, instead.

After hunting up a shovel, she dug a shallow trench about four feet out from the fence. Next she carried buckets full of water until the ground was soft and muddy. Night Fire didn't much like it when she snubbed him to the top rail. He was used to running free. "Don't blame you, fella," she murmured in a soothing tone. "I'm not big on being confined, either." And that was putting it mildly. Never mind that now, she told herself. Just keep busy.

It had been her intention, even after Spencer fired her, to shoe those saddle horses in the east pasture—to fulfill her contract with Rafe. She was shocked to look up from looping the last knot in Night Fire's lariat and see the school bus rumbling down the lane. Goodness, it was later than she realized. So, she thought with a pang, her successor, whoever he might be, would shoe the horses from the remuda—the group of ranch-owned horses the cowboys used during roundup. There wasn't a doubt in Liz's mind that her replacement would be a *he*.

The Spencer twins ran pell-mell toward her. She couldn't tell them apart. Each had a chipped front tooth, as well. "Hold it, guys." She stepped from the corral and snagged the closest boy's arm. "I've got a jumpy stallion here. Don't scare him."

"Okay." Speaking in unison, they skidded to a halt, matching plaid shirttails flapping around their knees. Ornery they might be, but someone had taught them a healthy respect for horses. Liz was thankful for that. The boys respected Melody, even though she was a girl, on the basis of her riding skills.

Liz smiled wryly. Melody could be tough when she wanted or a demure young lady—like now. She walked sedately down the lane, her clothes spotless compared to the mess the boys' outfits were in.

"Why don'tcha use the mud stall?" asked one of the twins, wrinkling his face as he looked up at Liz and into the sun.

She turned from watching her daughter. "Your dad's mare went lame," she said offhandedly. "She's in the refrigerated stall."

"Dad's home?" The twin she'd pegged as Rusty let out a whoop and started for the barn. Spinning, he called back to his brother, "C'mon, Russ, get the lead out. We gotta catch Dad before Ben gives him those notes from our teachers, or he'll never let us help look for that ol' cat Rafe told us about."

"He's gone to take a nap," Liz called, annoyed that she'd failed to identify them again. The two nine-year-olds were like matched bookends with their auburn hair, freckled noses and cleft chins. They did resemble their dad, except that his eyes were hazel to their green, and his hair a darker richer red. The boys' faces were rounder than his. Gil Spencer was taller, leaner—and younger—than Liz had pictured. If he had a cleft in his chin, it was hidden today by stubble. But she could imagine him with one.

She found herself speculating what the boys' mother looked like. Not that it mattered. The Spencers were nothing to her now. What should be at the top of her agenda was finding a way to break the news of their imminent departure to Melody. A sadness crept in, leaving Liz drained.

"Mom, wait'll you see what I got in my book bag." Melody hopped in circles. The red bow that held the girl's dark ponytail flapped like a bird in flight.

Liz loved seeing sparks of excitement lighting eyes that had been somber for too much of Melody's young life. But now... She got hold of herself. "Um, let me guess." She eyed the bulging bag. "Not a kitten. Tell me you didn't rescue another stray." She pictured the bedraggled ball of fur that had joined their household last week. If they went back to following the rodeo, how could they keep a pet?

Melody giggled, a dimple flashing in her cheek. "Not a kitten. We went to the liberry today. Miss Woodson let me check out *three* books."

Something about the number was obviously significant to her daughter, but Liz's thoughts had skipped ahead. This was Friday. Rafe Padilla was due back soon; shortly thereafter they'd be gone. How on earth would she get books back to the school? Liz put a hand to her forehead. It all seemed horribly overwhelming.

"What's the matter, Mom? Two of the books are 'bout horses. I figured you'd like those. The other's all 'bout a mouse named Frederick. It's mostly pictures."

"Honey, it's not that..."

"Then what? Don'tcha feel good?" Melody slipped her small hand into her mother's larger one and gazed up anxiously. She'd always been a worrier.

Suddenly Liz didn't feel well. Not well at all. It made her positively sick to think about disappointing Melody. So she wouldn't. Not yet. Not until she saw Rafe drive in. "Why don't you go change out of your school clothes, sweetie? After I finish here, I'll shower and then we'll read one of the books. Deal?"

Melody's smile lit her face. "Can we do it before bed? After I change, I'm goin' to the barn—to see if the twins' dad is as neat as they said."

He's not, Liz wanted to scream. She didn't, however. What was the use? "I don't want you bothering Mr. Spencer, hon. He just got home from roundup and needs to rest. Why don't you saddle Babycakes," she suggested, referring to Melody's pony. "We'll treat ourselves to a short ride."

Liz couldn't afford to keep a horse for herself, but the pony didn't eat much. So far she'd managed to trade shoeing for his vet bills. Liz hoped she could again. But what if some other farrier had moved in on her old job with the rodeo?

Dispiritedly Liz watched Melody skip toward the cottage. Sometimes Liz wondered if her father had put a hex on her when she ran off to marry Corbett—not that she believed in such nonsense. But he'd threatened dire consequences if she left the farm and broke her mother's heart. Toliver Whitley's most redeeming trait was that he loved his wife to distraction. Otherwise he was a cold harsh man. He certainly hadn't cared about his *daughter's* heart.

Sighing, Liz went back to rewet the ground beneath Night Fire's hooves. She figured he'd been restrained enough for one day and was loosening his bonds when Melody hurried past the corral juggling two paper plates. "What have you got there?" Liz called.

"Oatmeal-raisin cookies for me and the twins."

"You'd better ask Mr. Jones if it's all right before you dole out sweets to the boys. Didn't you tell me Rusty said they never get cookies?"

"That's 'cause they don't have a mother. And Ben says he's too old to make cookies."

Liz released the stallion and coiled the lariat. "People don't get too old to make cookies, Melody. My grandmother baked them up to the day she died, at eighty," she said nostalgically. "Mr. Jones can't be sixty."

"More'n sixty. And his bones hurt bad. Dusty said he got throwed from a mean horse and had to quit bein' a cowboy. That's why he hates his job."

"Surely he didn't say that to the twins," Liz exclaimed. "Maybe Dusty just told you that to gain your sympathy."

Melody shrugged.

"Well, never mind. Run along." Liz knew she shouldn't encourage Melody to speculate about her friends. But if this was true, it might explain why the twins swiped cookies, engaged in pranks and generally lacked discipline. Did Gil Spencer know how his house-man felt? She recalled the rapier gaze that missed little and decided he must. Anyway, by this time tomorrow, she'd be too worried about where Melody's next meal was coming from to feel sorry for a couple of kids who'd been born into the luxury of the Lone Spur Ranch.

THE BARN DOOR squeaked as it slid open. Gil glanced tiredly over the tops of his sons' heads. The sunlight hurt his eyes. It seemed he'd no more than dozed off when the boys bounced into his bedroom. He'd decided to check on Shady Lady and was glad. She needed a vet.

Once his vision adjusted, Gil saw that a petite dark-haired girl stood in the sun filtering through the door's narrow opening. A pretty child, with huge chocolate brown eyes. Gil frowned. The eyes looked familiar, but he couldn't quite place where he'd seen them. It was rare for his sons to have visitors he didn't know.

The twins swiveled to see what had claimed their dad's attention. "Melody," they chorused. "Whazzat you got?" Rushing to meet her, they grabbed from the plates she held. "Cookies. Um, yum."

"Wait," she said, jerking the plates away. "You're s'pose to ask if it's okay to have some. My mom said to ask Mr. Jones but— Is that your dad?" she asked.

"'Course it's all right if we have cookies, dummy," said the twin holding the biggest fistful.

Gil stepped out of the stall, his frown deepening. "Russell David Spencer. I don't object to your having a treat, but I do object to your calling anyone a dummy.

Apologize." As he spoke, Gil recalled the new farrier's complaint about his sons, and he realized the girl watched him with the same wide velvety gaze as...Lizbeth—wasn't that the woman's name? Yes, and now he recalled she'd mentioned a daughter.

"Hello," he said, smiling down at the girl. "Russell," Gil prompted. "No apology, no cookie."

"Oh, Dad, she's just a *girl.*"

That statement drew an even sterner look from Gil.

Dustin, quicker on the uptake than his brother, jammed an elbow in his twin's ribs. "Rusty's sorry, Melody. Aren't you, nerd?" he hissed.

"Dustin, it's no better to call your brother names. What's with you guys all of a sudden? I don't have time to get to the bottom of this now, but tomorrow we're having a family caucus."

"Now you did it, ding-dong," Dusty muttered.

"Me? You're the one callin' me names," Rusty shot back.

Gil placed his thumb and little finger between his teeth and issued an earsplitting whistle. All three kids jumped. "Enough. Go inside and ask Ben for some milk to go with the cookies," he said firmly. "I have to call Dr. Shelton to see if he'll take a gander at Shady Lady's leg, then I'm going back up to bed. Do you think you can quit bickering long enough to let a man get forty winks?"

As if their heads were connected by a string, the kids nodded of one accord. The twins raced off. Melody hung back and offered Gil a cookie. "Your horse hurt its leg?" she asked after he'd accepted one and thanked her.

"She stepped in a hole." One-handed, Gil punched out a number on the telephone that hung on the barn wall. "Do you like horses? Blast," he muttered, glaring at the bleating phone. "Vet's line is still busy." Scowling, Gil downed the cookie in two bites.

"My mom'll help. She knows everything about a horse's feet and legs. Hoot said she knows more'n a vet."

Gil choked on a crumb. "Well, if Hoot's your mom's boyfriend, then he's probably biased." After he dusted off his mouth, he dialed again.

Melody rolled her eyes. "Hoot's not Mom's boyfriend. He's the best rodeo clown alive. Want another cookie? My mom made 'em. 'Course, her chocolate-chip ones are better. And her brownies. They're the *very* best."

Gil listened to the insistent busy signal, trying to recall how long it'd been since he last ate a homemade cookie of any kind. Maybe at his friend and fellow rancher Morris Littlefield's home. His wife, Nancy, took pity on Gil and the boys every few months and invited them to dinner. Mostly she served apple pie for dessert because it was the twins' favorite. Come to think of it, the last time he'd had cookies that didn't come from a package was at the June breeders' meeting. Madge Brennan had made coffee and passed around a plate of molasses cookies. He really wished he could say they were better than these, but he couldn't.

The girl passed the plate again, and Gil sampled another cookie. "These are pretty good," he mumbled. "Shouldn't you hurry on inside before the twins polish off the milk?" Her solemn stare unnerved him.

"You should go get my mom."

Before Gil could say he thought her mother was probably busy packing, the phone rang. He grabbed it up and was drawn into an unsatisfying conversation with his ranch foreman. The next thing Gil knew, the kid had disappeared. Just as well, considering he'd used some pretty colorful language. And not solely because the brakes went out on the ranch truck, leaving Rafe stranded in Abilene, either. Gil did his fair share of chewing Rafe's tail over hiring that woman.

God, what next? Gil wondered as he signed off with a sigh. Mrs. Robbins wouldn't get her money today. And maybe not tomorrow unless he made an unscheduled trip into town. Rafe said the service center had to send to Dallas for parts.

Hell, she should know the Lone Spur paid its bills. His dad had let things go, but not Gil. He'd go hunt her up and demand an address where he could mail her a check. Dammit, what was wrong with Doc Shelton's phone, anyway? Gil hung up, then headed for the door. If he didn't get some sleep soon, he'd drop in his tracks.

He'd just reached the double doors when one slid open and Gil found himself face-to-face with the woman he needed to see. A light floral scent replaced the more pungent barn smells. Gil froze midstride. Gone were the accoutrements of a farrier. She looked dainty as a new filly in worn but clean jeans and a sleeveless flowered blouse.

"Oh!" Liz leapt back. "Sorry." She placed a spontaneous hand on Gil's arm. "I wasn't expecting anyone to be here, except maybe my daughter." She peered around him, or at least tried. His broad shoulders filled the doorway. "Melody was supposed to saddle her pony. I thought we'd take a last ride to sort of shake out his kinks before stuffing him in a trailer. Rafe let me ride Starfire," she said, referring to a balky gelding. "Do you mind if I take him out one last time?"

When the man didn't speak but stared, instead, at the supple fingers resting on his long-sleeved shirt, Liz lifted her hand and snapped her fingers in front of his glazed eyes. "Mr. Spencer. Are you all right? Has something else happened to your mare?"

"Nothing," he croaked, stepping abruptly back. "I was on my way to find you. Rafe called a minute ago. He's had trouble with the truck and won't make it to the ranch for a couple of days. If you bank locally, I'll have my accountant deposit direct. If not, you'll have to tell me where to mail a check."

Liz braced herself against the door frame. Now she'd have to explain her ailing finances, no matter how embarrassing. "Uh, I haven't opened an account here yet. And I'm short on cash for gasoline. I'll have to wait until Rafe returns."

Gil's eyes narrowed. "How short? Don't you have credit cards?"

"I, ah, no." She felt her face getting red and toyed with the gold-plated chain Melody had given her last Mother's Day. She'd long since sold the two real ones she'd worn when she left her parents' home. Those and her wedding rings had bought the plot to bury Corbett. It had taken her until last year to pay off the casket.

Liz felt Gil Spencer's eyes following the movements of her hand. She stopped twisting the chain and hoped she'd washed away the green ring it sometimes left. She imagined the women he knew wore only high-grade silver and gold. Lizbeth Robbins didn't need expensive baubles, and tried to convey as much to the owner of the Lone Spur with a carefree up-thrust of her chin.

Gil was too close to running on empty to pick up on any of her fleeting emotions. He could barely keep his eyelids ajar. The flash of sunlight on her gold necklace made him light-headed. "We'll settle this in the morning, Mrs. Robbins. If I don't get some shut-eye, I'm gonna pass out."

To Liz's surprise, he brushed past her and stalked across the yard and up the steps to his house. She'd barely closed her mouth when Melody and the twins came tumbling out the door that had so recently swallowed Gilman Spencer.

"My dad said for us to keep quiet," one twin announced. "He wants us to ride over and get Doc Shelton for Shady Lady. Can Melody come along?"

The boys had never asked her permission for anything before. They just took what they wanted, often convincing Melody to join them. But today... well, what harm in letting Melody accompany them one last time? According to Rafe, the vet was located near the west end of the ranch. Maybe a half-hour ride away. It would give Liz time to do some preliminary packing. "Okay," she agreed. "No side trips, though. Stay on Lone Spur land and come straight home afterward. It'll be suppertime."

"Yuck," confided the twin who'd done all the talking so far. "Ben's fixing liver and onions. I hate liver."

"Me, too," said his brother, making a gagging sound.

Liz turned abruptly toward the cottage. Secretly she agreed, but it wouldn't do to let those little rapscallions see. Lord knew what they'd tell Mr. Jones. Not that it made any difference now.

Back inside the cottage, Liz didn't know where to start. In two weeks she'd scrubbed, painted, sewed curtains, put down rugs and made this place into a home. Unless Spencer's next farrier had a wife, she doubted the pastel paint and lace curtains would be appreciated. Yet to leave the floors and windows bare seemed petty. In the end she elected to leave everything behind, not wanting any reminders of her sojourn here. That decision made, her chore shrank considerably. Liz poured a glass of lemonade and went out to sit on the porch. No need to box things up until Rafe returned. Tonight she'd make Melody's favorite supper. Chicken and dumplings. With chocolate cupcakes for dessert. Later they'd read her library books.

The evening sky was streaked with what looked like layers of raspberry and orange sorbet by the time the children galloped into the yard. The cooled cupcakes were frosted, and plump dumplings simmered on top of thick chicken stew. As Liz stepped to the door, all three children slid off their mounts and talked at once. The gist was that the veterinarian's house had burned down. According to his neighbor, the doctor and his wife were staying at one of the hotels in town. The neighbor didn't know which one.

"Rusty and me gotta go tell Dad," one twin said as he tugged on his brother's arm. "He wanted Doc to fix Shady Lady. Now what'll he do?"

"Mom, you'll take care of her, won't you?" Melody asked earnestly.

Liz wiped sweaty palms down the sides of her jeans. "Oh, I don't know, hon. You know I'm not a vet."

"But Mr. Spencer said it's her leg. You know 'bout legs."

The children formed a ring at the bottom of the steps. Three pairs of eyes clung to Liz. She shrugged and tucked her hands into her front pockets. "Your dad was done in," she told the boys. "I'd hate to have you wake him needlessly. Tell you what, after supper, I'll take a look at the mare. If I think I can help her, I will. If not, I'll call around and try to locate Dr. Shelton."

One of the boys sniffed the air. "Something smells great."

Liz smiled. "Nothing special. Chicken and dumplings."

Melody's eyes danced. "Yippee!"

"You got 'nuff for me and Rusty?" one boy asked wistfully. The one Liz had thought *was* Rusty. Turned out she was wrong again.

"I have enough, but Mr. Jones—"

"—won't care!" whooped the twins together.

"But your father—"

"—said for us to be quiet," Rusty finished sagely.

"Please, Mom," Melody begged, prancing around on tiptoe. "We haven't had company for supper since we moved in."

Liz leveled a stern look at the boys. "We almost did," she said pointedly. "I mean Macy Rydell's surprise visit."

The twins had the grace to look guilty, but neither admitted a thing.

Liz threw up her hands. If Melody wanted company, how could she say no? They were just kids, after all— kids without a mother. Liz didn't know what had become of Mrs. Spencer, but young as they were, they must miss her. "All right." She gave in. "Bed the horses, then see if Mr. Jones agrees. Melody, you go with them to make sure he knows it's me doing the inviting." For a minute it was difficult to associate the eager little boys with the hellions who'd harassed her for two weeks.

Supper went off without a hitch, even though one of the boys—Dustin, Liz thought—picked the celery out of his chicken stew and piled it beside his plate, and the other fed the cat under the table even though she said not to.

The cupcakes were, of course, the biggest hit. Both boys gobbled them up and conned her into allowing them seconds. It seemed like a good opportunity to satisfy her curiosity about their mother, but Liz struck out flatly when she asked a discreet question. Immediately thereafter, one twin spilled his milk. It was so quick on the heels of her query, Liz wondered if he'd done it on purpose. She cleaned up the mess without comment, and a few minutes later, when the boys insisted it was time to leave, she offered to walk them home.

"Boys ain't a-scared of the dark," one twin declared brashly.

Liz still trailed them to the door. "I'll look in on the mare," she promised, lingering on the porch until she saw they'd reached home safely. Not wanting to leave Melody alone, Liz suggested she don her pajamas and bring a library book to the barn.

Turned out it was a smart move. Shady Lady had managed to get twisted in the sling. Cold water no longer ran on her injured limb. Liz spent forty minutes loosening the sling and turning the horse. By the time she finished, Melody was asleep in a pile of fresh straw. Liz felt bad about not reading to her. She stroked a hand through Melody's bangs and wondered if the Spencer twins would remember the cupcakes long enough to grant her the favor of returning the books to school on Monday.

Near midnight Liz thought the mare's leg looked a little better. She had dug through the supply cabinets and found two ingredients, liniment and DMSO, an anti-inflammatory salve. Some vets eschewed using either or both. In the past she'd had some success mixing the two. Her father always stressed trying homeopathic methods before using steroids. On that they agreed.

Melody slept on, and Liz lost track of time as she alternated the applications with ice packs.

GIL AWOKE with a start and looked at the clock—2:00 a.m? He still lay naked and crosswise on his king-size bed. The last thing he recollected was toweling off after he'd showered and shaved. All at once Gil remembered Shady Lady. He grabbed the clock and shook it. Was that the right time? He'd sent the twins for the vet. Why hadn't someone come for him when Doc Shelton arrived?

Bolting off the bed, Gil searched his closet in the dark for a clean pair of jeans. He jerked them on, tugged on his boots, then hurried from his room and down the stairs, stopping at the second level to check on the boys. The pair were sleeping soundly in their bunk beds. The ranch house was big enough so each could have had a separate room, but every time he suggested it, they declined.

Smiling at the way Dustin slept with his rump in the air and Rusty lay curled around a raggedy stuffed dog, Gil backed out, closed the door and smothered a yawn. The teachers separated them at school, claiming that otherwise they couldn't tell the boys apart. Gil didn't understand that. He had no trouble. Dustin did everything with a swagger, sort of like his great-grandfather Spencer. That kid was a leader, a mover and a shaker. Lately, more of an instigator.

Gil paused on the landing to glance back at the closed door. Sobered, he headed down the next flight. Russell, now, was a thinker. A cuddler. He was also a follower, which worried Gil. He wished he had more free time to spend with his sons. Ben Jones, by his own admission, was slowing down. The boys needed someone caring yet energetic. A tall order.

Gil couldn't say why, when he stepped outside into the moonlight, his gaze strayed to the cottage snuggled beneath the live oaks—the ranch farrier's cottage. *She* fairly oozed energy. Clattering disgustedly down the steps, Gil jogged to the back door of the barn. He counted on the crisp night air to clear his head. He'd pretty well succeeded in shaking out the cobwebs when he burst through the barn's side door and tripped over the woman who muddied his thoughts.

"Oof!" Liz let out a muffled scream as she fell. She'd taken Shady Lady out of her stall and they'd ambled the length of the barn. She was bent over checking the mare's sore leg when a shadowy hulk barreled through the door, knocking her flat.

Gil grabbed for her and missed. His momentum toppled both of them to the hard-packed earthen floor. He sprawled over her, as yet unable to get his bearings.

She landed an elbow in his diaphragm, stealing his wind.

"Get off me." Instinct prompted her wild struggle. For a second Liz feared Macy Rydell had decided to take revenge for the twins' practical joke. It dawned slowly that she didn't smell Rydell's strong cologne; the warm skin pressed against her nose exuded the subtle scent of spruce.

Liz lay still, breathing deeply. It was silly to be attracted or repelled by a man's cologne, but from the first day she'd met Corbett, she'd been drawn by his clean scent of heather and sea breeze. When good memories sneaked in like this, Liz still had problems accepting the unfairness of Corbett's early death.

Her sudden quiescence allowed Gil time to scramble up. "What in hell are you doing in my barn at this hour?" he demanded, extending her a hand.

The warm feelings evaporated instantly. "Not stealing your horse, if that's what's running through your mind." She batted his hand aside and climbed to her feet unaided. "Twice we've met, Mr. Spencer, and twice I've bruised more than my pride. Haven't you ever heard of a handshake?''

Gil ignored her sarcasm. He'd bent to examine Shady Lady's trim ankles. It was difficult to tell which leg had been injured. "So, were you here when Doc Shelton came by? I thought the boys would wake me."

"Your vet had a house fire. According to the kids, he's temporarily moved his practice into town. His neighbor didn't know exactly where."

"Then the ice water did the trick. Guess that leg wasn't as bad as I thought."

Liz debated whether or not to mention her home remedy, and decided he needed to know. "I popped in here after supper. Your horse had managed to twist herself up in the sling. I rummaged around and found cold packs, then alternated them with a topical mixture my dad used on his thoroughbreds. I was just walking her, to see if the swelling stayed down."

Frowning, Gil ran a hand through his sleep-tousled hair.

Liz's eyes followed the play of muscles down his arm and chest. She'd assumed, because of the long-sleeved shirt he'd worn earlier, that the skin beneath would be pale. In fact, his tan was the color of Kentucky bourbon and covered every inch of his flesh she could see. And that was quite a few inches. No farmer's tan for Gilman Spencer. He bronzed nicely for someone with so much red in his hair. Liz studied his body with open appreciation.

Gil noticed. He ran a self-conscious hand over his bare chest. "Sorry if I offend your Southern sensibilities. I didn't expect to find ladies in my barn at this hour—except the equine variety."

Liz didn't flush or look away. "Who says I'm Southern?"

Gil crossed his arms and laughed. "You have that drawl, Miss Scarlett."

Whirling, Liz led Shady Lady to an empty stall she'd spread deep with sand and sawdust, then covered with fresh hay. "I was born and raised in bluegrass country. We don't consider ourselves Southern."

"That's right," he said lightly as he followed her. "You said your daddy raises thoroughbreds. So why aren't you home in Kentucky shoeing *his* horses?"

Liz felt a knife blade slide into her heart. How had their conversation taken this turn? Corbett and Hoot Bell were the only two people who knew about her permanent estrangement from her parents. Melody had never asked about grandparents or her lack thereof. Liz wanted to keep it that way. The poor kid had enough strikes against her having never known her father. Patting Shady Lady's silky nose one last time, she backed out of the stall and quietly closed the door. "I've left the mixture for her leg in the fridge. You should use it liberally two or three times a day until the swelling's completely gone. And don't ride her for a week. But I'm sure you know that." Liz strode briskly through the barn, stopping where Melody lay asleep in the hay.

Gil wondered at being so rattled by Lizbeth Robbins that he hadn't seen the child until now. He was even more puzzled by the woman's curt response.

"Wait," he called as she bent and slid her hands beneath the girl. "You aren't going to carry her, are you? She must weigh fifty pounds."

"Forty-four," Liz replied. "And I'm quite capable, Mr. Spencer."

Gil didn't know why it grated on his nerves when she said "Mr. Spencer" in that tone, but it did. "I'll take her," he offered politely, refraining from suggesting she call him Gil. "It's the least I can do to thank you for the time you put in on my horse."

Liz straightened, Melody draped over her arms. "I wasn't looking for gratitude," she said, moving carefully toward the door. "The only thing I want from you is the money I've earned. 'Nice' doesn't suit you, Spencer. Don't strain yourself."

Gil blinked as if he'd been slapped and watched her disappear into the night. The moon had slipped behind a cloud, swaddling the area beyond the barn in inky blackness. He debated the wisdom of chasing her down. But before he could make up his mind, he saw a light appear in the cottage. Then another. He stood a moment where he was, until he noticed a colored square lying in the hay where the child had slept. It was a book—a horse story, he saw as he picked it up. From the school library. The book had been checked out only today.

Guilt swamped him. There were many reasons Gil had fought for sole custody of his sons. A major one—with which the judge had agreed—was that Ginger's job with the rodeo necessitated her jerking the twins from school to school.

In firing his farrier today, he'd just sentenced that sweet dark-eyed little girl to the vagabond life he hadn't wanted his own boys to suffer. Gil dropped the book back on the hay bale. Damn Mrs. Robbins for being what she claimed. And damn Rafe Padilla for hiring her in the first place.

CHAPTER THREE

GIL SPENT the next hour with his mare, and the girl's library book mocked him the entire time. Damned if he wasn't forced to admit Mrs. Robbins had done a damned good job—which didn't mean that another farrier wouldn't have been just as astute. But...she'd also homed in on Night Fire's problem, something his previous farrier had missed.

It didn't matter, he argued. Throwing a woman—especially a pretty one—out on the range with a bunch of randy cowboys was asking for trouble. Take, for instance, Kyle Mason's experience at the neighboring Drag M. Last year he'd hired a woman cowpuncher and bragged to anyone who'd listen about being the area's first equal-opportunity rancher. Far as Gil knew, there'd never been a fight among Drag M hands till Maggie Hawser came on board. After, they'd had plenty. More accidents, too. Not that it was *all* Maggie's fault. And not to say she wasn't a good hand. Some of the men admitted they'd spent so much time mooning over her they'd gotten careless.

But lovesick cowboys were only half the problem. Maggie'd up and married the clerk at the feed store. She left Kyle shorthanded in the middle of branding. Drag M wranglers moped around for months and spent weekends in town raising hell.

Come to think of it, there'd been an unusually large number of Lone Spur horses throwing shoes this last week—meaning Gil's headaches had already started. It was a good thing Ben had sent Rafe out with the notes from the twins' teachers, or he might not have come in yet and learned what his manager had done.

Those notes spelled more trouble. Of a kind Gil didn't want to think about tonight. Giving Shady Lady's neck a final pat, he went back to the house and upstairs to bed.

IN THE MORNING at breakfast Gil contemplated the best way to tackle the twins' teachers' concerns. As usual when his mind wrestled with a dilemma, the boys' yammering passed right over his head. Suddenly, as if through a fog, Gil heard Dusty gloating about a "neat trick" they'd pulled on Melody's mother last night. That got Gil's attention.

"Sneakin' out to put those bats in Mrs. Robbins's bedroom after she went to the barn was easy as eatin' pie, wasn't it Rusty? I wish we coulda seen what happened when she went to bed. Buddy Hodges said bats always get tangled in girls' hair. I bet Melody's mom screamed up a storm." Dustin laughed around the mouthful of pancake he'd stopped to shovel in.

Gil choked, spewing coffee over his place mat as his second son wiped a milk mustache from his upper lip and ventured, "I think we shoulda waited, Dusty. That was a good supper she fed us."

"So? She wouldn't have if Melody hadn't bugged her. She didn't want us there. I could tell."

"Hold it right there." Gil raised a hand, then slammed it on the table as he gazed in horror from one boy to the other. "I can't believe what I'm hearing. You two know bats carry rabies."

Dustin looked smug. "We didn't touch 'em, Dad. They came from Rafe's bat trap. We opened the box and shook 'em out in her room. Same as we did that old bull snake we put in her bed last week."

Gil counted to ten under his breath, then he exploded. "Remember that rabid coyote I showed you last year? We discussed how painful treatment is for our horses. I assumed you knew it'd be as bad or worse for humans."

Dustin stuck out his lower lip. "Men are smart 'nuff to not get bit. Can we help it if girls are stupid?"

Livid, Gil rose over his sons. Grounding them for life was too lenient. Through a haze of anger Gil heard his white-haired houseman bang a cupboard door and grunt. "Spit out what's on your mind, Ben. It can't get much worse."

"Time somebody teaches them knot-heads some respect," he said. "Lord knows they don't listen to me. It's a cryin' shame, the shenanigans they pull on folks. I tell you, Gil, I'm too old to be kickin' the frost out of kids meaner than oily broncs." In cowboy lingo he'd likened the twins' need for discipline to breaking a bad horse—which, Gil knew, laid Ben's feelings squarely on the line. He loved the twins.

So, the lady had told the truth, Gil fumed. No doubt the teachers' notes regarding disrespect in the classroom were on target, too. Had he closed his eyes to behavior he should have seen all along? Well, they were open now. Gil wadded his napkin and threw it on his empty plate. Stalking around the table, he grabbed both boys by the shirt collars, marched them into his office and kicked the door closed. "Sit. We're going to have a frank talk about how men treat women."

Ten minutes later Gil slumped in his chair. The upshot of the twins' half of the conversation was that they held

some pretty unflattering opinions of the opposite sex—
which they claimed to have gotten from him. Gil was
stunned to learn his bitter divorce had translated as a total disregard for *all* women. "Boys...I don't hate women.
Just where, I ask, would the world be without women?"

"Shorty Ledoux says a man don't need women or
schooling to work horses," Dusty informed his dad sul-
lenly, quoting one of Gil's best but crustiest old wranglers.

"Dustin." Gil smacked a hand on his desk top, making both boys jump. "Nothing is less true. It takes a college degree in agriculture or animal husbandry or both to
successfully operate a ranch the size of Lone Spur.
Moreover, whether or not we have women on our ranch,
men treat them with respect wherever they are. Your behavior toward Mrs. Robbins is inexcusable. I'm angry
and disappointed."

Rusty started to sniffle. Dustin blustered. "Well, gol
dang, Buddy Hodges says we don't need women no way,
no how."

"I beg to differ with Buddy. Maybe it's time we sat
down and addressed the whole subject of the birds and
bees." Gil jumped up and paced the length of his office.

Both boys turned red and wiggled uncomfortably in
their chairs. Gaze locked on his toes, Dustin again spoke
first. "Buddy told us where babies come from. He
'splained exactly what happens in the mating barn." The
boy rolled his eyes. "Me'n Rusty made a pact. Ain't neither of us ever gonna get married. All that gruntin' and
squealin' is pure disgusting."

Gil's jaw sagged. Tugging at his earlobe, he stomped
out to get a cup of coffee and look for Ben. The old
wrangler was nowhere to be found. Sly old dog. Gil remembered he'd been thirteen when he and his dad had a

man-to-man chat. Thirteen had been too late, but
damn—nine—they were still babies.

Determined to meet his obligation head-on, he returned to the office and took the bull by the horns, so to
speak. But after stumbling through generalities as best he
could while the boys fidgeted and asked to be excused to
go to the bathroom three times each, Gil gained a new
respect for his father, who hadn't pussyfooted around the
subject of sex. Nor did Gil doubt that Buddy Hodges had
been more graphic in his portrayal. Gil only hoped he'd
corrected some of Buddy's gross misconceptions.

Weighing each word, Gil realized it was damned uncomfortable trying to explain the more heartwarming
aspects of sex when it'd been so long he'd almost forgotten them himself. As it turned out, his sons understood
a whole lot more about the mating ritual than Gil wanted
to imagine. They apparently also knew that a couple of
women in town had boldly invited their dad to sleep over.
And that friends had tried to set him up for more than
dinner a few times when he'd gone out of town on business. It appeared the twins had thrown a monkey wrench
in some of those trips by developing planned illnesses.
Why, the little devils— Not that Gil would have in-
dulged in any one-night stands with virtual strangers, but
he'd believed the boys sick on those occasions. The
thought of how easily they'd manipulated him made Gil
a little sick.

He plodded through the rest of his explanations and
finally touched on a gentleman's code of conduct before
calling a halt to their chat. Then he sent the boys crying
to their room as punishment for the episode with Mrs.
Robbins and the bats. "And there'll be no TV for a
week," he shouted up the stairs. "When I get back from
assessing the damage caused by those bats, I'll draw up

a list of chores. Maybe work will keep you out of mischief.'' Their door slammed midsentence.

Damn. He'd never spanked his kids and didn't intend to start now. Anyway, their most effective punishment was to be confined indoors on nice days; they hated that more than anything. They took it even harder if he happened to be home. As a rule Gil didn't believe in retroactive punishment, but this time he'd make an exception. And they'd better believe he meant business.

Gil plucked his Stetson from the hat rack. Normally he found it best to take care of all unpleasantness at once. Like it or not, he had to go see the Robbins woman. Hell, he'd stood at the barn door last night and watched her walk into that cottage—into who knew what kind of mess while he'd cogitated over some damned library book. The book. Gil snapped his fingers. What better excuse to go calling this early?

Shifting the book from hand to hand on the short walk to the cottage, Gil worked out his speech. Something he hadn't counted on was finding his ex-farrier outside on her hands and knees weeding a colorful profusion of fall flowers. He stopped short of the picket fence as his stomach fought his morning coffee. No one had planted flowers at the Lone Spur since his mother passed away— the year he turned sixteen. Without her constant loving care, the gardens had withered and died. Until now, Gil hadn't realized how much he'd missed the bright colors or the sweet aroma that used to greet him.

The sight before him hit Gil hard and stole what little defense he had mustered on behalf of his sons. ''You're wasting your time,'' he growled, slipping through the gate. ''If the drought doesn't get them, the deer that feed here at night will.''

Liz jerked around in surprise. She hadn't heard his footsteps. Removing her gloves, she wiped a bead of sweat from her brow. Lord, he *did* have a cleft in his chin. How had she missed seeing it last night? It softened his straight eyebrows and angular features. The effect had Liz throwing up her guard. "Not to worry, Mr. Spencer. I won't charge you for the plants or for the spring bulbs I already planted." She stood and dusted the knees of her jeans. "Have you brought my wages?"

"Uh . . . no." Gil took off his hat and moved from one foot to the other, remembering the book. "Your daughter left this in the barn. I didn't think you'd want to lose it . . . By the way, is she all right?" He squinted at the door. "I, uh . . . Is that her I hear crying?"

Liz glared at him. "Yes."

"Not from a bat bite, I hope. God, I'm sorry. I just got wind of the twins' latest escapade. Rest assured, Mrs. Robbins, they will pay. We'd better quit jawing, and I'll drive you to town. A bat bite is nothing to fool with."

Lizbeth plucked the book from his hand and marched up the porch steps. "Melody slept through my award-winning bat dance. She's sobbing her heart out because I finally told her we're leaving."

Once again Gil suffered remorse. No matter how hard he tried to shelter his sons from the fallout of his divorce, their lives had changed. But the twins probably still had more continuity day to day than Melody Robbins did tagging after the damned rodeo.

Not given to snap decisions, Gil made one. "Stay," he blurted. "Through the school year at least. I'll hold off putting out feelers for a new farrier until mid-May." Considering where they'd left things yesterday, Gil thought his offer generous.

"What?" Spots of red blazed on Liz's cheeks. "You propose that I let Melody make friends, and then you have the nerve to suggest I put her through this again in May? What's really behind your benevolence, Spencer? Are all the good farriers taken?"

"I haven't checked. Look, I'm trying to do the decent thing."

"A belated attack of conscience?" Liz laughed. "Touching, I'm sure. But all I want from you is my pay. And I'd appreciate cash."

"Dammit, the offer's got nothing to do with conscience. I sure as hell won't beg you to stay." He didn't know why he'd weakened in the first place. Insufferable woman!

It didn't help Gil's mood to have three of his best wranglers ride in off the range just then and pounce on him, all three willing to plead Mrs. Robbins's case. How they'd heard so quickly that he'd fired her Gil hadn't a clue. Sometimes he thought ranch gossip traveled on the wind.

"Check out the shoes she made for Firefly, boss. This dang horse always shuffled before," exclaimed Clayton Smith, one of Gil's steadiest hands.

However, Gil noticed that today even Clay had on his Sunday shirt and that he kept darting shy glances toward the farrier. In her favor, she didn't comment or do anything to solicit Clayton's endorsement.

It was obvious to Gil that Yancy Holbrook had also slicked himself up for this occasion. Gil almost choked on Yancy's cologne when the man brought his gelding over for Gil to inspect shoes he claimed Liz had fashioned to fit a slight deformity.

The third wrangler in the trio wasn't any big surprise. Luke Terrill was a flirt, a ladies' man, although not as blatant as Macy Rydell. Today, however, Terrill sported a fresh haircut, a newly trimmed mustache and laundry-creased jeans. Though he spoke last, Gil pegged him as the ringleader in today's mission. Luke got right to the point.

"The lady forges a fine shoe, boss. But more important to us lonesome wranglers, she's a dang sight easier on the eyes than any farrier we've ever had. Fire her, and some of us might just mosey on down the road, too."

It was a matter of pride with Gil that he had the reputation of treating his hands fairly. Plus, he paid above-average wages. Cowboys lined up to work here. The Lone Spur rarely had an opening because the men he hired usually stayed. He didn't take kindly to being backed into a corner over an administrative decision.

Gil smoothed a palm down the nose of Luke's strawberry roan. "I'd hate to lose you, Luke, but it's your choice. My CPA's got the ranch checkbook in town this week. You wanta pick up your gear and meet me at his office in a couple of hours, I'll cut you a check. Same goes for anyone else who's got a hankering to leave."

From the way Luke turned white, then red and back to white again, it was clear he'd hoped to bluff his way past Gil.

The tension between the two men grew and spread to the others. Even the horses shifted restlessly. Liz knew the gauntlet had been thrown. She blanked her expression, wishing Luke hadn't put her in the middle. Although, in all fairness, Spencer had given the men wiggle room to keep their jobs and still save face.

On the rodeo circuit, where men's egos were bigger than their hat size and belt buckles combined, a challenge of this nature always ended in a brawl. Liz had learned to keep quiet. Too many times she'd seen situations in which a woman tried to mediate, only to have a fist fight erupt. She reached for the screen door. Let them bay at the moon. By nightfall, she'd be history here. Unexpectedly the door flew out of her hand and Melody hurtled out. She threw her arms around her mother's waist and sobbed. "I saw you and Mr. Spencer talkin'. Didja tell him we don't want to leave, Mom? Say please. You told me 'please' always works."

Liz's heart wilted. Dropping to one knee, she gathered Melody into her arms. "Honey..." she said brokenly. But no explanation made its way to her tongue. *Talk about egos*. Gil Spencer had offered a reprieve and she'd turned him down flat. True, it had only been for nine months, but that was nine months in which to check out other jobs in the area. Liz hadn't really considered Melody's feelings when she'd thrown Spencer's offer back in his face to salve her own pride. Now she had to eat her words.

Straightening, Liz lifted Melody's chin. "Dry your eyes," she said in a voice that carried. "Mr. Spencer brought back the library book you left in the barn. And... he asked me to shoe some horses in the east pasture. Hurry, go saddle Babycakes. I doubt he's one to pay his farriers to stand around."

The wranglers were quick to jump on the out Liz provided. Crowding Gil, they asked why he hadn't said in the first place that he'd rehired her. The three men lost no time making tracks out of Liz's yard. If Gil hadn't been so dumbfounded, he might have laughed.

Liz let Melody work through her excitement without comment. She felt Spencer's eyes boring holes in her back and heard him dusting his Stetson rhythmically against his lean thigh. She didn't turn to meet his gaze until Melody had dashed off to the barn to saddle her pony. Actually Liz waited another moment to see if the cadence of the tapping changed from irritation to resignation. It didn't. So she fixed a smile on her lips before facing him.

Tap, tap, tap. "What happened to 'not on your life'?"

Liz tossed her head defiantly. "I changed my mind."

"I don't recall asking you to shoe any horses in the east pasture." *Tap, tap, tap.*

She shrugged. "They're from your remuda. Rafe assigned me the job on Thursday."

Tap. Tap. Tap.

Was a slower rhythm better? Unsure, Liz stood her ground. Lo and behold, the tapping stopped, and she felt the muscles in her jaw relax.

"Did Rafe also tell you we have a ridge runner raiding mares up that way?" Gil stopped messing with his Stetson and put it on.

Liz tensed again, knowing a ridge runner was what breeders called a rogue stallion. "No. But he said the horses I'm supposed to shoe are all geldings. I'll be driving my pickup, and I doubt a stallion would bother Melody's pony."

"Wild stallions are totally unpredictable. Dangerous. Plus, we've got a marauding cougar staking his claim in those foothills. He kills just to be killing."

"Are you trying to scare me, Mr. Spencer? It's dangerous going to bed at night, what with all the snakes and bats that find their way into the cottage."

Gil tugged at his hat brim to hide his discomfort. So, Mrs. Robbins had a dry wit? A trait Gil liked in the men he hired. Why, then, did the fact that she possessed a sense of humor bug him? "Well," he said gruffly, "since I'm here, I may as well go ahead and flush those critters out of your bedroom."

Liz stepped back to accommodate his large frame, which suddenly dwarfed her small porch. "What critters?"

"The bats. I assume you shut the door and slept elsewhere last night."

"You assumed wrong. I shooed them out the window with a broom. You think I wanted bat poop on my new rug and newly papered walls? Even at that, I was up washing and scrubbing till nearly four. Who knows what germs bats carry? I'm surprised you'd allow the boys to handle them. They might have been bitten."

Picturing her going after bats with a broom prompted Gil's lazy smile. Irritation at her insinuation that he condoned the twins' nocturnal activities made it slip. "To quote Dustin, boys are too smart to get bitten. I won't mention his thoughts on girls, but it's another reason the boys are spending a Saturday morning in their room. I don't *allow* them to do things that are harmful or disrespectful."

Liz barely heard his words. She'd gotten hung up on the brief peek at his smile. What a shame he didn't let it surface more often. If he did, she thought, there'd be nothing a woman could refuse him. Some men smiled with only their lips. Some let it reach their eyes, and that was better. A very few had killer smiles that came from the heart. Corbett had been one, and so, apparently, was Gil Spencer. However brief that grin, it left Liz weak at the knees. A funny flutter in her stomach drove her to sit down on the old porch swing.

"Mrs. Robbins... is something wrong?" Gil asked, abruptly breaking off his explanation concerning his theories on discipline.

"Wrong?" Liz blinked at him, her eyes sort of distant and unfocused.

"Here comes your daughter on her pony. Maybe you should reconsider making that run to the east pasture today. It doesn't sound as if you got much sleep."

Liz tore her gaze from his face. "I'm fine." She stood and walked to the end of the porch, away from him. She was about to suggest that Melody ride in the cab and lead the pony behind the pickup, when Gil spoke quietly from behind her.

"I believe I'll saddle up and ride out that way, too. It's been a while since I checked fence along the river."

Melody reached them in time to hear his statement. "Oh, goody. Can the twins come? They said there's a place on the river to catch crawdads." She flashed Gil a shy smile. "My mom won't let me swim less'n I'm with a grown-up."

It had been on the tip of Gil's tongue to say the boys would have to miss the fun. But all at once he wondered if he couldn't teach them more by being a role model than in leaving them alone to stew. "Right she is, young lady. If the boys led you to believe I let them go alone, they fibbed." He ran one hand through his hair. "I *was* going to make them stay home—but I've changed my mind."

Melody glanced at her mother. "Is it okay if I take my swimsuit then?"

Lizbeth hesitated, still thinking resentfully about the Lone Spur's owner tagging along. She'd bet dimes to doughnuts that he planned to hang over her shoulder.

"I promise there'll be no bats or snakes or skunks, Mrs. Robbins," Gil said in a calm voice. "And the river at that point is only knee-deep." He looked up at the low-riding sun. "We'll have frost on the pumpkins before long. You might want to take a suit and dip your own toes."

''I'm going up there to do a job,'' she said stiffly. ''When I'm on company time, shoeing horses is all I do.''

Gil backed off, touched the brim of his hat and nodded curtly. What had he been thinking to suggest she join them? He certainly didn't want to give her the impression that he mixed business and pleasure. Or that he was in the habit of letting women intrude on his outings with his sons. Once, he *had* included a woman. His wife. Too late he'd learned that she wasn't interested in spending any time alone with her husband and sons. ''You two go on ahead.'' He stepped off the porch and didn't look back.

Liz saw by the way the light went out of Melody's eyes that she was disappointed. However, the arrangement suited Liz. The less time she spent around any of the Spencers, the better. ''We don't need company to have fun, Mel. Take a book and a doll like you always do. I'll fix a lunch for us to eat down by the river.''

''But I want to swim and catch crawdads with the twins.'' Melody's eyes brimmed with new tears. ''I didn't mean to make Mr. Spencer mad.''

''Sweetheart!'' Liz hurried down the steps and clutched her daughter's knee. ''It wasn't you. What I said more than likely reminded Mr. Spencer that he's the boss, and I'm just a hired hand.''

''So?'' Melody continued to look stricken.

''Well, ah . . . honey. I don't know how to explain social hierarchy to you. When you grow up, you'll understand.''

''If it means you and me always got to be alone, I don't wanna understand. The other day at school we hadda learn how to spell 'family.' My teacher showed pictures of moms, dads and kids. Gretchen Bodine don't got a mom or dad. She's got two grandmas, two grandpas, three brothers and a sister. That's a family, too, Miss Woodson said. And...and I want one!''

"Melody Robbins. We're a family, you and I. And we have Hoot, don't we? He already sent you a postcard. Honey, I thought you understood why I can't give you brothers and sisters—because your daddy's in heaven.'' Liz tried a new tack. "You finally got a kitten. And we've got our own house. That's a start, Mel.''

"But I'm gonna be a pumpkin in the Halloween play,'' the girl blurted. "Families get to come. Not kittens. Not Hoot. He's gonna be at the rodeo in Kilgore.''

"I'm afraid you lost me somewhere, honey. How did we get from crawdad hunting with the Spencer twins to your Halloween play?''

"Rusty and Dusty don't got no mom, and I don't got no dad. We could be a family. The boys liked your cooking. And their dad loved your cookies.''

"Oh, no!'' Liz gasped. She hadn't had an inkling that such an idea lurked in her daughter's head. "Melody, baby, you can't just pick up stray people like you do stray kittens and make them part of your family.''

"Why not?'' A tear caught in thick lashes, then trickled down a round cheek.

"Well, because...because...'' Liz puffed out her lungs and expelled the drawn breath on a sigh. "Because you just can't. And whatever you do, promise me you'll never bring up this subject with Mr. Spencer or his sons.''

"But how will they think of it on their own? Boys only ever think about horses and food and stuff like that.''

"Never, Melody. Is that understood?'' Liz pursed her lips.

"All right. But gee whiz.''

"Never!''

"O...kay. But will you make enough sandwiches for them? On your homemade bread? And take the rest of the cupcakes. Please, Mom."

"Melody Lorraine. I can see the wheels turning. You will not lure the Spencers with food. Where on earth are you getting this nonsense? Certainly not from me."

"Am I in trouble?" The child sniffled. "You only call me Melody Lorraine when you're really, really mad."

Liz threw up her hands. "No, I'm not mad at you. I just want to make sure you know I'm dead serious about this, Mel."

"All right. But jeez!" With that, she slid off her pony and plunked down on the porch steps to wait, chin in hands.

Thinking it best to let matters drop, Liz went inside and slapped together some sandwiches. She made enough for five people, but she used store-bought bread. The cupcakes needed to be eaten, so she did put them in, as well as a big package of trail mix. If she had her way, she'd feed the Spencers sour green apples. Or maybe not. She liked to cook, and the boys had certainly scarfed down supper last night. Liz didn't know whether the twins lacked a mother through divorce or through death. Either way, it wasn't their fault. How could she begrudge lonely children a simple meal? She knew all too well what loneliness was like.

She secured the house, then put the picnic basket and a jug of cold water in the cab of the pickup. Although she gave Melody a head start, she still had to drive slowly. The pony had short legs. That was probably why the Spencers caught up with them well before they reached the river. Markedly subdued, the boys both muttered apologies of sorts.

Dusty and Rusty rode a matched set of well-gaited buckskin geldings. They were small, but not as small as Melody's Welsh pony. Gil Spencer rode a powerful bay gelding, instead of his injured mare.

The three children met and galloped off in the lead. Gil tipped his hat to Liz and cantered past without saying a word, even though she had her pickup window rolled down. She was so busy admiring the way he sat a horse that she almost broke an axle driving across a rocky arroyo. Darn, but she was a sucker for the way a man—a good rider like Gil Spencer—looked on his horse. He had an easy fluid grace that Liz considered the trademark of a real cowboy. The gelding recognized his mastery, too. He responded to the slightest touch of his rider's heel or knee.

The boys, now, were learning, and they were perpetual motion in their saddles. She could see daylight between rump and saddle. Liz grinned to herself. Melody was the more polished rider by far. She could handle a bigger horse. Deserved one.

The salary that went with this job was more than adequate to provide for their needs, and maybe there'd be enough left over each month to start saving for a couple of really nice horses.

Speaking of horses, off to her left, ankle-deep in grass, stood thirty or so buckskins, the sleek well-proportioned animals that put Spencer's name in the horse breeders' registry. Liz slowed her pickup to a crawl. The land they'd just gone through was barren and dry. These grassy knolls, outlined in a patchwork of fences, had obviously been seeded and irrigated. She'd guess it hadn't been an easy matter to pump water uphill from the river she could see winding through the stand of cottonwoods far below.

Gil noticed that she'd slowed almost to a stop. Turning, he galloped back. "Is everything okay? You crack the oil pan when you bottomed out back there?"

Just as Liz thought—nothing got by Gil Spencer. For that reason she didn't make excuses, only laughed. "For a few seconds I wondered that myself. But my pickup's running fine. I'm just admiring the scenery. Your irrigation setup took some ingenious engineering."

Gil thumbed back his hat, rested his forearm on the saddle horn and surveyed the pasture all around him. "I'm afraid I see five years of backbreaking work—not to mention buckets of money that both my dad and Ginger accused me of pouring down the drain."

"Ginger?" She'd noticed a bitter edge in his voice when he said the name. Liz knew someone named Ginger—but no, it was too much of a coincidence to think she'd be one and the same person. Maybe his dad's second wife? "A wicked stepmother, I presume," she teased lightly.

His eyes glittered angrily. "You presume wrong," he said, surprising the gelding when he choked up on the reins and wheeled him on a dime. Sod, damp from a recent watering, flew from the gelding's sharp heels and stuck to the pickup's windshield as Spencer cantered off. In the field the horses stopped eating and whinnied nervously. Liz sat in her idling pickup. "What in heaven's name was that all about?" she wondered aloud. Obviously it'd been a mistake to tease him about Ginger—whoever she was. But if Gil Spencer thought his terse remark would end her curiosity, he didn't know human nature very well. Although not prone to gossip, Liz did like to know what made people tick. She was intrigued by the little mysteries of life; she was also patient and content to bide her time.

Catching up to the children, Liz insisted Melody join her in the fenced-off pasture where three geldings grazed. No matter how cleverly the boys and her daughter cajoled her, Liz had no intention of allowing Melody out of her sight.

"I should be able to shoe two of those horses before lunch. Melody and I will meet you fellows at the crawdad hole. We'll share our sandwiches if you point out where you'll be."

Gil had dismounted to check a fence post nearby. "We don't expect you to feed us," he said. "But you're more than welcome to join us at the river. See that tall weeping birch?" Liz turned the way he pointed. "My grandfather planted two of them as seedlings," he added. "Grandmother wanted to build a home there when the trees got big enough for shade."

"What happened to change her mind?" Liz asked, assuming they built the Spencer ranch house.

"First big rain, and the river flooded the valley."

"Oh. Did it wash out the second tree? I only see one."

"It died when I was a boy, during the seven-year drought. Granddad packed water all the way out here from the house, and still he lost one. Even though they'd given up the idea of building here, they still planned to be buried at the foot of those old trees."

"So, are they? Buried under that tree, I mean?"

Gil shook his head and stared down at the solid gold key chain he'd absently pulled from his pocket—a gold spur linked by the arch of a golden horseshoe. Diamonds winked from the spur's rowels. His grandfather had entrusted Gil, rather than his own son, with the keepsake. He'd made Gil promise to look after the ranch he so loved—as if he knew his only son wouldn't. To Gil, the key chain symbolized the heart and soul of the Lone

Spur. "It's almost impossible to bury someone on private property," he said in a low voice.

"Yes. Corbett's rodeo buddies wanted him buried beneath that chute. I was relieved when the funeral home refused." Brushing a sudden tear from her eye, Liz hurriedly pressed a hand to Melody's shoulder. "Come along," she urged softly, "I have work to do. Run and tell the boys you'll see them later."

Gil watched the woman gather her tools and stride toward the horses to be shod. *Tears? At this late date?* He couldn't say why it annoyed him to see proof that she grieved for her husband, that she'd loved him.

It more than annoyed him, it made him damned uncomfortable. Because Lizbeth Robbins didn't seem to fit his image of rodeos and their hangers-on.

And, thanks to his wife, he knew plenty about those.

CHAPTER FOUR

AFTER LIZ FINISHED checking the hooves of all three horses, she started with the one that was hardest to fit. Rafe had told her cold-shoeing was the only method the previous farrier used. It was certainly cheaper to use ready-mades, but Liz had been taught by an old-timer who believed that a foot shod properly and at regular intervals would remain sound for the life of a horse. Forming a shoe to fit exactly corrected a multitude of problems and extended the animal's work life.

Liz slipped a lariat over the first horse and led him to a big oak tree. Its spreading branches provided shade and a relatively clean work space. From the notations Rafe had made on her clipboard—indicating each animal's identifying features and markings—she determined that this horse was called Sand Digger. Back at her pickup, Liz wrote his name on a three-by-five card, dated it and briefly listed what she intended to do. Then she placed the card in a recipe box, which would eventually include every horse she worked on, with the cards filed in date order. She believed in shoeing at six-week intervals, eight at the most, unless the animal threw a shoe. Good records were something else Hoot had insisted on, and another thing the Lone Spur's former farrier apparently hadn't felt was important. She was virtually working blind on these animals.

Gil trotted up just as Liz fired her forge. "Starting lunch?"

She slipped on her apron and gloves. "It's barely nine-thirty. Don't tell me your breakfast has worn off already?"

His gaze slid from its inspection of her trim figure to where his sons were energetically throwing a football. "I'd barely poured my coffee when our breakfast conversation turned to bats. Food was forgotten." He glanced at Melody, who played quietly in the pickup's cab with a family of plastic dolls. "Is she always so placid?"

Liz looked up from gathering her nippers, blade and rasp. Laughter bubbled spontaneously. "Rarely. She's trying to impress me so she can go catch crawdads later. Beneath that sweet exterior lies a total tomboy. You'll see."

Gil adjusted his hat. "That's good. Maybe my sons'll learn some respect. They seem to equate female with inferior."

"Imagine that," Liz said dryly. Then before he could take exception, she turned and made her way back to Sand Digger. Thanks to her sixth-sense antennae that were attuned to Spencer, Liz knew the moment he dismounted and followed her. Ignoring him, she arranged her tools carefully, then walked Sand Digger in a circle to check his gait. She reminded herself that a lot of owners preferred to watch their horses being shod. But for some reason it grated on her nerves to have Gil Spencer hunkered down beneath the tree, relaxed as you please. Evidently he hadn't spied on his other farriers. If he had, his animals might be in better shape. Sand Digger favored his right front foot. On closer inspection, Liz discovered that the last nails had been driven in crookedly.

"Something wrong?" Noticing her frown, Gil stood and removed his hat.

"What? Oh, nothing." She repeated the procedure with the other hooves and found the same crooked nails in all but one.

"You frown at nothing?" Gil tilted back his hat and sauntered over to take a look. By the third hoof, he whistled through his teeth. "Damn!"

"You swear at nothing?" Liz restrained a smirk.

"That jerk!" he exploded. "I had no idea..." Off came the Stetson again and he began the signature *tap, tap, tap* on his thigh. "I fired him because I smelled liquor on his breath. I don't tolerate anyone drinking on the job."

"I guess you didn't follow him around and check his work." She shrugged.

He paused in the middle of tapping; an expression of surprise then chagrin furrowed his brow. "Look, ten years ago my pop's weakness for alcohol nearly lost us the ranch. I sold off all but thirty horses, dropped everyone from the payroll but Rafe, and the two of us put in twenty-hour days, seven days a week, to dig this place out of bankruptcy. There weren't enough hours in the day. We handled breeding, training, shoeing, built fence, mucked stalls—you name it. Now I have twenty men on my payroll. All experts."

"Twenty men and one woman," she said. "And as an expert I recommend you let this horse run barefoot and riderless for about six weeks." She flipped her rope off Sand Digger's neck and walked back to change the information on his card. "I don't drink, and I drive a very straight nail, Mr. Spencer, so you won't need to check up on me, either. Maybe you can take that extra hour or so a day I'll be saving you and spend it with your kids."

Gil stiffened. She'd hit a raw nerve. Ginger complained to anyone who'd listen that he'd neglected her in favor of the ranch. Neglect was a big issue in the custody hearing, even though Gil had hired Ben and cut back to ten-hour days. Little by little, as the boys grew and spent more time with him out on the range, he'd let longer hours in the saddle creep up again. But he didn't neglect his sons and he didn't need some woman looking at him with sorrowful calf eyes, suggesting that he did.

"Are you fixin' to fire me again?" Liz drawled softly, wishing he wasn't such a hard man to read. She could see he'd worked up a head of steam but honestly didn't know why. "I only meant you can trust me to do a good job of shoeing."

Gil stared at her neat array of tools. The card she'd been writing on fluttered to the ground. He picked it up, realizing at a glance that if all her records were this precise, she was definitely telling the truth. "Guess I'm kind of touchy when it comes to my family," he said gruffly, handing her back the card.

Liz filed it and filled one out for the next gelding, Coppertone's Pride. Named for his perfect all-over tan, she reasoned—and then her mind flipped back to what Melody had said about her teacher's pictures of family. Mom, dad, kids. It seemed grandparents were acceptable, as long as there were two. But one parent and child? Apparently not. By Miss Woodson's definition, she and Melody weren't a family. But *of course* they were, the same as tens of thousands of other single-parent families in the world. Liz would have to have a talk with Miss W. She needed a new supply of pictures.

"C'mon, boys," Gil called. "Mount up. Time to check fence." He squinted at the sun. "We'll mosey toward the river about noon," he told Liz.

"Do we hafta go with you?" The boys stopped tossing the football. "Riding fence is boring. Can't we stay here and play? We brought a Frisbee, too."

"No. Remember, I said idle hands make mischief."

"Aw, Dad. We said we were sorry."

Gil turned back to Liz, giving an apologetic shrug. She wasn't sure if he was asking her to let them stay or if he was irked at having her witness a little family discord. "I'll keep an eye on them if you'd like," she murmured discreetly. She didn't want to be accused of aiding and abetting dissension.

His sudden grin was like the sun coming out from behind a cloud. "Thanks. I'll put the fear of the Lord in them so they won't cause you any trouble. Riding fence *is* boring. Someday they'll accept that it's part of the job. Now they're at the age where anything short of calamity is boring."

"Yeah, I know what you mean. I get so sick of hearing that word."

"You, too?" He laughed. "I always picture girls playing quietly with tea sets and dolls. Like Melody there." He gestured over his shoulder at the pickup.

Liz pointed out a fact he'd obviously missed. Mel had left the truck to join the twins and had just delivered a punt that sent both boys running back into the dry wash.

Gil was still shaking his head when he mounted up and rode north along the fence row. He'd been right to bring the boys along. Being around Melody and Lizbeth might be the best way for them to learn some genuine respect for women.

Liz appraised the way his soft blue shirt stretched taut across his broad shoulders and narrowed snugly down to lean hips that rocked gently against a tooled leather saddle. Heat struck her like a blast of hot wind. She jerked sideways, assuming she'd let the forge get too hot. In fact, the fire burned low and steady. Annoyed by her own response, she coiled her lariat and went to separate Coppertone's Pride from his companions.

His feet were well shaped and symmetrical. Liz finished the easy shoeing just as the three children charged up, begging for water. She poured them each a generous cup from her jug. "Your faces are red as beefsteak tomatoes. Why don't you go sit in the shade of that old oak to drink these?"

"I'm ready to jump in the river," one of the twins said. "What do you s'pose is keeping my dad?"

Liz checked her watch. "He hasn't been gone an hour. He said noon. It's not quite eleven."

"We don't have to wait for him," the twin with the reddest face declared.

"Oh, ho," Liz chuckled, thinking he was baiting her. "Guess again, young man." She'd almost called him Dustin, but caught herself in time as she wasn't certain.

"We don't gotta mind you, do we, Rusty?" the boy said, deliberately crushing his plastic glass beneath the heel of his boot.

So, it *was* Dustin. Instinct had served her well, Liz thought smugly. When it came to confrontations, she noticed he most often led. But this time, Rusty ignored his challenge. "You're absolutely right, Dustin," Liz said quietly, walking over to pick up his flattened glass. "The rules you have to go by are the ones your dad set down before he left. And only you and Russ know how he'll react if you break them." She walked past him to toss the plastic pieces into the box lid. Unfurling her lariat, she deftly roped the third gelding, Little Toot. At this moment Liz felt it described Dustin Spencer. With his flashing go-to-the-devil eyes and pouting lips, he was a little toot, all right.

"Hey, that was cool," Rusty exclaimed, running to meet her as she returned with the dun-colored gelding in tow. "Will you teach me how to throw a rope like that?"

Liz cast a surreptitious glance toward his surly twin. Dusty's head was down and he was digging a furrow in the dirt with a boot heel. She'd bet the contents of her lunch basket that he didn't want any part of her teaching.

"I'm not sure how long it'll take to shoe this horse." She patted the soft nose as Little Toot nibbled her collar. "There are several lariats behind the pickup seat. Melody can explain the basics. If I have time before your dad gets back, I'll be glad to show you some simple rope tricks." She pointed. "See that old stump?" It looked as if it'd been sheared off by lightning. "That's how I learned and how I taught Melody. You practice roping stumps by the hour."

Rusty let out a whoop that scared the horse. "Sorry," he muttered, dashing after Melody. "C'mon!" he yelled to his brother.

"I don't want some dorky girl teachin' me to rope," Dustin declared loudly. "Shorty said he'd show us how before the next roundup. Let's wait."

Rusty's steps slowed. He glanced back at his brother, then at the rope Melody offered him. Hunching his shoulders, he turned and raced Melody to the stump.

Good for you, kid, Liz thought as she bent to her task. Still, she did feel for Dusty. Tough guys took a lot of falls before they learned. Especially the ones who used stubborn pride as a defense mechanism. This child came by the trait honestly; Gil Spencer wore pride like a suit of armor. Rusty was the anomaly here. More open. You could even call him sweet. Liz hammered the first white-hot piece of metal into the proper curve and cooled it in the bucket of water. She'd have to be careful not to treat Rusty with more affection, she told herself. Who knew better than she that pride was sometimes all that protected a fragile heart? So many times she'd picked up a pen to write her parents. At least four times she'd slipped Melody's picture into an envelope. She'd thought that maybe if this job panned out... But now, of course, it wasn't going to last. Yes, she knew all about stubborn pride.

And Dustin Spencer showed no sign of relenting. Liz watched him slam rock after rock, hard as he could, against a rusted coffee can. She stayed silent, knowing there was nothing she could say to him.

She was driving the final nail into Little Toot's fourth shoe when Gil Spencer galloped toward them from the north, his horse blowing hard. "Hurry," he called. "You guys saddle up and follow me if you want a treat. The rogue stallion has his herd grazing just up the draw. It's a sight, I'll tell you."

All three children sprang into action. Rusty dropped the rope he was using and raced his brother for their tethered mounts. Melody coiled her rope and his and carefully returned them to the pickup. "Is it all right if I go?" she asked her mother.

"Go ahead. I'll stay and pack up. The engine noise would probably scare him off before we got within range." She wanted to go, though. Liz had never seen a true wild horse.

"It's not far," Gil said, riding up beside her. "Come on, ride with me." He leaned from the saddle and stretched out a hand.

Liz felt her eagerness fade in a rush of embarrassment, even though she'd made her living working with men since Corbett died. She'd learned to sidestep advances and had developed a no-nonsense handshake, but it had been more than six years since she'd slid her arms around a man's waist. And, Lord, when you weren't intimate with the man, what did you do with your hands? Just now Liz tucked them in her back pockets and gave a little shake of her head.

Gil didn't think he'd ever seen a woman with more expressive eyes. How could they remind him of rich dark chocolate drops when they were so transparent? It made no sense. But they did. Unfortunately Gil had a big weakness for chocolate. "I've gobbled up my quota of women this week. Come."

He sounded as prickly as the spiked cactus that dotted the terrain, and Liz realized she was acting foolish. The kids waited, their horses huddled together—they all seemed much too interested in her childish display. Before second thoughts could weaken her knees, Liz stepped up, slid her toe into the stirrup Gil had already kicked free and, clasping his hand firmly, heaved herself up behind him.

Startled by the sudden shift in weight, the bay crowhopped a few steps along the side of the hill, nearly unseating Liz.

"Whoa!" Gil tightened the reins. Liz's foot slipped from its tenuous position in the stirrup and smacked the bay's belly, causing him to do a little bucking.

Liz tucked her thumbs gingerly under Gil's belt loops, then felt one break and give way. Self-preservation had her flinging her arms tight around his waist and burying her nose in the center of his back.

Gil felt her heart hammering against his backbone. The unexpected tensile strength in the slender arms circling his waist, along with an engulfing cloud of her perfume, precipitated a shocking swell against his jeans zipper. "Whoa, dammit," he shouted at the bay, "or I'm going to feed you to the buzzards." Then, fearing that his frantic threats revealed the agony he experienced each time he landed against the pommel, Gil let the fool horse buck out.

The kids' gleeful whooping and hollering prolonged the calamity. Twice Liz felt herself bounce. Once she thought for sure she was going flying. She wrapped her legs tightly around Gil's thighs and clung like Spider Woman to a wall. It ended a few seconds later. The horse stopped and quietly flicked his ears. Still shaken, the riders were left to untangle their limbs.

"Sorry," Liz murmured as Gil lifted her left calf off his knee. She loosened her stranglehold on his waist, but wadded his shirt tight in both hands in case the horse surprised them again.

"Are you all right?" Gil asked Liz after he warned the three kids to hush. He should be okay—now that she'd freed him. But for some reason his body had other ideas. Ideas it expressed all too insistently. Shifting carefully, Gil forced himself to turn and see how she'd fared. If not for the hats that kept them apart, she sat so close their lips would've brushed. Gil fought an urge to close the gap.

Liz shook like a novice circus flier facing her first high wire—until she noticed Dustin's face all but telling her to keep her hands off his dad. "Sideshow's over," she announced briskly. "Let's go or we'll miss seeing the wild stallion." She was careful to release Gil's shirt and find purchase on the saddle.

Stung by her coolness, Gil spoke sharply to the kids. "Stallions spook easily. Pipe down. We don't want him to think we're a threat to his herd."

"I thought you and Rafe were going to capture him, Dad." One of the twins reined in beside Gil.

"Not that wily son of a gun. The best we've been able to do is steal back some of our mares. As Rafe says, it's more that we enjoy the chase."

The boy cocked his head. "I don't understand."

Liz couldn't see Gil smile, but she was positive he did.

"I think you'll understand when you see him, son. He's wild and he's dangerous, but some animals are born to be free. So don't even think about trying to track him. If you're out riding and he shows up, leave. Don't ever underestimate him."

"Where did he come from?" Melody asked.

Gil hunched a shoulder. "Nobody knows. He just appeared one day a couple of years ago. Frankly I wish he'd picked somebody else's ranch."

After that, Gil motioned with his finger against his lips for silence. He took the lead as they rode single file through a narrow cut in a rise. When they came out on a promontory beneath a row of gnarled mesquite trees, Gil indicated that everyone should dismount. Quickly and impersonally, he handed Liz down. He sat on the bay an extra moment to clear her perfume from his head. Then he dropped down and crept to the edge of the outcropping.

Moving in beside him, Liz caught her breath. Below, in a green valley split by the river, grazed a small herd. Across from his observers on a matching promontory stood the most regal horse she'd ever seen. Coal black, his coat gleamed blue in places. The wind ruffled a mane that nearly swept his knees and his finely arched tail brushed the ground. He wasn't Arabian, although Liz would bet Arabian blood flowed in his veins.

"What's his name?" she whispered.

"He has many," Gil murmured. "I call him Wind Dancer. The few times I've given chase, he's disappeared as if the wind lent wings to his feet." He broke off, apparently embarrassed by his unexpectedly poetic words.

"Yes." Still considering his description, she nodded. "I can imagine him in flight." Eyes shining, she clutched Gil's sleeve. "It's a perfect name."

One of the boys—Dustin, no doubt—wriggled in between them. "I'd call him Darth Vader," he announced gruffly. "He's black as night. Looks scary. And you said not to trust him."

The stallion must have sensed their presence, or maybe he heard the boy. At any rate, he rose on his hind legs, gave an almost eerie whistle that rode the faint breeze, and like magic, the herd dissolved before their eyes.

"Wow!" Melody exclaimed softly. "Where'd they go?"

"Into the foothills and on up to the caves in the canyons beyond," Gil said, straightening and dusting off his knees.

"Caves?" Melody asked, obviously interested.

"We can't go there," Rusty cautioned. "The cougar lives there."

"Can, too, if we go with Dad," Dustin put in. "Rafe said maybe some weekend soon we can go with him and Dad when they go huntin' that old cat."

Gil had just climbed aboard the bay and helped Liz up behind him. She heard him sigh deeply.

"Don't even think about it, boys. I can't imagine why Rafe would suggest such a thing. All the crazy stuff he's done lately, I wonder if the man's gone loco."

Liz knew one of those crazy things was Rafe's hiring her.

Dustin flung himself on the buckskin, his lower lip stuck out in a sulk. "Rafe don't treat us like babies."

"Well, son, you've certainly been acting like one lately," Gil said in the tone that warned he was running short on patience.

"Have not!" Dustin shouted so loudly all the horses flattened their ears. "I wish I'd stayed in my room, instead of comin' along on this sissy ride." He dug his heels into his mount's side and tore off along the fence row.

"Dammit," Gil swore. "Sorry," he said to Liz. "I'd let him go, except he's liable to kill himself and the horse."

Nodding, Liz gripped his waist. Even then, he took off so fast she had to slide her arms more firmly around him to keep from being unseated.

They overtook the boy in short order. "Pull up, Dustin," Gil ordered.

Scowling, the child slapped his reins against the buckskin's neck and edged ahead by a nose.

Gil barely signaled his mount. As the big horse surged forward, the man leaned out of the saddle and grabbed the buckskin's reins just below the bit. "I said pull up!"

Liz felt Gil's muscles bunch beneath her hands as he hauled both snorting horses to a standstill.

"Dustin Lawrence Spencer, what in blazes has come over you? The rest of us are going to the river to swim and catch crawdads. You, young man, will sit on the bank and twiddle your thumbs."

Dusty's face turned ugly again. "I don't care! I don't care!" he yelled. "You and Rusty only wanna show off in front of dumb ol' girls. I wish they hadn't come to our ranch. I hate them and I hate you."

Tears made dirty tracks down his cheeks, but Liz didn't think he was crying. She felt Gil's sharp intake of breath and knew he was about to erupt. She touched his upper arm briefly. "I imagine you two would like to settle this in private. If you let me down, I'll walk back and meet Rusty and Melody."

Gil frowned, but he saw the value in her suggestion. In fact, he should have thought of it himself. But Dustin's temper tantrum threw him for a loop. If his son pulled this crap at school, no wonder the teacher needed a conference. All he managed to do was nod. Belatedly he offered her a hand, but she'd already slid to the ground. Hells bells, what must she think? Of him and his brood?

Taking a deep breath, Gil tried to moderate his approach. "I've been pretty involved with fall roundup, son. Are you and Rusty feeling neglected?" Gil hoped that if he included Rusty, Dustin wouldn't think he was being singled out. The boy's behavior had him truly concerned.

Dusty refused to look at his dad, nor did he speak.

"This didn't start out as a pleasure trip." Gil tried again. "Mrs. Robbins came to shoe horses and I needed to check fence. I thought since we hadn't spent much time together, you boys might like to tag along and take a last run by the river before winter sets in."

"Ben told Luke you fired Mrs. Robbins." The words shot out as if blasted from a cannon.

"Well, Ben was wrong." Gil didn't intend to discuss reversing his decision with Ben or his sons any more than he had with his wranglers. "Why do you dislike Mrs. Robbins? Has she treated you badly?"

Dustin buried his chin in his chest and shook his head.

"Does Melody make a pest of herself at school?"

"While you were ridin' fence, Rusty asked *her* to teach him how to rope. I said Shorty's s'pose to teach us, but Russ went off with Melody, anyway. I'll have to 'splain to everybody why my dumb brother ropes like a girl."

"Ah. How do girls rope differently from boys?"

"You know . . . prissy. Like the way they throw a baseball and stuff."

"Well, Dustin, should that be true, and it's not, it would be Russell's problem, not yours. An old accepted response is simply 'I'm not my brother's keeper.'"

Dustin slanted him a peeved look from beneath sun-tipped lashes. "We're more'n brothers, dad. Sheesh, we're twins."

"Nothing—neither being a twin or a male—is license for the way you're acting. I see your brother and Melody have caught up. We're not going to discuss this any more right now, but I promise you it's far from over." Gil handed back the reins and forced his son to meet a gaze that said he'd better shape up or else.

The boy wisely held his tongue. Shoulders slumped, he plodded on ahead while Gil returned to pick up Liz.

"I better go see Dusty," Russell said, nervously eyeing his father.

"No," Gil snapped. He gave Liz a hand up. "Dustin needs to cool off. We'll drop Mrs. Robbins at her truck and head for the river. Your brother won't be wading or catching crawdads. And you will not crow or otherwise rub it in. Is that understood?"

"I wouldn't do that, Dad. Neither would Melody." Rusty's lip trembled.

Gil cleared his throat. "See that you don't." He wheeled the bay so abruptly Liz had to clutch his shoulders. He slowed the horse immediately, grunting something that passed for apology.

The silence stretched between them as the horses fell into single file. Liz thought about asking how Dustin was. On the other hand, it was quite evident that their chat hadn't gone well. She elected to grip the saddle's cantle and no part of Gil.

The sky, at least, was beautiful. Not a cloud marred the expanse of Delft blue. A slight breeze kept the day from being too hot. Here and there as they passed bloomed-out agave in an undergrowth of cedar bushes, songbirds trilled. If not for the tension emanating from every line of Gilman Spencer's stiffly erect body, Liz would have enjoyed this interlude. As things stood, she was relieved when her pickup came into sight. She dismounted quickly and without a hand.

"We'll ride on and you can follow when you're ready," Gil said. "There's a trail of sorts that leads to the birch. Meet us there and we'll walk to the river."

Shading her eyes with a hand, Liz gazed up at him. "Do you want to eat lunch by the tree or at the river?"

"Eat? Oh. I forgot you brought food. As I said, you don't have to share. We'll be home by two o'clock."

"Suit yourself. It's not gourmet. Roast-beef sandwiches, trail mix and chocolate cupcakes I had left from supper. I brought a jug of cold water to drink."

Rusty rubbed his stomach. "I'm starved, Dad. And I can say for sure them cupcakes are yummy."

Gil glanced at his other son, who remained in a sulk. Finally he shrugged. "By the river, I guess."

Liz repacked her tools and climbed into her truck. He didn't have to sound as if she'd coerced him into this picnic, she fumed. All he had to do was say no. She understood the word in three languages. If Melody hadn't had her heart set on going after those ugly crawdads, Liz would have left the Spencer troops to simmer in their own cauldron. Talk about Dusty's attitude. And his father's wasn't all that saintly, either. Liz didn't realize she'd slowed to a crawl while she seethed until she stared at the rumps of four unsaddled horses. They'd all gone to the river without her. Not that it mattered. She was a big girl. But if Spencer had really wanted to set a good example for his sons, he'd have helped carry the picnic basket or the heavy jug of water.

"No wonder Mrs. Spencer took a powder." Liz grumbled as she lifted them down. Immediately she felt guilty. After all, she didn't know if the Spencers were divorced or if Mrs. Spencer had died. Feeling slightly more charitable toward her boss, Liz balanced a container in each hand and followed the excited voices of the children through a thicket of underbrush.

Gil had his hands full trying to keep an eye on three rambunctious kids, or he might have seen Liz slipping and sliding down the steep incline. He was simultaneously watching Rusty and Melody, who teetered on a log that jutted out over the swiftest part of the river, and Dustin, who roamed upstream along the bank—just short of being out of sight.

Puffing, Liz slammed the basket and the jug down at Gil's feet. She'd left a trail of plastic glasses, which she stomped back to retrieve. "Thanks for all the help. Maybe you'll have more energy after you eat."

Gil felt the sting of her reprimand in a flush that moved up his neck. The fact that he hadn't been on a picnic in eight years where he was expected to bring more than a six-pack or maybe a bag of chips was no excuse for bad manners. She had him dead to rights. What was left but to hurry and take the cups from her hands? "Sorry," he said simply. "The kids were champing at the bit, and I didn't want them coming here alone."

Liz saw sincerity in his eyes, and her anger dissipated. "No problem," she mumbled as she knelt and opened the basket. Taking out a small red-checked tablecloth, she spread it on the ground. She'd no more than removed a packet of blue ice and set out the sandwiches than Rusty and Melody flopped down beside her.

"I'll go get Dustin," Gil said. However, he returned moments later alone, lips pressed in a tight line.

Liz glanced beyond him to where Dustin heaved sticks across the stream. "Why don't you take him a sandwich and a cupcake?" she said lightly, picking up one of each.

"No." Gil plopped down on a log a few feet away, where he could keep his stubborn son in full view. He shredded a dead limb of its bark, trying to stave off the dull pain licking around his heart. He couldn't help thinking that he was partly to blame. He and Ginger.

Liz made up a plate for each of the others and one for herself. Minutes ticked by. She almost hated to chew and swallow, it was so quiet. Even the birds had fallen silent. Liz was relieved when, after polishing off the food, Rusty and Melody claimed they didn't want to hunt for crawdads or go wading, after all.

Gil stood. "Just so you know we won't be making another trip out here this year. Understood?"

Rusty gazed longingly at the water.

Melody stowed the garbage, then clasped his hand. "Don't worry. The crawdads'll be bigger next summer."

Liz was proud of those two kids. She hoped Dustin would one day appreciate their sacrifice. Grabbing up the

basket and the jug, both much lighter now, she started
back up the trail.

Gil snatched the items from her hands, then called to
tell Dustin they were leaving.

Liz thought they must make a pathetic-looking cara-
van trekking home. Dustin streaked ahead and Gil gave
him room. Rusty's horse wanted to run, but the boy kept
him in check to stay abreast of Melody. Liz brought up
the rear, her heart leaden with sorrow for the owner of
the Lone Spur. She no longer thought of him as a man
who had everything. Gil Spencer's family problems
weren't going to be solved by any amount of money or
acreage. And underneath, she'd bet he felt just as lonely
as she did.

CHAPTER FIVE

DURING THE NEXT MONTH, following the incident at the river, Liz caught no more than distant glimpses of Gil Spencer. Her orders came from Rafe who, since his return, treated her politely but stiffly. And he refused to meet her eyes, as if she'd somehow tricked him into hiring her—which she hadn't. If the opportunity ever presented itself, she'd point that out.

Luckily the weather remained good. Liz settled into a comfortable, sometimes solitary routine shoeing Lone Spur stock. It reminded her of the farm where she'd been raised. Sometimes the similarities caused a wrench of nostalgia.

Night Fire's hooves did so well with the mud soaks and lavish conditioning that Liz figured in another few weeks she could remove his old shoes. He didn't like them, nor did the wranglers assigned to help when he was mated. News filtered back to Liz that he'd developed a nasty habit of lashing out with his back feet. But when she showed up at the mating barn unannounced to suggest covering the shoes with thick socks, her presence embarrassed the cowboys. "Look, guys," Liz protested, "I grew up on a horse farm. I've also been married and had a baby. Believe me, procreation holds no secrets for me."

Rafe escorted her out. "The men are superstitious, ma'am. We'll keep out of his way till you pull his shoes. And you keep out of ours." He left her standing outside the door, paying not a bit of attention to her indignant sputters.

Liz stormed back to her cottage. If she'd been the drinking sort, she would've belted back a stiff brandy. No matter how efficient she was, there were barriers on the Lone Spur she couldn't seem to cross—even though most members of the crew tried at one time or another to make a date with her. Her lack of a sitter for Melody allowed her to turn them down without ruffling feathers. She didn't want to date them; she wanted to be a colleague on an equal footing. Liz was sick of the double standards men deemed their gift at birth. Not *all* men, thank goodness. Times like these she missed Hoot—and of course, Corbett—more than she could say.

She held some hope that Rusty Spencer might grow up to be more enlightened. He often popped in after supper to hang around her kitchen while she baked bread or cookies. Without his brother, he seemed less constrained by the bonds of male convention and, to all appearances, enjoyed his visits.

Several Saturdays in a row, Liz saw Dustin ride off with two bigger boys. She didn't like their looks, but she wouldn't presume to interfere in Gil Spencer's domestic domain. Besides, she had problems of her own. Problems not related to work. Old nightmares had, for no reason, come back to haunt her. For more than a week she'd been plagued by dreams of being trapped inside the chute with the crazed bull that had killed Corbett. Why was this happening again?

Liz knew if she went to the doctor, he'd prescribe sleeping pills. Having been down that route, she tried other methods these days, such as staying up past the point of exhaustion. Nothing gave relief. Perhaps if she could keep her mind occupied . . .

So she volunteered to sew costumes for the school's Halloween play. The corners of her living room were stacked with pumpkin frameworks, over which she stretched neat gores of bright orange cotton. Green leaf caps for the children's heads took up any chairs not draped with witches' costumes. But despite working all evening, every evening, in the wee hours she still bolted wide awake, bathed in perspiration.

Liz guzzled warm milk by the quart and counted sheep by the score. By the time Thursday night of the second week of insomnia rolled around, she'd dropped six pounds and was beginning to feel like a zombie. It was the night before the school play, and all the sewing was done. Sleep continued to evade her.

As a last resort, she got out Corbett's guitar and retired to the porch swing. In the past, when she felt confined by the camp trailer she'd sometimes made her bed in the back of the pickup, where she'd gaze at the stars and serenade herself to sleep.

Tonight it was downright chilly. Liz went back for a quilt and slipped on fuzzy slippers to go with her favorite flannel nightgown. When she'd finally settled in, the stars had disappeared behind a layer of clouds. Lone Spur Ranch lay cloaked in darkness, except for a light in her living room and one in the foaling barn. Drawing comfort from the distant beacon, Liz began to strum the instrument she'd once had to pawn to buy Melody a crib.

As a surprise, Hoot and his pals had redeemed it for her the next payday. The old guitar, three worthless plaques and a dozen pictures of Corbett atop those ugly bulls were the only mementos Liz had left of her happy-go-lucky young husband.

God, but she missed him. Missed the warmth of his arms and the laughter he'd brought into her life, however briefly. Her parents were all work and no play. They simply didn't understand a man like Corbett Robbins. Nor were they pleased when he'd come to the farm with a friend to buy a racehorse and ended up stealing the affections of the Whitleys' only child. *Someday, you'll be made to repent falling in love with that shiftless cowboy,* her father had predicted.

Maybe insomnia was her penance. Swallowing a hysterical laugh, Liz coaxed the mournful wail of a train whistle from the taut strings. The bluesy sound suited her mood when she got like this.

Suddenly, without warning, she felt eyes on her from the darkness beyond the porch, and she broke off with a sharp twang. "Who's there?" she called, trying not to sound frightened or breathless.

At first there was only the chirp of a stray cricket. Then a shadow, darker than the outline of the oak, separated itself from the tree and fell across the porch steps. "Don't stop playing." Gil Spencer moved into the shaft of light. "Except isn't it a mite cold to be out here like this?"

"Did my playing disturb your sleep? Sorry. I didn't think it would carry so far."

"I doubt you can hear it in the house. I was on my way back from helping Lady Belle deliver. At first I thought the twins had left a radio on outside."

"Is Lady Belle all right? I heard Rafe tell Luke Terrill you expected trouble."

"Belle had twins, but thanks to Doc Shelton, we delivered both colts. One's the spitting image of Night Fire. The second one's a little squirt, but Doc thinks he'll make it. Equine twins rarely both live, you know."

"Yes, it's so sad." Liz watched him walk wearily into the bar of light cast by her living-room lamp. "I'll go have a look at Lady Belle's miracle tomorrow—if they don't throw me out of the foaling barn.''

"They who?'' Gil asked.

"Didn't Rafe tell you about our tussle? He thinks women bring bad luck to the mating barn.''

Gil leaned on the porch railing and raked a hand through his hair. "Of all the idiot ideas... We've got several women ranchers in the breeders' association. Does Rafe think they avoid the mating barns?''

Liz stifled a yawn. "Look, it's no big deal.''

"Hey, I didn't mean to bend your ear. I get so wired when we're pulling a foal I forget the time. I asked Doc to come up to the house for coffee. He acted as if I'd slipped a cog, it being so late and all.''

"I don't have coffee, but I have a thermos of hot chocolate.'' She patted something in the shadows at her feet. "I've had trouble sleeping,'' she murmured, not telling him why or how long it'd been. "If you don't mind drinking from the metal lid, you're welcome to share.''

"Thanks. I will, if you don't mind my smelling like a horse and a few other things. Last time I showered or saw food was sometime yesterday, I think.''

Liz glanced up sharply from filling the cup. "You mean you haven't eaten since then? I have chicken salad left from supper, and fresh pumpkin bread—if you don't need something more substantial, that is.''

"Sounds good, but I wasn't hinting. Don't go to any trouble on my account. Ben has leftover hash I can warm in the microwave. I'm sure there's plenty. The boys hate hash.''

"It's no trouble.'' She rose and gathered her blanket and guitar.

Gil automatically took the thermos.

She led the way, turning to place a finger to her lips when they got inside. Her nod indicated that Melody slept behind the partially closed door leading off the living room.

Gil gazed around at the piles of costumes. "Don't I pay you enough?" he whispered. "You need to moonlight as a seamstress?"

Waiting until they reached the kitchen to answer him, Liz explained she was sewing costumes for the school play. Then she snapped on the light.

Gil had been about to comment on the event—that it was a big all-community affair—when the light gave him a clear look at her granny nightgown. He was sure his face turned five shades of red. "I, uh, didn't realize you were dressed for bed," he stammered. It wasn't even that the gown was provocative, he decided. More that it suggested a casual intimacy he'd been a long time without. Suddenly Gil asked himself what in hell he was doing in this woman's kitchen at two in the morning.

Liz had her back to him and her head stuck in the refrigerator, apparently unfazed by the situation. Gil wiped nerve-damp palms down his thighs. So why was *he* bothered by it? Maybe because Lizbeth Robbins had sneaked into his thoughts so much this past month.

Liz set a bowl on the counter, got out a plate and scooped him a generous helping of chicken salad. Moving easily, she unwrapped a fragrant loaf of pumpkin bread and cut him two thick slices. Still brandishing the knife, she pointed to the small dinette table that sat in one corner. "It'll be sort of hard to juggle a plate and a cup standing up. Take a load off, why don't you?" She poured the contents from his metal cup into a ceramic mug and placed it in the microwave. "I'll warm this up."

Gil discovered he hadn't moved, except to take off his Stetson and maybe cleave his backbone to the connecting door. It flashed through his mind that his ex-wife wouldn't have been caught dead in a gown that covered so much flesh. Nor would she have been standing in the kitchen serving him food in the dead of night. Ginger had rarely even cooked supper. Her thoughts and her time were only for herself—and her rodeo obsession. It shocked Gil to realize he hadn't seen that when they dated—before they married and brought babies into the world.

Perhaps he would have if he hadn't missed the ranch so keenly when he went away to college. Ginger was the first woman he'd met who loved horses as much as he did. Not for the same reasons, though.

Liz gazed at him curiously as she warmed her own mug of cocoa. "Are you too exhausted to eat? I don't want to force this on you."

"What? Oh, no. It looks great. Sorry, guess I spaced out. For some reason I was thinking about the twins' mother." He ambled over to the table, set his plate on one of the green-checked place mats and then pulled out a chair. His back to her, Gil didn't see the way Liz abruptly stopped pouring and sucked in her breath.

"Tomorrow's All Hallows' Eve," she said, carefully carrying the mugs of cocoa to the table. "It's when we traditionally remember our dead. For two weeks I've been fighting memories of Corbett. Experts say the only grief harder to bear than losing a spouse is losing a child. So... your wife died? No one's said."

Gil stiffened, a forkful of chicken salad halfway to his mouth. "I didn't mean to imply that she died," he said curtly, "or that I missed her."

Startled by his bluntness, Liz flushed. For a moment neither spoke. What was there to say?

He finished swallowing that bite and then sampled a piece of bread. "Mmm. No wonder Rusty hangs out here. I trust you'll let me know if he makes a pest of himself."

Still disturbed by his callous dismissal of someone who'd borne him two children, Liz just stared at him.

He picked up the napkin that lay beside his plate and wiped his mouth. "Is that better? Did I have salad spread from ear to ear? Or bread crumbs?"

"Neither. Mr. Spencer," Liz began tentatively. "Rusty—in fact, both boys—exhibit classic behavior suggesting they miss their mother very much. I can see why, if you bite their heads off when they innocently mention her. Regardless of how you feel, they need to know they weren't abandoned. You should try ironing out your differences with their mother, at least for the boys' sake."

Gil looked from her to his barely touched plate of food. He folded the napkin as carefully as a road map and laid it precisely where he'd found it. "If I wanted a sermon with supper, I'd have gone into town to the Salvation Army." He started to rise.

Liz motioned him back to his seat. "Finish. I'm not usually given to messing in other people's lives. It's just that I thought I recognized the symptoms in the boys, having gone through all the steps with Melody even though Corbett died before she was born." Sighing, Liz picked up her cup of hot chocolate. "I think I've read every child-psychology book written on the stages of grief. Maybe I was misreading your kids' behavior. I guess a little knowledge can be a dangerous thing." She ended with a deprecating shrug.

Tension arced between them for several moments. Then Gil settled back in the chair and toyed with his salad. "My divorce wasn't what you'd call amicable. Sounds as if your marriage was good. Has he been gone long?"

"Gone?" She wrapped her hands too tightly around the mug. "You make it sound as if he's visiting Houston or Kansas City. Corbett's been *gone* six years, four months and twenty-two days. And our parting wasn't amicable, either. It was courtesy of a bull called Sudden Death." Without lifting her eyes, she let her story spill out—including the part about her recurring nightmares of finding herself in the chute, and how the fear manifested itself in debilitating claustrophobia. By the time she finished, her knuckles were white.

Gil leaned forward and gently parted her fingers. Rising, he dumped her cold cocoa down the drain. When he poured her another cupful from the thermos, he brought it back to the table. "Drink this," he said quietly.

Dazed, she met his eyes. Up close the hazel took on many hues. Chestnut, bronze and saffron, in addition to flashes of green.

"Lizbeth." He said her name with a rough embarrassed catch. "If you expect a man to eat, don't stare." Picking up his fork, he deliberately attacked the salad.

The way he'd said her name sent a chorus of vibrations along her limbs. Liz crossed her arms and massaged the soft flannel of her gown's long sleeves. "I didn't mean to stare. Has anyone ever told you that your eyes are a collage of colors?" she asked dreamily. "Probably not," she muttered when he choked on a bite.

She leapt up and thumped him on the back. "Hey, sorry for making you listen to all my woes."

Gil pushed his now empty plate aside and stood. "Frustration, grief—they gotta go somewhere." He took her hand, dropped it at once and reached quickly for the knob to the back door. "I break horses. A lot of horses. And if that doesn't do it, I set fence posts until I'm numb."

She trailed him to the door, a frown wrinkling her brow. "Yes, but I pound the daylights out of a ton of iron. Mr. Spencer," she said, feeling they'd circled back to an employer-employee standing. "I wouldn't want my story getting out. It's important for the wranglers to see me as a professional. As a farrier and not as a woman."

"Everybody who works on the Lone Spur calls me Gil."

Shivering in the doorway, Liz looked down at the toes of her fuzzy slippers. A stab of conscience had her darting a furtive glance toward the barns and corrals. She doubted any of the hands were lurking there at this hour, but what would the men think if one of them did see her saying good-night to their boss in her nightgown?

"It's very late, *Mr. Spencer,*" she muttered, quickly withdrawing. "Good night."

"Gil," he said again as the door closed in his face. And he stood there even when he'd heard the lock engage. *Damn,* he thought. Talk about damaging tales—what would happen if Rafe or the doc saw him leaving Lizbeth Robbins's place this late at night? Whirling, Gil peered at the foaling barn where a light still burned. Considering how difficult Lady Belle's delivery had been, something could have gone wrong with her or the weaker foal—something that might have sent Rafe in search of him at the house. And if the foreman hadn't found him in his bed, what then?

Double damn! Gil had known from the minute he laid eyes on her that Lizbeth Robbins was going to cause trouble at the Lone Spur. He chanted the reminder like a litany as he circumvented the silent bunkhouse and re-checked the foaling barn. But Lady Belle and her babies were alone, all of them fine. Phew. Gil breathed easier. He didn't ever want the men whispering, pitying him again, the way they had when Ginger took off with Avery Amistad.

Nice as tonight's interlude had been, Gil wasn't one to fool himself—he'd just eaten his last midnight snack with the Lone Spur's farrier. Trudging up the two flights of stairs to his bed, he did everything humanly possible to comply with her wishes, to think of her as a profes-sional, not a woman. It'd be easier if he didn't keep hearing the lonesome wail of her guitar, or if the way she looked in that voluminous white nightgown would quit playing behind his closed eyelids.

Gilman Spencer had made at least one decision by the time the morning sun blazed through his east window. He was going to stay the hell away from his farrier, by damn, at least until May. By then, he'd be sure to have her re-placement hired. When he rose, bleary-eyed, the first thing he did was draw a big black X through October thirty-first on his wall calendar. This would mark the beginning of a new regimen, with the chief task of avoiding Lizbeth Robbins. Day by day he'd get through, just as he had following the breakup with Ginger.

True to his word, he made it to the end of day one without laying eyes on Lizbeth. He knocked off early to shower and get ready to take the boys to the Halloween play. Gil's eyes still burned from lack of sleep. He'd sooner fight a bobcat than socialize tonight. All his friends from the neighboring ranches would be there, and

Gil expected they'd rag on him about his latest hire. What if they badgered him to introduce her? Scowling, he dropped in on the twins to hurry them along.

"Dustin!" he exclaimed, aghast. "You can't wear that shirt. It's about two sizes too small. And the pants are miles too short."

"I wore 'em last year. It's the only black stuff I got. I can't be one of the headless horsemen less'n I got on a black shirt and pants." He ended on a wail of desperation.

Gil stood in the doorway, hands bracketing his hips. "Did you just find this out today?"

Rusty stuck his head out from behind the closet door. "We got our parts a long time ago, Dad. He knew."

"Shut up," Dustin ordered. "I told Ben more'n a week ago."

"So, Russell?" Gil faced his second son, trying to hide his mounting frustration. "What do you have to wear?"

"Nothing."

"Nothing?" Gil's brows shot up.

Rusty giggled. "Nothing special, I mean. I'm gonna be a ghost. My teacher's bringing sheets. She took 'em home to cut eyeholes."

Gil felt his good mood slip away. "I'm sorry, Dustin, you'll have to be a ghost, too. Change into your jeans and a shirt that fits. And step on it, or we'll be late."

"Not gonna! Not gonna!" Dusty stamped a foot. "I ain't gonna be no weenie ghost. The headless horsemen are cool. We already made our horses!"

"Dad," Rusty howled, "ghosts aren't weenies. Tell him they're not." He shoved his brother against the bed.

Gil's jaw went slack. Violence was so untypical of Rusty. God, was he losing all control over his sons' behavior? Lizbeth's words from last night flashed through his head like the neon beer sign hanging downstairs over his bar. Hell, he'd sooner chug a six-pack of Red Dog than ask to borrow those child-psychology books of hers. And he was a two-beer-limit man.

About the time Dustin hauled back and slugged his brother in the eye, Gil jerked them both up by their shirt collars and dangled them like a mother cat does her kittens.

Ben Jones limped into the room. "What's all the racket?" The old man struggled to catch his breath. "Oh, you're here, Gil. I thought these two was killin' each other."

"Ben. Dustin claims he told you he needed black pants and shirt for this shindig tonight. Did he?"

The leathery face fell. "Danged if he didn't. I wrote it down to tell you. But I plumb forgot."

He looked so guilt-ridden, Gil was afraid he'd have a stroke. "Never mind. A man's allowed to make a mistake now and then." Trouble was, they both knew there'd been more than a few lately. Deciding he'd have to deal with the problem when he had more time and less stress, Gil steepled his fingers. "We have two choices, fellas. Stay home." He paused to let that option sink in. "Or," he said softly, "Dustin can wear a pair of newer jeans and a navy blue shirt. You have two minutes to decide. What'll it be?"

It took less than a minute for Dustin to opt for the jeans. Both boys seemed to know their dad had been pushed to the limit. Surprisingly, when they piled in the Suburban, tough guy Dustin dropped a remark that floored Gil. "If we had a mom, 'stead of Ben, this wouldn't a happened. The other horsemen all have moms who bought them the right stuff to wear."

For the second time within an hour, Lizbeth's prophetic words regarding his sons rattled Gil's composure. As if having her words smack him in the face wasn't bad enough, he drove down the lane and saw her standing with her daughter under the old oak tree. The hood was up on her blue pickup, and she appeared to be fiddling with the engine. Gil had never seen her in a dress before—a summery thing with little straps that left her shoulders bare. What was she doing, working on a car in a floaty pink dress? It was fall, dammit. Once the sun set tonight she'd freeze.

Rusty craned his neck as they went by. "Looks like Mrs. Robbins has car trouble, Dad."

Gil slowed but didn't stop. After all, she'd said not to treat her like a woman. He hunched his shoulders. *Was it any wonder Dustin had an attitude?* Gil winced. Again Rusty pricked his conscience.

"Dad, aren't ya gonna see if she needs help? Mrs. Robbins has got most of the costumes for the play."

Shoot and sugar! Gil reached the end of the lane and did a U-turn. He swung in close to the ailing truck and stepped out of his vehicle. "Problems, Mrs. Robbins?" he asked, half under his breath. But she heard.

"Water pump, I'm afraid." Liz wiped her hands on a remnant of towel. "I'd hoped it was a hose and I could manufacture one. But I think the pump itself is shot." She slipped an arm around Melody, who'd started to cry.

"Dad," Dustin whined, slumping lower in his seat, "It's bad enough I ain't dressed right. Now we're gonna be late, too."

Gil's hesitation was brief. His sigh was longer. "Get out, boys, and give me a hand. We'll transfer all the costumes into the back of our rig and give Melody and her mom a lift into town." Gil could practically hear the

smart-aleck remarks his rancher friends would make
when they got a load of the five of them driving through
town—all cozylike. He dared not even *think* any of the
swear words crowding his mind, lest he spill a doozy in
front of the boys.

Rusty scrambled out, brimming with enthusiasm. Sullen, Dustin ignored his dad's orders.

"Shake a leg, Dustin," Gil reminded him none too
gently.

Each time Liz carted a load of costumes to the Spencers' vehicle, she darted a sidelong look at Dusty, who
only slumped lower in his seat. Partway through the
process, she poked her head in his window. "Aren't you
feeling well, Dustin?"

He muttered something she didn't quite catch.

"What's that? You don't like your shirt? I think it's
quite handsome." She was glad to hear it wasn't a bad
stomachache, as was common with kids about to per-
form.

"It's s'pose to be black. So'er my pants," he grumbled, kicking his feet aimlessly against the back seat and
picking at a shirt button held on by a thread.

"Oh." She straightened, darting Gil a puzzled look.

"He's fine," Gil snapped. "Everyone there'll be
watching their own kids. I'll bet you no one even no-
tices."

"Will, too." Dustin gave a final twist and the button
came off in his hand. "The guys'll all laugh at me. And
you and Ben don't care."

Liz noticed Gil's jaw bunch as he spun and went back
for another load. When he returned, she caught his arm.
"Before we moved, a friend gave me a box of clothes she
thought Melody might grow into. I know there are two or

three pairs of black jeans and probably at least one black shirt. What size does Dustin wear?''

"Seven, jeans. Eight or ten in a shirt. What about that, son? Do you want to take a quick look-see?'' Gil looked hopeful, if not relieved.

"Ain't gonna wear no girl's pants,'' Dustin declared.

Liz laughed. "I wouldn't have offered them, Dustin. My friend had four boys, and these clothes came from Patrick, her youngest. It won't hurt to check them out while your father finishes here. I know right where the box is in my closet.''

Dustin climbed out at his brother's urging and shuffled after Liz. She led the way to her bedroom, never saying a word. After the incidents with the snake and the bats, she figured he knew his way to her room. With luck, this might change the tide and put them on better terms.

By the time Dusty appeared in the doorway, Liz had laid two pairs of nearly new black jeans on the bed and two black Western shirts complete with black pearl snaps. She noticed the boy's eyes sparkle.

"Wow. Those are cool shirts.'' He reached for the one with red piping. The other had black piping, but it also had a small black rose appliquéd on the pocket. She could tell that he wasn't one for flowers.

He'd almost unbuttoned his shirt when he suddenly stopped. "You ain't gonna watch, are you?''

"Heavens no!'' Liz raised both palms and backed from the room. "Try on the newer pants first. I think they're the right size. And hurry,'' she called. "The teachers will be panicked about those costumes as it is.''

He was fast. Faster than Liz had anticipated after all the times she'd had to nag Melody. "Looks good. How do they feel?'' She had to put her hands behind her back to keep from combing tufts of his hair that stood on end.

"Spiffy. Thanks, Mrs. Robbins." His grin was her reward. She was amused by the way he swaggered over to the Suburban. Rusty and Melody were already buckled into the back seat. Dustin charged ahead of Liz to show off his finery, snagging the center. That left Liz next to Gil, although she'd planned to sit with the children.

"You kids keep an eye on those pumpkin frames," she cautioned, trying to hide her nervousness as Gil hurried to open the door for her.

"Thanks," she mumbled, thoroughly thrown when Gil not only handed her in, but pulled out her seat belt, which hooked to the wall above and behind her right shoulder. He smiled then, so close it froze Liz in her tracks. Twice she fumbled the fastener.

"It's me who should be thanking you," he said quietly before he slammed her door and traversed the front of the vehicle to climb in. "I hated it when my dad started a sentence with 'When I was a boy.' But I swear, when I was their age, I didn't give a damn about the color of my clothes." He started the engine, smiling back at his son. "I have to say you made his day—and mine. You see, he's a whole different kid when he's content. I just wish I knew what comes over him at times."

His smile faded after he pulled out. Never big on talking while driving, Gil was uneasy about what she might expect of him in the way of conversation. It wasn't just Lizbeth; he felt the same when one of his friends' wives cornered him at gatherings. Gil knew horses inside out, and weather as it affected the land. He could quote the current price of grain, but he knew next to nothing about art, novels or music—subjects dear to the hearts of most women he'd met.

As the silence grew, Gil cast a furtive glance at his passenger. He was surprised to find her looking relaxed.

Ginger had always gabbed nonstop whenever they traveled. Furthermore, she'd bugged him if he didn't answer her quickly enough. Apparently Lizbeth was different. No apparently about it. She *was* different.

He settled back. Well, maybe this wasn't going to be so bad. Except, what happened when they arrived together, looking like a couple? Would she follow him around? Did offering her a ride constitute being her escort for the evening? Gil had planned to deliver his sons into the care of their separate classrooms, follow up on last week's conference with their teachers, then go hang out with other ranchers. Most smoked, so the group gathered behind the gymnasium. Gil had never developed a taste for tobacco, but he tolerated it for friendship's sake.

"Here we are," he announced inanely, pulling into an already full parking lot. "Boy, looks like we'll have to tote these costumes a long way." For some reason he was reluctant to offer to round up his friends. It seemed too much like an all-out declaration that they'd come as a twosome. Gil would rather make ten trips by himself than give that impression. Ranchers were the very worst when it came to ribbing one of their fellows.

Liz eyed the distance thoughtfully. "If you trust me to park this thing later, you could drive right up to the back door of the gym. Then you take off with the boys or whatever you were planning to do. I'll find students or volunteers to help me unload."

Gil's astonishment must have shown in his eyes.

"I'm a good driver," she said defensively over the din of the children's yammering. "I've backed stock trucks as big as my house, for goodness' sake."

"I don't doubt you," Gil told her. "Sit down, kids. We're driving to the gym."

"Hey, Dad!" Rusty exclaimed. "There's the Little-fields. Oh, yummy. Miss Nancy's carrying two apple pies. I hope I get a piece at the potluck."

Liz was mildly surprised when Gil whizzed past the couple without giving any sign he'd seen them. But perhaps he hadn't. He seemed distracted.

"C'mon, boys," Gil called the minute he'd shut off the engine and handed Liz his keys. "I'll go with you to find your teachers. Just pocket the keys," he instructed Liz. "No need to come huntin' me. We'll meet you later." The Spencer trio melted into the twilight.

Liz wasted no more than a moment puzzling over Gil Spencer's odd behavior. She was late with the costumes. The minute she was recognized, volunteers descended on her with open arms. Once everything was carted into the gym, she hurried to repark in the lot. Then, since she'd offered her services backstage, too, Liz was busier than a bee in a new hive. Too busy to give the Spencer males any thought, other than to restaple an ear on Dustin's stick horse and adjust Rusty's ghost costume so he could see through the eyeholes.

Nor did she look for them in the cafeteria following what was declared the most successful play yet. Liz hardly had a moment to breathe between storing the costumes and racing around, helping in the kitchen, heating and dishing out food for the potluck.

Strangely enough, Gil found himself getting worried when he wandered the length of the cafeteria several times and failed to find her—*after* he'd stopped looking over his shoulder every five seconds, thinking she'd pop up wanting to be introduced to his friends. The Little-fields were the only ones who'd seen Gil with a woman. Being his best friends, they were discreet in their curiosity. They seemed to accept his declaration that the girl they'd seen in his Suburban was a friend of the twins; he went on to say he'd given them a ride because her mother's truck had broken down.

Other women gathered around, giggling and sniffing at his heels. All wore too much makeup to suit Gil, and they came on way too strong. Halfway through the ordeal of fending them off, Gil realized he'd been comparing each of the women to Lizbeth, and that they'd all fallen short by far.

Long before the whole shebang wound down, Gil was plenty peeved that Lizbeth had made no effort to rescue him. It made him wonder who'd she'd slipped off to eat with, since he'd seen Melody twice in the company of classmates.

He'd gone beyond peeved by the time friends started coming up, saying goodbye and leaving. Finally, to avoid questions about why he was hanging around, Gil herded the twins to the Suburban. He was flat-assed mad when she finally sashayed up to their vehicle—one of only three left in the parking lot.

"Where in royal blue blazes have you been?" he roared, uncurling his length from the hood of his vehicle. "You have the only set of keys."

Liz clutched Melody's hand, her steps slowing. She dug the key ring from her pocket and slapped it into his palm. Her voice crackled with anger. "Frankly I didn't think you were in any rush to leave," she said as he unlocked the doors. "Every time I looked, you were surrounded by a bevy of women."

"Wives of neighboring ranchers. We're all close friends."

Liz recalled the pert blonde in the lavender linen suit and the redhead who wore the clingy teal. "Um . . . I saw how close. Don't their husbands mind?" She lifted Melody into the back of the Suburban and climbed in after her.

"What's that cryptic comment supposed to mean?" Gil asked icily, turning to pluck a sleeping Rusty from the hood.

Dustin slid off, covering a yawn. "Dad, she probably saw that dorky Suzette Porter hanging all over you." Clambering into his seat, the boy made urping noises before adding, "Shorty Ledoux says her top deck's full of bird's nests, but that most men don't care 'cause she's got big bazooms." He motioned with both hands.

"Dustin Lawrence Spencer, that's quite enough." Gil plopped Rusty into the passenger seat Liz had occupied on the drive to school and yanked out his seat belt.

"It's true, Dad," the boy insisted. "And Rafe says she's got 'em aimed at you."

Under the glow of the auto's interior lights, Gil's face turned a mottled red. "Not one more word out of you, young man. Not one!" He shook his finger in Dustin's face.

On the drive back to the ranch, it was so quiet you could have heard an ant sneeze. Liz wanted to laugh—but she didn't dare.

CHAPTER SIX

DURING THE DAYS between Halloween and Thanksgiving, Liz felt especially restless and housebound without her truck. The repair shop in town had ordered a water pump, but since her pickup was an import, she'd been told delivery would take longer than usual.

If only Hoot had been able to come for the holiday. But he wrote to say the rodeo was performing in Austin that weekend. The wife of a retired clown who lived nearby had offered to cook turkey and trimmings for Hoot and his buddies. The news depressed Liz. Maybe because the ranch buzzed with everyone else's plans. Even crotchety Shorty Ledoux had a sister to visit.

"We could invite all the Spencers to eat with us," Melody announced one evening when her mother complained grumpily about cooking all day for just two people. "Rusty said the turkey Mr. Jones cooked last year was tough as an old porcupine."

Liz made no comment, although she actually considered Melody's suggestion—at least until she rode into town the next day with Rafe to collect her repaired pickup. Away from the ranch he seemed friendlier.

"Say, Liz, would you keep a eye on Marshmallow Girl this Thursday? She's due to foal by week's end. Her last, a filly, surprised us by coming early."

"That's Thanksgiving." Liz halted, half-in, half-out of the ranch vehicle. "Won't the boss want to watch her himself?"

"He and the twins are going to Morris Littlefield's. Their holiday spreads last half the night." Rafe chuckled. "Gil will probably wish he'd stayed home. According to Luke, Nan also invited the divorcée who opened that new fluff-duff shop in town. Morris's wife is always trying to find Gil a woman."

"What's a fluff-duff shop?" Liz asked, to cover a swift unexplainable wave of jealousy over a woman she'd never met.

"Again according to Luke—who's p.o.'d, mind you, 'cause he's been nosing around her trying to get a date— her shop's full of glass doodads. Polly, that's her name, conned Luke into helping dust all that junk. Can you picture it?"

"Rafe—" Liz looked him square in the eye "—the Spencer twins never talk about their mother. What happened to her? Is it a big secret?"

Rafe wrinkled his nose and assumed an interest in the knobs of the tape player. He hemmed and hawed, then in a rush told her how Gil's wife had skipped out with a rodeo cowboy by the name of Amistad.

When he finished, Liz blanched. "Avery Amistad? That guy's a jerk!"

"You're being generous. If you know him, you probably know Gil's ex. We heard she married Amistad before the ink on her divorce papers had dried. You may know her as Ginger Lawrence. She kept her maiden name for barrel racing."

"Ginger Lawr— But they're not—" Liz swallowed and lowered her gaze. She'd started to say Avery and Ginger weren't married, only living together when they weren't fighting.

"They're not what?" Rafe prodded, his interest piqued.

Liz shrugged. "They're not friends of mine." And that was no lie. "Listen, we're blocking the auto shop's driveway. I'd better run. Oh, and hey, I'll be glad to look in on the mare. No problem."

"Okay. Thanks." Rafe leveled a look that said he didn't buy her attempt to switch subjects. But before he could press, she slammed the door, waved and left.

"Ginger Lawrence. Phew," Liz muttered. And she'd thought it wasn't possible for Gil's Ginger to be the one she knew. A statuesque redhead with cold seafoam-green eyes—a perfect example of beauty's being only skin-deep. The woman was totally devoid of scruples. How could someone as ethical as Gilman Spencer have married someone like that? Before Liz reached any conclusion, the mechanic showed up to discuss her truck, and she was forced to table the shocking news for the time being.

But her mind returned to it as she bought groceries and then drove home. So much made sense now—Gil's wariness of women, his dislike of anyone connected to the rodeo.

Liz wished she didn't know these things about his ex. She'd had two run-ins with the barrel racer over toe weights. Avery had convinced Ginger that weights made a horse run faster. Liz knew *any* extra weight fatigued a horse and decreased agility. Her argument with Ginger was legendary among the rodeo set.

But that wasn't all. Ginger's cream-colored buckskin was spoiled rotten. The mare had a nasty habit of biting and leaning on a farrier. Liz had never thought it was her job to teach a horse manners. But neither did she court broken bones. Ginger pitched an ugly fit the one time Liz tied the mare down to shoe her.

Brother! Of all the women in the world her boss might have married, why did he have to pick the one who'd done her level best to get Liz barred from working the rodeo? Ginger hadn't succeeded, but she'd forced some good people to take sides. In Liz's opinion, the woman was devious. Memories plagued her all the way home.

Liz hadn't seen Gil for more than two weeks. So why, when she pulled into her drive—in the middle of rehashing a bad scene with his ex-wife—did he happen to be sauntering down her porch steps with that easy sexy roll of his hips? Gilman Spencer's walk tended to stall Liz's breath somewhere between her lungs and her diaphragm.

"Hi." He smiled as he opened her door. "Rafe said he'd given you a lift to town to get your truck. He didn't say you'd stopped to shop. Here, I'll lend a hand."

"No need." She declined his offer. "Since I was already in town, I decided to buy groceries and save going the day before a holiday. Did you come to ask about a particular horse?" She mentally ran through all the animals she'd shoed in the past week and couldn't think of any problems.

"Two actually." He grabbed a grocery sack and was surprised by its weight. "Feels like brick," he said, scrambling to keep from dropping it.

"Our Thanksgiving turkey," Liz explained, taking the sack. "First one I've bought in a while. The oven in my trailer was too dinky to cook anything this big. And I'm planning to cook enough to have leftovers for a week...." Her sentence trailed off. "Are you saying we have two horses with problems?" she blurted.

Gil picked up a gallon jug of milk and a second sack. "Rafe said he mentioned our pregnant mare. I'm not expecting trouble but figured I'd give you the Littlefields' phone number just in case. I don't like carrying my cell phone to a social gathering. And there won't be anyone here. All our wranglers who don't have family to visit are going to the Drag M for a gymkhana. They chipped in, and Kyle Mason's camp cook is serving everyone dinner after the riding and roping competitions. So I'm grateful you're willing to look in on the mare."

"That takes care of one horse and problem. What's the other?" She unlocked the door that led directly into her kitchen. Funny how he purposely avoided calling the men's competition a rodeo. A gymkhana was nothing more than a mini-rodeo.

"Westwind." Gil went straight to her refrigerator and began making room on the top shelf for her milk. "Rafe sold him to a rancher east of town—Pete Markham. He claims the gelding has a bad foot. I'd like you to give him the once-over."

"Sure." Relieved to learn he hadn't come to complain about her work, Liz passed him perishables. "Hey, you're a master packer. Is there room for my bird on the bottom shelf? Big as he is, he'll take the rest of the week to thaw."

Gil shifted a few more items. "Afraid not. That sucker'll feed a regiment. I thought Rusty said you'd only invited your friend, Hoot. Hope he's a big eater."

"As it turns out, he can't come." She gestured Gil aside and began combining leftovers. "Darn," she muttered. "Still won't fit."

"You mean you aren't having company next Thursday?"

"No. But Melody and I will be here, so I'll keep an eye on your mama-to-be."

"Then you aren't sticking around just because Rafe asked you to check up on Marshmallow Girl?"

"No. Who on earth named that horse?"

"I did. Why?"

She laughed. "No offense, but it's hardly a name I'd expect from a man. Westwind—now that's more like it."

"That mare has a history. She was a runt I gave Ben to bottle-feed in the dead of winter. She hated the bottle, and they fought something fierce. One day when his back was turned, she ate a whole bag of marshmallows, sack and all, that he'd bought for the boys to take to school."

"I hope she didn't get sick."

"Nope. Amazing, isn't it? The name sorta stuck, though."

"So it seems." Liz laughed. "Getting back to your second request, I'll take a run to Markham's after I store all this. Jot down the address, will you? I think there's a pad and pencil beside the phone." She nodded toward the corner.

"You may as well ride with me. I guarantee my stock, so I'm taking a trailer in case I have to swap him for a new horse. Say, I have a second fridge on my screened porch that'll hold your turkey. You finish here, and I'll swing by and pick you up."

Liz glanced at the clock. "Will we be back by three? I may be a single parent, but Melody's not a latchkey kid."

"We should be back in time. I feel the same as you, which is why Ben lives with us. In case we run late, why not leave Melody a note telling her to go have a snack with the twins? I'll mention it to Ben."

"Will he mind? He always seems so . . . so stern. Probably due to his arthritis," she said hurriedly when it appeared Gil was about to launch into a lengthy dissertation. "I shouldn't judge him. I hardly know the man. But Melody likes him. And a lot of people think Hoot is gruff, too. Mel and I know he's an old softie." She handed Gil the rock-hard turkey. "Here. And thanks. I'll be ready."

Gil let the icy bird roll against his chest. Suddenly, without warning, he leaned close to her ear and sniffed.

"What?" She dodged to the side. "Do I smell like garlic? I bought some at the store."

"Flowers. I should know what they are," he muttered. "Lilacs?"

Tongue-tied by his nearness, Liz blushed. "Violets. They're purple, but darker and smaller than lilacs. When I was growing up, we had huge beds of them around the house. I haven't seen any growing in Texas," she said with a dreamy look.

"Violets." Smiling, he bent and sniffed again. "Nice."

Now her cheeks ignited in flames. Liz ducked her head to hide the rapid beating of her heart. It had been so long since she'd fielded a compliment from someone she might care to encourage. "You'll suffer frostbite if you don't get that bird home and into your fridge," she muttered.

Gil hesitated, wondering if he'd somehow offended her. Cursing himself for being so tactless, he all but bolted out the back door. He was home before he'd completely rid his nostrils of her sweet scent. Damn, but that stuff could turn him from Jekyll to Hyde with a single whiff.

No doubt about it, Lady Lizbeth is trouble. Any woman who shook him up with her *perfume*, for God's sake, needed keeping at arm's length. Part of his anatomy could use a little frostbite—unfortunately not the part holding the bird.

Liz folded the last sack. Because Melody didn't read yet, she called the school and asked the secretary to relay a message. All the hassle the woman gave her, grumbling about how she couldn't be expected to give personal messages to four hundred kids, left Liz feeling uneasy. What would Melody do if some accident befell Liz out on the range? Most kids had *someone* to contact in an emergency. Her daughter had no one. Not here. Not anywhere.

This fear stuck with Liz even after she joined Gil in the cab of his pickup.

He darted several glances at her between the time they left the cottage and the time he stopped at the main road. "Right turn takes us to Mars. Left to the Milky Way," he teased.

"Um...okay." Liz continued to make restless patterns with her fingers on her knee.

Gil signaled and turned left. "You're a million miles away."

Liz blinked at him. "Do you have a will?"

"As in willpower?" His eyes twinkled.

She made a face. "As in last will and testament."

He tromped on the gas and the truck leapt forward. "Why would you ask a thing like that?" Suspicion doused his ready smile.

Drawing her knee up, she faced him. "I started thinking...if I died suddenly, like Corbett did, I don't know what would happen to Melody. I just wondered if you've arranged for a guardian for the twins or what?"

Gil gripped the wheel hard. "You sound like my lawyer. I plan to live a long time. But I've set up a trust to deal with the ranch, and it provides for the twins' basic needs."

"I don't even have life insurance," Liz murmured, gazing out the window.

"Wouldn't your dad step forward and claim Melody?"

"That would be difficult, since he doesn't know she exists."

Gil shouldn't be shocked, considering how she avoided talking about her parents or her life in Kentucky. But he was, all the same. However, she had that cornered look again, so he fettered his curiosity for the moment. "My attorney's convinced I'm the biggest fool on earth," he said conversationally. "I spent twenty thousand dollars in legal fees fighting my ex-wife for custody of the boys. If I died today, the court would hand them back to her. I should name my friends Morris and Nancy Littlefield as guardians and be done with it. But they're both pushing sixty. I keep thinking it wouldn't be fair to dump two rambunctious kids on them."

"So is that why they keep trying to find you a woman? I mean . . . a wife?"

He almost put the truck in a ditch. "Who told you that?"

She grinned. "An unimpeachable source."

"One of my men? Damn!"

"Well, it would solve your guardian problem—a wife would."

He snorted. "Marriage creates problems. It doesn't solve them."

Considering the length of time since his divorce, his vehemence surprised Liz. "All marriages aren't bad," she said gently, remembering the cozy nights of loving and laughter she and Corbett had shared. Problems had seemed so insignificant then.

"Here we are at Pete's, or I'd argue that point."

Liz straightened and studied the ranch with interest. Markham's fences were barbed wire where the Lone Spur's were rail. Suddenly her eyes came to rest on a massive tan bull with an almost black hump. He swung his head toward her. Spittle dripped as he pawed the ground. Riveted to the seat, Liz saw another bull—a dirty white chute. And Corbett's broken body.

"That's Gibraltar," Gil volunteered. "Mean dude, according to Pete. But worth a big chunk of change."

Her eyes remained locked on the beast even after Gil opened her door.

"Lizbeth?"

Gil's voice reached into the swimming void to draw her back to reality. Sweat pooled between her breasts, and she wiped damp palms down her denim-clad thighs. *This bull's name is Gibraltar—not Sudden Death.*

"We walk from here. Pete keeps his horses in a field behind the house. Lizbeth, what's wrong?"

Unconsciously Liz resisted the pressure Gil applied to her elbow. "You didn't say he raised Brahmans." The hollow words sounded faintly accusing.

Gil read something more in her eyes. "Stay in the truck. I'll go get Westwind."

"No," she said weakly. "I have to get over this fear. It's dumb. After all, he's penned. Give me a minute. You go on. I'll get there eventually. I'm assuming one of the two men who just walked around the house is Mr. Markham. Go on, Gil, or he'll think something's wrong."

Gil continued to stroke her upper arm as he turned to check. "It is Pete. And Morris Littlefield. I didn't see his rig when we drove in. Oh, there—that black truck."

"The one with the two rifles in the window rack?" She slid out, steadier for having found a new focus. "No wonder you hesitate to make him the boys' guardian."

"A rifle is a necessity for a rancher. You should carry one, and a cellular phone, too. Never know when something'll come up out on the range."

"I intend to get a mobile phone when I can afford it. No rifle. My best childhood friend accidentally shot and killed her little brother. She never got over it."

"One accident, Lizbeth."

"Do you know how many gun accidents kill children each year?"

"As do boats, cars and planes. Kids have to learn gun safety, same as you caution them about all the other dangers involved in living." Gil broke off his lecture as the two men walked up. The older and taller of the two clapped Gil on the shoulder and gave Liz a careful once-over.

"Quite a philosophical speech to reel off to a pretty lady, Gilman. I don't believe I've had the pleasure," the rancher boomed, reaching around Gil to pump Liz's hand. "Morris Littlefield's the name. There's Pete Markham." He nodded toward the lankier man. "I hope you don't hold this boy's lack of social grace against him, darlin'," Morris said gravely to Liz, dropping her hand to doff his high-crowned hat. "Out at the Lone Spur they go for months at a time without laying eyes on a woman."

"Really?" Liz didn't have to feign shock. It was obvious Gil hadn't told his friends about her. That hurt. Why, if he wanted to keep it a big secret, had he brought her here?

"You mean the word isn't out?" Gil studied the tips of his boots. "I figured the phone lines would hum. Gen-

tlemen, meet the Lone Spur's farrier, Lizbeth Robbins.''
His friend's astonished expressions tickled Gil purple.
Morris in particular liked to think he was on top of everything that went on in Crockett County. But Gil should
have guessed he didn't know, or Nancy would have hotfooted it to the ranch by now.

Morris snapped his fingers. ''Son of a gun. This is the
lady we saw in your Suburban at the Halloween fest.''

Gil admitted nothing.

''Nancy'll croak. You said you'd just given a ride to
the mother of one of the twins' friends.''

''He did,'' Liz said coolly. ''That'd be my daughter,
Melody. Speaking of kids, I'd like to be home when the
school bus drops her off. Could I see Westwind?''

She spoke with such authority Pete Markham immediately turned and started for his pasture. Morris tried to
detain Gil, but he shook off the man's hand. ''Say hello
to Nancy. See you Thursday.'' Gil touched two fingers to
his hat and hurried after Liz.

Liz knew which horse was Westwind the instant she
laid eyes on him. He had long legs, a deep chest and the
burnished red coat of his sire. A throwback, rather than
the trademark buckskin. He definitely favored one front
leg when he trotted up to greet them. She saw the worried look that passed between Pete and Gil just before she
climbed through the fence and picked up the gelding's
foot.

Relief swept over Liz. She set the hoof down gently and
smiled. ''Westwind has a corn, gentlemen. It's large and
tender, but easily treatable with Pine Tar. If you don't
have any on hand, I'll drop some off. He'll need three or
four treatments.''

''A corn.'' Gil hugged Westwind when he really wanted
to hug Lizbeth. Sobered by the thought, he turned to

Pete. "Your foreman, Murph, had me believing it was cancer. I brought the trailer—I was positive I'd have to run him to the vet. So, let me take him to the Lone Spur for treatment and I'll lend you another."

Pete shook hands to seal the bargain. "Murph knows cows, but I trust you to know horses, Gil."

"In this case we'll both trust Lizbeth." Gil smiled into her eyes.

It warmed her to her toes and helped ease the slight she'd felt earlier, thinking he had deliberately kept her employment at the Lone Spur a secret. The affable feeling lasted even after they loaded Westwind, though they spoke little on the way home. Gil slipped a tape into the cassette player. After humming along for a few minutes, he seemed lost in his own thoughts; Liz used the time and the mellow bluegrass music to unwind after that nasty business with the bull. It was a good thing, because they entered the lane immediately behind the school bus, and when they all tumbled out of their respective vehicles, it became clear that Dustin Spencer sported a black eye and a bloody nose.

"Buddy Hodges did it," Rusty and Melody both piped up. "Buddy told everybody the black shirt you gave Dusty made him look like a dime-store cowboy."

"You fought over a shirt?" Gil exclaimed. "Buddy Hodges has four inches and a good twenty pounds on you, son. We've discussed how nothing is ever solved by using fists."

Liz had gone to the cottage for an ice pack and returned in time to hear Gil's charge and Dustin's reply.

"It was 'bout more'n a shirt. Buddy said *she's* suckin' up to me and Russ just to get in your bed." Dustin glared at Liz with his one good eye.

She gasped and dropped the ice pack.

Gil's brows drew together as he picked it up. After affixing it to Dusty's eye, Gil hustled both boys into the cab of his truck. He jumped in, slammed his door and drove off without a word to Liz. A vein throbbing in his neck attested to his anger.

Liz remained motionless until Melody's puzzled question prodded her to life. "Why would you want to sleep in Mr. Spencer's bed, Mom? I'm gonna tell that dumb Buddy Hodges that you got a p'fectly good bed of your own."

Liz shooed Melody toward the house. "Stay away from Buddy Hodges, honey. He's a troublemaker."

"But, Mom."

"Feed your kitty, sweetheart. Then come with me to the barn. I've got a horse to treat. Afterward, how about if we go for a nice ride?"

Fortunately for Liz, Melody was easily distracted. While treating Westwind, Liz imagined how she and Gil would laugh tomorrow over the incident and the fact that Buddy Hodges was hell on wheels.

Several days went by before Liz realized Gil was deliberately avoiding her. Rusty stopped visiting her kitchen, too. Surely Gil didn't give credence to Buddy's allegations?

By Wednesday—Thanksgiving eve—Liz began to think he did, especially when Gil sent Rafe by with the Littlefields' phone number and the key to his sun porch so Liz could get her turkey out of his fridge.

As a result, Liz took none of the anticipated pleasure in making holiday pies, dressing and cranberry sauce that evening. She only kept up appearances for Melody's sake. Well after midnight, while readying her turkey for the oven, Liz gazed at the Spencer's dark house. She again lamented the loss of a budding relationship. One that now appeared to have no hope of getting off the ground. If it ever had. Maybe she'd read the signals wrong. Did the attraction she thought they shared exist only in her mind? Lord knew she didn't have a lot of experience to go on.

As she faced the long, empty day Liz realized something profound: unlike Gil Spencer, she wasn't afraid of falling in love again. What did terrify her was the prospect of falling in love with the wrong man—a man who didn't love her in return.

With that, she banished the Lone Spur's owner from her thoughts and didn't allow him to intrude again until midmorning when Melody came moping in, saying the Spencers had left to go to the Littlefields' and she was bored. "Mr. Spencer said we might get snow today," she informed her mother without enthusiasm.

"Snow?" Taking note of Melody's pink cheeks, Liz ran to the window. She'd been too busy at the stove to pay attention to the weather. "It does look blustery. Good thing the crew cut and baled the winter hay," she said more to herself than to Melody. "You'd think he'd have brought the horses in off the open range."

"He did. Rusty said." Melody hung her jacket on the peg beside the door and swiped a sugar cookie. "Oh, and Mr. Spencer ast me to remind you to look in on Marshmallow Girl. He said she's gonna have a baby."

"That she is. I hope she waits until the weekend. Last baby I helped deliver was you," Liz teased.

Melody perked up. "How do babies get borned?"

Liz stood at the sink peeling sweet potatoes and wished she'd held her tongue. "Human babies are usually delivered by doctors or midwives, honey. Animal moms aren't quite so wimpy. Your baby book is on the top shelf of my closet if you want to see how much you've changed."

Melody took off like a rabbit. Liz didn't see her again until nearly two, when she popped back into the kitchen. "The turkey smells yummy. When can we eat?"

"Around four. Get your jacket, Mel. We'll go take a look at our expectant mom."

They stepped outside into a cold north wind. Halfway to the foaling barn, stinging ice crystals slapped them in the face.

"Snow!" Melody danced around.

"Sleet." Liz shivered and turned up her coat collar. The ground sparkled with it by the time they reached their destination. Both welcomed the rush of heat that embraced them as they entered the barn.

Liz needed only one look at the mare to know she was in distress. Stripping off her coat and gloves, she knelt in the stall and smoothed a cool hand down the mare's sweating neck.

"Mom?" Melody's obvious fear spilled out in that one word.

Liz had seen a number of foals born. She didn't think this was normal. Not the easy birth Rafe had predicted. Nor had Liz exaggerated her lack of experience in her earlier discussion with Melody. She stood and rolled up her shirtsleeves. She did know how to check the mare's progress. Only she didn't want to do that in front of an impressionable six-year-old. Perhaps if it was a routine birth or if she knew exactly what she was doing... But she didn't. Not really.

"Honey, I may have to call Mr. Spencer. I left the Littlefields' phone number taped to the wall by our kitchen phone. Would you run to the cottage and get it for me? Rafe said Mr. Spencer installed a phone in each barn. See if there's one by the door on your way out."

The girl turned and ran from the stall.

Ten minutes later Liz went to see what was keeping her daughter. The mare's condition didn't look good. Instead of moving down the birth canal with each contraction, the foal seemed to be jerked back as if by some unseen hand.

Heavenly days! The wind ripped the barn door from Liz's hands and stole her breath. Icy barbs whirled so fast and furious she could barely see a foot in front of her. Venturing a few steps, she cupped her hands and called, *"Melody!"* Was that an answer or the wind's whistling? Liz cast a worried glance back toward the barn, then pushed her gloveless hands into her coat sleeves for warmth and set out for the cottage. She was gasping for breath when she and Melody collided, unable to even see each other in the slashing snow.

"Mama," Melody sobbed, "I thought you was lost. I had to get kitty. He went under the porch and I was scared."

"I had no idea it was so bad out." Liz wrapped her arms around the child and the mewling cat. "Sweetie, we have to go back to the cottage for a minute. I want to check the turkey. Plus, there're a few things I might need. Then I'll drive us to the barn."

"Okay." Melody's voice was shaky. "You left the radio on. Some man called this a blue norther. He's silly. Snow is white."

Liz's steps faltered. Fear clutched at her throat. She'd read about ice storms that blew up out of nowhere and claimed untold numbers of lives. She shook off remembered stories of people found dead five feet from shelter. "Hang on tight to my hand. Don't let go for any reason. Do you understand?" She thought Melody answered, but her own teeth chattered so hard she couldn't really tell. And unless her mind was playing tricks, in the direction of the corrals the nearly obliterated skyline had a cobalt hue.

It seemed they stumbled along for a lifetime before Liz tripped over the back steps of the cottage. Almost giddy with relief, she refused to release Melody's hand until they'd both made it safely up the five slabs of slick concrete. Liz sobbed for joy once they were inside and had closed out the storm. Her fingers and toes were numb. Somehow she wasn't surprised to find the telephone dead.

Drawing strength from the need to remain calm in this crisis, Liz did what needed to be done swiftly and methodically. The turkey was near enough cooked that she set it out to cool, marveling that they hadn't yet lost electricity. She collected extra blankets to cover Marshmallow Girl, and buckets for water. Among her medical supplies, she found a mild muscle relaxant. She didn't know the ramifications of administering it to a pregnant horse; she'd use it only if she had to. But with any luck, the phone in the barn was on a different circuit, and she'd be able to reach Gil and maybe the vet. If she didn't save both mother and foal, it certainly wouldn't be for lack of trying.

She bundled Melody up until she waddled, and they left the house again, all but crawling to the truck over the slippery buildup of sleet. Only once, when the engine stalled about halfway to the barn, did Liz have second thoughts about what she was doing. She knew it was a straight shot from her cottage to the foaling barn. Hadn't she sat on her porch, basking in the barn's light the night she fed Gil that midnight supper?

Absurd thoughts to have now. Her hands shook as she restarted the engine, and not entirely from the chill. She hoped Gil wouldn't be so foolish as to try to come home from the Littlefields in this, yet she was gripped by a premonition that something was terribly wrong. Liz recalled similar feelings the day Corbett met his fate with the bull. It didn't change one thing in the aftermath to know she'd begged him not to ride.

"What's that?" Melody asked when they'd fought their way into the barn again.

"The horse is having a hard time breathing, sweetie." Liz shook the sleet off the blankets and rushed to the stall to check the wild-eyed mare. "Take this number," she urged Melody, thrusting a paper into her hand. "Look—there's the phone." She pointed. "I want you to keep trying to get through, and ask for Mr. Spencer. Tell him I think the foal is caught at an angle. I don't want him to come, but I need him to tell me how to turn the baby. Come get me, and I'll talk to him, okay?"

Eyes big in a pale face, Melody nodded. She slipped silently out of the stall, and Liz went to draw two buckets of water. Next she felt the mare's belly. It was rigid with a contraction. A prayer for guidance passed her lips as she reached carefully into the birth canal. Weakly thrashing hooves were all she felt.

"There's no dial tone, Mom." Breathless, Melody hovered in the opening to the stall. "Is Marshmallow Girl gonna die?" Huge tears rolled down her cheeks. "Why is your arm all bloody?"

Liz washed in one of the buckets of water, remaining calm to allay Melody's fears. "I'm doing my best, honey. Trust me. I need you to be strong right now. I'll try and explain all this later."

"Can I watch?"

"I need you to keep dialing that number. Pray that the men working for Ma Bell get those lines fixed soon."

Melody withdrew. From then on, Liz worked as though in a daze. She injected the muscle relaxant to slow the contractions. Then, with each new one, she reached carefully inside until at last she determined which direction she needed to swing the foal. And she developed a special bond with the plucky mare. Liz knew what it was like to go through a tough delivery, relying only on strangers. Her encouraging murmurs calmed the mare. Liz just wished she knew if what she was doing was right.

At a point when Liz was dangerously close to giving up and on the verge of tears, she heard a loud noise at the front of the barn. Her thoughts flew to Melody, but for the life of her, Liz couldn't rise to go see. Her clothes were drenched in blood and sweat, and her limbs shook with fatigue. Putting every bit of strength she possessed into one last effort, Liz felt a sudden gush and a plop, and a spindle-legged filly landed in her lap. Through a curtain of tears, she watched the mare struggle to her feet.

The next thing Liz knew, strong arms circled her and she felt her feet leave the floor. Either she was dreaming or cool lips brushed her ear, her cheek, her chin, and whispered lightly over her mouth. "Lizbeth," a rough voice shuddered. "She's beautiful. What on earth happened? Melody said—and I can see—you ran into trouble."

Liz clung helplessly to the wet wool that covered Gil Spencer's broad chest, drinking in his sight, his touch, his smell. He was warm to the eyes, cold to the touch and smelled faintly foresty through the metallic odor of blood.

"I . . . she . . . we . . ."

"Never mind," Gil whispered, catching her close again. "You're fine. We're okay. Mother and baby are A-okay. Wash up and I'll pour you a cup of coffee. Nan

Littlefield sent along a hot thermos. She thought I was
crazy to forgo a meal and set out in a storm, but I was
worried about you and Melody being here alone.''

Joy filled Liz's heart and released another flood of
tears. Eyes glistening, she skimmed Gil's craggy features. ''We've all got a lot to be thankful for,'' she sighed
softly. ''Coffee's a bonus.'' She didn't tell him, but feeling his strong arms holding her was better than a bonus.
It was a return of hope.

CHAPTER SEVEN

"I NEED TO TAKE FEED out to the horses and break the ice
off their water troughs before I worry about getting anything to eat," Gil said once he'd finished checking the
new mother and her foal. "This little lady's buddies are
out there freezing their tails. She's the lucky one." He
patted the mare's sweaty neck.

"Lucky?" Liz grimaced. "*You* have a baby, pal. Then
let me hear you say that."

Gil watched Lizbeth towel her arms vigorously after a
quick douse in the bucket. Their pale undersides stirred
an ache in his loins. Whirling, he decided to let her remark slide rather than get embroiled. He called for the
boys to bring the thermos from the truck.

All three kids ran to the stall, then crowded close to see
the new filly. The twins joked about her lack of coordi-
nation and her knobby knees. Melody stood up for the
baby. "Bet you guys didn't look any better when you
were borned. My mom says people babies are all red and
wrinkled at first."

"Are not," Dustin declared. "You're makin' that up,
ain't she, Dad?"

Gil passed a plastic cup filled with hot coffee across the
stall to Liz. "As a matter of fact, she's not, son."

Liz read disgust on Dusty's face. She lowered her cup,
attempting to side-track the questions she saw heading
Gil's way. "Wrinkled or not, every parent thinks his or

her child is perfect. Look how proud Marshmallow Girl is. Who's going to name her baby?''

"I ain't gonna name no girl," Dustin said. "Are you, Russ?"

He gazed wistfully at the awkward filly, then shook his head.

Liz found Rusty's swift capitulation a bit disappointing, but kept her thoughts to herself. "Give me a minute to finish my coffee," she told Gil, "and I'll help dole out the feed. I still can't believe one minute it was fall and the next, winter. Brr."

"Old-timers call these blue northers or blue whistlers. I've only witnessed one other one—when I was a teenager. Today the temperature fell forty degrees in fifteen minutes. A frigid north wind swept down across the plains and hit a warm gulf breeze, and we got caught in the middle." Overhead lights blinked twice, then went out, ending Gil's explanation.

"Oh, no. First the phones, now the electricity." Liz set her cup down, and groped for her coat. "I could hardly see when I drove the truck from the house to the barn. Is it any better out there now?"

Gil clipped a blanket around the new mother. "It's a nightmare out on the roads. I hope none of the wranglers try to leave Kyle's before it clears."

"You did, though," Liz reminded him.

"Yeah. Well, it's my ranch. And the Suburban is a big four-wheel drive."

So it was worry for the ranch and not for her that had brought him back. "I assume you have room for all of us and the feed in your *big four-wheel drive?*" She gathered the children.

"I plan to hitch a flatbed." Gil registered her sarcasm. He missed the source—unless . . . "No one expects you to help, Lizbeth. I have to stop at the house to change clothes and start the alternate generator. You and the kids can stay there and keep warm. The generator puts out enough amps to run low heat and lights in a couple of rooms."

"I'm already dressed for the weather," she said as she pulled on her gloves. "I thought you'd welcome an extra pair of hands."

Gil, whose eyes had begun adjusting to the lack of light, gazed at her a moment, trying to read between the lines. Failing that, he dumped his coffee, herded everyone out and closed up the stall. "Then let's get at it. I want to see everyone wearing boots, hats and gloves. There's a box full of extras on the back porch."

Outside, it looked much later than her watch said. Liz knew at once where the name "blue norther" came from. The icy fog, in the murky half-light, took on varying shades of blue, from pale powder to bright indigo. The wind was so intense it stole her breath and made talk impossible. By the time Gil drove—inched along, really— from the barn to the ranch house, everyone understood the severity of the storm.

It was much warmer in the house even though the electricity had been off some fifteen minutes. Gil started the gas generator first thing. Soon the kitchen lights flickered and grew steady.

Liz and Melody chose hats with earflaps while Gil and the boys went to change into work jeans and long johns, then waited at the door. When the heavily jacketed trio of males waddled back, looking like they'd gained weight, the laughter they shared over it felt good.

"Oh, look. You have a red light flashing in that alcove," Liz informed Gil in a low voice as he reached for the door. "Does that mean something's wrong with your generator?"

"It's my answering machine. Someone called before the phones went out. Probably Rafe or Luke. I'll retrieve it later. Let's go."

Liz cast another glance toward the winking light as he opened the door to the howling wind. "Wouldn't they have called you at Mr. Littlefield's?"

He frowned. "Or on the cellular. Wait, kids." Gesturing them back inside, he closed the door and strode to the alcove.

Liz heard a beep, a buzz, then a second beep, followed by a woman's frantic voice. She was too far away to hear what the caller said, but there was no mistaking Gil Spencer's string of curses.

"Dad? What's wrong?" Rusty sounded alarmed. "Is that our mom?"

"No. It's Ben, or rather his sister." Gil passed a hand over his eyes and jaw, then took a deep breath. "Ben's been injured in a car wreck."

Liz covered her mouth with gloved fingers. "Bad?" she gasped.

"Bad enough. Shattered his hip, his thigh and the opposite knee. They're waiting for the storm to let up so they can fly him to a better equipped orthopedic hospital. She said he figured with the men gone I'd need help, so he left to come home. He slid off the road and over a bank a mile from her house."

"Did she leave a number? Maybe you can reach her on your cellular."

"She did. Russell, find me a pencil, will you?"

It was a silent group who raced through stinging sleet to his rig, already slick with ice.

"I'll drive, you make the call," Liz said, sliding behind the wheel. "Where to?"

"South pasture." Gil seemed distracted. "Thanks to Ben's gut feeling yesterday, we brought the majority of the herd in closer." Gil helped the children buckle in over their extra clothing before he punched a number into his phone. He drummed his fingers on the dash while it rang and rang. "Nobody there. She also left a number at the local hospital. Man, this is some Thanksgiving." Rechecking the scrap of paper, he fed in a new series of numbers. His call was answered immediately. Gil greeted Ben's sister briefly, then asked about his old friend.

Liz heard only Gil's side of the conversation, but knew from his deepening frown that the news wasn't good. After a lengthy discourse he clicked off. The twins bombarded him with questions.

"Ben's been thrown a lot of times, but it sounds like he's in for a heap of surgery. Peg said they discovered he broke his left wrist, too. All in all, he'll be looking at several months of casts and therapy." Gil didn't want to scare them, but he wanted to be honest.

Dustin's lower lip quivered. "I shouldn't a said Ben's cookin' was awful. He's always home after school. What'll we do without him, Dad?"

"I don't know, son. Right now, pray he gets well."

Liz cleared a place to see through the frosty windshield. "You guys are welcome to tag along with me. I always meet Melody's bus."

"Will you teach us how to rope?" Rusty asked excitedly.

"Rope?" Gil snorted. "You'd better be asking her to teach you how to cook."

That set both boys back. The misery on their faces touched Liz's heart. "If you could get by at breakfast and lunch, I'd be glad to fix your suppers."

Gil rasped a thumb over his afternoon stubble. "I appreciate the offer, but we can't impose. There's cleaning and laundry and a hundred other tasks. I'll ask around town and see if I can hire someone."

Dustin leaned forward. "Aw, Dad. You know who'll wanna come. That dorky Mrs. Porter."

"Suzette?" Gil chuckled. "I don't think washing a man's socks has ever been one of her ambitions."

Liz wondered if Dustin noticed the smile that lingered on his dad's lips. She glanced in the rearview mirror and saw Rusty and Melody exchange glances. Now what did that mean? Before she could delve into what their little minds were hatching, the headlights picked out a shadowy fence row that Liz fervently hoped ringed the south pasture. Driving with almost no visibility was nerve-racking, even though they were just creeping slowly along on Spencer land. She eased up on the gas and turned expectantly to Gil.

"Here already?" He seemed surprised. "Hey, good going." He reached across her to flip on a spotlight he used for finding lost or strayed horses.

His fingers so close to her breast brought a moment's distraction to Liz. Her foot slipped off the gas pedal just as Gil told her to turn west. There was a sickening crunch on the right side of the vehicle. She automatically hit the brakes, overcompensating. The heavy flatbed trailer bounced and slid sideways, pulling them into a spin. Liz braced herself and turned the wheels into the slide.

Gil fought a desire to rip the steering wheel out of her hands. He did move close enough to see the pulse hammering in her throat. Knowing his own pounded in sequence, he casually stretched out a hand to massage the back of her neck. "I forgot about that stump," he said evenly. "There're three more along here. The first lean-to isn't far now."

Liz marveled at his mastery over his nerves. She was determined to follow his lead, but her voice broke and gave her away. "Do...do you think I damaged anything?"

His eyes crinkled at the corners. "Other than your pride?"

She couldn't look away, especially as his fingers and thumb continued to rub the tense cord below her ears. "I was thinking m-more of the hi-hitch."

"I'll take a look-see. Sure you're okay?" he murmured.

"I'm fine. I should be the one to slog around out there. This was my fault."

"Dad?" a shaky voice queried from the back seat. "Did Mrs. Robbins get us stuck?"

"We're not stuck. And it's no one's fault, son," Gil said over his shoulder. "By jove, I think it's warming up."

Liz felt the icy slap of the wind as he climbed out. "Sure it is," she muttered. But he was barely gone seconds before he was back, bringing another blast of Arctic air.

"Brr. The iceman cometh." Liz scooted into her corner as he shook ice crystals from his hat and jacket.

"Crimp the wheel left and pull forward a foot. Straighten her, go three feet to the left and hold her steady."

"Easy for you to say. How about if we trade places?" It did nothing to bolster her confidence to have all three kids readily agree.

"You've made it through the worst, Lizbeth. The rest is a piece of cake. Another two hundred yards or so is the first shelter. Drive slow. I'll get out there on the flatbed and look for any problems as I shovel out the hay."

"Not while I'm moving. I'll stop and we'll both shovel hay."

"Look, it's hard work even for a man." Smiling, he brushed a thumb lightly across her chin.

Liz neither budged nor returned his smile.

"If you aren't the most stubborn female I've ever . . ." Gil let his sentence trail off, given pause by the soft sheen of her cheek and the sudden realization that her offer to stand shoulder to shoulder had been what he'd always wanted from Ginger.

Sensing something more in his silence than mere capitulation, Liz abruptly faced forward and edged the automatic transmission into low gear. The first lean-to proved to be precisely where Gil had said. It loomed dark in the crystal mist. Inside, Liz identified a huddle of horses, rumps all turned into the wind. Her heart splintered. "Those poor creatures. They need more than food. Can't we take them back to the barn where they'll be warm?"

Melody and Rusty hung over the back of her seat, echoing her sentiments.

"Be reasonable, Lizbeth," Gil chided. "You're talking stalls for two hundred and fifty horses or more." When he saw her crestfallen expression, he framed her face with his gloved fingertips. "Darlin', quarter horses are bred to withstand the elements. They're cow horses. Cowboys ride the range in all kinds of weather."

"But you said blue northers are rare."

"We get storms of all kinds. That's why I built big sturdy lean-tos."

The children slumped back in their seats, apparently accepting Gil's edict about the horses. Although Liz nodded, set the brake and opened her door without a word, Gil knew her nurturing instincts still balked. For a moment, he longed to take her in his arms and kiss away whatever doubts lingered—a moment that passed as quickly as it'd come. And as Gil slipped out his door to join her at the trailer, he wondered how someone so small could have such a large impact on his normally unshakable logic.

They worked side by side without talking. Liz tossed hay over the fence and Gil spread it among the animals. He used the handle of his pitchfork to break the thin layer of ice that had built up on the water trough. Raising his voice, he told her that according to Ben's accounts, blue northers rarely lasted more than a couple of days.

Speaking of Ben, how would he replace the old wrangler-cum-houseman? As he checked a leg here and patted a nose there, the question continued to disturb Gil. It was still on his mind when he returned to the vehicle, automatically climbing in on the driver's side. Liz stared at him openmouthed.

She heaved herself into the car and slid into the passenger seat. Stripping off her gloves and hat, she shook out her damp curls. "Hey, thanks for driving, Robbins—but I'll take over now. Show you how it should be done," she said, trying to mimic Gil's deep voice.

"What?" He looked startled, then sheepish as he gripped the wheel. "A purely reflex action, Lizbeth. I'm not used to anyone doing the driving but me."

Her backbone relaxed. "Sorry. Hoot always said I was too touchy when it came to man-woman roles. Guess I've been in the driver's seat too long." She gave an offhand shrug that drew Gil's gaze to her slender shoulders.

He smiled. "I thought only old bachelors got set in their ways."

"Yeah, right!" A grin bowed her mouth. "And old single moms."

His full-bodied laughter bounced off the ceiling. "Touché."

Liz's heart gave a funny hitch. Laughter etched appealing creases in his lean cheeks. A playful Gilman Spencer had chased away the blues that always came with a gloomy day. Suddenly Liz underwent a painful collapse of her jubilation. Corbett had been the only man to have that effect on her. Until now, he'd been the only man to provide a total infusion of sunshine into her life. Oh, she'd known that someday she'd probably take another mate—so Melody would have a father. Liz just hadn't expected to meet anyone who'd brighten those empty corners of her life, the way Corbett had. The ease with which the man seated on her left had accomplished it left her feeling terribly disloyal.

Her abrupt withdrawal reminded Gil of a night cereus at daybreak. Like the pretty white blossom his mother had once let him stay awake to observe, Lizbeth folded in on herself—the light gone from her eyes. Unfortunately they'd reached the second lean-to, and she bounded out of the vehicle before Gil could ask why.

And afterward they were too busy. Although the wind had definitely slackened, and also the sleet, they had more difficulties with this second group of animals. A young unbranded mare had given birth in the past few days to a long-legged colt. The mare was more than half-wild and nipped at Gil when he tried to get close. "Dammit," he muttered, risking the mare's teeth again. "Her colt's gonna die if we don't get him warmed up."

"He's the son of your rogue stallion," Liz breathed, moving silently up behind Gil. "Why don't you toss out the feed and let me try coaxing him? If I can get the little guy on the trailer, the mom will follow us, don't you think?"

"She won't let you. And he's so weak, he'll fall off."

"I'll ride back there with him. Do you have some sort of blanket?"

"Yeah, but you're not riding in an open trailer. Even if that wild mare doesn't trample you, you'll freeze."

"I won't. Please, Gil? He's worth a little frostbite, isn't he?"

Gil had no defense against her pleading eyes. "All right. *If* you catch him, and *if* the mare follows. Only I'll ride back there with him and you'll drive home."

His statement had a ring of finality that did not invite argument. Liz inclined her head and handed him her pitchfork.

Gil stared at it a good two seconds, wondering why he felt as if he'd been seduced by the devil. He didn't give her an iceberg's chance in hell of catching that little varmint. And dammit, she'd probably get herself horse-bit to boot. As he spread the hay, Gil warmed to the idea of treating her. Rubbing in salve could be damned erotic. Then he pictured teeth marks marring Lizbeth's pale skin, and he promptly went back to tell her she wasn't to fool with a wild mare.

Once again Gil had misjudged his farrier. Lizbeth already had the colt on the flatbed wrapped in two lap robes she'd found behind the Suburban's back seat. The mare stood beside him and sniffed at the blankets suspiciously—but showed no sign of wanting to bite. "Well, I'll be," was Gil's only comment as Liz adroitly switched places with him and went to start the vehicle.

On the drive home, he not only froze his fanny but had to balance the colt and put up with fish faces made by all three kids, who had their noses pressed to the rear window. Gil did his best to look content. Somehow he imagined that the twins, if not Melody, kept up a running commentary on his tribulations for Liz's entertainment.

Apart from a near mishap—when Gil lost his grip on the gangly colt and almost tumbled them both off the trailer—things went fairly well. Still, he was stiff, cold and miserable by the time Liz braked in front of the barn. And she was entirely too cheerful, hopping out, dancing around, light as one of the snowflakes that had begun slapping him in the face.

"You okay?" She laughed, trying to catch one of the soft fluffy flakes on her tongue.

"Abso-damn-lutely!" But of course he wasn't. His teeth nearly cracked when he jumped down, and Gil feared his joints would never work again—which turned out to be the least of his worries. Now that they had the renegades, the mare refused to set foot in the barn. Yet the minute they took her baby inside, she reared and battered at the door with both front feet.

Both Gil and Liz were afraid she'd break a leg or hurt one of the children, who were laughing and chasing around in the snow.

Liz stuck her head back outside. "Kids! I know you're excited. But you're scaring the mare. Why don't you three go feed the birds? I have half a bag of birdseed under the kitchen sink."

"I know where it is," Melody said, sounding important. "But you can help me throw it under the trees," she informed the twins.

With all this discussion of feeding horses and birds, the twins immediately claimed they were starved.

Gil gazed at their empty house. A sigh escaped his lips, melting a lazy snowflake or two. "Ben cleaned out the fridge before he took off for his sister's. I suppose there's some sort of leftovers in the freezer."

"Leftovers—on Thanksgiving? Yuck, Dad!"

"Boys, boys!" Liz clapped her hands. "You'll have turkey, I promise. I bought a twenty-pound bird. Please, let your dad and me finish up here, then we'll eat."

Amid high fives and a loud chorus of "All right!" the three children scampered off toward the cottage.

Gil's sigh was bigger this time. "You sure speak with authority and they mind you. Maybe I'll hire a drill sergeant, instead of a housekeeper."

She clicked her heels and saluted. "Does that mean if I say, 'Hut, two, three,' the mare will fall in and march into the barn?"

"Stand aside. Let a wily old horseman get this show on the road. I'll prop the door open, and you put that colt in the first stall yonder." He tipped his hat. "I'll rattle the food, like so. See?" He grinned as the mare poked a wary head inside. "I just hope she doesn't tear out the side of the barn making her getaway."

"Surely not. When she sees oats—and that her baby looks warmer..."

"I'll even add a carrot or two. But dammit, Lizbeth, you can't let yourself get so attached. These are horses, not human beings. You sound as if you think they can reason."

Taking tiny backward steps, she went beyond the stall door. "Maybe it's not exactly reasoning," she said stubbornly. "But instinct in caring for their young is shared by all mothers in the animal kingdom."

Gil dumped oats into the feed trough and climbed a ladder to reach a rack of carrots suspended overhead. When he landed beside her and slapped the vegetables into her hands, his lips had taken on a harsh set. "You're asking the wrong man to buy that philosophy. My ex-wife has no instinct for mothering. I have to track her down three weeks in advance of the twins' birthday and remind her to send cards." Turning, he walked away.

Liz heard the heartbreak in his voice. She wanted to call him back—to say that he must be mistaken, that no mother could possibly forget her kids. But she knew Ginger Lawrence too well to dispute him. The sad thing was that he still held all the hurt and anger inside. Her eyes filled with tears that Gil Spencer couldn't shed.

The carrots were shredded tops in her hands and her eyes were dry when Liz rejoined Gil outside. All the same, her heart ached for him and his sons. Corbett might have left her in a financial bind and to bear their child alone. But he'd laid a foundation of love before he died. It didn't sound as if the Spencer family had many good memories to get them through bad times.

Liz was determined to do what she could to change things. She began by insisting they needed a candlelit Thanksgiving supper. Those tough Spencer males could do with a bit of romantic atmosphere, she decided.

Catching the spirit, Gil offered to bring the food from her cottage. "I've got a sideboard full of china and silver that belonged to my mother. Let me clean up first, then I'll dig it out."

It was on the tip of Liz's tongue to tell him she'd do it—until she saw by the wistful look in his eye that he wanted to help. "All right. But I'll bring the food. I need to go home and shower."

Gil's generator was a godsend. Her cottage had a decided chill, and she nearly froze in a cold shower. By contrast, Gil's home was cozy. Soon holiday odors permeated enough corners to entice the kids into the kitchen. Preparing the dinner was mostly a matter of reheating. Liz hummed while she set things to simmer.

"Do we get gravy?" Rusty asked as he peered into the various pots. "Mrs. Littlefield makes the *best* gravy. Ben's always has a ton of lumps."

Liz never made gravy. Corbett had watched his waistline, and Hoot and his pals worried about cholesterol. But how hard could it be?

She found out when they were all seated around the table. Her hasty concoction was so thick, lifting the spoon practically picked up the gravy boat, as well.

"This stuff's like cement," Dustin declared a moment after their napkins were unfurled.

"Shall we say grace?" Liz asked brightly.

"Bless the meat, damn the skin, turn over your plates and all begin," Melody singsonged.

"Mel!" Liz blushed to the roots of her hair.

"Well, isn't that what Hoot always says?"

"That doesn't mean you're allowed to repeat it."

Rusty raised himself onto his knees. "I can't see. And those candles stink. What happened to the lights? Did the generator quit?"

"No. Hush," Gil scolded. "I think everything looks great." Beaming at Liz, he passed her a steaming slab of white meat. "I guess the boys have forgotten last Thanksgiving. Ben caught a wild turkey—or a buzzard. Dang thing was full of buckshot."

Liz tested her meat with her knife. "Oh, no," she wailed, "this isn't quite done." Probably because she'd taken it out of the oven early.

Gil shrugged and cut around the really pink parts. He told the boys to eat.

Liz dug around on her plate. The dressing was cooked, and she knew the pies were fine. All in all it wasn't quite a disaster; neither was it a roaring success. It might have been better if Gil hadn't kept insisting everything was great. If he used that word one more time or if the boys bellyached about one more thing, Liz thought she'd scream. Remembering her earlier vow to bring positive change to the Spencers' lives, she pasted a smile on her face and kept it there until she thought her face would break.

It was just as well that the power came on when it did, and that the boys and Gil dived for the TV to see the football game. Liz savored the peace and quiet of cleaning up.

"Melody fell asleep on the couch." Gil popped into the kitchen at the end of third quarter. "Come watch the end of the game. One of the teams is my old alma mater. When it's over, I'll see you back to the cottage."

She would have gone along, had he not praised her ill-fated meal yet again. "No sense in my trying to play catch-up with the game," she said a bit testily. "I think I'll go check on our two babies. Uh...I mean, *yours*," she stammered.

Bracketing her face with two weather-roughened hands, he said, "You got it right the first time. If not for you, neither of those foals would see daylight. They're yours when we wean them, Lizbeth."

Her irritation melted like the rum sauce had over her warm mince pie. Not because he was giving her two expensive pieces of horseflesh but because of how he said her name. He had a way of pronouncing it that sent the hot blood racing to her toes. She couldn't help it. She rose to the tips of those toes and kissed him full on the mouth—intending to end with an impassioned thank-you and be on her way to the barn.

At the touch of her lips, Gil's palms slid around her neck. His fingers tunneled beneath her thick curls, and his mouth opened, eliciting an entirely different kind of kiss.

Surprised and then pleased, Liz accepted the honeyed investigation of his tongue. Her hands circled his lean waist, and she settled her slim body neatly between his splayed legs. It'd been so long—too long—since she'd enjoyed the feel of a man's burgeoning erection. And Gil's was instantaneous. A slow suffusion of heat started low in Liz's stomach. It spread deliciously outward, weakening her limbs.

Gil flamed like a torch. He couldn't remember when he'd last held a woman this close. Couldn't remember when he'd wanted to—or when he'd wanted more than kisses. It seemed a lifetime since he'd thought that he would die if he didn't bury himself in a woman's soft-ness—since he'd wanted to wring every bit of emotion from both of them—to end in a tangle of hot bodies and cool sheets. He wanted that now with Lizbeth Robbins, and he didn't want to wait. Lifting her, he pressed her slight frame against the kitchen counter.

Suddenly airborne and weightless, Liz clung to Gil, her thighs circling his narrow hips. The rasp of denim on denim nearly sent her over the edge. She ripped open the pearl snaps down the front of his shirt. She wanted to feel the bronzed skin she'd so far only seen. Running her fingers through the crisp hair that fanned across his chest was almost her undoing.

The untimely arrival of his sons, coming to let him know the fourth quarter had started, shocked Gil back to reality. Dustin's voice came at him through a red haze.

"Game's on. Whatcha doin', Dad? Is somethin' wrong with Mrs. Robbins?"

Mrs. Robbins. That cut through his passion fast. Gil plunked Liz unceremoniously on the counter, heedless of his mother's good dishes. One saucer fell to the floor and broke while Gil endeavored to refasten his shirt and Liz blinked at him through luminous eyes.

She teetered on her precarious perch, taking longer than Gil to make the transition. When she finally did and quickly reached for the cupboard above her head, more of the dishes she'd stacked on the counter threatened to fall. "Your father's helping me put these cups on the top shelf," Liz said in what she thought was a remarkably calm voice. "Thanks for the boost," she told Gil, all the while cringing at the skepticism lacing the twins' silence. As well she might. For the top shelf was totally filled with the popcorn popper and the slow cooker. Nary a cup in sight.

Just then Melody wandered in, giving a sleepy yawn. "When are we goin' home, Mom? I'm tired."

"Right now." Liz jumped down and picked up broken china. Dumping the pieces into the trash, she said, "You're welcome to the leftovers. Don't bother to see us out. We know the way."

Gil hardly had time to marshal his thoughts before they'd gone, leaving him to face the narrowed gazes of his sons. "Who's winning?" he asked lightly.

"You were kissin' Melody's mom, weren't you?" Dustin demanded.

Feeling exposed by the two open shirt buttons, Gil crossed his arms. "What if I was? I think I'm old enough to kiss a woman without asking your permission."

"Ick. Suck face." Rusty circled his neck with his hands and made gagging sounds.

"More'n ick," added Dustin in his know-it-all fashion. "Buddy Hodges says after kissin' comes marriage, then makin' babies. How could you, Dad? How *could* you?" Both boys ran from the room, pounded up the stairs and slammed their bedroom door so hard the old house rocked.

Gil winced. He gazed at the swaying light fixture overhead for a long time—until the tension drained from his neck and shoulders. Buddy Hodges wasn't so smart. If things had been allowed to run unchecked, he could well have been making babies *before* marriage. Lordy, how could he have let a few kisses get so out of hand?

Then Gil recalled how Lizbeth Robbins felt in his arms and he grew hard again—which left him two choices. Stay away from her or pay a visit to the drugstore. Considering the twins' reaction, he'd have to weigh those two options carefully. Except that he was very much afraid his feelings for Lizbeth overshadowed any ability to remain impartial.

HAD GIL BEEN ABLE to keep a housekeeper more than three days running, he might have been granted the time to work things out with regard to Liz and the boys. Unfortunately things kept happening. First, he hired Mrs. Wagner, an acquaintance of Ben's sister. They'd met at the hospital the day Gil visited Ben. The boys dubbed Mrs. Wagner the dragon lady. Three days of their usual tricks, and she packed her bags, demanding Rafe take her home at once. She didn't even wait for her pay.

She was followed by a sweet but timid former nun, whom Gil had found through a friend of a friend. Miss Farnsworth claimed to have an excellent rapport with children. She'd just failed to list on her application that she had an almost phobic fear of creepy-crawlies. A fact the Spencer twins discovered in the first hour she was installed in their home. Terrorized and terrified, Miss Farnsworth left the Lone Spur on day two of her employment. Five minutes into cleaning out the boys' lunch boxes after school.

Liz witnessed the woman's flight. She'd just left her cottage with Melody, taking her to one of the pastures where she was shoeing a horse for a new wrangler who'd recently come on board, when she heard Gil's housekeeper scream. No amount of cajoling on Liz's part could convince the woman to wait and talk with Gil. Miss Farnsworth didn't care that the tarantula wasn't real, that it was left over from Halloween. She called a cab and marched to the end of the lane to wait for it.

Angry on their dad's behalf, Liz lectured the twins for five full minutes. "I can't leave you alone. You've got no choice but to come with me."

Almost meekly they saddled their horses and followed her to the line shack above the west pasture. Dustin didn't like it a bit when she made them stand under a tree. Too bad. Liz wasn't in any mood to take his lip. She'd heard Ben might make it back mid-February. This was only the second week of December. She couldn't imagine what Gil would do in the meantime. Complacent about Miss Farnsworth's ability to manage things, he'd gone off to deliver a gelding to Morris Littlefield. There was no way of knowing when he'd make it back.

She and the kids arrived at the ranch just past suppertime, and Gil hadn't yet returned. Tired, dirty and out of

sorts, Liz fixed supper at the ranch house. She had just
sent the boys to change into their pajamas when Nancy
Littlefield dropped by to welcome the new housekeeper—and mistook Lizbeth for Gil's ex-nun.

Liz understood the woman's shock. Dressed in a tiger-
striped leotard and tight raggedy black jeans, no one
looked less like someone who'd been cloistered for ten
years than Liz. Once the two women stopped talking at
the same time and got to the truth, they fell together
laughing.

Her bad mood dissipated, Liz happily left the twins in
Nancy's capable hands. She went home to clean up and
put Melody to bed.

Gil walked in two hours later. Nancy met him at the
door and then bent his ear for another twenty minutes—
until, against his better judgment, Gil agreed to take the
Lone Spur's farrier up on her original offer of fixing
supper and keeping an eye on the boys after school.
Standing in the doorway watching Nan drive off, Gil had
a sinking feeling he'd been had. He'd been on the receiv-
ing end of Nan's matchmaking efforts too many times
not to recognize that insidious gleam in her eye.

CHAPTER EIGHT

IN THE MORNING Gil rose early to fix breakfast. He burned the toast and let the Cream of Wheat stick, but by the time the boys donned their yellow slickers and trudged off to meet the school bus in the rain, they knew he meant business. They should. After all, he'd been awake half the night drawing up an expanded list of chores. This morning he'd laid out his expectations in no uncertain terms. The one thing he didn't do was bring up Lizbeth's name, preferring to speak with her first.

Determined to get this settled, Gil phoned her. "Hi, it's Gil. Do you have time to stop by for a cup of coffee?"

"Uh...sure," Liz agreed warily. But then, she supposed he wanted to hear firsthand about Miss Farnsworth's hasty departure. "No problem. I'll see you in a bit."

Gil assumed he'd be able to clean up the kitchen before she arrived, but he'd barely started when Lizbeth banged on his back door.

"Whew. Not fit for man nor beast out there." She shook rain off her Stetson, scraped the mud from her boots and looped her slicker over a peg on the porch. Hovering on the threshold of the Spencers' kitchen, she wrinkled her nose. "Wow, did you have a chimney fire or something? It's smoky in here."

Gil glanced around, expecting to see flames. She'd brought in the freshness of the rain and the ever-present

flowery scent of what he now knew was violets. It filled
his nostrils. If she hadn't walked straight to the stove and
sniffed at the corroded cereal pot, he wouldn't have connected the smoke to his cooking efforts—at least not until her eyes swept over him in pity.

"It helps if you put things like this to soak right away."
She carried the singed pot to the sink and ran it full of
water.

"I'll manage. Ben knows every quirk of this cantankerous stove. I haven't got the hang of it yet."

"I see. But Miss Farnsworth's problem wasn't the
stove."

"I know." Gil poured her a cup of coffee and refilled
his own. Clearing a space at the round oak table, he offered her a chair. "Nan Littlefield told me the whole
story. Thanks for trying to salvage things, Lizbeth."

She gave a hitch of one shoulder as she sat and accepted the cup. "What are you going to do now?"

He cleared his throat. "If you're willing, I have a
proposition."

Liz had just taken a sip of hot coffee, which refused to
go down. She spewed it all over the table. "Sorry." Color
rose to her cheeks. Her gaze made a restless foray of the
room before meeting his.

"Not *that* kind of proposition." It was Gil's turn to
flush. "Although," he mumbled, "the way I acted a
couple of weeks ago, I can see how you might get that
impression."

"So, now that you're actually admitting *something*
happened between us on Thanksgiving..." Liz stood,
grabbing a towel to mop up her spill. "Let's hear what's
on your mind, Spencer." She'd be darned if she'd let him
wriggle off the hook.

"Here's the deal, Lizbeth," Gil said solemnly. "I need your help with the boys until Ben gets on his feet, but I don't want us to get *involved*. You and me, that is."

Well, he couldn't have been more blunt! Liz got quickly to her feet, went to the sink and started rinsing breakfast dishes. Since the ardent kiss they'd shared in this very room, she had admit to having thoughts along the line of *involvement*. Disappointed to hear he felt differently, Liz was determined not to let him suspect she'd entertained any romantic ideas, either. "Well, that's a relief. I've wanted to tell you that I got carried away by the generosity of your gift of the foals and...and the emotional aftermath of the storm. Frankly I felt unfaithful to Corbett." That, at least, was true.

Gil frowned at the soft slope of her shoulders. The pale skin of her neck peeked out between her pink sweater and the dark bob of her short curls. He had the damnedest urge to press his lips to the curve below her ear. What did she mean—unfaithful? Corbett Robbins was dead. Lizbeth was alive. So was he.

Damn—when she wasn't around, his plan to keep things strictly business seemed so easy.

She turned to glance over her shoulder to see why he hadn't jumped to agree with her. The intense look on his face surprised her—a mixture of hunger and passion. It struck her then that he might be more involved than he'd let on. But for mercy's sake, why deny it? They were both single and unencumbered. Obviously it had to do with his bad marriage. Quickly she bent to fill the dishwasher. When she straightened, the longing was gone from his eyes and he got down to business.

"Last night, Nancy pointed out that, with Ben away, I have an opportunity to spend more time with my kids. I realize I've spoiled them. Overcompensation for their lack of a mother, I guess." He stared into his cup for a long time. "Thanksgiving, you suggested letting the boys tag along with Melody after school, and maybe fixing us supper. If you haven't changed your mind, I'd like to see how it works. Only I won't let you do it for free."

The amount he named staggered Liz. "I can't take money. Not after you gave me those foals. Don't insult me. What are friends for? I'll just make extra when I fix our evening meal."

Gil's teeth worried his lower lip. *Friends.* That had a nice safe ring to it. "Okay, or we can all eat here. But if you have second thoughts, say so. Plus, I insist on buying all the grub. I'm going into town today to make arrangements for our laundry. Would it be a problem to write up a grocery list by noon?"

She started the dishwasher and wiped down the surrounding counters. "I'll check your fridge and cupboards while I'm here. No sense buying stuff like flour and eggs if you're already supplied."

"Ben buys milk and eggs from Florence Ames. She lives in an old farmhouse up the road. Her husband died a while back and her son took a job in Tulsa. Flo should move into town, but she can't bear to leave the farm Buck bought when they got married. Ben keeps an eye on her woodpile. When it gets low, I stop by for coffee and chop some more. Morris drops off feed, and Doc Shelton attends to the health of her cows. I'd appreciate it if you'd fill in for Ben."

Liz's eyes teared. "No problem. That's a sweet thing you're doing."

"It's neighborly." Gil brushed aside her praise as he strode to the door and collected his jacket and hat from the pegs. "Oh, in case you aren't aware—the boys hate liver and corned-beef hash. They gobble down pigs in a blanket. We all like fried chicken, cold or hot. Make things easy on yourself. Keep it simple. Leave that list on the table, and I'll be back to pick it up after I see how Luke's doing—he's breaking two-year-olds. If you like, I'll meet the school bus today and lay down rules for the kids."

These last two speeches were the longest Liz had ever heard him make. She recognized his uneasiness—felt a little nervous herself. It was silly. Nothing had changed. She was still his employee. Her duties had expanded into the domestic arena, that was all. It wasn't as if he'd proposed they set up housekeeping together. What shocked Liz was that she didn't find such a thought abhorrent.

"Suit yourself." She shrugged, hiding her discomfort. "I'll be close by if you get tied up. Rafe told me to muck out the big barn." She made one of Dustin's gagging sounds.

"Since when does our farrier muck out barns?" Gil began the rhythmic slap of his hat against his thigh.

"It's okay. I was making a joke. When Rafe hired me, he said it was part of the job. It's just that I don't like being cooped up inside. But unless it's blowing rain, I'll open both front and back doors."

Gil scowled. "It might have been okay if Rafe'd hired somebody with a little more muscle. Mucking out stalls is hard work."

"As is scrubbing floors, doing laundry and having babies." Her chin came up. "My mother's mother picked tobacco, chopped cotton and sold home-baked bread to feed and clothe a fatherless brood. She outlived two sons. And I doubt she ever weighed more than ninety pounds in her life. Go on, break your horses and quit worrying. I'll do my job fine."

A smile broke free of Gil's penetrating gaze. "Yes, ma'am." He angled his Stetson jauntily. "Then I guess there's no need for me to take the laundry to town. I'll just drop it by your back porch every morning."

Liz's groan was lost in the echo of his boot steps and the subsequent slam of the back door. Well, she'd certainly asked for that. She'd walked right into it with her eyes open. Plunking herself down at the table in front of her now cold cup of coffee, she laughed until the tears ran. Wait until she relayed this episode to Hoot. He was forever saying she had foot-in-mouth disease. Still, she knew Gil wouldn't really leave her his dirty laundry. He was too proud.

Even though it rained steadily all morning, Liz never made it to her chores in the barn. Thick mud out on the range played havoc with the lightweight shoes on some of the wranglers' horses. She set her forge up under the umbrella of an old oak tree and was kept busy molding heavier shoes until lunchtime. From her vantage point on the hill, she saw Gil return to his house for the grocery list. If her heart gave a little flutter kick at the sight of his wide square shoulders, the swing of his narrow hips, she blamed it on a fat raindrop that plopped off her hat, slithered beneath her collar and trickled coolly between her breasts. It was the only thing cool about her—which was why, when she heard his vehicle splash to a stop outside her cottage a few hours later, Liz didn't look up. She didn't think her heart could stand the strain of watching him make all those trips into her place with enough groceries to feed a family of five. Because they *weren't* a family.

The bad thing about shoeing horses was that her mind had too much freedom to wander. Once Liz started thinking about Gil, her brain seemed stuck in a rut. It dwelled on the odd fact that the men never gossiped about their boss's romantic alliances. In the four months she'd been at the ranch, no one had talked about who he dated. There was open discussion about the other men's love lives. For instance, Liz knew that Rafe exclusively dated Joyce, a visiting nurse. Luke had fallen hard for Polly, the owner of the "fluff-duff" shop, and Macy Rydell played the field far and wide; his exploits made history for a week. Most of the others were vocal about what they liked or didn't like in a woman. Only Gil shied away from romance. Thanks to Ginger Lawrence, Liz presumed.

Liz rarely ran across a person she didn't like. That woman was an exception. Something puzzled Liz—if Ginger had always been grasping, why on earth would she throw away the Lone Spur for the likes of Avery Amistad? Maybe someday Liz would work up the nerve to ask Gil about his marriage. But not anytime soon.

Goodness! There was the school bus turning into the lane. She'd wasted half a day mooning over Gil Spencer. She made her way as quickly as she could toward the drop-off point. And wouldn't you know it, just then he rode up on a feisty high-stepping filly. It was the first time she'd seen him in a pair of chaps. When he dismounted and looped his soft leather gloves around his belt, she had difficulty expelling the air trapped in her lungs. By the time she'd covered the short distance that separated them, blood swished in her ears, leaving her light-headed.

"Hi." His greeting did little to slow her heart rate. Liz said nothing as he wrapped the reins twice around the fence and gave a good yank. "I thought for a minute I'd be late. Got more than I bargained for uncorking this lady." He smoothed a palm over the filly's withers. The rain had stained her coat a dark rich shade of butter-scotch.

"Threw you, did she?" Liz smiled. "Sorry I missed that show."

"Next time I'll sell tickets. Luke knew, damn his or-nery hide. I should've guessed when so many hands came out of the woodwork to gawk."

"That's usually a clue something's wrong. I get the same thing when somebody brings me a rough horse to shoe. An audience materializes out of the dust." Her gaze meandered over his backside. "You must have stayed with her. I don't see any mud."

"We're using the covered arena. It was costly, but worth every dime. I've never met a cowboy who liked getting wet."

"Likewise farriers."

As the faded yellow bus rumbled to a stop and she sauntered toward the opening door, Gil eyed her mud-spattered jeans. Like him, she'd cast aside her rain gear in favor of jeans and a flannel shirt. When she stepped aside to let the boisterous children alight, he could see the way her shirt molded the generous swell of her breasts. In an unconscious movement, Gil cupped his palms, imag-ining the damp fit. The minute he realized what he'd done, he gave a start and tried to bury his hands in his front pockets. Brought up short by his chaps, he felt sil-lier than ever.

"Hey, there's Dad! Cool," yelled the first twin off the bus. "Look, Dusty, we don't have no crappy ol' house-keeper meetin' us, like you said."

Dustin swung down. He plowed through a puddle his brother had managed to avoid. But his steps slowed, leaving him standing in ankle-deep water as Melody Robbins and her mom joined his father.

"Boys," Gil said lightly. "The day we learned about Ben, Lizbeth offered to let you guys hang out with her after school. She also said she'd fix us supper every night. I decided today that's what we'll do for a while."

"Cool," Rusty said again, and promptly danced a jig with Melody.

Slogging out of the puddle, Dustin marched right up to his dad. "Ain't it kinda chummy, callin' her Lizbeth? You didn't use those other housekeepers' first names."

Liz knew that if either one of the boys grumbled, it'd be Dustin. But she hadn't anticipated such outright belligerence.

Neither had Gil, although he could trace its roots to a certain kiss—which wasn't to say he condoned his son's behavior. "We call Ben by his first name, and Rafe and Shorty. Besides, Lizbeth isn't our housekeeper. She's a friend doing us a favor. I want you to keep that in mind, Dustin. No more shenanigans, mister." In spite of the fact that it had begun to drizzle again, Gil knelt and met his son eye to eye.

Dustin kicked at the book bag he'd dragged through the mud. "What'er shenan . . . shenanig . . ."

"Tricks. Pranks. Jokes," Gil said sternly. "And every night at suppertime, Lizbeth is going to give me an accounting of how you've behaved. So don't think I won't know."

Liz coughed. When Gil glanced in her direction, she discreetly sliced her finger across her throat. "We'll do fine," she said with more confidence than she felt. In the same sweet tone, she added, "Your saddle's getting wet. Maybe you'd like to help us muck out the barn while it dries."

"What?" Wheeling, he saw that she was right. Splotches of rain darkened his hand-tooled saddle. The humor in her voice annoyed him. Obviously she knew how cowboys felt about climbing aboard wet leather. Blocking out her knowing grin and the probability of chafed privates, Gil sprang into the saddle.

"Dad, do we hafta muck out the barn?" Dustin jogged alongside the horse, splattering mud in all directions.

The green-broke filly, still unused to dealing with a man's weight, sunfished with a twist. "Look out, son," Gil shouted as he rose clear out of the seat. He slammed back, unable to get a firm grip with his knees.

Liz ordered Melody and Rusty to head for the barn. Certain they'd do as they were told, she sprang forward and yanked Dustin out from under the filly's flying back feet. The boy flung his arms around her waist and hung on for dear life until she boosted him over the fence. Climbing to the top rung, she turned and caught the rest of Gil's wild ride. No lady, the filly tried every trick imaginable to dislodge her passenger. Gil was equally determined to stick with her.

He had, as they said in the rodeo, a gold-buckle ride. With no hazers to flank him at the end of an eight-second buzzer, Gil went the distance. Liz held her breath and mentally counted the time. He was beautiful. His knees jackknifed high on the filly's neck, his right arm whipped high over his head, and his long body lay flat out over the horse's rump. Just when Liz thought Gil couldn't possibly take the punishment a moment longer, the filly quit pitching and tore out on a run.

"Golly-dang!" a white-faced Dustin exclaimed. "I'm . . . I'm sorry. I didn't mean to spook my dad's horse."

Liz draped a shaky hand over the fence to ruffle his shock of auburn hair. "He knows that, Dusty. But sometimes it pays to think before we act. If it'd been me up on that animal, I'd probably have broken my neck. Come on.'' She knew he felt bad; no sense making him feel worse.

Gil's brush with danger had a sobering effect on everyone. The four talked little as they cleaned out old bedding and put new hay in the stalls. Since the children worked hard to help her finish before dark, Liz decided to treat them to chicken potpies for supper. That, green salad and cinnamon-sprinkled baked apples should fill a jittery stomach after a rainy unsettling day.

Liz didn't look forward to winter. Short dark days often triggered terrible bouts of claustrophobia. Spring couldn't arrive fast enough to suit her.

Because the boys had homework and Melody didn't, Liz elected to cook at the ranch house. She showered, gathered some pots and pans, plus the ingredients she'd need from the sacks Gil had left on her counter and loaded them in a picnic basket. It would serve as well to bring her food and Melody's home to the cottage. So much back and forth sounded involved, but once she worked out a routine, things should go smoothly. The year she started junior high school, the farm cook had had a family crisis. Liz recalled how her mother fixed food in her kitchen and transported it to the stable hands in baskets similar to this one.

She paused, locked in memory, seeing her mother's smile in the rain-streaked window. A sudden jarring recollection of her father's anger wiped it away. He didn't want his wife and daughter exposed to stable riff-raff, he'd said. And that was the end of that. The Whitleys, unlike her mother's family, were such snobs. Even then, sometimes Liz wished she could turn back the clock and play that scene over. And others like it. . . .

Crazy thoughts. Thrusting them aside, Liz hurried to finish, determined to get to the ranch house and on to more pleasant things. The twins balked at sitting down to homework, until they discovered that Liz was willing to help them.

"Ben never went past fifth grade," Rusty informed her when she peeked over their shoulders and discovered, to her consternation, that neither twin could subtract.

"Quit whining," Dustin admonished. "Ben said he wasn't paid to teach us. Said they should give us time to do this stuff at school. It's Miss Burke's fault," he said, laying the blame squarely on his teacher.

"Did you discuss this with your father?" Liz sorted through page after curled page, all ungraded because of incomplete work.

"Naw," Dusty said. "We're usually ready for bed before he gets home."

"I see." But she didn't. Especially as she knew Gil had had conferences with both boys' teachers. Surely they'd explained to him how poorly the twins were doing.

She sighed, pulled up a chair and started with basics, using sugar cubes to explain subtraction. The Spencers' cupboards revealed boxes of sugar cubes. Treats for the horses, she supposed. The twins thought it was a great game. Melody had been asking what she could get the boys for Christmas. Liz made a mental note to buy flash cards and maybe a money game. The twins learned quickly and were soon delighted to have their homework done in time to watch TV.

As Liz set the table, she noticed a lot of little things that had been let go around the house, things she hadn't seen before. Junk piled in corners. Spills not cleaned from the beautiful old hooked rugs. Dust buildup. Things a man with aching bones would naturally let slide. But

Liz didn't think Gil Spencer would appreciate a woman going on a marathon cleaning spree in his home. Too bad.

She happened to be staring out the dining-room window when Gil arrived home. Apparently his joints weren't doing so well, either. She noted the tired slope of his shoulders and the stiff-legged way he negotiated the stairs. He was—what? Thirty-two or -three? Not old, but too old for a steady routine of breaking horses.

Walking in on the wondrous odor of cooking food surprised Gil. "Hey, hey," he said as the boys charged through the kitchen and slammed into him with bear hugs before he'd even cleared the door. "Take it easy on your old man. I've seen the wrong end of a bronc too many times today." He glanced at the kitchen clock. "I thought it was a lot later. Because it got dark so early, I guess. I know why you guys aren't in your pajamas yet, but shouldn't you be hitting the books?"

Liz stepped around the corner. She passed Melody a jacket and shrugged into her own. "Since you're here, I guess Mel and I will go home." She gestured to the boys. "They finished yesterday's and today's lessons. Let them get into their pajamas while you shower. By the way, I set a bottle of Ibuprofen beside your plate. And liniment may stink, but it'll do wonders, too."

He straightened immediately. "Why would I need all that?"

"Why indeed?" She went to the stove, removed two potpies and two baked apples and put them in her basket. "There's salad in the fridge. No reason the boys can't clean the table later and put the dishes to wash."

They grumbled, but nodded when she said that if they wanted her to continue fixing supper and helping with homework, they'd better do their part.

"Wait." Gil placed his hand on her arm. "Why don't you two stay and eat with us? No sense letting your food get cold on the way home."

Looking over his shoulder, Liz noted that Dustin wasn't at all pleased by his father's invitation. "My basket's insulated. You'd better hurry, though. I turned the oven down, but everything's ready."

Disappointment flickered in Gil's eyes. Rusty, too, begged them to stay. Dustin clung to Gil, so it was easy to see that *he* didn't want to share his dad with Liz. For the first time she wondered if Dusty harbored a dream of his mother coming back. She'd read in more than one psychology book that it was common for some kids to feel that way, even years after a divorce.

As she and Melody walked back to the cottage, Liz reflected on that telling look of Gil's. She was still thinking about it after they'd eaten. Given their present situation, it'd be easy for him to succumb to the slightest bit of TLC. Not so Dustin. He was brimming with resentment. Suppose a relationship did develop between her and Gil—not that it would. But if it did, Liz wasn't sure she had it in her to fight a jealous child.

She set aside her thoughts about the Spencers long enough to read Melody a story before tucking her into bed. Then she washed dishes, straightened up the living room, sorted through bills. Finally, stealing a few minutes for herself, Liz relaxed at her kitchen table with a cup of tea and a book. All at once the man who still hovered around the fringes of her thoughts rapped sharply at her door.

As each was plainly visible to the other through the small-paned window in the top half of the door, Liz closed her book and rose to let him in.

"Hi! This is a surprise. I thought you'd be home coddling those aching joints. You shouldn't be out traipsing in the rain."

Gil stepped inside and set her empty pans on the counter. "There's no such thing as a fair-weather rancher." He smiled. "Anyway, I think the storm's blown over. The stars are out. It's turning cold." He blew on his hands. "Fireplace weather. I came to check on your wood supply."

She leaned around him to look at the clock. "Midnight—and you're offering to chop my wood?"

"Well . . ." He removed his hat and slapped it against his leg. "Thought I might work it in tomorrow. Thanks for supper. We finished everything."

"Didn't I make enough?" She sucked in her lower lip.

"Plenty. Too much." He laughed. "If we eat like that every night, the boys and I will soon resemble Pudgy Ralston. He owns the bakery in town."

Liz's gaze followed the hand that stroked his midsection. She remembered vividly how those same fingers felt massaging her neck. How they felt sliding up and down her back. "Pudgy?" She cleared her throat. "Shame on you. Nicknames of that sort seal a person's fate. What kind of lesson is that for your sons?"

"I didn't give him the nickname. In fact, he prefers it to Angus."

"Oh. Then use his middle name perhaps."

"Ulysses?"

"Well." Their eyes met and they both dissolved into laughter. "Would you like a cup of tea?" she asked in the awkward moment when they stopped laughing.

"Is that what you're drinking?" He sniffed the air.

"Yes, aniseed."

"Smells like licorice."

"It does. I have sort of a scratchy throat tonight. I'm hoping this will help ward off a cold." She stroked thumb and fingers down either side of her neck.

Gil stood a moment, as though mesmerized by the slow movement of her hand. "I, uh, I'd better let you get to bed. Sleep is the best medicine for a cold. Maybe looking after the boys and the extra cooking is too much. I can make other arrangements."

She stiffened, letting her hand drop to her breast. "Whatever you like. You'll want to add a tutor to your list. Did you know the boys are having major trouble in math?"

"Trouble?" He stepped forward and gripped her arms. "Are you saying my kids are dense?"

"On the contrary. They're very bright. But they're missing the boat because no one at home is taking the time to see that they understand what's being taught at school." She wrenched out of his hold, wishing, when she saw the pain darken his eyes, that she'd minded her own business.

He raked a hand through his hair. "The teachers said they're falling behind, yet Ben insists they work like beavers on their homework. When Dustin's teacher referred to him as incorrigible, I'm afraid I walked out on the conference."

"Could you maybe get the boys up an hour earlier?"

"They're not what you'd call morning people. We're so far from town, I wonder where I can find a tutor."

"I'm willing to help after school like I did tonight. Really, it's no trouble. If they tune me out, I suppose you'll have to get someone else—or when Ben gets back."

Gil eased her into a full embrace. Nuzzling his face in her hair, he sighed. "Lord knows why you're so willing, considering the way we started off."

She pulled back. "It's not for the reasons Buddy Hodges said."

"I know. Just as I've known the job was too much for Ben lately. But he gave me a hand when I couldn't find anybody willing to take on two squalling babies."

"It's all right," Liz murmured, running her hands over his back. "I know what you mean. Hoot did the same for me. Let's give this a few more weeks. Till after Christmas. New Year's, we can reassess."

"Christmas. Don't remind me," he groaned. "I hate shopping for presents and wrapping them. I lie awake nights plotting how to hijack a dozen elves."

Liz's throaty laughter shook both their bodies. "So now you know what we women have gone through for generations. Cleaning, shopping, cooking, wrapping and hiding gifts. Not to mention decorating. Don't expect me to have any sympathy."

He leaned back, stretching out his arms to their full length. "Bah, humbug. Get rid of all the fuss and mess— except the food and mistletoe." Bending, he nibbled at her ear. "One thing we have plenty of on this ranch is mistletoe."

She pushed playfully at his face. "Just like a man. Thinking only of food and sex. We women happen to *like* decorations and presents."

"Then you're stuck with the whole ball of wax." He captured her lips and kissed her soundly. A kiss that went from fun to serious in a heartbeat. By the time it ended, they were both breathing raggedly.

For a long moment Liz gazed into sparkling hazel eyes that had come alive with passion. His head had begun a second descent toward her lips when she untangled herself from his arms and crossed to the window. She stared out into the dark. "Gil, the situation with me filling in for

Ben isn't the only one that needs time. Dustin has a mile-high chip on his shoulder when it comes to women. It's not so surprising, Gil. You've locked away your mother's things and stripped the place of any sign of their mom.''

"What makes you such an authority on my life?" Nothing sobered him like the mere mention of his ex-wife.

"I'm not. But why else would Dustin hate to see you touching me?"

Gil tucked a thumb under his belt, his lips pressed for a moment in a tight line. "Do your psychology books say parents should let kids manipulate their love lives?"

"Certainly not. But they do say to be aware of problems and try to help your kids resolve them."

"How do you feel about my touching you?"

She waved a hand. "That's hardly the point."

"I think it's very much the point," he said curtly, making his way stiffly toward the door. "This is between you and me. Leave the boys out of it. I'll handle my kids."

Unhappily she watched him jerk the door open and leave in a huff. She could have called him back and answered his question, said how much she liked being touched by him. On the other hand, she would've thought he could recognize for himself that she turned to gumbo in his hands. What would it take to get through to that man? And what had happened to that firmly stated decision of his about not getting *involved*? Did he want to or didn't he? She wasn't a Ping-Pong ball, for goodness' sake.

For the rest of the week Liz worked close to home. Her lessons with the boys went well, even though she insisted on doing her cooking at the cottage. The minute she saw

Gil drive in, she loaded the basket and sent the twins home. Every morning, the basket reappeared on her back porch, filled with clean dishes and accompanied by a terse note of thanks. Lord, she missed their casual visits. Should she be the first to try to bridge the rift? If only she had more experience in such matters....

By Friday a chilly wind had kicked up, and her scratchy throat grew worse. Not only was Liz hoarse when the school bus pulled in that afternoon, her hands and face were chapped and sore from spending so much time shoeing out in the weather. She had little patience when the boys complained about being forced to go back with her to the south pasture. *She* was the one with six horses left to shoe, not them.

Her lack of patience, she suspected later, was the catalyst that resulted in Melody's cat, Mittens, ending up stuck in the top branches of the tallest oak tree. She'd only gone into the house for five minutes to get Melody changed into play clothes and hadn't even realized the cat had escaped. The twins, already in jeans, were instructed to drop their book bags on their sun porch and come right back to the cottage.

Liz was positive that in the few minutes they were apart the boys had, out of spite, terrorized Mittens and chased the poor cat up the tree.

"We didn't," they denied, in the midst of Melody's bawling and Liz's frantic raspy cries of "Here, kitty, kitty. Nice, kitty. Come on, Mittens, there's food inside."

No amount of cajoling or rattling a box of dry cat food dislodged the frightened animal from her perch. After ten more minutes, by which time Liz's voice had given out, she decided she'd have to personally rescue the cat.

Which is how she came to be at her worst when Suzette Porter, of the big bazooms, drove in.

The woman apparently spied the Spencer twins shivering beneath the spreading limbs of the oak. She stopped her silver-gray Mercedes and hopped out to check on the little dears.

Halfway up the tree, Liz was afforded a bird's-eye view of everything happening below. The acoustics weren't bad, either. Sound carried upward on the wind.

"Boys," the newcomer cooed in a too-sweet voice. "Whatever are you doing standing out here in this freezing weather? Why aren't you inside by the fire?"

Liz watched the woman wrap her thigh-length mink coat tight around her short winter white wool dress and stoop to look where Rusty pointed at the branches.

"I just learned about dear Ben's accident," she gushed. "Russell, are you saying the woman your father hired to care for you is up in that tree? I can't believe your daddy would condone such behavior. Where is he, by the way?" She straightened and gazed toward the barn.

Liz found herself wishing Melody's cat would take it upon himself to piddle instead of just yowl. The spitting feline crouched on a limb slightly out of Liz's reach—but directly above their visitor's salon-styled hair.

Dustin, the very same child who'd claimed at Halloween that Suzette Porter had her sights set on his father, pointed to the weanling barn and offered to go fetch Gil.

Let him, thought Liz, creeping out on a swaying branch. "Cat," she croaked, "I'm gonna wring your scrawny neck, and then I'm gonna start on a couple of boys."

Unfortunately her words also carried. Melody sobbed harder and Rusty began to cry. All but clucking, Suzette Porter gathered the twins beneath her mink and announced they should forget that horrible woman and go to the house for some of the chocolate cake she'd brought.

Liz made a lunge for the cat just as the Mercedes whizzed off. Having missed, she dug her fingernails into the bark and choked on diesel fumes. If that wasn't indignity enough, the darned cat chose that moment to scamper across Liz's head and down the tree.

She clung there, afraid to move a muscle, feeling like a monkey on display. Which was how she came to have such a clear view of Gil's untimely return to his house.

Following what Liz would term an effusive greeting from Gil, Suzette Porter gestured toward the oak.

Hands on hips, he sauntered to the edge of his porch for a closer look.

Liz would be darned if she'd give him one inkling that anything was wrong. Ignoring her scratched palms, she released one hand and gave a carefree wave. She wasn't so far away as to miss the amused pucker of Gil's brow. Soon—but not soon enough in Liz's estimation—the group, Gil included, turned their backs and waltzed back into the ranch house.

Left to find terra firma alone, Liz ached in every spot imaginable by the time she touched ground. All she could think of was taking a long soak in a nice hot bath. The hell with finishing those horses in the south pasture. Hobbling into the cottage, she grumbled to her now beaming child that it'd be a cloudy day in you-know-where before she took supper to Gilman Spencer and his lady friend. Let them eat cake!

CHAPTER NINE

"AHH." LIZ'S SIGH of relief as she slid up to her neck in a steamy bath was cut off by someone pounding on the back door of the cottage. She tensed, hearing Melody scurry through the house. "No, hon," she rasped. "Don't . . . Mob's in the tub." Liz couldn't help remembering the night Melody had escorted Macy Rydell into this very room when she'd been draped over the commode hanging wallpaper. Liz hadn't set foot in here since without locking the door. It was locked—right?

"Lizbeth?"

Recognizing Gil Spencer's resonant voice, Liz slid lower, covering what flesh she could with a ridiculously small loofah. No one said Lizbeth quite the way he did. Half formal, half caress. Why was he here? What did he do with Miss Kitten Britches? That was Hoot's apt description of women who draped themselves in dead animals.

"Lizbeth? Are you all right?" The question was followed by a light tap. "Melody says your cold's so bad you can hardly talk."

Liz croaked something that was meant to be "Go away."

"You sound terrible. Why did you work outside today?"

Liz's next attempt at speaking was less fruitful.

"I'm coming back in ten minutes with Ben's cold remedy. I expect to find you in bed wrapped up in that white flannel thing you wear. The boys and I'll fix soup or something for Melody and you, if you feel up to eating."

"I hate it when you're nice, Spencer." For some reason—the steam perhaps—her voice had returned.

"Feisty again, eh? That's more like it." Gil smacked the flat of his hand against the door frame. "Rusty explained what happened with Melody's cat. I'm sorry, Lizbeth. Mel said you're all scraped from the bark. Why didn't you send one of the boys to get me, or at least yell when you saw me on the porch? I thought you were clowning."

Liz slid lower and rested her head against the back of the tub. The slightest movement of the water made her cuts sting, and she'd discovered a new bruise on her hip. "It was safer not to. Where's your guest, addyway? Shouldn't you be hobe entertaining?"

Gil pieced together her froggy histrionics. "Mrs. Porter had to leave. She *said* she wanted to help. But when I told her the floors needed scrubbing, she remembered a prior appointment. Lizbeth, I'd apologize for Dustin, but dammit . . . there's no excuse. I honestly don't know him lately. Normally he loves animals."

Liz didn't want to say that she thought Dustin's aim was to drive her off the way he had the others. Since her feelings still felt bruised, she said nothing. Besides, she and Dustin needed to work things out on their own.

"I'm leaving now. Remember what I said about bed. I want to find you there when I get back." His footsteps echoed along the hardwood floor of the hall.

Liz held her breath until the outer door slammed. Already her bathwater was cooling and her throat felt scratchier.

"Mommy, are you goin' to bed before supper? I'm hungry."

Hearing the plaintive quaver in her daughter's voice, Liz sighed and pulled the plug. She stood up, and a shiver overtook her as she reached for a towel. "Mob's getting out, sweedie." Liz hated being sick. Melody worried so much. But who could blame her? Chasing the rodeo was like riding a roller coaster over shifting sand. Her psychology books said few children thrived on constant change; they needed a steady anchor.

Liz wondered if there was enough farrier work in Crockett County to support her and Melody if she freelanced for small ranches. Come May, she'd have to find *something,* and she preferred to stay in this area, for her daughter's sake. Unfortunately her time was limited as long as Melody attended elementary school—not an ideal situation for a farrier in business for herself. Lord, but life was complicated, she thought as she pulled the nightgown over her head. Not the gown Gil had suggested; this one had a pink background dotted with sprigs of roses. It was soft and comforting. Oh, how she wished she could just crawl into bed and make the world go away.

She'd no more than slipped into her fuzzy slippers and stepped into the hall than she heard a commotion in the kitchen. Shivering from the cooler air, she grabbed a robe and went to see what Melody was up to.

Two steps into the living room, and she tripped over a Hot Wheels track the Spencer twins were busy assembling. "What...?" The intended question began in bass, rose to alto and disappeared in a squeaky soprano. The three children gaped. Dustin shuffled his feet and growled an apology. One intended to cover the cat caper, she guessed, as well as the near accident in her own living room.

Gil appeared in the kitchen archway. Their gazes met, skipped away and connected again. "I figured I could handle something simple, like heating canned vegetable soup and making microwaved hot dogs. How's your throat?"

Liz gestured toward it with both hands, tried to speak and gave up with a helpless shrug.

"Detour past here on your way to bed. I've mixed you a shot of Ben's snake oil. Guaranteed to cure what ails you." He waved a tablespoon.

She picked her way across the room looking doubtful, stopping when Dustin declared, "Accordin' to Ben, it'll kill a cold and put hair on your chest at the same time."

Liz tried to laugh, but it hurt.

"Ben tends to make up things to fit the circumstances. I'm sure he'd tell the ladies it would curl their hair. I checked once, and his concoction actually has less alcohol per dose than commercial cough syrups."

"Okay," Liz strained to whisper. "I'm never sick, so I have nothing on han—"

Gil had poured a thick substance from a mixing cup into a spoon, and he popped the spoon into her mouth before she'd finished speaking. "Sorry," he said as her eyes began to water. "Tomorrow you'll thank me." On that prophetic note, he disappeared into the kitchen.

The whiskey burned a path the length of her throat between gasps. Her whole face puckered from the lemon. Fortunately the honey soothed and covered a bitter taste she thought might be Chittam. Through her tears, Liz saw the boys gaze at her with interest. She tried to smile but figured at best it was a grimace.

Damn Gilman Spencer. He knew. He knew she couldn't gag or spit it out in front of the kids. If she went to the kitchen now, she'd kill him. Instead, she ran to her bedroom. She had to let the last bit trickle down her throat, and by the time she'd kicked off her slippers, ripped back the covers and thrown herself into bed, Liz had to admit that she already felt better.

Gil glanced over his shoulder, expecting a rear attack as he rinsed the cup and spoon. The minute he heard her bedroom door slam, he felt guilty for not warning her. He'd wanted to strangle Ben after experiencing his first dose. But the stuff did help, and as Ben said, no use punishing your palate a sip at a time.

"Does your mom have some kind of serving tray?" Gil asked Melody after he'd called the kids and settled them at the table with soup and hot dogs.

"I dunno." She shrugged.

"Where's your bowl, Dad?" Dustin climbed to his knees and scanned the table.

Gil looked up from his inventory of a bottom cupboard. "I'll eat with Lizbeth if I find trays."

"In her bedroom?" his son demanded. "She's wearin' a nightgown."

"She's sick, dodo." Rusty elbowed his brother.

It was a telling moment. Gil wrestled a pang of regret. Through no fault of their own, his sons had never seen him wait on a woman. It was way past time they did; Lizbeth had done a heap of nice things for them. Gil hadn't realized how much he looked forward to ministering to her for a change. But what did it say about him that he'd never done anything like this for Ginger? Those days, he'd skipped more meals than he'd eaten—and she'd been completely involved in training the buckskin he'd given her as a wedding gift. Once she got the horse trained, she'd spent all her spare time traipsing around the state to rodeos, only coming home when she needed money for entry fees.

He didn't often have free cash then. But he'd managed to find it—somehow. Especially when she met him at the door wearing tiny scraps of black lace. It had taken him a while to see that she was using him as a means to an end.

Hell, he would have given her the money; he wanted to give his wife more. The only thing Ginger coveted that he hadn't given her was the gold-spur key chain that had belonged to his grandfather. Outside of the property, it'd been the most valuable thing he owned at the time they split. As it was, she'd done her level best to break him. Fortunately he hadn't had much stock then, and his land was mostly unimproved. Today she'd have walked away with a helluva lot more.

Gil stared at the set of three nested bamboo trays he'd finally unearthed. All these years, and he was just beginning to get over that feeling of being used. The boys knew how he'd felt. Did Dustin see history repeating itself with Lizbeth?

Impossible. Gil had never met a less designing woman in his life. He knew that with Lizbeth, he could let go of the past. It was what he needed, what he intended— though it might take his sons longer to come around. As Nan Littlefield had so bluntly put it, what he had to do was set the example. And there was no time like the present to start.

Aware of Dusty's disapproval, Gil filled two trays with food. "The door will be open, son," he said as he balanced a tray in each hand. "Give a yell when you're ready

for more soup or hot dogs. I don't want you kids getting
burned helping yourselves.''

Hands full, Gil wasn't able to knock on Lizbeth's
bedroom door. It sat ajar, and he nudged it open with a
hip. When he turned, a clever greeting fizzled on his
tongue. She'd fallen asleep. Her face was flushed a soft
pink beneath a dark cap of tumbled curls that made her
look scarcely older than Melody. A scrawny cat with big
feet took up half her pillow. As Gil paused, his gizzard
turning to pulp, the calico cat opened a lazy eye, yawned
and flicked his tail.

He hovered in the doorway on the balls of his feet until both soup bowls rattled against their respective trays.
Except for a gallery of photographs showing Melody's
growth on one wall, Lizbeth's room was sadly spartan.
An iron bedstead sagged. A two-drawer dresser and un-
matching nightstand both had books propping them up.
Gil didn't think even Goodwill would take the rickety
straight-backed chair. Only a bright cheery oval rug
looked new. It picked up colors from the frilly curtains.
Clean wallpaper with faint stripes in the same shades as
the rug covered a multitude of imperfections.

Gil wanted to snatch her from this room. He wanted to
whisk her away—wanted to lavish her with *things*. Nice
things. Pretty things. She always seemed so happy Gil
had never guessed she had so little.

"Gil?" Liz leaned up on an elbow and stifled a yawn.
She tried to clear the cobwebs from her brain and attach
a reason to his forbidding look. She sat up abruptly, dis-
lodging the cat, and retied the neck of her gown. "What
time is it?" She reached for a small plastic Mickey Mouse
clock she'd placed on the nightstand beside her only
framed picture of Corbett. "Six o'clock? Is that a.m. or
p.m.?"

"Evening. Don't you remember you have a bad cold? I said I'd bring you a bowl of soup."

The day's events came flooding back. She felt her cheeks with the back of her hand and then rubbed her throat. "I remember that rot-gut tarantula juice you stuffed down me earlier. What kind of Texas lightning did you dump in my bowl of soup?"

Her sarcasm dragged a laugh from him as he watched her scoot upright. "Eat it and see, Ms. Sassy Mouth. I should rate a thank-you for giving you back your voice."

She accepted the tray he held out, her eyes suddenly aglow with mischief. "Beware. I make a green-chili cheeseburger guaranteed to singe your eyebrows. I rarely get mad, Spencer. I *always* get even."

"Forewarned is forearmed." He hunkered down on his heels beside her bed, as he might have done by a camp fire.

"I'll move over and you can sit on the end of the bed. That looks uncomfortable."

Gil cast a nervous glance toward the door, expecting to see Dusty's scowl of disapproval.

"Looking for help?" she teased. "What? You think I bite?"

"How's the soup?" he asked, unwilling to cast his son in a less favorable light than she already viewed him.

"Good. I never get waited on. I could get used to this."

Setting his bowl aside, Gil picked up his hot dog and broke off a piece to feed the cat. "I can name at least five of my wranglers who'd fall all over themselves for the opportunity to jump at your beck and call."

Liz's cold left her chuckle slightly rusty. "A woman who wants to wallow in velvet doesn't choose a cowboy. They want a servant-mother-mistress all rolled into one package."

"I thought you had a perfect marriage."

"I like to think it would have lasted fifty years or more," she said wistfully. "I'm not so foolish as to believe it wouldn't have taken work. Corbett operated on whimsy, me on practicality. He spent money we didn't have on flowers that wilted before nightfall, or silk teddies that weren't me." She gazed into her soup as if remembering.

Gil pictured her in cool pastel silk. Shifting his weight from one heel to the other, he tossed the remainder of his second hot dog to the cat. The ceiling had been wallpapered, too, he noticed, which must have taken some backbreaking contortions. Suddenly his mind was imagining contortions of another sort.

"Dad!"

Gil sprang to his feet. His tray tipped and his bowl clattered to the floor. The words *guilt, guilt, guilt* pulsed in a brain throbbing with less-than-pure thoughts.

Liz broke off what she'd begun to say about Corbett's not having the word "domestic" in his vocabulary. "Did your foot go to sleep? I told you to sit on the bed."

He gazed at her helplessly, still envisioning her swathed in something clingy and pink. Sitting on her bed wasn't going to be any help.

She frowned; his guilty expression seemed exaggerated for someone who hadn't even chipped a dish.

Dusty stopped just inside the door, suspicious hazel eyes sweeping the room. "Whatcha doin', Dad? You said to holler and you'd come, but you didn't."

Gil bent to pick up his scattered utensils, using the time to collect his thoughts. "I was on my way. Are you kids ready for more soup?"

"Melody is. Rusty'n me want more hot dogs. Then we wanna go home. Melody said she'll take care of her mom." He flashed a sullen glance in Liz's direction.

"We'll go when I say so, young sprout," Gil shot back. "Doing acrobatics in a wet oak tree didn't help Lizbeth's cold. Is there something you want to tell her?"

Dustin's eyes narrowed and his hands balled at his sides.

Liz was surprised at the force of Gil's anger. "It's all right. Dusty already apologized." She softened her expression. "Besides, I didn't actually see anyone chase Mittens up the tree. 'Tis the season to forgive and forget, is it not?" she added gently.

"That reminds me." Gil snapped his fingers. "Let me go refill their plates, then I have something to run by you."

"Okay." Her voice changed octaves again. "Don't look at me like that. And don't even *think* about fixing me a second dose of that sheep dip." Trying for a stern expression, she passed Gil her tray.

"But see how much better you feel already."

"No." She crossed her arms.

"At least promise me you'll stay inside tomorrow. I can't think of a horse needing shoes that can't wait. Anyway, we've got a thunderstorm brewing."

"A day off would give me a chance to bake some holiday cookies. All three kids brought home notes yesterday saying they need to take some to school on Friday. You do remember they're on vacation starting Monday until after New Year's?"

"That soon? Like I said, let me get them seconds on hot dogs, and then I want to talk to you about the holidays."

He sounded so serious Liz immediately began to wonder what on earth he'd have to say. She didn't have long to wait. He was back within minutes.

"Mitch Wilson of the Running W out of Fort Worth ordered a matched set of buckskins for his daughters for Christmas. I promised I'd deliver them personally."

At first Liz couldn't see how his delivery concerned her. Then it dawned. "Oh, so you're wondering if I'd mind taking care of the boys? No problem."

"Ah…" Giving her a peculiar look, Gil plunked down on the end of her bed. "I'm, uh, asking you to go along."

"Go? With you…to…to Fort Worth?" she stammered. Perhaps it was the lingering effects from Ben's cold cure, but her heart seized, then began to pound.

"The stores in town are already picked over. I don't know what you want to get Melody for Christmas, but shopping's a lot better in Fort Worth."

"Shopping. Uh…yes."

"Did you think I wanted you to go along to shoe the horses?" He reached out to pick up her hand.

"I didn't know what to think." She liked the feel of his hand and let hers lie still. Little by little she warmed to the idea. "We can take turns watching the kids while the other does Santa shopping. Sounds like heaven. I've always had to shop over top of Melody's head. It's nearly impossible now that she's older and wiser."

"Actually Nan Littlefield offered to keep all three kids. Last year I roped her into helping me buy their gifts. I think she's still frazzled." He smiled.

"Gil, the boys haven't said a word to me about what they want from Santa. And I've never shopped for boys. Do you think Dustin even believes in Santa?"

"He does and he doesn't. You have to get up early to put something over on him. But Ben's sneaky—he managed it last Christmas. Darn, I miss that old coot."

"So do the twins. It's good they'll get to hang out with you while they're on vacation. I'm afraid they think I keep them on a tight rein."

The light went out of his eyes.

"What is it?" she asked.

"Wish I'd known those dates. First week the kids are on vacation, we're scheduled to geld. I may be old-fashioned, but—"

"I agree," she said in a rush. "There's still the second week."

Gil shook his head. "That week we've got Night Fire lined up to cover six mares. Something else I don't let them watch."

"I thought Rafe oversaw the mating barn."

"He does, but a horse stepped on him a while back. The bones never healed right. His doctor was able to schedule his surgery that week."

"The boys will be terribly disappointed, Gil."

"It can't be helped. I'm not running the ranch as a hobby. I'll try to get away early every day. That's the best I can do." He might have elaborated, but Dustin barged in on them. He didn't look at all happy to see Gil sitting on Liz's bed, holding her hand.

"C'mon, Dad. Let's go. Me and Rusty have school tomorrow."

With some reluctance, Gil stood. "So we're on for Fort Worth?" he asked, trying to keep his voice low.

Liz watched a range of emotions skitter through his eyes and wished they were more easily read. In the end what swayed her was the fact that Gil apparently wanted her to agree. She nodded slowly, even though her heart quickened. "I guess so—if you're sure three kids won't be too much for Mrs. Littlefield to handle."

"I'll check with her again. And we're agreed you'll take tomorrow off?"

"You don't have to twist my arm." She flashed Dustin a smile. "You boys come straight to the cottage after school. I'll save making sugar cookies, so you can help."

"I'm not makin' any dumb ol' cookies. Ben bought the cookies we took to school. 'Sides, me and Buddy Hodges are gonna hunt wild turkeys tomorrow."

"Not on the Lone Spur you aren't," Gil said. "You know I planted five acres of prairie grass to entice wild turkeys back here after the older Hodges boys annihilated the flock. You guys are not starting on this one. You be here tomorrow after school, and you do what Lizbeth says. As many cookies as you eat, you should bake a few." He strode to the door. "We'll be leaving now, Lizbeth. If you need us, call."

He was gone almost before Liz could blink. He and Dustin were still bickering after they'd left the house. Her window faced the clearing, allowing her to hear every word. Dustin wasn't happy with anything. Not his dad, Rusty or Liz. When Melody bounced into her bedroom a few minutes later, Liz thanked Providence for her daughter's sunny disposition.

NEXT DAY, Liz stumbled out of bed to see Melody off to school, then crawled back under the covers and slept late. By midmorning, she felt a hundred percent improved. She'd just finished wrapping her sixth fruitcake in rum-soaked cheesecloth when Gil knocked at her kitchen door. She glanced up and motioned him in.

"Whew! What in blazes . . . ? It smells like a saloon in here." He removed his Stetson and approached the table with caution.

"My grandmother's fruitcake recipes. I made three dark and three light. I plan to give them as Christmas gifts to some of the neighbors, so I hope they have time to cure. I'm getting a late start."

"Don't light a match between now and Christmas. This place will go up like a Molotov cocktail."

"The alcohol smell will disappear by the time I close the tins. Sure you're not peeved because I haven't made the kind of cookies you want to snitch?"

"I stopped by to see how you're feeling. I met Melody when I rode out this morning. She said you were going back to bed."

"There's no such thing as privacy when you have kids."

"Isn't that the truth. No secrets, either. Those little monkeys heard what I said last night about going Christmas shopping. At breakfast they each laid a list for me about a mile long."

"So there went the Santa mystique, huh?"

"I don't know. They begged to go to Fort Worth. Claimed the Santa in our mall is a phony."

Liz went to the stove and poured him a cup of coffee. She set the timer to tell her when to seal the cakes. "Have you had lunch? I was about to stop for a sandwich."

"You talked me into it." He shook his head. "Those kids. Always trying to pull something."

She uncovered a loaf of fresh bread and cut four slices. "Did it occur to you they probably want to chaperon us?"

"Actually it did. By next Friday I predict both twins will be sick. However, I'm on to their tricks."

Liz cleared half the table of her cooking utensils and
set sandwiches at right angles. Gil pulled out her chair,
and as his arm brushed hers, she felt as if she'd taken a
jolt from an open electrical circuit. When he sat, their
knees touched, upping the voltage. For weeks, Liz had
known her feelings for him were deepening—and her attraction growing. She wasn't sure what he felt. "Gil," she
said suddenly, "maybe I shouldn't go to Fort Worth."

He paused, the tuna sandwich halfway to his mouth,
and watched her mangle a napkin. "That's what they
want. Dustin, at least. You'll be playing right into his
hands."

She leaned back and crossed her arms. "Since
Thanksgiving, I've been getting a lot of mixed signals
from you. Forgive me for being direct, but is this trip really about Christmas shopping?"

The air left Gil's lungs in a whoosh. He set his sandwich down, closed his eyes and massaged the bridge of
his nose. "And if I said it wasn't...altogether?" His eyes,
when they cracked open a slit, were guarded.

Her heart expanded with love for him. If putting a
name to her emotions made *her* cautious, Liz imagined
how difficult it would be for Gil. She hadn't risked her
feelings or her heart in more than six years, and it took
courage to do so now. "I'd want to know if this is something you do annually, like I do holiday baking." Nip-
ping in her lower lip, she studied her fingers.

He rose half-out of his chair. "Hell, Lizbeth, what
kind of a question is that?"

The minute his chair scraped, her gaze flew back to
him. "A fair question, I think. I'm not interested in being a new link in a long chain of one-night stands. On the
other hand..." Drawing a shaky breath, she got up and
went to the stove. "On the other hand," she said, not

facing him, "my stomach curdles when you say Lizbeth the way you do."

It took Gil a minute to digest her remark. Once he ran it through a second time, he stepped up behind her and rubbed his hands over the points of her shoulders. Bending, he placed a breathy kiss at the juncture between her neck and ear. "There isn't any chain. Not a single link. Would it sound like I'm playing games if I suggest we take it slow? Just let whatever's developing between us set the pace?"

She leaned back against his flannel-covered chest a moment, then covered her mouth to smother a chuckle. "No one playing those kinds of games would kiss a woman who smells of rum and Vicks."

Barely a heartbeat passed before Gil scooped her up, whipped her around and swung her high, his laughter chasing hers. "I reek of tuna. Probably reminded you of Melody's cat."

"Your nose is warmer." She shrieked as he pretended to let her drop, but abruptly fell silent as he gripped her waist and let her slowly slide the length of his body. A quivery pulsing spasm shot through her stomach. One trembling finger lightly traced his straight eyebrows, his angular cheekbones and the creases that bracketed his lips. Secure in his arms, Liz dipped her head and placed a soft kiss on his lips.

Gil felt as if his muscles had decomposed. Liz hooked her legs around his hips; Gil tightened his hold and increased the pressure on her lips. Soon they were lost in a tangle of tongues. A need for air forced them apart, but not before his hands had found their way beneath her shirt and she'd popped a few snaps down the front of his. Who knew how long the exploration might have lasted—

had the timer she'd set to remind her to cover the fruit-cakes not gone off, shattering the moment.

With a nervous laugh, Liz reached behind her and silenced the noise. Since he looked like he'd been run over by an eighteen-wheeler, she balanced against the sink, instead of circling his neck with her arms again, the way she wanted to. "Um, if this is your idea of slow, Spencer, I think we're in trouble. The kids get out of school at two today and it's one-thirty now. Teachers' meeting or something, the notes said."

He nodded, released her and drew in a slug of air as he backed slowly toward the door. He'd fumbled it open by the time she hurried to hand him the rest of his sandwich and his hat. Rising to her toes, she set the Stetson on his head. On her way down, she let her lips graze his, then his chin, and lastly the front of his shirt.

"Stop that, Lizbeth," he groaned.

"Um . . . yes?" She edged back, barely suppressing a grin.

"The trip to Fort Worth—it definitely isn't just about shopping." The door closed on that tantalizing note, and Gil clattered down the steps.

She ran to the window and watched him slosh through mud to where he'd left his truck. Little fingers of heat walked up her spine. Something good was happening between them. The smile that lodged in her heart refused to be shaken. Not even when Rusty and Melody burst through the door an hour later. Without Dustin.

"He went with Buddy Hodges," Rusty wailed the minute the two children cleared the door. "Said he's not comin' home till Ben gets back."

"Of course he is. What kind of nonsense is that?"

"I think he means it." Rusty's lower lip trembled and his eyes teared. "He doesn't want you goin' to Fort Worth with Dad."

That news came as no surprise. It screamed from Dusty's every pore. He must have overheard their discussion, Liz figured. Her joy began to fade. Dustin would do anything to drive a wedge between her and Gil. Why hadn't she seen it sooner? Rusty was easygoing like Gil; Dustin had inherited a few traits from his mother. No. It was unfair of her to attach a full-grown woman's foibles to an innocent child. And her relationship with Gil could only work if her love extended fully and completely to his children. It was up to her to scale Dustin's barriers.

"I gotta go find my dad." Rusty trudged toward the door, shoulders bowed. "When I tell him 'bout this, he's gonna be madder than a cross-eyed bull."

"Rusty, wait." Liz brushed flour from her hands. A plan took shape in her head as she covered the cookie dough and put it into the fridge. "It's me Dusty's mad at. I'd like a chance to talk him into coming home before we involve your father."

The boy's hazel eyes narrowed warily.

"Please, Russ? If he refuses to come back with us, I'll help tell your dad."

"Okay," he sighed. "I don't want my brother gettin' into trouble."

"I know, sport. Believe me, I don't either." And Liz found she meant it.

CHAPTER TEN

THE MINUTE she turned down the deeply rutted lane that led to Buddy's, Liz knew she'd misjudged the extent of Dustin's unhappiness. Compared to the Lone Spur ranch house, the Hodges' place was a shack. The roof had patches on top of patches, and the windows were lined with foil to keep out the cold. Chickens scattered when she parked. Pigs wallowed in the mud at the feet of a sad-eyed cow. "Rusty, what does Mr. Hodges do?"

"Raises melons. But Buddy says the kids do all the work."

"Kids? Brothers and sisters, you mean?" Liz asked idly as she opened the pickup door and wondered if she could jump the huge mud hole at her feet.

"Only brothers. Buddy's got two bigger brothers and three little ones."

"Six kids and two adults live in this house? Are you sure, Rusty? It doesn't look as big as my cottage."

"Do I hafta go with you?" Melody whined. "Buddy's brother Coulter is mean."

Rusty shifted in his seat. "All the Hodges are mean-er'n snakes. Maybe I'll stay here with Mel."

Feeling abandoned, Liz gave thought to hightailing it back to the Lone Spur—and Gil. But she hesitated too long. The front door of the house flew open, and a tall thin woman with chapped hands and graying hair stepped out onto the sloped porch. "State yer business, missy. I ain't gonna stand here freezin' my expectations."

Liz recognized the twang of a native West Texan. She was relieved to see that the woman looked more harried than mean. "I'm Lizbeth Robbins—from the Lone Spur."

"Figures." No other word, no greeting. But she was obviously waiting for Liz to explain why she was there.

Liz knew West Texans weren't big talkers, but she didn't intend to discuss the reason for her visit with anyone other than Dustin. "I'll be right back," she murmured to the kids. "Don't move a muscle." She shut the cab door gently and picked her way through chickens and mud, pasting a smile on her lips as she reached the house.

"Dustin's mentioned ya. You'd be the floozy that's a-livin' with Gilman, I guess. What a man does is his business, but I don't hold with goin' agin the good book."

Liz swallowed her smile. "Mrs. Hodges." She placed both hands on her hips. "I'm the Lone Spur's farrier. I *live* in a cottage well apart from the Spencers' house. I'm caring for the twins after school until Mr. Jones recovers from his car accident. Rusty said his brother left school today with Buddy. I need a word with Dusty. Do you know where I might find him?"

"Inside. They're fixin' to go huntin' gobblers."

Liz shuddered. Kids that age had no business messing with guns. "A private word, Mrs. Hodges. Please send Dustin out."

The older woman must have seen her determination. She gave a curt nod before withdrawing. Liz could just imagine what tales Dustin must have spun about her to give Buddy's mother such a terrible impression. But mortified though she was, Liz knew she wouldn't get anywhere with Dustin by taking an accusatory stance. If he even agreed to see her. What if he wouldn't? Or he might already be gone.

He did eventually appear, although Liz held no illusions that it was for any reason other than the fact that he was nine and she an adult. With that small advantage, she decided to strike first. "Dustin, if you go hunting, it will greatly disappoint your dad. He told you exactly how he felt about this expedition. Right now, you still have a choice. Get your book bag and come with me. Your dad will never be the wiser. Stay, and you take the consequences."

Dustin hooked his thumbs in his belt loops. "You mean you won't tell?"

If he'd actually gone hunting, Liz would have had to think twice about such a promise. As it stood, she couldn't see any harm in keeping his aborted rebellion between them. "Why hurt your dad? Isn't this really about us?"

His head shot up and Liz backed away from the dislike flowing from the hazel eyes that were otherwise so like Gil's.

"Why don't you just go? Nothin's been right since you moved in. You made a sissy outta Rusty, and now you got Dad cookin' and fetchin'. Ben's comin' back, you know. Then things'll be the way they usta be."

Liz gasped. "Dustin, it isn't unmanly to be thoughtful. I was sick last night. And if we stand out here in the cold much longer, I'm liable to be sick again. I believe I'll wait in the truck with Rusty and Melody while you say goodbye and get your things. It's your decision, but I think you should know that Rusty is pretty upset, too."

"You better tell Rusty not to fink on me to Dad. That wuss came cryin' to you, didn't he?"

Liz watched him stomp back inside. She hadn't thought about Rusty saying something to Gil either way, but of course he might. Liz knew from experience that kids were prone to do the very things they were told not to. Perhaps it would die a natural death if Dustin simply came home with them.

Thank goodness he did. Liz thought she concealed her relief admirably, although on the drive home the brothers remained as divided as Cain and Abel.

Back at the cottage, their estrangement was even more pronounced. Rusty and Melody threw themselves into making and decorating Christmas cookies. Dustin sat moodily in the living room, refusing even to sample the first batch. Although his attitude didn't dampen the other kids' enthusiasm, it took all the fun out of the afternoon for Liz. Not to mention the pall it cast over her proposed trip with Gil. But as she baked chicken and corn bread for their supper, Liz realized Gil was right. They shouldn't play into Dustin's hands.

Gil came to the cottage after work. He tapped lightly on the back door and walked in, a broad smile on his face. "Luke and I went to the timberline this afternoon. I cut a couple of Christmas trees. I don't suppose anybody here would be interested." He snatched a warm cookie from the counter as Rusty and Melody ran outside.

Gil's eyes sought Lizbeth's. She had the distinct feeling he'd like to be stealing a kiss to go with that cookie.

"Dustin." Liz stepped to the arch. It was the subtlest way she knew to let Gil know that all the children hadn't dashed out. "Your dad cut Christmas trees, Dusty. Don't you want to go have a look with the others?"

Dustin charged past her. It was the most animation he'd shown all afternoon. "Our tree. Great, Dad! Can we decorate it tonight?"

"Whoa, son." Gil caught him around the waist. "It's still wet from snow. I thought I'd put it in the stand and let it set a day. Tomorrow night maybe Lizbeth can fix supper at our house, and she and Melody can help with decorations. If the storm breaks, it'll be a good night for popcorn and hot chocolate. After we put the angel on of course." He turned to Liz, his eyes glowing. "It's a tradition of my mom's that the boys and I sort of carried on."

Liz realized Gil couldn't see Dustin's face. His pleasure died the minute his dad had invited her to share their evening. "Gil," she murmured, "that's *your* special tradition. Mel and I have our own. You said you cut two trees, didn't you?"

"Yes, but..." Gil seemed confused. Crestfallen. "But I thought Melody said you'd never had a tree because there wasn't room in your trailer."

"All the more reason to start some traditions." Liz failed miserably to telegraph the real reason behind her refusal. Yet how could she spell it out in front of Dustin? For his sake, she overrode her own disappointment.

Gil wasn't successful at hiding his. All afternoon he'd pictured the fun they'd have together decorating those trees. Obviously Lizbeth had changed her mind about a lot of things since noon. Damn, did all women have to jerk a man around? "It's your call," he said stiffly. He might have said more, but Melody and Rusty ran back inside just then, exclaiming that the pines were the most beautiful trees they'd ever seen.

"You've seen one tree, you've seen 'em all," Gil snapped.

Liz wished he'd noticed the smile that replaced Dustin's scowl, or the fact that his moody son had suddenly whooped and dragged his twin outside for a second look. Had Melody not stayed in that time, Liz would have set Gil straight.

Only too aware of the tension that had developed between them, she turned to dish out the Spencers' portion of the evening meal. Dustin had lost the first round today; he deserved to win this one. Although if the way Gil grabbed the basket of food and left was any indication, Dusty might win the whole shootin' match. Surely Gil wasn't so blind he couldn't see . . .

A little miffed herself, Liz stayed up half the night moving furniture around in her tiny living room, deciding where to put her tree. With hard work, her anger dissipated. She brewed a cup of soothing tea and reconsidered talking things out with Gil.

Next morning, after the children's bus had come by, Liz hurried to the barn in hopes of catching Gil before he rode out. Instead, she met Rafe saddling up.

"The boss took five men and rode out at dawn. Macy found where a big cat downed one of our mares yesterday. Yancy and I were planning to comb the canyons for strays today, so I got the twins ready for school. Why're you lookin' for Gil? I thought you had horses to shoe. But it's okay to let them go if you're still sick."

"Um...no. I'm better. The question I have for Gil can wait till I take them supper tonight. And Rafe, if I finish early, I may run into town. Mel and I don't have any decorations for the Christmas tree Gil cut. Can I get anything for you while I'm there?"

He dug in his pocket and handed her a crumpled hundred-dollar bill. "Would you buy something slinky for me to give Joyce for Christmas? Size eight."

"Slinky, huh? Come on, Rafe. Can't you be more specific?" Liz teased.

"Uh, you know. Nightwear."

"Oooh...a sexy nightgown?"

His face turned three shades of red.

"Rafe, wouldn't it mean more if *you* bought her present?"

"M-m-me? I couldn't go in one of *those* stores. By morning it'd be all over town. Can't you imagine what guys like Luke and Macy would say?"

"They'd probably say you lucky devil, you." Liz shook her head. "Oh, all right." She folded the bill and tucked it in her pocket. "Better yet, why don't I pick up something on my shopping trip to Fort Worth? They'll have more of *those* stores."

"Are you still going? I thought the way the boss talked this morning that maybe you'd canceled out."

She gave Rafe a funny look. Just how much had Gil told his foreman about that proposed jaunt? "I didn't cancel, Rafe. Question is—did I *get* canceled?"

"Hey, don't ask me. Maybe I misunderstood. You oughta talk to Gil."

Liz laughed. "Exactly. Isn't that where this conversation began?"

"Right," he drawled. "If I see the man, I'll send him around. Oh, hey—I guess you've got the night off, too. Gil asked me to meet the twins' bus after school. They'll eat with me in the cookshack."

Now Liz knew something was definitely up with Gil. All day, she kept an eye out, but to no avail. As it turned out, Rafe needed her to feed the boys, after all. He left her with three kids who were in snits because they'd all counted on decorating their respective trees after supper. Liz couldn't even interest them in tacos. Not only that, Dustin blamed her for Gil's lateness. She'd barely gotten them all to sleep at midnight when Gil dragged in.

"What are you doing here?" he asked curtly on finding Liz pacing his kitchen. "I expected Rafe." He slapped his hat on the rack and shrugged out of a muddy sheepskin-lined jacket.

"He expected *you* home by seven," she shot back, then wished she could retract her words, he looked so weary. "Gil, I know it's late, but we need to talk. There's hot coffee, and tacos to put in the microwave if you're hungry." Without giving him an option, she went to the fridge.

"I have to wash up," he said, carefully skirting her.

Well, she thought, *this is going to be a dandy conversation.* She had his food on the table and coffee poured by the time he returned.

"What's this about, Lizbeth? You sure blow hot and cold."

"Funny, all day I've thought the same thing about you." As he sat down, she saw uncertainty shadow his eyes. "Eat," she said softly, trying to figure out a way to sneak back the coffee she'd doctored up a bit because she'd been feeling vexed at his attitude. But it was too late. He moved the cup to the right of his plate, out of her reach.

Gil polished off half a taco, leaned back and washed the final bite down with a hefty swig from his cup.

Liz winced the minute he bolted out of the chair, gasping to breathe against the triple shot of Jack Daniel's. He gazed at her through watery eyes. "So... if you're not mad, I guess this means we're even," he choked.

She pursed her lips, but not in time to hide those mischievous dimples.

Gil foundered on the urge to kiss her again. Damn, but he'd never met a woman who could scramble his brains like this one. He might be dead on his feet and furious with her, but his body had other ideas. So, apparently, did his heart, whether he wanted it that way or not.

"It's late," she muttered, as if she knew precisely where his thoughts lay. Standing, she picked up his plate and bent down to put it in the dishwasher.

Gil's temperature shot up twenty degrees. He was contemplating what he might do about it when she set the dials, turned and said, "I shouldn't have provoked you tonight. I'm sorry you didn't get the cougar, Gil."

"Me, too." Suddenly all his long hours in the saddle came crashing back. And the easy way Lizbeth had read his discouragement surprised Gil. "That damned cat has more than nine lives."

"Bad, huh?"

Gil leaned his elbows on the table, dropped his head into his hands and massaged an ache in his forehead with both thumbs. "He's killed three mares in as many days. We're bringing the main herd in off the winter grass. It means twice the work hauling hay. Worse, I'll probably have to have some of the hands cancel their holiday plans."

"Oh, so that's what Rafe meant about our trip being canceled." The tight lines in her face eased. "You're not going to Fort Worth, after all. I'm afraid...that is, I thought...well, never mind." She beamed at Gil.

He straightened, studied her carefully, then shrugged. "I still have to go. It involves a big sale. Are you saying I read things wrong? Didn't you give me the brush-off?"

How to proceed without betraying her promise to Dustin? "Yesterday, you told me yourself, 'Slow down. Let things progress naturally'. Gil, as I said the other day, this isn't just about us. Ben's accident shook the twins. They rarely had you to themselves before, and now they have to share you with me. I'm becoming a wedge between you."

"Nonsense."

"As an outsider, I see things you don't."

"Sure that's not a convenient excuse for cold feet?"

"I'm not the one who turned my duties over to Rafe and then ran for the hills. I'd like us to spend some time together, just the two of us. But only if the feeling's mutual."

"It is." He looped a hand behind her neck and tilted her face up. "So mutual I haven't thought of anything else for two days. You tie me in knots, Lizbeth."

She saw the truth of what he said in his eyes—and saw there the risk he feared in baring his soul to another woman. "Then why are we having this discussion at midnight? I'll have my bag packed by noon on Friday. See that you don't stand me up, Spencer."

The delay in Gil's reaction attested to his long tiring day. Smiling, Liz leaned over and nibbled his lips with a soft kiss. Just as quickly she jumped up, hurried into the living room and plucked Melody from the couch. They were gone before Gil came out of shock. He yanked back the kitchen curtain and watched her cover the short distance between their homes.

In bed later he dreamed of what it would be like to end the night with more than a simple kiss. He awoke at dawn in a rock-hard state that not even a cold shower could alter. Strangely enough, Gil felt young and carefree again. He left the house, counting the hours till Friday.

JUDGING BY THE SCENE unfolding on Nan Littlefield's front porch Friday at noon, Gil should have spent less time counting and more time preparing his kids. Dustin threw a fit to rival all fits. He used language that prompted Gil to give his son a hard shake. It was harsh punishment coming from Gil, and Dustin promptly started to howl.

Dustin's behavior at least was expected. Melody's fit of tears was not. Admittedly Liz had never left her with a sitter before. The little girl's sobs threatened to wake the dead. Gil didn't have to be a magician to interpret Lizbeth's guilt. Was he being selfish to want this trip in spite of the children's tantrums and tears?

"Morris knocked off early today," Nan told him, peeling Melody away from Liz. "He rented a ton of movies, and he's itching to teach the boys how to play pool. We have two foundling calves that have to be fed by hand. I'm going to need Melody's help with that after we settle her cat and her stuffed animals in her room. Go on, you two—shoo!"

Gil was the first to see wisdom of doing exactly what Nan suggested—leaving quickly. Liz continued to spout instructions as he tugged her backward toward his Suburban. Then she sat so still and looked so forlorn he pulled off to the side of the road before they reached the interstate. "Do you want to go back? You can give me your list. I'll try to do your shopping and mine. Although I don't know one Barbie doll from another."

The first item on her list had nothing to do with Barbie. It was Rafe's request for sexy lingerie. Finding humor in that, Liz started to laugh. "I think you might prefer Barbie over an hour in Victoria's Secret." Smothering a laugh, she explained.

"Well, whaddaya know. Didn't realize ol' Rafe had it in him. I think I'll buy the most risqué little nightie I can find, just to see his face."

"Don't you dare. Put this thing in gear and hit the road. I never should've said a word. He trusts me, Gil."

Gil checked behind him before pulling out and negotiating a ramp leading to the freeway. "So, zipping my lips puts you in my debt." He waggled his brows.

This was a flirtatious, fun-loving side of Gil that Liz had never seen. Unless he was simply trying to take her mind off leaving the kids. Nevertheless, she was happy enough to join in. "It would serve you right if I dragged you into every lingerie shop in Fort Worth, Gil Spencer. Think how you'd feel traipsing through bras, slips and panties in every size, shape and color of the rainbow?"

That got to Gil. "Guess I'd better stick to buying boots and saddles. However—" he slanted her a sidelong glance "—I'd better tell you that I have a pretty active imagination."

Liz did, too. She'd listened in on enough conversations around the rodeo to know most cowboy-types preferred to sleep in the raw. And if he was imagining her in flimsy lingerie, she was imagining him in...nothing. Clearing her throat, Liz dug out her shopping list and proceeded to read it aloud. "As well as Barbie, I want to buy Melody a frilly nightgown, a quilted satin robe and bunny slippers. Oh, and flowered leggings if I can find them. She rarely comments on her friends' clothes, but she talks about those leggings all the time."

Her smoke screen didn't fool Gil, but because they'd hit the outskirts of Abilene and traffic had grown heavier, he deemed it safest to play along. "Mitch Wilson, the man who's buying Butterscotch and Toffee—" he jerked a thumb toward the trailer "—plans to meet us at a friend's ranch at six. He's boarding the horses at the Double Bar Seven till Christmas. From there, I figured we'd go check into the hotel, unpack, call our brood. Then we'll find something to eat. How does that sound?''

Her smile blossomed. ''How did you know I'd want to call home?''

''Hmm. I wonder.'' He glanced over. ''Lizbeth, don't worry about Melody, okay? She'll be fine with Nan.''

Liz nodded, then laced her fingers together and bent them back nervously. ''Speaking of offspring, yesterday I checked out the mare we rescued on Thanksgiving. Her little guy's looking great.''

''*You* rescued. Come January, I'll be weaning your foals. You do know, don't you, that your wild mare will probably try and take her colt back to the herd?''

''She seems content. Are you sure it won't be the other way around? Maybe she'll spread the word, and Wind Dancer will come in.''

''Lizbeth, I declare.'' He took one hand off the wheel and snagged a dark curl. ''Board your damned colt with somebody on the other side of town until he's old enough to geld. I don't want him disappearing—and you disappointed. And I sure as hell don't want that stallion killing him.''

She slid her hand around his wrist and felt his pulse leap. She stroked his hand, cuddling her cheek into his palm, although not in any attempt at seduction. ''You're such a caring man,'' she said, holding his callused hand in both of hers. ''It's hard for me to imagine any woman leaving you.''

He pulled out of her grasp—because they were approaching a hill, he told himself. But not before he saw the troubled flicker pass through her eyes. ''My divorce was messy and bitter. I don't want it to come between us, Lizbeth.''

"I know this is a big step for you, Gil. It is for me, too. You're touchy. The boys are touchy. I feel caught in the middle and I don't know which way to turn."

He drummed his fingers on the wheel. "It's complicated."

"We've got more than a hundred miles to go."

Gil knew she meant there was time to talk. But he let a few of those miles go by in silence. It was so quiet he switched on some music. A tape of traditional Christmas songs. He'd bought it hoping to please her. Lizbeth didn't look pleased. Only silent. More miles slipped past, and he sighed. "When Ginger took off with Amistad, I was hurt. My lawyer wanted me to file for sole custody, but I didn't do it at the time—she hadn't taken any interest in the boys, and frankly I didn't want to face her in court. About a month after the twins' third birthday, she filed a petition for joint custody. I refused to consider it. We went back and forth in court until she ran out of money. Our fight upset the boys. I agreed that Ginger could visit them at the ranch whenever she wanted, but she didn't bother. About the time they turned four, she made and broke so many appointments I wanted to kill her. The few times she showed up, she and Ben got into shouting matches. The boys were in kindergarten when she filed for full custody. I offered her cash to leave us alone. She took it and I made sure my lawyers closed all the loopholes. Maybe I was wrong..."

"No, Gil." Liz thought her heart would break. "Don't turn yourself inside out like this. Let's start from ground zero. Hey, I'll check your shopping list, why don't I?"

There was nothing he'd like better than to switch subjects. Gil unsnapped his shirt pocket and pulled out three pages. "I'm warning you, those boys would be happy owning Toys R Us."

Liz laughed. But on reading the pages, she was appalled. "Gil, surely they don't expect *all* these things."

"Too much, huh?"

She sneaked a peek to see if he was joking. "Well, it's your money."

He tipped back his head and guffawed. "And at that rate, I'd go broke in a year. I do set some limits for them, Lizbeth. Like those electronic gadgets I've never even heard of. Will you help me pick four gifts apiece, hopefully ones that don't cost a mint?"

"Eight gifts, plus my list. Wow, I don't know if we've allowed enough time."

"I guess we could start tonight," he said reluctantly. "If it's anything like San Antonio, the major stores stay open till midnight this close to the holiday."

"Midnight? Oh, no, you won't catch me tramping through malls with nine million people that late at night. I plan on hitting the sack long before then." The instant Gil drew a sharp breath, Liz realized what she'd said. Too late to retract her words, she decided to go for broke and met his smoldering gaze with a lazy smile. Talk fell off as Gil kicked the Suburban up to five miles above the speed limit.

Her insides bounced from dizzying anticipation to paralyzing apprehension. Why, for goodness' sake? This wasn't the first gamble she'd taken looking for love. She knew better now than to count on the everlasting brass ring.

MITCH WILSON was waiting when they pulled into the Double Bar Seven at dusk. He and his friend, the Double Bar's owner, greeted Gil effusively. The men immediately went to unload the pair of buckskins. Liz felt awkward about getting out to stretch her legs, since Gil hadn't offered to introduce her. No sooner had she examined the hurt feelings this caused than he did that very thing, telling Mr. Wilson she was the best darned farrier the Lone Spur had ever had. Boy—talk about touchy. She had her moments, too.

Gil handed over the registration papers, which Wilson pocketed without a second glance.

Liz found that simple action a testament to Gil's character. It spoke of trust. And men born in the West didn't trust lightly. As they drove away, Liz felt totally at ease with her decision to be with this man. And maybe he felt it, too. They exchanged warm smiles that lasted until Gil entered the city limits and stopped beneath the awning of the Worthington Hotel, blithely handing his keys to a uniformed valet.

Liz brushed at her worn jeans and raked a hand through her windblown hair. "Gil, what are we doing here? I'm not dressed for a place this fancy."

He hefted their bags before giving her a cursory once-over. "You look fine. This town was built by cow people. Catering to horse folks should be a step up." He took her arm and winked as they passed the doorman.

"Gil Spencer, you're incorrigible. Is it any wonder the teacher slapped that label on Dustin?" She laughed, yet when he left her standing beside an elegant silver-and-white Christmas tree while he went to register, she was *sure* that everyone who passed knew she didn't belong. And the longer Gil stayed at the polished marble counter, the more certain she became that everyone on staff knew exactly what they were doing here.

At last he turned and started back. Liz held her breath. She almost bolted when he picked up their bags without a word and led her to a bank of elevators.

"This brochure explains the athletic and tennis clubs and includes a map. Here, I got you a key card even though I figured we'd be going everywhere together."

The elevator was empty; still, she sidled close and whispered, "Do they know?"

"Know what?" Gil frowned.

"You know," she murmured as the elevator glided to a stop.

He removed his Stetson and raked a hand through his hair. "Lizbeth, are you feeling okay? You're white as a ghost. Is your throat sore again?"

She snatched her bag from his hand and stomped out onto the deep pile carpeting of the gilt-encrusted hall. Checking the number on her key-card folder, she marched to the door and waited for him to catch up. Her jaw dropped when he walked past her to the next room and stuck his card in the door slot. She rechecked her key card just to be sure of the number.

By then Gil understood. Propping his door ajar with his bag, he came back, took her card from her limp fingers and repeated the process with her door. "I thought you'd like the privacy of your own room. I meant what I said about letting things develop naturally. But—" he flashed her a grin "—there's a connecting door in case—"

He never got to say in case what. She slugged him on the arm. "You might have clued me in. And you know darn well my throat's just fine." Flying past him in a huff, she slammed the door. Then she stood, holding her breath, waiting for his protest. Waiting for *him* . . .

Two minutes later he appeared at the connecting door, looking hesitant. "You left your key in the slot, Lizbeth. Even in a swank hotel that's dangerous."

"Thanks. Throw it to me."

She caught the key card and tossed it on the dresser. Suddenly playful, she stripped off her leather jacket and fell across the massive bed, laughing as she bounced. "Leave the connecting door open, Gil. This is as natural as it gets. If you've got a dime, I'll flip you to see who gets to call home first. Then I think you promised food. Gad, I'm so hungry I could eat a mule."

"Shh." He dashed across the room and covered her mouth. "This town's got the finest steak houses in the West. But mules... well, lady, them's fightin' words."

Giggling, Liz placed an openmouthed kiss in the center of his palm.

He jumped back as if he'd been bitten, instead of kissed. "Lizbeth, I swear..."

Her eyes rounded innocently. "Yes?" She uncurled her hand. "The dime, Spencer. I'll do the flipping."

He gazed at her so long, lids lowered, eyes smoldering, that her heart rate quickened. Maybe she wasn't as hungry as she'd thought. "Gil." Her voice held the barest hint of a tremor as she flattened her fingers along his chest.

Gil sailed his Stetson halfway across the room, missing the chair. Catching both her wrists, he slowly pulled her upright. "It's powerful between us, Lizbeth. And getting stronger."

Gentling his grip, he lifted her fingers to his lips and kissed them repeatedly. "If I join you on that bed right now, I'll last about two seconds. You deserve a whole lot better." Sliding his hands along her arms, he gathered her up and held her close. "Make your call to Melody. I'll go to my room and call room service. While we're waiting for our food, you can shower and, uh, get into something more, ah, comfortable—and I'll... I'll call the boys."

Liz framed his face. "I forgot how long it's been for both of us. Maybe we should go shopping first. I, uh, I'm not on . . . anything, Gil."

Smiling, he dusted his knuckles over her cheek. "I guess now I have to confess. I've been planning this for a few weeks. Not to worry, I came prepared."

"Oh." Liz felt her cheeks heat. She wasn't as modern or as bold as she'd wanted to appear.

Gil saw. Enchanted, he tipped up her chin and helped himself to a long lingering kiss. A sample of what would come later. Loving the glow his kisses left in her eyes and on her cheeks, he backed through the door into his room. He didn't *want* to say it but felt he had to. "No rush, Lizbeth. If you'd rather, we'll go shopping after supper."

Liz fully expected the delay would ruin the mood—so she slipped into sweats after showering and tucked her shopping list into her jacket pocket, betting they'd go to the mall.

But when Gil came out from his bathroom, he was barefoot, wearing only the bottoms to silk pajamas. They hadn't been out of his drawer since he'd spent a weekend in Mexico at the home of a rancher friend—*after* his divorce was final. He'd missed the boys and the ranch so much he didn't even look at the women his friend had invited.

Gil certainly *had* planned his part, Liz thought, feeling very overdressed. She might have commented, but just then someone knocked at his door. She made herself scarce while he accepted the cart from room service. The aroma soon brought her out of hiding. "Oh, look—what a gorgeous centerpiece."

"Comfortable?" he asked, handing her a slender silver vase holding one delicate white rose surrounded by Christmas greenery.

She nodded. But heat coiled inside her, and she nearly dropped the vase as she carefully set it back on the cart. "Were, uh, how were the boys?"

"Fine." He smiled, seating her in a chair by the window that overlooked the lights of the city. "The rose is for you, Lizbeth."

"I... You shouldn't have, Gil. I told you I don't need flowers."

"We're not kids, Lizbeth, struggling to make ends meet. I can afford roses."

Reaching out, she touched the translucent petals. Gil was right about their not being kids. A fact made evident to Liz now as she sat here staring at the dusting of dark hair sprinkled generously across Gil's upper chest.

Tongue-tied, she inhaled the seductive scent of spruce wafting from Gil's still-damp body, and the appetizing aroma of steak and lobster from the platter he held out for her inspection. And Liz knew she was going to enjoy every morsel of this meal—and every moment of his seduction.

"Wine?" He indicated a bottle of white and one of red, and reeled off their vintages.

Liz chose white, knowing nothing about wine. Before the meal ended, she knew more. She knew that it relaxed her and took away her inhibitions. Yet alcohol had nothing to do with her willingness to skip the dessert of crème brulée. That had only to do with Gil. "Excuse me," she murmured, as she pushed the small silver dish aside. "I can't possibly eat another bite." Rising, she picked up the flower he'd given her.

"At least stay and have some coffee." He stood, slipped both hands around her hips and turned her to face him.

She rose on tiptoe and grazed his cheek with her lips. "Bring the other bottle of wine to my room, why don't you?"

Gil watched her hurry out. She was so small and delicate. Had he frightened her with his need? His stomach knotted. He couldn't blame her for having reservations, but damn, he didn't want to ply her with more wine. He wanted her to know exactly who was making love to her. So Gil arrived at the connecting door empty-handed. And it was a darned good thing. He would have dropped the bottle, and red wine made such a mess.

Lizbeth walked out of the bathroom, the only light in the room behind her. All she had on were cotton string bikini panties in an icy mint color and a matching short tank top that stretched over the full mounds of her breasts and clung to her narrow ribs.

She looked up, saw Gil and would have apologized for not owning any sexy lingerie. But the crushing all-consuming kiss he gave her as he tumbled her across the bed showed Liz plainly that Gilman Spencer wasn't a man to be fooled by the trappings of satin and lace. He was, however, way off base concerning his staying power. He kissed and suckled her into a frenzy. Three times she begged him to join with her and put out the fire that raged unchecked. As many times, he explored every inch of her body and still made her wait for relief.

Finally, when it seemed as if they'd both explode, he entered her in one long stroke and dived with her over the edge to fulfillment. To a sense of sated contentment and pure happiness.

Panting and peppered with sweat, they reentered the real world and crawled beneath the covers, each asking nothing more than to enjoy being held in the other's arms. Gil lazily stroked her hair. She skimmed her fingers and lips along the salty rim of his collarbone. They didn't need words, only an occasional approving murmur to convey how they felt about what had happened between them. Neither mentioned home or children or shopping. For this moment, all trouble was left back in Crockett County.

In the night when Liz awakened in the throes of one of her terrible claustrophobic nightmares, Gil was there to drive her fears away. They made love again, so tenderly this time it brought tears to her eyes.

The next day Gil served her breakfast in bed. Afterward they wandered along streets resplendent with the trappings of Christmas. They shopped holding hands and made short work of both Christmas lists. Many times throughout the afternoon, the hardships of single parenting dissolved in the face of shared laughter. Like children, they tried out every noisy toy they could lay hands on.

In a card shop, Gil bought special cards for several close friends. Liz selected one for Hoot. She picked a sentimental one for her folks, then before reaching the cashier, she stepped out of the line and put it back. Maybe she'd call them, instead.

That night they made love and promises—till dawn brought a horrendous thunderstorm and an abrupt end to their idyll.

They dressed in separate rooms and spoke little on the drive home. Gil concentrated on watching the highway through sheets of rain. Liz did her best to keep the windshield cleared of steam. "Has this all been a dream?" she asked once when they stopped for coffee and to calm their nerves.

Gil threaded his fingers through hers as they dashed back to the van. "It's no dream, Lizbeth. It's the start of something real. I'm not good with words, sweetheart, but I think it's pretty evident how I feel about you."

"But the children," she murmured, watching him fumble for his keys. "Dustin answered the phone this morning. He was more than cool. He didn't say two words to me before Nancy called Melody to the phone. I think he knows what's gone on, Gil."

"We'll take it slow for a while. Date." He bent and kissed a fat raindrop from her nose. "By spring foaling, they'll see we're serious." A drumroll of thunder forced him to hustle her into her seat and race through puddles around to his side. After that, they were both so preoccupied with the dangers of the drive, their new relationship was temporarily put on hold.

CHAPTER ELEVEN

CHRISTMAS BLEW into Texas in the company of a hail-storm.

Liz prepared a beautiful standing rib roast that dried out before Gil got back from checking the horses for cuts and bruises.

Rafe had developed minor complications from his surgery. Christmas Day, Gil worked long hours, short-handed. *Welcome to ranching,* Liz thought wryly as she sat alone admiring the winking tree lights while Gil dozed fitfully in the chair. The boys had put aside their re-mote-controlled big-wheel trucks and dragged their new hand-tooled saddles upstairs to use as pillows. Melody slept on the love seat, buried in Barbie dolls, books and games. She'd insisted on wearing her new nightgown and robe.

Liz's hand kept straying to one of Gil's gifts to her—an elegant boot-length, dark red velvet dress with a sweet-heart neckline etched in antique silver studs. It came with matching boots of the softest leather. She'd never owned anything so rich. For the Littlefields' New Year's Eve party, he'd told her offhandedly when she couldn't find words to thank him. Liz wondered now if that meant he'd be embarrassed to be seen with her in something she'd bought herself. She shook off the thought, not wanting to create problems where none existed. Stretching, she rose, shut off the lights and woke him gently. "Go to bed,

Gil. Time for me to get Melody home. There's finally a break in the storm. The stars are out.''

He jumped up, rubbing the heels of his palms across his eyes. "What time is it? Don't tell me the boys have crashed? God, Liz, why didn't you poke me sooner?"

"It's okay. You needed the rest."

He pulled her to him and nibbled softly on her bottom lip. "Fort Worth seems a lifetime away, doesn't it? I hate to impose again, but could you watch the twins tomorrow? I know they were supposed to ride with me, but Rusty's not feeling all that well."

Her reluctant "Sure" was swallowed by a more passionate kiss, and Liz forgot what her objections might be.

The next day she remembered. Because she was forced to deal with Dustin's post-Christmas blues, as well as his surliness. By midday, she'd about had it with running inside every ten minutes to break up arguments he'd provoked between Rusty and Mel.

What had Gil thought? That she'd ride herd on the kids all day, never mind her job? Did they turn some corner in Fort Worth that she wasn't aware of? But no, they'd agreed to date. That was all. She was neither official housekeeper nor mother to the boys, a fact of which Dustin Spencer was well aware. She remained the Lone Spur's farrier—a job she took pride in doing. The frozen ground caused many of the wranglers' horses to throw shoes. Knowing the men were having a rough enough time battling the weather, Liz erected her forge in the Spencers' front yard to save the men from having to ride unfamiliar mounts while she played nanny to the boss's kids.

Considering all their new toys, Liz assumed the trio would play quietly inside while she worked. Wrong. They interrupted her so many times with their bickering she finally sent Dustin out to play by himself in the barn. The glare he aimed at her was fierce. Liz was almost glad to see Buddy Hodges ride in a half hour later.

She shoed two horses. The cold wind left her fingers numb. Liz decided to break for coffee before starting on Yancy's dun-colored mare. She'd just reached the porch when a shout, followed by a bloodcurdling scream, rose from the barn. Liz wanted to run, but her legs refused to function. When they did, horrible images dragged at her steps, making her stumble.

Moments later, bursting into the barn, it was as if her worst fears were realized. Dustin lay on the earthen floor beneath the hayloft—and there was blood everywhere. Dear Lord, how bad was he? Should she move him? Or call an ambulance? She'd wanted to try the new cell phone—another of Gil's extravagant Christmas gifts— but not for this reason. *God in heaven, how badly was he hurt?*

Buddy Hodges hovered in a corner. What was wrong with that boy? Why didn't he go for help? Liz dropped to her knees on the cold floor. Her legs shook so hard she couldn't have stood much longer. Her tongue had difficulty forming words. "D-did he fall from the l-loft or the ladder?" She ripped off her jacket and covered Dustin, paying no heed to the crimson stain that spread across the light-colored leather.

Liz thought she heard Buddy choking. Obviously he was crying and trying to be manly. Liz had just placed a hand on Dustin's pulse when he jackknifed into a sitting position and burst into peals of laughter. "Told ya so, Buddy! I said I could make good fake blood out of catsup."

Stunned, Liz went through a dozen emotions ranging from relief to fury, and still she couldn't control her internal shaking. They were kids, she told herself. Boys who didn't know the seriousness of their actions. And it wasn't her place to chastise either of them. It was Gil's. She fully intended to tell him the whole story.

But once her heart had resumed its normal pace, she began to wonder if there'd been something of a challenge in Dustin's eyes—daring her to make trouble for him with his father. After much soul-searching, Liz decided to let the incident pass. Maybe it was typical boy behavior. What did she know about raising boys? If it was some test he'd dreamed up for her, heaven knew she wanted to pass it.

The rest of the day slid by without incident. And the next and the next. Before Liz knew it, a week was gone. She and Gil hardly managed more than a word in passing between Christmas and the Littlefields' New Year's Eve party—a big family affair.

Gil showed up late to collect Liz and Melody. He looked wonderful in his suit and top coat.. So handsome. Liz stumbled over a fitting compliment.

"You look lovely, too," he said, thrusting a gardenia into her hands.

To Liz, who ached at the sight of him, the words sounded like nothing more than a polite tribute. Too polite coming from a man with whom she'd made hot steamy love a couple of weeks earlier, she thought, murmuring a self-conscious thank-you.

But maybe she was reading things wrong—again.

The party was in full swing when they arrived. Gil sent the kids off to play, then introduced Liz to all his horse-breeder cronies and their wives. Everyone seemed to genuinely like her. She and Gil were invited, as a couple, to attend both Valentine and St. Patrick's Day events. Still, Liz didn't relax until she overheard one of the wives tell Nan that it was the first time she'd seen Gil look so happy at one of their gatherings.

He did, Liz realized. He looked happy. In love. Willing to accept what she could validate with her eyes, she curled a hand possessively around his arm and passed him a glass of champagne.

Smiling, Gil pulled her closer.

Experiencing the warm familiar brush of his lean body against her softer curves, Liz imagined for a moment how they'd look together when they were Nan and Morris's age. It was a fleeting image. Gone within moments, because someone began counting out the old year. Soon others joined in, shouting and laughing amid the popping of corks.

Gil tightened his arm around Liz's waist and guided her into a secluded corner. His midnight kiss was close to being X-rated—and extended well into the new year. He was far less flustered than she over the good-natured ribbing they got from his pals.

Talk and music flowed. Couples danced until nearly dawn. Liz enjoyed herself so fully she paid scant attention to the dark looks Dustin Spencer cast her from an adjoining room.

Only after the adults crowded into the kitchen for Nan's traditional country breakfast did anyone realize winter had set in outside with a vengeance. They quickly ended the festivities to hurry home to their ranches.

Unfortunately a series of storms kept Gil busy in the ensuing weeks—too busy to fulfill a single one of his outrageous New Year's resolutions. The one Liz had particularly looked forward to was a promise to duplicate their weekend in Fort Worth. He'd confided it in a whisper on the harrowing ride home from the party. This was at a time when all three kids sat on the edge of their seats, and Liz couldn't even seal the bargain with a kiss.

Nevertheless, she dreamed about it often over the next two months as West Texas was pounded by one storm after another. She and Gil passed like falling stars in an endless night. Liz began to wonder if he'd actually made the wanton promise, or if it'd been wishful thinking on her part. Many times she gazed longingly at his back as he walked away with Rafe. Really, she would have settled for a hug.

School was closed more than it was open the month of January, what with ice storms followed by melting rains that caused flooding, followed by a series of tornadoes, one of which lifted the roof off the foaling barn. Through it all, Liz had more ups and downs with Dusty. He was forever dragging her off the job with pranks that too often sent her on wild-goose chases. Each time, he dared her with mocking eyes to run and tattle to his father.

Once she almost did—the day Buddy Hodges tied Melody's cat to a makeshift parachute and tossed him out of the barn loft to Dustin, who stood below. Liz should have gone to Gil, but darn... he looked so harried these days she longed to ease his burden, not add to it. As a result, she took on a greater portion of the boys' daily care. And the more she took on, the more Dustin resented her.

Rusty was a joy. A trooper. He and Melody sorted and folded laundry, cleaned their rooms and made their beds. They never fought unless Dusty egged them on. Dustin, who deemed manual labor and playing with a girl, beneath him.

"I wish Ben'd get back," he declared one Saturday in mid-February. "Then Dad wouldn't let you order us around no more. He only asked you to help out 'cause he's busy, you know. Ask Shorty. My Dad said it ain't 'cause he wants a *wife.*"

Liz told herself five times that day it was childish pique talking. On the other hand, Gil rarely found opportunities to be with her these days. When he dragged in at night, he didn't try to sneak her away from the kids to hug her or kiss her.

Although... Last Wednesday he'd brought her violets. The purple blooms filled the kitchen with their sweet scent, despite the pouring rain. He'd gone to town for feed and said he saw the potted plant in the florist's window. On the way home his truck had slid into a muddy ditch. He'd spent hours digging out. The heavy ceramic pot had tumbled off the seat and overturned, crushing a few stems and his cell phone. The pot of violets exchanged hands with little fanfare.

Had she even thanked him? Or had she snapped because dinner was ruined and she'd been worried sick when he didn't call? Did he suspect that some nights she ached for him? Everything would be much easier to bear if once in a while they could just hold each other. Maybe now that Rafe was back, the pressure would let up on Gil.

It didn't. If anything, the pace grew wilder. To top it off, Ben's sister called one Sunday in the early part of March—about the time everyone expected Ben back. She said the doctor wanted Ben off his feet another month or more. It was the "or more" that concerned Liz. Underlying it was an implication that he might not return. Since she'd taken the phone message, it was up to her to relay it to Gil. As she trudged up the path to the foaling barn, where several men, Gil for one, worked steadily on the new roof, it came to Liz that this last bit of news might open his eyes. Gilman Spencer *did* need a wife. His sons needed a mother. And she wanted both roles.

"Lizbeth." A smile chased away the weariness in Gil's eyes the moment he saw her. "Hot coffee. Mmm. How is it you always know when we're flagging?" He climbed down the ladder toward her and wound a dark curl that had escaped from beneath her hat around his finger. His features softening, he brushed the wispy tip across her nose. "Are you letting your hair grow?"

"When have I had time to get it cut?" She yanked the curl from his grasp. Sighing, she reached for the men's cups that still lined the fence from an earlier break.

"It's been a tough winter and now spring is late. I don't know what I would have done without you, Lizbeth. When Ben gets back—"

"Gil, Ben's sister phoned while I was making coffee." It was her bad luck that the twins and Melody galloped up just as she finished telling Gil what the woman had said.

Dustin flung himself off the horse. "He's gotta come back. He's just gotta. Next week is spring break. I thought him and me and Rusty could do something."

Liz noticed Dusty's plans didn't include her or Melody.

"Straighten up, Dustin, and stop whining," Gil said. "This is no one's fault."

Not wanting to intrude on the heated discussion developing between father and son, Liz filled the cups and asked Rusty and Melody to deliver them while she returned to the house. She felt as if a yawning hole had opened where her heart belonged. Judging by the look on Dustin's face, he'd never accept her as his stepmother.

No wonder Gil had applied the skids to a romance one of his sons so adamantly opposed. He *must* have noticed her ongoing struggle with Dustin. Not long ago Gil had asked her how the two of them were getting along.

It was the day after the incident with the cat. She shouldn't have fibbed and said "okay." But the last thing she wanted was to have Dustin label her a snitch.

Gloomy weather and gloomier thoughts chased Liz back to the cottage. It seemed unfair—when she and Gil had been so happy in Fort Worth—to have their hopes and dreams dashed by one small boy. But love didn't seem to be in the cards for a lonely rancher and his equally lonely farrier.

Less than an hour later Liz happened to look out the kitchen window and saw Dustin riding his horse through her flower beds. The animal's sharp hooves trampled new shoots just beginning to poke up through the harsh Texas soil. The boy's thoughtless act snapped the last thread of her control. Not even realizing she was crying, Liz ran from the house. She fell to her knees and tried to salvage something. Anything. But the shoots were broken, beyond saving. Through her tears, she watched Dustin and his pal, Buddy Hodges, hightail it out of sight.

Gil, returning to the house for a tool, glanced toward the cottage and saw Liz amid tears and mud. Afraid she'd hurt herself somehow, he tore across the clearing. "Lizbeth, what's wrong? Are you hurt?"

Equally impervious to his entreaty and to the dampness soaking her, she continued to cry. Huge wrenching sobs shook her body.

Gil gathered her in his arms so gently that the words tumbled out between sobs. She was hardly aware of telling him what had happened.

"Why? Why would he do this?" Gil wiped at her tears with his thumbs. "I'll see he buys you new plants with his allowance, and by hell, he'll replant every one. I may paddle his butt. Please, Lizbeth, stop crying."

"Don't, Gil. He misses Ben. I know Dusty's hurting. I don't think he understands."

"*I* don't understand, dammit."

"I didn't, either, at first. He needs attention, Gil. Yours. You have to set aside some time to spend with him." A series of sniffles punctuated her plea.

"Time, Lizbeth?" Gil said bitterly. "Haven't you noticed that I can't even find time for you lately?"

She straightened and gazed up at him through tear-spiked lashes. "It helps, knowing you want to."

He ran his hands down her neck and over her back, steadily pulling her against his chest. "I want to, Lizbeth. The world can tell how much I want by looking. The hands see it whenever you walk by. It's so obvious how I feel I'd be willing to bet the men are tiptoeing around you."

"Now that you mention it, I have become a wallflower."

"I'm sorry we missed the Yeagers' Valentine bash, honey, but the tornado hit and—"

"I don't care about parties, Gil. I *have* wondered, though, if you'd come to regret what happened between us in Fort Worth. You'd tell me the truth, wouldn't you? I deserve the truth."

Groaning, he tightened his arms, cradling her head in the rain-soaked curve of his shoulder.

As he drew her close, Liz thought she glimpsed someone peeking around a shutter in the hayloft. She blinked and the face disappeared.

"The truth is, Lizbeth," Gil said fiercely, "you haunt me day and night. You think I don't see the weight you've lost—working like a slave to keep up your job and Ben's? Just when things get to where I think I can spare an evening to take you and the kids to town for dinner and a movie, another bomb drops. Like tomorrow—we're chasing our killer cougar again."

"Oh, no, Gil."

"Can't be helped. He brought down a yearling last night in the corral behind the weanling barn. Two days before, he took down a steer at the Drag M. We know it's the same cat. He's got an old leg injury that shows in his tracks."

She shuddered and gripped the front of his jacket. "Tomorrow is the start of the kids' spring break. Will you take the boys with you?"

"Lizbeth, I can't. The environmentalists are on our case. They don't want that cougar shot. And, hell, I'm out of tricks to catch him. I have someone coming from the San Antonio Zoo who's an expert at trapping big cats. This time we're staying out till we get him. A trip like this is too dangerous for the boys."

"You're right, of course. But I'm scheduled to shoe out in the east pasture all week. The twins won't be thrilled if they have to tag along. Especially Dustin."

"Too bad for Dustin. I'll tell him myself, and I've got a few more things to say to that young man."

"Go easy, Gil. I want him to like me."

"Like you? Why wouldn't he, the ungrateful kid?" Seeing her distress, Gil relented. "All right. I won't bust his tail. Neither will I tolerate any monkeyshines while I'm gone. You're right about my making more time for the boys. *We* need to make time. I want them to see us together. How about if, after we get the cat—well, I mean *if* we get him and they decide to keep him at the zoo— how about we take a couple of days and visit San Antonio? Do you think it'll make the boys feel important to know we had a hand in finding the cat a home?"

"Maybe. Oh, Gil, that does sound promising. If only
Dusty isn't too unhappy about having me go along."

"He'd better get happy, then." Gil pushed her hat back
and helped himself to a taste of her lips. One kiss dragged
into two, then three. It was some moments before either
of them realized how long they'd stood there in the open,
exchanging heated kisses.

Fully aroused, Gil swallowed a moan and set her away.
"I really came to ask another favor. Will you feed the
boys and sleep over at the house until I get back from the
hunt? Luke, Rafe and I are hauling some of our vulner-
able stock to the Running Z down near Ozona. That's
where they'll stay between now and the time we capture
the cougar. I'm including your two foals, Lizbeth. We'll
leave for the hunt from there."

Liz rubbed at an uneasy knot in her stomach. "You'll
be careful, won't you, Gil?"

In answer, he kissed her again. They parted only when
Rusty and Melody rode in looking for Dustin.

Gil sighed and detained his son. "I want a word with
both of you boys, Russell. Come along, let's go find your
brother."

Liz's heart fluttered as she watched Gil stride off. The
knot and now the flutter were reminiscent of warning
signals she'd had before—like the time Corbett had called
her premonitions silly and climbed on that killer bull
anyway. Running, Liz grabbed Gil's arm. In a rush, all
her fears poured out in one long stream.

"Lizbeth." Gil touched her nose, her cheek, and lastly
smoothed the rough pad of his thumb along her bottom
lip, over and over. "Don't worry. Everything will be
fine—you'll see." He bestowed a last reassuring kiss before catching up with his son.

Liz gazed after him through the gray mist, and this time there was no mistaking that someone watched through the upper window of the barn. *Dustin.* Liz recognized his jacket. Now he'd be sure she'd squealed to Gil. If only she'd had a chance to talk with him first. Maybe it was naive, but she still believed that, given time, she and Dusty could arrive at a truce. With Gil away, she'd have to make a point of sitting down with Dustin tonight—to explain again that she wasn't trying to divide the family or take his dad from him.

"Mom!" Melody yelled from her pony's back. "I'm going to go put Babycakes away. Then can we eat? I'm hungry."

"Feed Mittens and get your sleeping bag, kiddo. We're camping out at the big house tonight. The twins' dad is going on a short trip."

"Goody! That'll be fun." Melody tossed Liz a gap-toothed grin as she urged her pony into a trot.

"Fun," Liz muttered, squaring her shoulders against a feeling of impending doom.

That word "fun" mocked her many times during the evening as she suffered Dustin's silent treatment. It proved impossible to find any time alone with him. And what if she had? He flatly refused to speak to her.

Liz noticed he seemed to have a lot to say to his twin and to Melody. Every time Liz looked up from her chores, those three were huddled—with Dustin doing the talking. "Big whoop," she heard him say once to some muffled comment his brother made. Their arguing didn't worry Liz; their intensity did.

"What were you kids talking about this evening?" Liz asked as she tucked Melody into her sleeping bag.

Melody's eyes grew solemn. "It's a secret, Mom. I crossed my heart and promised not to tell a soul."

Liz knew Melody couldn't be swayed when she'd crossed her heart. But she was confident her daughter wouldn't be party to anything really bad. Very likely it was nothing and she was letting her concern for Gil spill over onto the kids' silly games.

Next morning Liz's heart was less heavy. A thin sun shone down through patchy clouds. It was the first sunlight in months, and everything seemed brighter. The children were going to accompany her to the east pasture; Gil had done as he'd said and talked with the twins about it.

Apparently he'd made an impression. Not only did Dusty empty his piggy bank into her hands to buy new plants, but they all surprised her when she returned from readying her truck. They'd fixed peanut-butter-and-jelly sandwiches and packed them with apples and cookies in individual knapsacks for the outing.

"Well, look at this," Liz exclaimed happily. "Keep up this behavior, and we'll knock off early and go into town for a treat."

Dustin smiled. He actually smiled at her as he hustled the other two off to the barn to saddle up. By the time all three kids galloped out ahead of her, Liz found herself humming a jaunty tune.

She received another nice surprise when she drove into the east pasture. Dustin rode his buckskin close to her pickup and greeted Liz with a grin very like Gil's. For a moment the scenery tilted, then Liz happily returned his smile.

"Dad said we're to ride fence," Dusty announced.

Liz thought his eagerness a far cry from the boredom he'd claimed the last time they were here. "Fine by me." She nodded, then tensed. "You aren't thinking of heading south toward the river." She made it a statement.

"Naw. North." He pointed.

Liz recalled the promontory overlooking Wind Dancer's herd. "You kids don't have any plans to chase wild horses, do you?"

"No way."

He said it so quickly and sounded so sincere that Liz believed him. "All right." She finally relaxed. Obviously Gil had made headway. Or maybe it was a condition of his taking them to San Antonio. In any event, why question success?

"Stay within shouting distance." Liz raised her voice to include the other two, who waited a few feet away. She stood and watched as all three wheeled their horses and cantered off along the northern fence row. Now this was more like it. Liz could hardly wait to tell Gil.

Soon, busy trimming heels and shoeing horses, Liz forgot how long it had been since the trio had checked in. When she took a break from working on a cantankerous horse, she realized the sun had slipped a bit into the west.

Straightening, she cupped her mouth and called, "Melody!" A breeze kicked up a clump of weathered grass, and the geldings in the pasture flicked their ears. No answer floated back on the wind. Liz called again. And again. The last time she heard a faint faraway response—or thought she did. It might have been a bird, but perhaps the kids had just ridden farther than they'd intended. After all, the day was beautiful. And they'd all eaten big breakfasts, so it was unlikely they'd be spurred by hunger to return at exactly noon. If they weren't back by the time she finished this ornery roan that belonged to Shorty Ledoux, she'd shake out his kinks and go see what had become of her little charges.

She had two shoes nailed when she heard the rapid staccato of hoofbeats sweeping down the ridge. Liz hadn't even realized her stomach had clenched until it suddenly unfurled at the sound.

"Mom! Mom!" Melody shouted the moment she got within range. "You hafta come quick."

Liz glanced up from cooling the third shoe. Melody and Rusty galloped down from the ridge, their horses showing signs of having been run hard. Straightening, Liz shaded her eyes. Poor Babycakes's sides were heaving. "Melody Lorraine, you know better than to ride your pony into a sweat."

"You gotta come," Rusty implored, hauling back on the reins and sliding his long-legged buckskin to a stop beside Liz's hot forge. "Dusty fell down a hole."

Liz felt her heart plummet. At least it did until she remembered the catsup blood and the three times since that Dustin Spencer had cried wolf. "Did he now?" she said, deliberately fitting the cooled horseshoe to the roan's left hind foot.

"A deep hole," Melody cried, her voice quavering. "Me and Rusty peeked in, but we couldn't see him."

Liz paused, reminding herself that they were talking about the boy who'd caused her more bouts of anxiety than she cared to count. "A fence-post hole isn't that deep, Mel. He's probably hiding behind a stump having a good laugh."

Rusty shivered. Fat tears tracked his pale cheeks. "The hole ain't near the fence. I'm sorry we let Dusty talk us into goin' after Dad. He never said it'd be so far. Mel and me wanted lunch. Dustin said he'd stop 'cause we were babies. He got off his horse to look for a good place to eat—and he . . . he disappeared."

"Rusty Spencer, you know very well your dad went up to the caverns after that cougar. If you three have decided to play a trick on me, it's not funny. Cool out those animals and go sit under a tree until I finish Shorty's horse.''

The boy scrubbed at his cheeks, but the tears fell faster. Melody, too, began to sniffle. Liz's blood started to simmer. This behavior of Dustin's had to stop. How dare he involve the other kids? Any minute now he'd show up; Liz could all but see that cocky smirk he'd fine-tuned to get her goat.

''Now, Russ,'' she chided gently, stepping up to heat the final blank, ''surely you don't expect me to believe that even Dustin would cook up a crazy stunt like that after your dad laid down the law yesterday?''

Rusty's head bobbed. ''I told Dusty that Dad would get mad. He said, 'Big whoop.' He said Dad wouldn't send us back to the ranch alone in the dark.''

A chill shot up Lizbeth's spine. She had heard Dustin make that retort last night—the ''big whoop'' part. The rational portion of her mind continued to deny that anything had happened to Dusty. It had to be another of his pranks.

But something in Melody's eyes scared Liz. That, and the fact that Dustin had yet to ride in, crowing over his victory.

As if she wasn't already beginning to suffer real anguish, Shorty's horse nipped her thigh. ''Damn,'' she said, biting back a stronger word just in time. She looked from one stricken face to the other, begging them to be wrong. The sweat popped out on her brow. ''Kids,'' she said in a shaky voice, ''can you find the hole again?'' *Please Lord, let it be nothing!* All thought of riding Shorty's nag fled her mind. She chose, instead, a powerful chestnut whose back was broad and smooth—perfect for riding bareback.

Bestowing a last prayerful look into the distance, Liz grabbed a spare saddle blanket from the truck, clipped her new cell phone to her belt and vaulted aboard the big gelding. Dread gripped her throat as she urged Rusty into the lead. With each rolling hill they crowned, Liz scanned the horizon, expecting Dustin to appear and prove her fears unfounded. She wondered where Gil was right now. Had they captured the cat? Were they headed back to the ranch? *Please! Let them be.*

She paused once, berating herself for having let the kids leave her work site. For having believed Dustin's apparent willingness to ride fence. But that didn't matter now—she had to find the boy. Resolutely she flipped open the phone and hit one of the numbers Gil had programmed into her phone.

Rusty reined in beside her. "You callin' Dad? Don'tcha remember? He broke his phone the night he went in the ditch. It's not fixed yet. That's another reason Dusty figured Dad wouldn't send us home."

Her heart sank. "Maybe your dad's already back at the ranch." Crossing her fingers, Liz keyed in that number. But it rang and rang. She listened to the bleat long after she should have clicked off. The sound was like a link to the Lone Spur, and Liz hated to sever it. She finally did when they topped the next rise and started down into a grassy field littered with rotted ore boxes and rusty mine cages. Good heavens, had Dustin fallen into an abandoned mine? Funny, Gil never mentioned trying his hand at mining.

"We've crossed over to the Drag M," Rusty said as if reading her mind. "We're not 'spose ta be here. Dad would skin us alive if he knew."

"The Drag M runs cattle. I wonder what they were mining up here. Do you know, Rusty?"

He shook his head. "Nope. But we ain't ever 'spose to come up here." He jerked a thumb west. "We ain't 'spose ta go there, neither."

Liz felt a wave of nausea.

Melody's pony trotted as fast as his short legs would go. Liz waited until she drew abreast of them. "How much farther?" she asked, eyeing the Welsh pony's sweat-stained coat. What if they'd come too far already?

"Over there." Melody pointed to a circle of matted grass.

Not a mine. At least Liz didn't think it was. Her apprehension grew more pronounced the closer they got to the field. "Stay back," she warned Rusty when they rode close enough to see rotting planks that appeared to have been broken through. Liz slid off the gelding and slowly approached the spot. *A well.* "Dear God," she whispered, falling to her knees. Not an abandoned mine, with an opening big enough to crawl through, but a well.

"Dustin!" she called, thrusting her face near the dark opening. His name echoed back eerily. She felt faint as her own claustrophobia set dark spots dancing before her eyes. The children must be wrong—it was all a joke, she thought frantically. Then from far away, deep in the bowels of the earth, Liz heard a faint mewling cry. "My God, he's not fooling." First pinpricks of heat, then icy swells of terror swept over her. Liz fought to keep from throwing up.

Gil had trusted her with the two most precious things in his life, and she'd failed his trust. Just like she'd failed Corbett. Here she was, alone except for two kids, miles from help. What on earth should she do? *Think, Lizbeth!* She pressed unsteady hands hard against her quiv-

ering lips. *Think, darn it. What would you do if it was
Melody in that hole?* But all she could recall was how—
if she'd yelled—she might have saved Corbett. And how
she'd frozen. Just like now.

CHAPTER TWELVE

AFTER A WHILE Liz became aware of two small warm bodies pressed tightly to hers. Aware, too, of muffled sobs. Her fingernails bit into her palms. This had nothing to do with Corbett. It was a different time, a different place. Anyway, no one in the arena that day believed she could've saved Corbett.

But she could save Dustin Spencer. She had her phone and she had her wits. And she had two other children to calm and be brave for.

"Listen, you guys." Liz gently dislodged them and put on a false smile. "Crying won't help Dustin. I want you to tether the horses, take this blanket and sit right there." She indicated a solid plot of ground adjacent to the well. "Talk to Dusty. Happy talk. Yell if you have to. He needs our strength right now."

"I want my daddy," Rusty sniffed. "I'm scared."

She hugged him, then Melody, who'd grown deathly still, her eyes huge and fearful. "I'll keep trying the bunkhouse. The minute one of the hands gets in, we'll send him after your dad. Meanwhile, I'm going to contact the police and fire departments. Agreed?"

They didn't seem at all sure. But they obeyed her and already seemed more composed. Liz hoped they didn't see her shaking fingers as she dialed the local authorities. She wanted Gil, too. Oh, how she wanted him here.

But thank God Gil had had the foresight to program emergency numbers into her phone.

In the next hour he was never far from her mind. She was overwhelmed with relief when she tried the bunkhouse for about the fortieth time and Clayton Smith answered. Tranquil reliable Clayton. Liz believed him when he promised to have Gil out there before dark. *Dark*. She shivered. She wanted Dustin out of that hole *long* before dark. A wave of nausea threatened again.

Unwilling to do nothing while she waited for the police, Liz called Nan Littlefield and got the number of the nearest drilling outfit. Nan put up a good front, but Liz knew how worried she was. She promised to gather Morris and the other ranchers and organize the women in town to provide food, tents, blankets and coffee for the rescue team that would soon assemble. She had no illusions that they'd get Dusty out any time soon.

The man at the drilling company asked Liz a lot of questions she couldn't answer. He wanted to know the type of well. The depth. The size bore, and if she'd tried to pull Dustin out with a rope. "What difference does any of that make?" Liz demanded. "Time is the enemy. Come, and bring everything you've got to reach him. Hear what I'm saying—he's a long way down." Apparently taken aback by her vehemence, the man, Jarvis, agreed to bring a crew by helicopter. His questions left Liz wringing her hands and feeling terribly inadequate. She had ropes back in her truck, of course. But now that she was here, she hated to leave Dusty alone to go get them. Nor did she feel comfortable sending Rusty and Mel. Was it so wrong of her to want to keep them close?

The three of them were hoarse from shouting down the well, and Liz's nerves were frayed by the time the first group of rescuers pulled in. Hot on their heels was a horde of reporters. Liz detected a coolness in their attitudes when they discovered she wasn't Dustin's mother, but merely an employee who was supposed to watch him. *Someone who hadn't done a very good job of watching him.* Was that how Gil would see her when he finally arrived?

If only she'd been on better terms with Dusty. Liz was swamped by if-onlys as more men—rough-hewn strangers—started rolling in. The policemen and firemen were solicitous of Liz and the kids; they just didn't have any experience with well rescues. Liz's stomach began to churn acid. Jarvis was a different story. Big and barrel-chested with iron-gray hair, he'd been in oil drilling forty years. Liz wanted to kiss his solid-looking backhoe and the derrick affair he called a rat-hole rig. But she still wanted Gil. She wore bare patches in the prairie grass, pacing and eyeing the descent of the sun.

It had fallen behind the distant foothills by the time a very dirty, very tired Gil Spencer climbed out of a chartered helicopter. Rusty flew into his arms, leaving Liz and Melody behind like so much excess baggage. After that, Gil was involved in conversations with Jarvis and the police. Liz couldn't fault him for wanting to get reports from all the authorities first. She just felt so sick and helpless—and responsible.

Or maybe she needed him to rail and accuse her of being negligent. Anything but ignore her.

He sought her out when she least expected it. When she was at her lowest ebb. Not to accuse, but simply to hold her and bury his face in her fragrant hair. "Lizbeth." He said her name three times, his breath a ragged sigh against her ear. "Rusty told me what happened. I can't believe Dustin would be so...so foolish. He knows damn well this area is off-limits."

"It's me," she sobbed into the front of his shirt. "He wouldn't be in this mess if Ben had come back on time."

Gil lifted her off the ground and cradled her cheek to his. "I won't have you condemning yourself, Lizbeth. It's an accident. No one's at fault. Or if anyone's to blame, it's the fool oil driller who pulled out without filling in that shaft. Kyle Mason thought he had. Now he's trying to take the blame, too."

Her toes dangling, Liz slumped into his arms. "Will they get him out, Gil?" It was a question she'd been afraid to ask even Jarvis.

"They will. *We will*. Just like we got that old cat today—spitting, but in one piece." He planted a hard determined kiss on her lips. "Thanks to your quick action, they have a generator in place, lights on, and oxygen being pumped to Dusty. They've already started digging a rescue shaft about ten or twelve feet from the well—to avoid a cave-in. Jarvis said the way you barked at him over the phone, he expected you to be ten feet tall, instead of a scrawny lightweight." He tapped her chin with his lucky spur key ring that had somehow found its way into his hand.

Gil's lopsided smile was exactly what Liz needed to boost her spirits, which had dwindled in the chaos developing around the site. She shivered as he pocketed his talisman and left. Luck. They needed all they could get. Liz wished she could be as certain as he that everything would turn out.

Darkness brought a chill to the high desert, and renewed desperation to the drillers. The optimism that had risen and beaten back fears earlier slipped away.

"Mrs. Robbins, is the boy wearing a jacket?" asked a man with a miner's light on his cap. "He's probably cold and damp, although we're mighty grateful this is a dry oil shaft and not an old water well. The boy's lodged about forty feet down."

"That far?" Liz swallowed the bitter taste of bile and wrapped her arms more tightly around the two children, who'd come again to seek her comfort.

"He had on his red Western shirt and a jacket like this," Rusty piped up. "He's my twin, you know."

"I know, son." The man patted Rusty's head. "Hey, there's a woman over there in the blue tent who says she brought you kids sleeping bags and stuffed toys. It's gonna be a long night. You might want to grab some shut-eye."

"That'd be Nan." Liz directed the children to a small tent someone had recently hoisted. "Get something to eat, too. And tell her I'll be along shortly."

"Where's Mr. Spencer?" she asked after the children left. "What's taking so long to get Dustin out?"

"Spencer's down in the pit. It's frustrating work, ma'am. We've hit rock. Nasty rock. She's breakin' our tungsten bits like they were Popsicle sticks, and there's evidence the kid's slipped a few inches in the last hour."

Liz stood there blinking as he walked back toward the other men. Old fears mingled with new. Gil was in a pit, Dustin in a black void. She wanted to scream, to run, to hide. Visions swirled behind Liz's eyes, shooting terror to her heart. Her only solace came from the solid wham, wham, wham of the drill. Each time it stopped, Liz held her breath and prayed until it started again.

New helpers arrived every hour. Liz forced herself to stay busy; she handed out sandwiches, losing count of the number of pots of coffee she brewed. Cups and plates appeared like magic as more people heard and local ranchers rallied round.

Sometime after midnight, Gil found her and led her into a quiet corner. His shirt was ripped, his pants filthy. Dried blood arced in a half-moon across one stubbled cheek. Liz saw that his bravado had disappeared. This time she offered him relief in her arms. "Gil, you should rest. Yancy called to see how it's going. He said you were up all night tracking the cat."

"Could you rest if it was Melody down there?"

"No." She smoothed a hand over the tense lines on either side of his mouth. "I can't rest knowing it's Dusty, either. Knowing I should have guessed he was up to something. There are things I didn't tell you, Gil." She turned aside and crossed her arms, cradling both elbows. One incident after another tumbled out.

"Hush, Lizbeth. I should have taken a firmer hand with him." Gil spun her around and kissed her quiet. Drawing away, he gazed into her bleak eyes. "What's done is done. Sweetheart, I'm sorry you suffered through Dustin and Buddy's antics. You did what you thought was right. I wish I'd known so I could help, but—"

"I love you, Gil," she said solemnly. "I want your sons to love me. I thought if you ever saw they ne-nee-needed m-me..." she stammered. Tears glazed her eyes and she closed them against the confusion that suddenly darkened the hazel eyes staring back at her.

"You pick a helluva time to tell a guy you love him, Lizbeth." He gripped her so tightly to his chest he almost smothered her in the smoky flannel of his shirt.

Her heartbeat picked up speed to match the tempo of his. "Are you saying you...you c-care for me?"

"I passed caring before Fort Worth, Lizbeth. And after...well..." He flushed and broke off when a man stepped up and tapped him on the shoulder.

"Mr. Spencer, Jarvis hit an impasse. He says we need a large-bore, multihead cone and a good diamond bit. Wonders if you know any ore miners? All we got here are oil rigs with small bores."

Gil shook his head and Liz felt his despair. "Kyle had an outfit in here looking for precious metals. Far as I know, they took all their equipment when they left."

Suddenly the area around them blossomed with light and two men holding video cameras dashed up to flank Gil. "Mr. Jarvis said the quickest way to get what we want is for you to go on TV and ask for help. Here, he wrote down the particulars. Start out by saying who you are. Tell what's happened to Dusty, then read this list. I'll wind down with a shot of the well and a phone number folks can call. He also said setting up and taking down a multihead rig is expensive. Can you handle it or should we ask for donations?"

"Money is no object," Gil snapped. "But I don't know about going on TV." He reached for Liz's hand. She felt the sweat on his palm and knew—private man that he was—he wanted to bolt. Clamping her fingers around his wrist, she held him fast. "For Dustin," she whispered.

Taking his cue from her, drawing strength from her, Gil stumbled through the ordeal. His nervousness made his plea more poignant.

The production drew a crowd of gawkers. The minute Gil read the last word, he disentangled his hand from Lizbeth's and left her to field questions from reporters. The media swarmed out of the darkness like locusts. By the time they got what they wanted from her and departed, Liz felt sucked dry of all emotion.

But something positive happened as a result of Gil's ordeal. Not ten minutes after his plea went out on live

TV, a mining company out of Denver called to say they could meet his requirements. Not only would they fly in equipment free of charge, but the owner volunteered his safety inspector, as well. A big hurrah went up when the word spread. Liz dabbed at the corners of her eyes. Too often there was nothing in the news but disasters and reports of misery. Looking around her now, she was seeing good news. An outpouring of love from grown men who teared up each time someone coaxed a sound out of Dusty. And the women who worked quietly in the background to fill the bellies of exhausted workers with warm food or to tend scrapes and cuts of men whose names they didn't know. Friends and strangers linked by a silent vigil for a small boy many had never seen before.

The men used jackhammers while they awaited the larger bore. The rock was so hard—a hundred times harder than granite—that ten to fifteen minutes was the most a man could take in the hole. Normally a burly driller managed four hours before taking a break. Watching them crawl out of the pit after fifteen minutes, their muscles turned to mush, sent a pall of gloom over everyone at the site.

Liz and Gil took refuge together whenever their breaks coincided. A touch seemed to shore up wilted energy faster than words. Gil's knees buckled and he leaned heavily on Liz when two doctors came to discuss their fears of dehydration and hypothermia. Her fingers bit into Gil's waist as one physician suggested cutting back on the amount of oxygen they pumped to Dusty. "Oxygen dries the air," he said.

"I can't— Won't that slow his breathing? Liz?" Anguished, Gil turned to her.

"These men are experts in their field, Gil." But her stomach quaked as she said it. What if they'd misjudged his weight? They were going by school records.

Gil kissed her anxious upturned face. "Okay, do it," he instructed, a tremor in his voice. "How long has he been down? Does anybody know?"

"It's been sixteen hours since Mrs. Robbins arrived on the scene," said the younger of the two men.

Liz expelled a sharp breath. "It feels like a hundred."

"I'm sure it does," said the older doctor. "Why don't you two hit the sack for a while?" Because both Gil and Liz looked at one another and turned red, the flustered speaker cleared his throat and scurried off.

Gil crooked his index finger under Liz's chin. "So much for our reputations," he murmured. "Once this is over, remind me to make an honest woman of you."

His kiss sent a tingle all the way to Lizbeth's toes. His words dashed heat all the way up her spine. Before she could ask if he was teasing or if he meant it as a proposal, he was called away by yet another dust-covered volunteer.

Night was gradually replaced by the purple streaks of dawn. With the rising sun and the long-awaited delivery of the multihead bore came renewed hope.

Sunlight also brought a new complication in the form of Gil Spencer's ex-wife. She descended from a beautifully restored 1960 white Cadillac, her flame red hair brighter than the struggling sun. The fringe on her white boots kicked up puffs of dust. White twill pants caressing every curve were cinched at the waist by a goldsmith's trophy—a buckle declaring her three-time world-champion barrel racer. Her hat—a Charlie One Horse—flashed when she walked, or rather the hat band of gold-tone conchos did. Her caped Western blouse bore

the trademark lightning strikes of Brooks and Dunn. A
hush fell over the mass of workers as they parted to let
her pass.

Liz closed her mouth with a snap and brushed at her
dirt-encrusted jeans. Lord, the woman sashayed through
the tents like a queen. A *rodeo* queen, Liz reminded herself. What, she wondered, was Ginger Lawrence doing
here with the rodeo due to play its biggest money-stake on
the circuit next weekend? Liz learned soon enough.

Ginger spotted Gil climbing out of the pit. She ran to
him and began pounding on his chest. "It's your fault!
Your fault!" she screeched. "You've neglected my babies again. I knew this would happen when that lousy
judge gave them to you. All you ever really cared about
was this damned land."

Surprised by the unprovoked attack, Gil grabbed Ginger's upper arms and thrust her away just as Liz raced to
his side. Flashbulbs winked and video cameras whirred.
A case of hysterics like this was always news.

Gil released her the minute he realized they were becoming public spectacles. He was dog-tired from his stint
in the pit and more than forty-eight hours without sleep.
He didn't know who the hell had summoned Ginger, but
he'd learned long ago that arguing only spurred her on.
About then, he spotted Liz, her eyes wide, a hand flung
over her mouth. Smothering a curse, he went to blow off
steam.

One glance was enough for Liz to recognize the tired
slump of Gil's shoulders and the despair in his eyes.
Blotting out the crush of bystanders, she marched up to
the sweetheart of the rodeo and spun her around. "You
have some nerve yelling at Gil. You can't even remember
the twins' birthdays. And they're not babies. They're
growing boys. Did you know or care that Dustin grew

two inches and needed new clothes twice since school started? It was Gil, not you, who sat through teacher conferences and cheered at their Halloween play. Gil who tramped through twenty toy stores buying their Christmas gifts. I'd watch who I was calling neglectful, if I were you."

The redhead's green cat-eyes narrowed. "Well, well. I thought there was something familiar about the female creature clinging to my husband's arm in that television blip."

"Your *ex*-husband," Liz said. "I can't say I've missed shoeing your spoiled buckskin, Ginger. The horses *and* the horse owners on the Lone Spur have much better manners."

Ginger's eyes frosted. Leaning toward a skinny man busily writing in a notebook, she said in a low voice, "If you're looking for a real story, gentlemen, check with the rodeo commission. I lodged complaints against Lizbeth Robbins on two occasions for cruelty to my horses. This is the type of person Gilman chose to care for our twins. Is it any wonder my precious baby had an accident? He was probably trying to escape this... this meanie."

The last part of Ginger's barb struck too close to home. Liz felt her skin go pasty, and she knew the moment heat stung her cheeks that Ginger had scored ten points to her two. The man with the notebook backed her into a corner. Liz shoved him aside. "Oh, for pity's sake," she snarled. "Our main concern here should be to pray for Dustin Spencer's safe recovery. Excuse me please, there are hardworking men out there who need food and fresh coffee."

When Lizbeth didn't join him at the tent, Gil worked his way back through the onlookers to see why not. He had a ringside view of Lizbeth's passionate performance on his behalf. Her loyalty was beautiful to see. *She* was beautiful. And the way she'd flown to his defense... Admiration for her still shone in his eyes as the man in front of him left and Gil glanced up to encounter Ginger's cold stare. He felt its chill even more when she bounced a venomous glare off Lizbeth's retreating back. Gil might have warned her away had Jarvis not sent someone to get him just then. Ginger was capable of shedding realistic tears at the drop of a hat, and she was a darned convincing liar. However, Gil didn't think her malice extended beyond him. There'd be time to deal with her later, to find out what she really wanted.

Gil went to join Jarvis in the shaft they were slowly sinking next to the one that trapped Dustin. Meanwhile, Ginger wound through the crowd, planting seeds of doubt about Lizbeth's competence. Of course, people didn't really know Gil's farrier well. Catching comments here and there, Liz ignored Ginger's remarks—until she began to experience the fallout. The volunteers, with the exception of Nan Littlefield and Kyle Mason's wife, weren't quite as friendly to her as they'd been before.

"Where's your fancy-dancy cowboy flash-rider?" Nan sniped at Ginger.

The rodeo queen gazed down her too-perfect nose. "Gone. Maybe Gil's little farrier knows where he went. She threw herself at him enough times when I hired her to shoe my stock."

Liz blanched. "That's not true." Only no one listened, because Ginger had spied the sleepy-eyed Rusty, and everyone in the tent shed a discreet tear at the touching reunion of mother and son.

Rusty barely recognized his biological mother, but given his brother's situation and the fact that his world had suddenly turned topsy-turvy, he reveled in the attention the flame-haired woman seemed willing to lavish on him.

Standing a few feet away, Liz heard only concern in Ginger's voice. If that concern was for real, how had the woman—the twins' mother, after all—managed to stay away so long?

By midday Dustin had been in the well for longer than twenty-four hours, and in spite of the new bit, the rescue shaft had yet to reach his level. Time grew longer between his responses. Rescuers alternated between panic and fatigue. Gil looked and felt like death. As he hunted for Lizbeth, he heard vague rumors floating around about her prior run-ins with Ginger. But of course they'd both followed the rodeo. Coming upon Lizbeth suddenly, Gil grabbed her arm. "Why didn't you tell me you already knew my charming ex-wife?"

Her heart thundering madly, Liz led the way into an empty tent. "You never asked," she said lightly. "You knew I shoed horses for rodeo contestants. It's not important, Gil. What's important is that you need to eat. Stay here. I'll run and get you something nourishing."

Gil found himself shivering as he watched her hurry away. Probably exhaustion. It was typical of Lizbeth to worry about filling his stomach, but what he really needed was rest. Looking around, Gil spotted the children's sleeping bags.

He was stretched out flat across both Melody's and Rusty's bedrolls, sound asleep, when Liz returned to the tent with his soup. Handing the bowl to a passerby, Liz lowered the tent flaps. Praying the crisis would be over when he awoke, Liz lovingly covered him with a spare blanket.

A shaft of sunlight winking in through a loosely tied tent flap awakened Gil. He rolled from beneath the covers, pulled back the flap and was shocked to discover that the sun had swung into the west. Dropping back to the rumpled makeshift bed, he saw that someone had propped an afternoon newspaper there. As if he wanted to read other people's hard-luck stories. Gil tensed and listened for the solid thunk of the drill. On hearing it, he relaxed and gave in to a yawn. The news headline caught his eye. Not too surprisingly, the well rescue had made the front page. Automatically Gil skimmed the first column—until he reached a paragraph that hinted at a love triangle between Lizbeth, Ginger and him.

Disgusted, Gil flung the paper as far as his aching arm could hurl it. "Damn Ginger." She'd made him a laughingstock among his friends once. How dared she do it again—and in the middle of their son's tragedy. And what about Lizbeth? Had *she* seen the paper? Gil stomped off to find her. One smile from her was all he needed before descending into that hellish pit once more.

Though he searched in all the usual places, he didn't find her. It was Ginger he met up with, instead. Ginger and Rusty, looking cozy as two clams in a shell.

"Hello, Gil." She smiled and took Rusty's hand. "Why are you scowling? They're making wonderful progress. Two more feet, that nice Mr. Jarvis said. Then it only needs a ten-foot cut across to the shaft Dustin's in, and our family will be reunited."

Gil started to say they weren't a family and never would be, but something in Russell's wan face made him ask, "Where did you lose Amistad?"

Pouting prettily, Ginger brushed at her son's shirt with nails polished a bright red. "With one of his floozies. It's over between us, Gil. Has been ever since I caught him behind a chute making out with your little farrier. But that's old news on the circuit. Ask anyone," she said as she sat cross-legged on the ground and pulled Rusty into her lap. "We all wondered where she'd run off to. Word got out, and people quit taking their horses to her. And then she ended up at the Lone Spur. Well, well."

Heat exploded behind Gil's tired eyes. Lizbeth had said she left shoeing horses at the rodeo to take the job Rafe offered because Melody needed roots. For no reason at all he remembered their weekend in Fort Worth. She hadn't been shy when it came to lovemaking. Images tumbled around his sluggish brain. Lizbeth's gentle touch. Her simple scent. Her open smile. "No," he said, shaking his head. "If you found her with Avery, he forced her against her will."

Ginger laughed. "Oh, Gilman, you are so gullible."

"Dad?" Rusty hopped up and stood between the two adults. "Why are you yelling at my mom?" Gil caught his son close. The child's body shook. "I'm so scared about Dusty." Rusty's voice quavered. "He's been down there a long time, and he won't talk to me no more. Please go get him, Dad."

Gil hugged his son and met his ex-wife's guileless smile. His stomach did a flip as Ginger pulled Rusty away and cradled him back in her arms. Dammit, something was wrong with this picture. Either that, or Ginger had changed. Was that even possible? But Gil didn't have time to analyze it now. Rusty was right; his twin had been in the well too long.

Gazing down on the pair, Gil muttered darkly, "We'll get Dustin, son. Before long, I hope. Why don't you run and play with Melody? She looked pretty lonely the last time I saw her."

Rusty settled more firmly on Ginger's lap. "That's okay, Dad. Mel's got her mom. And now I got mine."

Unable to respond, Gil was supremely glad when a stranger walked up just then and said Jarvis wanted him ASAP. Gil caught a glimpse of Lizbeth as he strode off. She appeared to be filling one of the large coffeemakers from a water barrel someone had trucked in. Because her back was to him and because the man had said Jarvis's request sounded urgent, he decided not to stop now. He'd talk to her later.

"What's up, Jarvis?" Gil asked, vaulting onto the platform.

"Good news and bad," the stocky driller returned. "Good news is we've started the cut across—between the two shafts. The bad news is Dustin didn't slip as far as we thought. From the soundings, it appears the pipe he's in narrows. Doc's afraid the kid's circulation has been restricted."

"You're the expert. What do we do?" Gil murmured.

"I recommend making the cut as fast as possible. Jackhammers are the only way. One man down and one standing by. The air's thin and the dust will be murder. Plus we gotta haul the waste rock outta there, else our crawl space will fill up. If a driller starts puking, I want him out of there like a shot."

"I'll go first," Gil said, reaching for a lighted helmet and a mask. No one argued, but a hush fell over the stalwart drillers. They were close, yet still so far from rescue. Not a miner present relished spending time in a stifling manhole—the nearly airless runway between two shafts.

Liz knew some change had taken place. No longer did the whump, whump of the bit drilling into the rock ring out across the valley. She left her post at the coffeemaker and worked her way through the milling throng to the rescue site. She saw only a flash of Gil being lowered into the shaft. She felt a painful tightening around her heart. Last time she checked, he still slept fitfully. Though she'd wanted them to talk, she'd been reluctant to wake him. He needed his rest. But she'd thought he'd hunt her up when he did awaken. A wrong assumption obviously. The tightness in her chest made it almost impossible to breathe as the top of his hard hat disappeared completely. For a moment Liz felt trapped. Around her pulsed the horrifying smell of death. But no—Gil hadn't gone into a chute with a crazed bull. And Dustin was alive.

Hands clenched, Liz forced her feet to cover the distance to the platform where there seemed to be a renewed surge of activity. "Are they getting close?" she breathlessly asked a muscled dirt-streaked driller who stood bent over, drinking in huge drafts of air.

"Close? That's the hell of well rescues, ma'am. Close only counts when you got the kid—and the fool going after him—safe on the surface again."

"Fool? Is his father going after him now?" Her fingers bit into his work-toughened arm.

"Naw. We're barely into the cut. The hole won't be very wide thanks to that cussed rock, so the guy Jarvis actually sends across to get the kid will have to be agile as a monkey and strong as an ox."

Liz gazed at the huddle on the platform. To a man they were broad-shouldered and thick-chested. Some of them had arms bigger than her waist. She scanned the police and firemen, then the paramedics. They were all a sturdy lot. Presumably Jarvis knew what he was doing. He must have his man waiting in the wings. The acid in her stomach eased a little.

Looking around for Melody, Lizbeth saw Ginger Lawrence and Rusty Spencer. She smiled at him, but he only edged closer to the woman in white. Liz frowned. Rusty wore his heart in his eyes and on his sleeve. What was in that woman's head, building him up like this— leading him for a fall when this was over and she went away again.

Suddenly the two women locked eyes above the child's auburn flyaway curls. *No.* Liz backed away from the smile that was at once mocking and challenging. A smile reminiscent of Dustin's after one of his pranks. Wheeling, Liz stumbled out beyond the crowd to where the air was fresh. She wasn't sure how she knew, but she did. The ex-Mrs. Spencer had no intention of leaving when this came to an end.

Surely she was wrong. Under the circumstances, her nerves were frayed and everything seemed colossal, out of perspective. Gil would never take Ginger back, would he? That was a question Liz intended to ask the first chance she got.

The chance eluded her all afternoon. Time and again, Liz saw Gil climbing out of the shaft, but whenever she managed to get to his side, Ginger and Rusty reached him first. Liz couldn't bring herself to interrupt.

News coming out of the pit wasn't encouraging. Once, they drilled through a layer of rock into wet loamy soil. Twice, the pipe they put in to shore up the mud slid on them. Frustration ran high, tempers short.

The one time Gil did come to the tent for coffee, he was besieged by reporters, and Liz never got close to him. For a second their eyes made contact. His looked so bleak, so utterly dismal, Liz couldn't have said anything to add to his stress if her life depended on it. She loved him. Had told him so, and he'd more or less said the same. For now, it would have to do. For now, Dustin needed everyone's devotion.

"Are you okay?" Nan Littlefield stepped behind the table to relieve Liz.

"Fine." The word sounded brave, but didn't fool Nan.

"I hope you aren't letting the witch of Crockett County get you down. She has more gall than a flock of turkeys. You aren't worrying about the possibility of Gil taking her back, are you?"

Liz shook her head.

"Good. 'Cause she'll show her true colors before long. Her kind always does."

"It's Rusty I'm worried about, Nancy. He's eating up all the attention she's giving him."

"Step easy there, gal. I overhead that viper tell Kyle Mason you were alienating her from her sons."

"It's not true! I told Gil the boys needed to see their mother more. Mr. Mason didn't believe her, did he?"

"Men are fools for a pretty face and a wiggly butt."

"He did believe her." Liz looked stricken. "What's to say Gil won't be hoodwinked by the same…attributes?"

"Attributes? Hmph. Fancy word for the crock of bull that woman's peddling. But Gil's sampled it all before."

Liz laughed at that. "You do have a way with words, Nan. And you're right. I should trust Gil. It's just…when you love someone, you don't want to see him hurt."

"Off with you, missy. Why don't you go take this tray of coffee up to the platform? Our beauty queen won't dirty her jeans to climb up there. I haven't met a rancher yet who doesn't appreciate it when his woman pitches in with the chores."

"Really? I thought you just said they like pretty faces and wiggly butts."

The older woman gave a wicked smile. "Time you learned that a rancher's wife has a passel of talents up her

sleeve . . . and, um, in other places." She winked and
shoved the big metal tray into Lizbeth's hands.

People parted automatically to let Liz through. Jarvis
greeted her with a heartfelt sigh. Liz knew the big man
had taken very few breaks in the many hours since this
ordeal began. His eyes were red-rimmed. The stress was
beginning to tell.

"I got nine grandkids about that little duffer's age,"
he said in answer to Liz's suggestion that he take a break.
"I keep seeing their faces. Time's running out."

"No." Liz thrust the tray into the hands of his assis-
tant and grasped his arm. "Don't even think it. Where's
Gil?"

"Just comin' up. That lad's gonna kill himself if he
doesn't ease up."

Liz turned in time to see Gil crawling off the sling on
his hands and knees. His face was ashen and his sides
heaved.

"We busted through the well," he gasped as Liz and
Jarvis rushed to his side. Gil flopped over onto his back,
struggling for air. "I was too far below him to get a grip
on his leg. The well's narrower than we thought. Can't be
more than fourteen inches in diameter."

"Shit!" Jarvis threw up his hands, saw Liz and apologized.

"That's okay." She shrugged his apology off. "Is
fourteen inches bad?"

Jarvis paced and rubbed his crew cut with a beefy
hand. "We'll have to expand the balloon below him at
the juncture to keep him from slipping. Go in above him
with the hydro-drill. It's our best option."

"Won't work. The shaft he's in is sunk in the middle
of that damned rock. It would take us hours to angle up
and drill through it. He's getting weak, man—I don't

think he has hours." Gil turned away, but not before Liz saw him blink back tears. In fact, there wasn't a dry eye among the men who gathered around the platform. Men who'd given their all and now saw hope slipping away.

Jarvis closed his eyes and rubbed at them with callused thumbs. "There must be somebody small enough to get through that dad-blamed hole. Got a circus playing in town? We need a skinny contortionist."

"What about me?" Liz stepped up, forcing the man to open his eyes.

"You a contortionist?" The driller's eyes lit up until Liz gave a shake of her head.

Gil reached for her and spun her around. "No, Lizbeth. You don't know what you're saying. It's pitch-black in the cutaway. There's no room for a breathing pack. You'd freeze up. Do you understand me? There's not enough air down there to light a candle."

Liz shivered. Nausea rolled over her at the thought of being confined. Fear gnawed at her insides. But they were talking about Dustin—Gil's son. It looked to Liz as if she was the smallest adult around. "You have a better idea, Gil?" she asked quietly.

"Ma'am, if you'll pardon me for saying so," another driller said, "you aren't any bigger than spit. It takes more than guts to get even a weak kid on a backboard and haul him out. It takes muscle."

She looked the speaker right in the eye. "I've been a farrier for six years. I pack my weight in iron every day, and I can throw a cantankerous horse when I have to. If you've got a better plan, tell us. Otherwise, get out of my way. I love that boy, and I'm going after him."

CHAPTER THIRTEEN

GIL SCRAMBLED to his feet. "Lizbeth, no. You don't know what it's like down there. It's blacker than night. Scary as all hell."

"I'll wear a lighted hat. Gil, I want to do this. I *have* to."

"No." He gripped her hard.

Jarvis eyed them both. "Duke it out, you two. Fast. Otherwise, we've gotta drill some more. Time's a-wastin'."

Liz gently disengaged herself from Gil's grasp. She grabbed a hard hat and tightened the cinch. Her nerves stretched tighter than guitar strings. Six years' worth of fear screamed through her head, taunting her. Calling her all kinds of fool.

"Take off your necklace, your watch and that belt," said one dirt-streaked driller, his eyes gleaming with admiration. "You hafta crawl both ways on your belly. You don't wanna wear anything that'll snag. I've done this type of rescue once—in a mine. Take it slow and don't freeze up."

Out of the corner of her eye, Liz saw Ginger and Rusty pushing their way into the front row of onlookers. Nan came from the other side holding fast to Melody's hand. A hush sank over the crowd.

"I'd like a word with my daughter, then I'll be ready." Liz wanted to get on with it with as little fanfare as possible. She didn't want anyone talking about the possibility of freezing up. Already her insides lumped like lead.

Dusk swooped in even as Liz hurried to meet Nan. Ginger's gaze skipped over Liz as she yanked Rusty into the circle of light. "What's going on?" Ginger demanded. "Why has the drilling stopped?" Her voice rose shrilly. Liz tensed, then forced herself to relax.

A man readying the backboard told Ginger that Liz was going down the shaft and across the cut to rescue Dustin.

Ginger flew into a rage. "I won't have it! I want a paramedic. A professional, not some amateur. Oh, my baby! My baby's going to die!" she wailed, pointing a finger at Liz, who'd just bent to give Melody a hug. "It's her fault he's in that well."

"Shut her up!" Jarvis roared. He stormed off the platform and hustled Lizbeth up the steps toward the sling.

She pulled up short in front of Gil. "Isn't there anyone else?" he asked, sounding desperate.

Behind her, Jarvis snorted. "Not who can wriggle into a fourteen-inch shaft at the other end. Gotta hunch your shoulders and reach up to grab him, missy."

Fighting off an icy wash of fear, she nodded.

Gil barely touched Lizbeth's chin. "I'll go on TV like I did to get the drill. There'll be someone. I'll fly him in."

Liz ran her tongue over her bottom lip. "Don't you trust me, Gil?"

"With my life. But—"

"Then trust me with Dustin's." She wrenched her eyes from his anguished ones and stepped around him.

Gil gazed at her narrow back. He hated this feeling of desperation. He was a man who liked to protect the ones he loved. Spinning on a muddy boot heel, he stalked to the platform's edge and scooped up Rusty and Melody. Within seconds he rejoined Liz, leaving Ginger raving to anyone who'd listen. And there were some. Newsmen whipped out cell phones so fast one would think war had been declared.

Just standing there, peering down into the rescue pit, made Liz's stomach roll. "Gil." She faced him squarely. "If anything happens to me, anything, uh, you know," she whispered, "notify my folks." Quickly she reeled off the name of her parents' thoroughbred farm. "If you have to call, go easy. It'll be a shock." Liz vowed that when this was over, she'd tell them about Mel.

"Lizbeth. For God's sake, it's okay to back out." Gil touched a curl that had escaped the hard hat.

"No. I'm going." Jaw clenched, she swung out onto the monkey board.

Gil set Rusty down and lurched to grab the cable. "I've been all the way to the juncture. It's the pipe where Dusty's lodged that's skinny. If you don't think you can squeeze in and out, get the hell back here immediately. We'll drill up through that bedrock and open a bigger hole closer to him. I mean it, Lizbeth. Don't take chances."

"Mommy?" Melody's whimper expressed an anxiety that linked all the volunteers clustered around the winch. The rustle of the wind and the squeak of the winch blended with the pump that ran oxygen to Dustin. Over that rose Ginger's raucous protest.

Gil had never felt so frustrated, so powerless, but he knew by the look in Lizbeth's eye that objecting was useless. "Lizbeth...dammit. Here. Wait. Take my lucky piece." Digging into his front pocket, he pulled out the golden spur that had belonged to his grandfather. Its tiny diamonds winked as he kissed the warm gold and shoved it into her hands.

Gil's back was to Ginger. However, Lizbeth saw the twins' mother break off her tirade and glare at Gil. "I'll give it to Dustin," Liz promised, hoping to avoid a backlash. She might as well have saved her breath for Ginger raged. To top it off, Gil leaned out as far as he could and gave Lizbeth a kiss no one could misinterpret. As the volunteers broke their silence to whistle and clap, Ginger's cat-eyes narrowed dangerously. Liz withstood the full impact.

Oblivious, Gil stepped back and gathered both children in his arms. He hugged them tight as Liz began her descent. She stood no taller than the backboard on which someone had strapped a thin blanket and a large tube of lubricant jelly.

The monkey board spun and Lizbeth sank out of sight. Gil's heartbeat thundered wildly. He wanted to snatch her back, but he couldn't. Dustin had now been in the well approximately thirty-two hours. Oh, the drillers talked about children who'd survived longer, and Gil knew that Lizbeth was strong and capable—but it wasn't right. None of it. He felt like howling at the moon. Not wanting the kids to witness his frustration, he lifted them off the platform.

Neither child wanted to leave, but Gil insisted on escorting them back to wait with Nan Littlefield. He needed to stay near the shaft—unencumbered—in case... He refused to finish the thought.

Morris clapped him on the back and Nan squeezed his hand. "God bless," she murmured. "I hope you know you have a treasure in that woman."

Rusty darted off the minute Gil set him down. The adults saw he'd rejoined Ginger.

Gil rubbed at the tension clamped to the back of his neck. "*Buried* treasure if my darling ex-wife has anything to say about it." A thin sigh escaped his lips.

"Why would she?" Nan scowled.

"Come on, Nancy. She's the twins' mother. You know the courts are biased in favor of mothers."

"Then they have a different definition of one than I do."

Morris looped an arm around his wife's neck. "Melody's ready for dessert. Pris Naylor just brought in a whole tray of brownies. Let Gilman get back to business, Nan. I, uh, we have a little pitcher with big ears."

Gil nodded, happy to let Morris deal with his wife.

"Mark my words, Morris Littlefield," Nan hissed. "That hussy's up to no good."

"Who, hus-hussy?" Melody asked, tripping over the unfamiliar word. "Do you mean my mommy?"

"Told you," Morris said, motioning Gil to take off.

Nan turned to Melody. "Land sake's no, child." She grasped the small hand. "I can practically taste those brownies. Can't you?" Waggling her brows at her husband, she made a beeline for the food table.

Grateful not to be caught in the middle, Gil left his good friends and all but raced back to the platform.

DEEP IN THE BOWELS of the earth, Liz might have enjoyed the humor in being referred to as a hussy if she hadn't been shaking in her boots. Hussy would be preferable to the names she called herself. Names like coward. Chicken. Or Dustin's favorite, wuss. Overhead the winch creaked and moaned. The cable swayed. Near the bottom the air grew oppressively close. When darkness swallowed her, Liz fought nausea and rising hysteria.

Closing her eyes, she held tight to the memory of Gil's last kiss. She conjured up how he'd looked just now, his strong arms circling both kids.

As the monkey board bumped to a stop, she envisioned how happy they'd all be when she returned with Dustin.

Through a fog, Liz accepted a few words of advice from the paramedic Jarvis had recently stationed at the bottom. At once she crawled into the cross-over tunnel—and nearly passed out. It was as if she'd zipped herself into a sleeping bag, body, head and all. Fear clawed at her insides. No one had said it was like being in a grave. Her throat closed. She nearly fainted, until she remembered that Dustin had been trapped for more than thirty hours. Shuddering, Liz stiffened her spine. After another delay, she crept onward.

Before long, her eyes burned like fury. Yet she was afraid to blink lest she lose the thin beam of light attached to her hat. Lord, she thought she'd known darkness before. But night was nowhere near this black.

As she paused to haul in a deep breath, her lungs seemed to shrivel. A ribbon of fire burned the length of her esophagus. Panicking, she froze, tried to scream, but couldn't. She felt dizzy. Time drifted in slow motion. Caught in the throes of vertigo, Liz lost the signal rope Jarvis had told her to affix to the backboard so the waiting paramedic could help pull Dustin out. She scrabbled around trying to find it. No use, it was gone. And the light on her cap didn't penetrate far enough into the blackness of the cave to find it. Bile welled, along with a crushing terror. Without signals, she and Dustin could both be trapped forever.

Gradually she got hold of herself. Ten feet. They said the tunnel was ten feet long, for crying out loud. Babies passed through the birth canal into a much scarier world. Now she was getting punchy. She might havé laughed, if only she could breathe. Somewhere she'd read that air was weightless. Not true. It weighed a ton. It wouldn't hurt this much if an elephant sat on her chest. But her fears loomed larger than elephants. Lord, oh, Lord, she felt sick. What if she vomited?

Fighting off hysteria again, Liz gave herself a hard mental shake and eventually snaked forward on her elbows. She paid scant attention to jagged rocks that tore through the fabric of her sleeves and into her flesh. Soon she lost track of time. Ten feet seemed to turn into twenty. Forced to stop and pant like a puppy, Liz almost gave up twice. Each time the image of Gil's face drove her on.

Just when she thought they'd lied about the length, she reached the hole they'd cut into the well casing. The air there was marginally cooler, but fetid.

At this point she was supposed to signal with a solid yank on the rope. Since that was out, she called to Dustin. Her voice caught and rasped out in little more than a grainy whisper. Once again her lungs seized, and Liz succumbed to a fit of coughing.

"SHE LOST THE ROPE," the young paramedic hollered up to Jarvis as he reeled it in. "What do you think that means?"

"Shit!" The experienced driller slammed a fist against the winch. "It means if she's not dead in there, she's gotta push the kid out without help. How much did we figure he weighs?"

"Seventy pounds, give or take a few," someone behind him said.

"And she weighs, what? Ninety? A hundred? Dammit all to hell!"

Gil returned in time to hear the exchange. "She's no weakling. You should see her at her forge," he said, wanting to shake the men who looked doubtful. "She's tough," he reiterated through clenched teeth. "All muscle. And she's *not* dead!" he shouted, daring anyone to argue with him.

Jarvis slanted Gil a sharp glance even though he was more than half-cloaked in night shadows. "I wish we could be sure of that, son. You don't by chance have a private channel to the Almighty? If so, it'll save me gettin' more gray hair."

"How much time did you allow for her to reach Dusty and get out?" Gil ignored the churning in his gut.

"An hour max." Jarvis ran a hand over his head and shrugged. "Damn, I shouldn't have listened to her. I knew it was a long shot. Rogers," he yelled at a dirty driller, "get over here so we can come up with plan B."

"No." Gil stayed him with a slash of his hand. "We'll give her the full hour. I don't wear a watch," Gil said. "Who has the time?"

Jarvis flipped out a beat-up pocket watch. "Half-past eight," he said.

"Expect her by nine," Gil stated firmly. "It's a good omen. Dustin came into this world at nine-o-two, squalling his head off." The memory of how he'd felt when Dr. Stevens placed his firstborn in his arms brought tears to Gil's eyes and a decided catch to his voice.

"I'm impressed you remember the exact time. Most guys don't even know the date," said one husky driller.

Jarvis straightened away from the hole. "Me, I only know that nine is the number of grandkids I got. In my book that makes nine a doubly good sign. Nine it is.

We'll wait." He picked up a thermos and poured Gil a steaming cupful. "When this is over, son, you and me'll celebrate with something stronger than this rotgut coffee."

Gil agreed. But he'd never been one to like waiting, and with both Lizbeth's and Dustin's lives hanging in the balance, this wait was pure torture.

"Hey," shouted one of the doctors assigned to monitor Dustin's vital signs. "I hear some sort of scratching in the shaft. Sounds like mice."

"Mice, or one damn brave lady," Jarvis yelped, running heavily toward the man holding the equipment. Gil wasn't two seconds behind him, oblivious to the hot coffee sloshing out of his cup.

Jarvis listened a moment, then handed the earphones to Gil. "Sounds like she's slathering that old pipe with lubricant unless I miss my guess."

Straining, Gil thought he heard a faint scrape. "Shouldn't we hear them talking? Lizbeth ... Dustin," he shouted down the hole. "Hey, guys, answer up!"

Everyone strained to hear. Nothing but an occasional scratch, scratch wafted back.

Jarvis placed a gnarled hand on Gil's arm. "Your boy's getting tired, Spencer. And I expect the lady's short on air."

"How short? It'll take a lot of oomph to drag Dustin back across ten feet of rock."

"We may want to kick down a wee bit more oxygen. What do you say, Joe?" Jarvis deferred to the doctor who manned the oxygen tanks. He nodded and fiddled with a gauge. "Seems to be a lot of space between noises. I just don't know."

Tension built on the platform as the men waited out the hour, and hoped.

LIZ WORKED as though in a thick fog. As she'd crawled hand over hand, she'd repeated the steps Jarvis had given her so many times in her head that now she went through each one precisely and methodically.

Her courage slipped farther, if that was possible, when she finally wriggled into the opening, reached up and tugged on Dusty's outstretched legs, only to have him moan but refuse to budge. Lord, was he caught on something? Had she hurt him? Alarm bubbled in her throat. Cold sweat beaded her brow and dripped between her breasts. Just breathing sapped her strength.

"Dusty," she gasped hoarsely. "It's Liz. H-hang on, I'll get you out."

He grunted, or she thought he did. Liz wanted to shout for joy. Instead, knowing she needed to save her breath, she grabbed hold of his jeans and yanked as hard as she could. All her efforts would be in vain if she didn't jar him loose. Doctors could fix cuts or broken bones.

At first he tensed up, as if he was afraid of falling. "I'll catch you," she promised. Next yank he slid free, and Liz almost cried. Except that her eyes stung painfully, and she discovered she had no fluid for tears.

Her reward came when in the dim light cast by her hat, Liz saw his feeble attempt to smile. Gil's lopsided grin. Hallelujah! Did she imagine it, or was that a shout from above? A chorus of shouts? Had something gone wrong? Terror squeezed out her joy.

Doubts plagued her again as she realized she'd have to squeeze out of the hole in the pipe first, then pull him out onto the backboard. No. That was wrong. Jarvis had distinctly said she should *push* him ahead of her through the tunnel. The man they'd stationed in the hold would be watching. The minute he felt two jerks on the rope, he'd help pull Dustin out. The rope. Damn, she'd lost the rope. Liz clutched Dustin tightly as the old phobia returned with a vengeance.

As if sensing something was wrong, Dustin started to whimper. "I'm s-sorry, Lizbeth," he mumbled over and over in a broken raspy whisper.

He sounded almost like Gil when he said her name, and since he'd only ever called her Mrs. Robbins before, she choked up. "It's okay, honey." Her attempt to comfort him sounded breathless, and the words ran together. They might have been indecipherable, but Dustin relaxed as she stroked his grimy face with a finger she'd managed to wiggle close to his cheek.

Was he okay? Dusty couldn't seem to move his left arm. Maybe it was because her light was feeble, but the fingers on his left hand looked puffy and blue to Liz. *Just get him out,* a little voice nagged in her ear.

"Out," she repeated, drawing confidence from her own voice. Gil was out there waiting. Somehow, some way, she'd get his son to safety. Oh, God, she had to. Despite Gil's earlier assurances that no one was to blame, it *was* her fault that Dustin had wandered off. She should have questioned the sudden change in his attitude.

The contortions Liz engaged in to get Dustin through the hole first would have put an acrobat to shame. By the time she had him strapped on the board, Liz swore and begged and pleaded for air. She knew she was in bad shape when she shoved with all her might and the backboard slid all of two inches across jutting rocks.

She sobbed, but not a sound came out. And the real trial didn't start until she was stretched flat in the tunnel. The battery pack on her hard hat fizzled and the light blinked out. Terror slammed into Liz. Sweat slicked her body as darkness settled around, ominous and debilitating.

The screams, trapped in her lungs along with stale air, threatened to strangle her. She couldn't move. They would die here the way Corbett had in that chute. Gil had put his faith in the wrong person. He'd put his trust in a coward. Lying on her stomach, fighting for sanity, Liz felt the fiery imprint of Gil's lucky piece pressing relentlessly against her hipbone. Luck—it was for fools.

FOR THE RESCUERS milling about on the platform, the minutes ticked by with maddening slowness—especially once the initial exultation had passed of knowing that Liz had reached the trapped child.

Doubly impatient, Gil paced a circle around the rescue shaft. Every five seconds he asked the time. Something was wrong. He felt it in his bones. He tried conjuring up a vision of Lizbeth and his son. It scared the hell out of him when the vision refused to form. He reached for the winch and would have raised the monkey board if Jarvis hadn't restrained him. "Let go. I'm heading down."

"Be sensible, man. We need a trained paramedic down there."

Releasing the winch, Gil twisted from his grasp and again asked the time.

"Eight-fifty," droned a voice from the darkness. Ten minutes sounded like a life sentence to Gil. The others, reacting to his increasing anxiety, fell silent. With each passing minute, worry deepened, and the group grew more restive. When nine came and went, not a soul spoke.

Suddenly they heard a shout from below. "I've got him," yelled the paramedic. "Thank God, thank God, he's moving and breathing." Then with less exuberance and more professional detachment, he reported Dustin's condition. "He's suffering some hypothermia. Get the doctor and ready a chopper. We may be dealing with gangrene in his left arm. Make way above—I'm putting him on a sling and sending him up."

Gil met the sling. Relief weakened his knees with his first look at that dirt-caked little face. Overwhelming joy held him upright while cameras whirred and confusion ran rampant around him. All the workers wanted to see the child for themselves, and Gil wouldn't deny them. Amid unabashed tears, the physicians who'd stood by monitoring Dusty's vitals throughout the long ordeal, prepared him for transport. Two subordinate members of the medical team raced for the chopper, calling for Gil to follow. He ran automatically, then all at once it dawned on him that Lizbeth was still below ground.

Stopping, he turned back to check. From behind, a massive hand attached itself to his upper arm and literally shoved him in the direction of the waiting helicopter. Gazing helplessly back over his shoulder, Gil strained to see any sign of dark curls swinging up and out of the shaft. But the winch remained still. Then before he knew what was happening, someone placed a flat hand on the back of his neck, bent him double and landed him in the chopper. As he scrambled to catch his breath, other hands buckled him in next to his son's stretcher.

With a whump-whump and a roar, they suddenly rose above the crowd and were whisked away into the starry night. Away from Lizbeth and Rusty. Gil pressed his nose to the glass, trying to see. Too soon darkness engulfed them, and Dustin cried out. Gil turned back to the son who needed him.

IN THE PIT, things looked bad for Lizbeth. She was cut, bleeding, in shock. "I need supplies down here," the paramedic shouted. "Drop me a Ringer's and O2."

Those were the last words Liz heard.

She woke up in a sterile emergency room, retching and fighting the oxygen mask that covered her nose. She felt as if her lungs were seared. Breathing the oxygen was like trying to swallow a cactus. She had no idea what was happening.

The first face she saw and recognized was that of Nan Littlefield, who hurriedly told her that Melody was just outside the room with Morris. Slowly, memory of the grueling experience came back to Liz. "Dusty? Gil?" she whispered, stretching forth a bandaged hand.

"Safe." Nan patted a patch of skin above the gauze and smiled. "They flew Dustin to the Children's Hospital in San Antonio. We just got word—his left arm may need skin grafts and plastic surgery because his circulation was cut off for so long. But, Liz, his fingers are going to be all right. And it's all thanks to you."

Liz burst into tears. "I'm sorry," she mumbled. "I should be happy. I don't know what's wrong with me."

"Child, you're exhausted," Nan said. "The doctor wants to keep you in the hospital overnight for observation. We'll take Melody home with us, if that's all right."

Liz suffered a moment's panic. "Hospital? No. I want to leave. I'm all right." She struggled to sit.

Morris Littlefield poked his head into the room and strode with Melody to the foot of the bed. "Let them pamper you tonight, darlin'. Gil just called to see how you are. He insists you stay."

"Okay—but where's Rusty?" Liz's brow crinkled.

"Uh..." Nan made faces over top of Melody's head. "WWW took him."

Morris wagged a finger at his wife and Liz continued to look blank.

"Wicked Witch of the West," Nan said with a wink.

"I see." But Liz didn't. She couldn't understand why Gil had let that woman take his son anywhere. The fine hairs at the nape of her neck prickled, but she was too tired to formulate clear thoughts. Then an orderly came to take her to the room where she would spend the night, and there was no need to think at all.

The next day, when the doctor redressed her scrapes and let her leave with Nan, Liz was even more confused by the sense of dread that was somehow attached to going home. Yet she turned down Nancy's offer to stay with them for a few days.

As Nancy drove beneath the iron arch on the Lone Spur, the first thing Liz saw was Ginger's Caddy parked, big as you please, in Gil's driveway. The owner of that car sat on Gil's porch swing, painting her nails.

Things became decidedly clearer after supper when Gil called. "Ah, good, you're home." His voice sounded weary and strained. "The doctor thinks you should have complete rest for a few days."

"Really? He didn't say that to me."

"Well, he told me. I let Rafe know. Listen, I haven't even thanked you properly for saving Dustin's life. It doesn't seem right, doing it long-distance."

"How is he?" Liz wrapped the cord around her finger. Gil's earnest husky tone sent shivers up her spine.

"Minimal tissue damage. When I think of the time it would have taken to drill through that rock if you hadn't—Liz...I—"

"Don't, Gil. It was a nightmare and it's over. Just hurry home, okay?"

"It'll be a week or two. Remember how you said I needed to spend more time with the boys? Well, I'm staying here until they let Dustin come home."

"And what about Rusty?"

"Ginger volunteered to watch him. I know she made a bit of an ass of herself, Lizbeth, but did you see Rusty's face? This is the first interest she's ever shown in the boys. Lizbeth, are you there? Hey, you're the one who said the twins should get to know their mother."

Prickles of denial sent goose bumps up Liz's arms— more or less the same sensation she'd had on learning Dustin had fallen into a well.

"I miss you, Lizbeth. Take care of yourself."

"I will. You, too. Bye, Gil." She held the receiver a long time after he clicked off and gazed at his lucky piece that lay on her nightstand. There'd been no way to give it to Dustin as she'd intended. She ran a fingertip lightly around the sparkling rowel and felt a sense of peace. Until Gil returned home, she at least had his talisman to keep her company.

That night Gil invaded Liz's dreams. Dreams so real she felt the warmth and comfort of his arms, and she barely stirred the entire night. On awakening, fully refreshed, Liz marveled at the absence of the plaguing nightmares. Could it be that in facing her demons in the tunnel, she'd not only rescued Dustin but healed herself, as well? Liz couldn't wait to discuss the possibility with Gil.

Except that he didn't call the next night or the one after that. It was on the third day, when Yancy stopped by to see how she was doing, that she found out Dustin had undergone his first skin graft. Later that evening Luke brought her a horse to shoe and more disturbing news.

"Ginger hired a woman to cook and clean. Six-foot Amazon. Old battle-ax makes us come to the back door if we need to get anything from Gil's office."

Liz thought Luke might be stretching the truth until Rusty showed up in her kitchen after school the next day complaining about the same thing. She hadn't seen him since the accident. Before week's end, he'd become a regular again.

"Does your mom know where you are?" Liz asked the following Wednesday. It was nearly dark, and Rusty showed no sign of wanting to go home.

"She don't care 'bout me. All she does is fix her face and read those horse magazines of Dad's. Buddy Hodges says it figures. His older brother told him all women are fic...fickle. I asked my teacher what that means. She said it's like if a person says one thing and does another."

"Rusty, if your mother didn't care, she wouldn't be here. Have you mentioned this to your dad?"

"Naw. 'Sides, he likes Dustin better'n he likes me."

Liz plunked down on her knees next to his chair, then winced because she still had bruises. "That I know is false. Your dad loves you equally, Rusty. It's just that Dustin needs him more right now. Honey, parents don't run out of love like we do milk or eggs or flour. What makes you think such a thing?"

Rusty sucked in a sigh. "Buddy..."

"Ah. I should have known. Another Buddyism. Russ, do me a favor. Go home and give this some time."

He gathered the crumbs from his cupcake in a neat little pile and brushed them into his hand. After dumping them in the trash, he confided, "Mrs. Morley yells if I drop crumbs on the table. *She* does, too. It's awful."

"Hmm." Liz assumed the *she* meant Ginger. A touchy subject at best. She didn't want to interfere; however,

Rusty looked so pitiful and sad she hugged him the way she did Melody when someone had hurt her feelings. "You're welcome to hang out here, sport. I don't mind if you come with Melody, after school. You can both meet me wherever I'm shoeing."

"Yippee!" Both kids danced around the kitchen table. Liz walked Rusty to the door and watched till he got home. She wondered if anyone met him at the door.

When she'd read Melody a story and tucked her into bed, Lizbeth tried calling Gil. He didn't answer at the hotel. She phoned the hospital and was told he'd just left—for his ranch. Surely not. Just in case, Liz waited by the window. Sometime after midnight, she saw his Suburban pull into the lane; she knew that Rafe had taken it to him in San Antonio. Her heart tripped over itself when he stopped alongside the cottage.

Liz didn't wait for him. She flew out the door and into his arms. The kiss they shared was everything she remembered and more.

"God, but you do feel good." He wrapped his arms tightly around her and nuzzled her ear.

She peeked into the vehicle. "Gil, where's Dustin?"

"I'm just home to sign paychecks and get clean clothes. He contracted a staph infection and they have to do the graft again."

"Oh, no! Gil, that's terrible. No wonder you look exhausted. Come inside. I'll heat some of my potato soup. And I baked cupcakes tonight." She clung to his hand. "Besides, I want to talk to you about Rusty."

Gil followed her into the bright familiar kitchen and hung his Stetson on a peg beside the door. Lord, but he'd missed this. Missed her. He stole another kiss before she took the soup from the fridge and popped it into the microwave. "So," he said, taking a seat at the table, "don't tell me Russell's been up to tricks. I'm not sure I can face dealing with another rebellious son.''

"No.'' She placed a steaming bowl in front of him. "From what Rusty's told me, I gather he's being unnecessarily reprimanded at home and often neglected.'' Liz plunked a plate with two slices of bread beside him and poured a mug of coffee.

Gil paused, spoon halfway to his lips. "Neglected? According to Ginger, they're getting along very well.''

"Really? When have you talked to Ginger?''

He finished that mouthful, then another. "She's called nearly every night to check on Dustin. She's changed, Lizbeth. I think she's trying to be a good mother.''

Liz's mouth fell agape. "A good—'' Snapping her teeth closed, she whirled, picked up a sponge and began wiping down the counters. "Well, excuse me, Gilman Spencer. I think you've gone soft in the head. Why don't you ask Yancy and Luke what they've observed?''

He set his spoon aside and rose. "Yes, let's talk about Yancy and Luke. I understand they spend more time here than they do wrangling horses.''

Liz dropped the sponge. "They've stopped by to see how I'm doing. I injured my hands, Gil. I didn't realize I was in quarantine.''

Gold lights smoldered deep in his hazel eyes. "The way I hear it, your place has a revolving door when it comes to those two. Dammit, Lizbeth, the neighbors know we've been dating. They gossiped about me once. I won't have it happen again.''

Heat worked its way up her throat, to her cheeks. "A revolving door to my place? Just what does that mean, Gil?''

"I think you know, Lizbeth. I'm waiting for you to deny it.''

"Deny that two men I work with every day care about me? Gil, this is silly. Why are we arguing?"

Wheeling, he snatched his hat. Shoulders stiff, he said, "If you won't deny flirting—or worse—with all my employees the minute my back is turned, maybe there's some truth to that story of Ginger's. She announced to me and half the world that she caught you and Avery in a compromising situation. I even saw it in the paper! Frankly, I looked for them to print your rebuttal. Perhaps there wasn't anything to rebut. And now you don't deny that you've been entertaining wranglers. What am I supposed to think?"

Liz felt her breath leave her lungs in one long hiss. So *that* was where all this had been leading. His unwarranted accusation hurt so much she thought she might die of it. No one on the circuit who knew her had believed Ginger's filthy lies. Apparently the man who professed to love her did. "Get out," she said the minute the pain let up enough for her to speak.

He went. Without a word and without a backward glance.

Numb, Liz couldn't move until after she heard the door of the Suburban slam and the ping of gravel striking her east wall. If he loved her, how could he believe such a thing?

All night she was haunted by the knowledge that she hadn't denied his accusation. She loved him, after all. She thought he loved her. She sighed. They were both too proud and stubborn for their own good. One of them would have to bend.

Next morning, after the school bus left, Liz made up her mind that she was going to see Gil and talk this out. She quickly wrapped the present she'd had Luke buy in

town for Dustin and marched up to the kitchen door of
the big house, fully ready to extend a peace offering.

Mrs. Morley informed her that "Mr. Spencer" was too
busy to be disturbed. Before Liz could object, the woman
whisked the gift from her hand and shut the door in her
face. Simmering, Liz strode off to the corral. She'd catch
him later.

Only she didn't. Midday, in the process of shoeing a
balky horse, Liz saw Gil's Suburban roar down the lane,
leaving a rooster tail of dust. She'd no more than finished when Rafe stopped by, and in the course of their
conversation, he made a curious statement.

"You might want to find someplace to board those
horses Gil gave you. Ginger's got her eye on the filly. She
thinks Snowbaby has the look of a champion barrel
racer."

"I'm sure Gil will tell her they belong to me."

"I told her. Didn't seem to faze her."

Liz stuck a hot shoe in cold water and watched it siz-
zle. She wondered if Rafe could see the steam coming out
from under her collar, too. Ginger was a spoiled willful
woman, obsessed with owning a winning horse. Liz knew
those things for a fact. But in this case it wasn't her re-
sponsibility to set Ginger straight. It was Gil's. "Well,
Rafe, I don't want to board them. As soon as I have time,
I'm going to start their training."

"Oh, so you're taking them when you leave?" Nodding, he turned toward the barn.

His deceptively casual question nearly bowled Liz over.
What was that all about? Surely Rafe didn't still think she
was leaving in May? Liz wrestled with a sinking sensation as she watched him saddle up and ride out. Gil had
never come right out and said that the situation between

them had changed, that they'd eventually be getting married. She'd just assumed.

Her mood shattered, Liz finished putting Bell Boots on a sorrel gelding that Yancy claimed was throwing his right front shoe. The horse wouldn't do it for her, and Liz didn't want to shoe him wrong. She'd run him in soft boots and keep him close in case she needed to experiment with leather shims.

The sorrel was her last project for the day. Since she had a couple of hours free before the school bus was due, Liz decided to take a run over to the Littlefields' ranch, on the off chance Nan had talked with Gil.

"Nary a word," Nan said as she ushered Lizbeth into the kitchen where she was making strawberry jam. "I didn't know he'd come home. Morris has to take some beef into San Antonio tomorrow. I'll have him stop by Children's Hospital. I hear Ginger's charging stuff all over town in Gil's name."

"Well, she is running his house. Rusty told me she went to Fort Worth last week to pick up a mare someone was breeding to Night Fire. Gil must have authorized it."

"Don't you stick up for her, Liz. She's badmouthing you every chance she gets."

"I know. Our rift goes way back. To when I had to shoe her spoiled horse."

"Yeah, well, watch out. Morris and Kyle Mason think she's been snooping into Gil's finances. He was land-poor when they got divorced. Obviously the Lone Spur's worth a lot more now. You have time for coffee?"

"No. Mel and Rusty will be getting home soon."

"How's Rusty getting along without his brother? Those two haven't been apart more than a schoolday since they were born."

"He misses Dustin of course. I think he misses Gil more. Poor kid spends all his free time at the cottage. At least I can try and provide stability. Although I don't want to do anything that would undermine Gil."

"You hang in till Gilman gets back for good. Things will change. You'll see."

Boy, howdy, did they.

That evening, while the children were in the barn checking out a new litter of kittens, Ginger paid Liz a visit. "How soon can you vacate the cottage?" she asked without prelude. Liz had just turned back to the sink to finishing slicing fresh spring carrots.

Liz dropped the knife in the sink with a clatter. "Vacate the cottage?"

Ginger studied her crimson nails. "Didn't Rafe tell you? Gil hired a new farrier. The best. You may have heard of him. Lex Burnaby."

Liz had. Burnaby free-lanced a huge area south of San Antonio. It wasn't that Gil hadn't warned her he'd be looking for a new farrier come May—but that had been *before*. She'd just thought... What had she thought? Sorrow, then anger bubbled in her chest. Tears pushed at the back of her eyes. She'd be darned if she'd let so much as one tear trickle its way out in front of Ginger Lawrence.

Drawing up to her full height, Liz said coolly, "I can be out of here as soon as Gil pays me in full." And there it was—she'd come full circle.

Ginger smiled. "No problem. He asked me to give out the checks." Cocky as hell, she fanned through a sheaf of envelopes and pulled out one bearing Liz's name. "Oh, one other thing." Ginger jerked back the check and tapped it against her bloodred lips. "Gil changed his mind about giving you those two horses. Really, he's letting you off easy, considering all it's costing us for Dustin's care.''

''Dustin's care?''

Ginger hunched a slim shoulder as she passed Liz the envelope. ''You *were* in charge of looking after Dusty. We could press charges of neglect.''

Liz's heart cracked. Gil couldn't have struck a lower blow. With trust between them in shambles, there was no hope at all of salvaging their love. But then, how could she be so obtuse? Those two little words of Ginger's— ''us'' and ''we''—should have been her clue. They went hand in hand with Gil's earlier proclamation that Ginger had changed.

''Excuse me,'' Liz said. ''I have things to do.'' She wouldn't break down. Not in front of that horrible smug woman.

BRIGHT AND EARLY the next morning, Melody's tears put the first chink in Liz's armor. The second came when Rusty flung his arms around her waist. ''Why? Why are you going away?'' he cried. ''I don't want you to.''

''I have to, Rusty. Ask your father why.'' Liz gently pulled free. She had to physically put Melody and her cat into the old pickup's cab. The truck bed was filled with their ragtag belongings. Everything she owned in the world.

''I love you,'' Rusty sobbed, ''and now you're leaving me, too. Please don't go. Stay. Please!''

''Oh, honey, no. Look, your mom's waiting on the porch. G-go to her,'' Liz stammered, her throat clogged. In the end she left him sobbing beside the lane while she tried to gauge the road through a shimmer of tears. She drove between the iron gates of the Lone Spur ranch, never finding the strength to look back.

Running. She was always running. Melody deserved better. She deserved roots, dammit. A home.

It was past time she met her grandparents. The Whitleys might be stern, but they weren't monsters. Home was the place to heal old wounds. And new ones.

Stopping at the crossroad, Liz remembered Gil's teasing once that a right turn led to Mars. But really, a right turn led to the interstate—and if she stayed on it, to Kentucky. Liz had never gotten around to writing her parents, but home was where a person went for comfort when there was no place else to go.

CHAPTER FOURTEEN

MELODY HUGGED Mittens and sniffled for twenty miles. Then she fell asleep, leaving Liz to deal with her conscience and memories and might-have-beens.

Among her more distressing concerns was the fact that she'd taken Mel out of school early again. There'd been no logical excuse she could give Melody's teacher; anything she said would be twisted, embellished and bandied about town, thanks to Ginger. Liz didn't care about malicious gossip for her own sake or Gil's, but she'd hate it if the twins got the wrong impression of what she and Gil had been to each other. What they'd shared in Fort Worth had been beautiful and real. For her at least.

Liz wiped a tear from her eye and gripped the wheel tightly. It was best to forget the Spencers and concentrate on meeting her parents. What could she say to them, just showing up on their doorstep after all these years? Calling ahead seemed pointless, since this was something she had to do. What if they refused to let her come home? Could she blame them? Sorry didn't always make things right. It was so easy to see now—with her life in shambles again—how they'd both erred, she and her parents. But still, she had to face the possibility that an apology might not be enough.

After three days of hard driving, of twisting herself into knots over the upcoming reunion, she was there. Home. She pulled into the lane leading through fields of bluegrass to the farmhouse. In many ways, going into that black hole after Dustin had been easier. Anxiety. Fear. She felt overwhelmed by both as she eased her foot off the clutch and drove the mile to the house. Now she wished she'd prepared Melody, who gaped at the acres of grass and demanded to know why they were stopping.

"You'll see in a minute," Liz murmured, parking under a spreading elm that once hadn't seemed half this big. The tree provided ample shade for the trailer carrying Melody's pony. Clinging tightly to her daughter's hand, Liz marched up the porch steps and rapped soundly on the door—before she could chicken out.

Toliver Whitley, stooped and nearly white-haired, opened the door just a crack. For a moment he stared at Liz through the screen, shock entering the dark eyes so very like Melody's. Abruptly and without a word, he flung the door wide and engulfed Liz in a trembling bear hug. "Mother! Mother!" he shouted back into the house. "Come see who's here. It's a miracle, I tell you, a miracle!"

Her parents' ready acceptance of her and Melody was both gratifying and humbling to Liz. She was grateful that her dad declared a holiday from work on the farm. That in itself surprised her. In the days before she'd run off with Corbett, nothing short of death would have taken her father away from his beloved horses.

The humbling part came with his tearful confession. "We thought you were lost to us forever, child. Did you know we hired a detective to find you? His agency gave up after three years. Where on earth have you been? We more or less assumed you'd go back to Montana with Corbett's people."

"Oh, Dad. He had no people, except for foster homes and me. It's one reason I always wanted to write and tell you about Melody. *He* would have wanted me to. I can't tell you how many times I started letters. I'm ashamed that I never mailed them."

"All that's past," her mother murmured, gazing lovingly at a grandchild who still didn't quite know what to make of finding out she had grandparents. "We won't speak of regrets, my dear. Toliver and I have many, as obviously you do. Tell us about your life, Lizbeth, and don't leave out any details." She patted a couch cushion next to her. A happy smile took years off her lined face.

They sat for hours catching up in a living room that was familiar to Liz, yet changed. Fabric worn. Colors faded. For the first time, the house she remembered wasn't spotless. There was a bit of clutter that, strangely, made Liz's confession easier. The severity of this house and the endless bleakness of her daily routine had been closely tied to her leaving here. Now, fortunately, her parents had mellowed; so had she.

Liz spoke with pride of Corbett's rodeo successes. She glossed over the last few months on the Lone Spur. "My love of horses—actually my decision to become a farrier—came from you, Dad. Horses are in the Whitley blood, I think."

The older man beamed. "You always had a gentle hand. Perhaps I should have let you be a jockey like you wanted. Then, I didn't think it seemly for a woman. Now I've hired two." His eyes held frank apology.

"Really? Maybe you'll give me a job shoeing your thoroughbreds. I drive a true nail and the shoes I forge fit like a dream."

"I have no doubt of that. But…Lizbeth, I've just sold the farm."

"Sold? Are you sick? Mother?" Liz flashed a troubled glance between the two.

"Not sick, tuckered out. Owning horses is demanding work. With you gone, there seemed little point in continuing to build a legacy."

Liz winced. She understood, and her understanding brought poignant memories of another horse owner. Gil, who ran on empty much of the time. Gil, who worked day and night to build a ranch worthy of his grandfather's dream. Because it made her feel closer to him, she pulled his lucky piece from her jeans pocket and ran a thumb idly over the diamond chips that outlined the delicate horseshoe and the spur's heel band. There'd been no time to give the key chain back. She hadn't been able to make herself go up to the house and hand it over to Ginger. She'd have to mail it to Gil.

"What's that you have?" her mother asked. "It's pretty. Was it something Corbett won?"

Melody came to swing on her mother's knee. She giggled as her cat leapt up to bat the dangling spur. "It's for luck—for when Mommy went down the hole after Dusty. Nan told me Mommy saved Dustin's life," she said importantly.

The color drained from the older woman's face. "Dusty? Not the family whose child fell down a well? The story made our local paper. Toliver still refuses to contaminate our home with television. My goodness, you knew those poor people, Lizbeth?"

"Yes." She sighed. "I worked for Gilman Spencer. I'm surprised you didn't read that Dustin was in my care when he took the tumble. He and I had a history of sorts." She sighed. "He loved to play tricks on me." In a few words she recapped what had led up to those horrible few days. Her tone grew somber when she added that the twins' father apparently believed she'd been negligent. Liz minimized the part she'd actually played in Dustin's rescue. She didn't want to talk about anything that followed.

Mrs. Whitley knotted her hands. "I can't believe Mr. Spencer would blame you for a child's willfulness. However, if it's the reason you've come home, I can only be thankful that he's such a callous man."

"He's not. As a rule Gil is kind, caring and generous." Liz broke off, feeling a rosy flush stain her cheeks. Why was she defending him? Not long ago she wouldn't have believed him capable of the pettiness involved in taking back the foals he'd given her. To say nothing of letting Ginger do his dirty work. It wasn't at all like Gil. At least it wasn't like the man she *thought* he was—the man with whom she'd fallen in love.

Her father lifted a brow. "I don't think your mother meant to malign him. If anyone knows the damage done by words spoken in the heat of the moment, we do. Hasty accusations have a way of coming back to haunt you. Loneliness makes a person repent quick enough. Let the dust settle, then give this Mr. Spencer a call, Lizbeth."

"Me?" she flared, the fire in her cheeks stinging again. "It'll be a cold day in he—"

"Lizbeth!" Her mother jumped up and steered Melody toward the stairs. "Melody and I will go make up your rooms. I'm sure you'll want to shower before dinner."

Dinner in Kentucky was supper in West Texas. Supper she normally cooked for Gil and the boys. Liz could only nod and blink rapidly as she stood and stuffed Gil's lucky key chain deep into her front pocket. Gil wasn't lonely— he had Ginger. And therein lay the crux of her problem. If he'd thrown her over for anyone else... But Liz couldn't bring herself to admit any of this to her father.

Toliver Whitley frowned. "Lizbeth, you help your mother with the rooms. It'll give you two a chance to catch up. I'll show Melody the stables and we'll bed her pony."

Rising, Liz nodded.

Melody skipped ahead of her grandfather and opened the back gate of the horse trailer. As they walked the pony toward the stables, Toliver Whitley asked, "How does our farm compare to that Lone Spur ranch?"

Screwing up her face, Melody looked around. "It wasn't green, but it's . . . my home. I didn't wanna leave. I hope we get to go back." Then her stories tumbled out—about her good experiences at school and Christmas and the fun she and her mom had with the Spencers.

"Sounds like Mr. Spencer's being unfair over this incident with his son, considering all the extra things you say your mom did for him around the ranch."

"Would you tell him that, Grandfather? I wanna go back and finish school." She gazed at him, her lower lip quivering. "I think Mommy really likes him a lot."

"Maybe I can, honeybunch, maybe I can. It just might make up for the terrible wrong I did your daddy once."

GIL SPENT a grueling seven days waiting at the hospital, worrying whether Dusty's latest skin graft would take. Though it was touch and go for days, when they finished the results looked good. Monday of the second week, Dustin's doctors said he was improved enough to recuperate at the Lone Spur.

Driving in past the cottage, Gil suffered a jolt of guilt over how he'd left things with Lizbeth. Jealousy carved up a man's heart and made mush of his brain. More than once he'd picked up the phone to apologize for wanting her to deny something he knew deep inside was false. But somehow, saying sorry over the phone stuck in a man's craw. So yesterday he'd foundered about in one of those ladies' shops and had come out with a scrap of emerald silk he hoped would make apology a lot sweeter for both of them.

And for afterward—once he'd convinced Lizbeth to forgive his horrible stupidity—a ring with a pink diamond. He patted his jacket pocket to make sure the black velvet box was still there. That was when Gil noticed a stranger in his corral. A big dark-haired man. "Who's that with Shady Lady?"

Gil braked beside Ginger's car and craned his neck to see over Dustin's head. It brought stabbing memories of the first time he'd laid eyes on Lizbeth Robbins.

Dusty stared out the side window. "I dunno."

Gil climbed out and put the same question to his second son, who'd just raced from the house to fling his arms around Gil's middle.

"That's Mr. Burnaby. Gosh, Dad, I'm glad you're home." Wriggling out of Gil's hug, Rusty dashed around the car and yanked the door open for his twin. Suddenly he seemed shy with his brother, or possibly ill at ease with Dusty's bandages.

Gil circled the hood more slowly. "Lex Burnaby? The farrier?"

"Yep." Rusty grabbed Dustin's duffle. "How long 'fore you can go ridin'? Buddy's been askin'," he informed his twin.

"So you did miss me, nerd." Dusty peered behind his brother. "Hey, where's your shadow?" Cradling his injured arm, Dustin awkwardly disembarked. "Melody, birdbrain," he elaborated when Rusty's brow furrowed.

"Russell," Gil interrupted, clamping a hand on his son's bony shoulder. "Why is Burnaby shoeing Shady Lady? Where's Lizbeth?"

"Gone." A tear sneaked out from beneath a dark eyelash. "Her and Melody. They left last week. But who cares? It's *her* fault Dusty fell in that dumb well. 'Sides, she's nothin' but a big ol' thief."

"Gone? Thief? Rusty, where in thunder do you come up with such farfetched notions? Stop it and tell me what's going on."

"I am. Mom told Mrs. Morley that Dusty wouldn't a fell in that hole if Lizbeth had been watchin' us like she shoulda been. That was right before she called the cops 'cause Melody's mom left and took your grandpa's lucky spur with her."

"Ginger called the cops?"

"It wasn't a cop, 'xactly. A detective, I think."

Gil didn't like the picture he was getting. Nor did he like the pool of acid beginning to slosh in his stomach.

Dustin fiddled with his sling, then squinted at his dad. "Mom called me the other day when you were out—to ask if I had your lucky spur. She 'splained that it's diamonds'n stuff. I guess you're pissed 'cause Mrs. Robbins stole it, huh, Dad?"

"Dustin Lawrence Spencer! Bandaged or not, you're cruising for a mouthwash. And just for the record, I *gave* that key chain to Lizbeth. For luck—when she crawled in the tunnel to haul you out. Boys, do you have any idea what a brave thing she did? Dustin owes his life to Lizbeth!"

Each boy mumbled something unintelligible. Dustin finally admitted he'd been pretty glad to see her. "I thought 'bout all the mean stuff I'd done. I said I was sorry."

Gil gazed at the house a long time, his hands splayed on his hips. "You fellows will have to trust me on this, but your mother is about to pack up and leave us again. Then we three are going to sit down and have a long-overdue talk about honesty, integrity and love. Stick close to your rooms, okay?"

"Gol-ly," said Rusty as his dad strode away. "All this comin' and goin' around here is makin' me dizzy."

"Yeah," his brother muttered, "'cept Dad's right. What Mrs. Robbins did *was* pretty cool. I'm tellin' you, Russ, I was scared shitless."

"No kiddin'? You ain't never scared."

"Well, I was. I hope she comes back. Things'll be different. I won't be mean to her no more. I swear on a stack of Bibles."

"Then I don't 'spect Dad'll mind you said 'shitless.' I think he likes Mrs. Robbins a lot."

"Let's you'n me go watch the fireworks 'tween him and Mom."

"Sure. I hope Dad sends that mean ol' Mrs. Morley with her."

"So, you ain't gonna miss our mom?"

"Naw. She's not much like a real mom. She's kinda mean. And she's always yellin' at me to go away. 'Sides, I think she likes horses more'n she likes me. Or Dad."

"Boy, Russ. Bein' an adult sucks."

"Yeah. So does bein' a kid. I wish we knew how to get Mel and her mom back."

"Let's ask Buddy Hodges. He knows everything 'bout women."

GIL STALKED UP the front steps, his tread deliberately measured as he passed the housekeeper. Backing up, he said, "Mrs. Morley, you're fired. I'll draw your check when I finish speaking with Ms. Lawrence." Ignoring the woman's indignant sputter, he entered the living room, where Ginger lounged on the couch.

"I'd like a word with you—in my office." Gil waited as she took her sweet time. He pointedly shut the door. "It's time for you to pack and leave," he said calmly. "And where in hell is Lizbeth?" he asked, his tone a shade more demanding.

Ginger's face contorted as she stamped a booted foot. Almost before Gil saw what was coming, she snatched up a genuine Frederic Remington bronze sculpture and heaved it at him. He ducked in time, although it gouged a hole in the wall. She proceeded to spew unkind names in a shrill voice and wound down threatening murder, kidnapping and all manner of lawsuits.

Gil dodged a clay ashtray made by one of the boys. He drew the line when she grabbed a watercolor of Night Fire the Littlefields had given him last Christmas. "What did you think?" he shouted. "That I'd take you back, and everything would be hunky-dory? Anything we felt for each other died years ago, and you damn well know it. Suppose you cut to the chase and tell me why you're putting on this act?"

"I want my babies, Gil. A mother has a right to see her kids."

"Then buy a house where they'll have decent beds. We'll work out visitations for vacations and holidays. They deserve a home, Ginger, not living like nomads."

"Sure. Buy a house, just like that?" She snapped her fingers. "You cheated me in the divorce settlement, Gil. I know now what the Lone Spur's really worth, so don't try and lie to me again."

"Is this about money, Ginger, or the boys?"

"It's about you giving me a fair share."

He sat down and wrote her a check for fifty thousand dollars. "The ranch was on the rocks when you left me with two babies to raise. I busted my butt to build the place up. Use this as a down payment on a reasonably priced home. Then show me you mean to make a go of it, and I'll even pay off the rest of your mortgage. Take it or leave it," he said coldly. "It's more than you deserve, and we both know it."

He watched as she folded the check and stuck it in her shirt pocket with a smirk.

"You have a filly and a colt I want, too." She described Lizbeth's weanlings to a tee. "You're worth a fortune now, Gil. I can and will cause trouble in court. How do you think the judge would feel about the week-end trip you took with your little farrier? Pete Markham mentioned he'd seen the two of you when I picked up his mare the other day."

Gil felt a kick to his midsection, but he didn't blink. "The horses you want aren't mine to give. I'm sure you know damn well I've already given them to Lizbeth. Pick two others. Night Fire's issue all have papers."

Ginger whined, threatened and cajoled. Gil sat dispassionately through her tirade. Money and horses—they were always the answer with Ginger. Her daddy had done a good job of teaching her to think the world owed her a living. Too bad he went belly-up in one too many real-estate scams and landed in jail.

It galled Gil to dicker, but perhaps that was a small price to be rid of her deceitful meddling. "That black colt you think you want will never be put to stud. He's the son of a rogue stallion. Technically he's not worth zip."

"Okay," she said, pouting. "I'll take two of Night Fire's foals. I also want the gold-and-diamond spur when you get it back. You know I've always hankered after it."

"No. Absolutely not. Out of the question."

When she saw he didn't intend to budge, Ginger said she'd go pack her things and meet him in the barn. "I'll be needing a horse trailer, as well."

Gil escorted her to the door. "I'll tell Rafe to *lend* you a trailer. And now there's something I want. Tell me exactly what you said to drive Lizbeth away."

She smirked again, spun away and ran up the stairs.

He went back to his office, deciding to call off the damned detective she'd hired. The thought of Ginger's taking ranch matters into her own hands made his blood boil. The minute he'd shown Rafe which horses to give Ginger, he'd go out and beat the bushes looking for Lizbeth himself. Her friend—that rodeo clown, Hoot something—maybe he'd know where to find her. Convinced it would be a simple matter of explaining to Lizbeth what had gone on in his absence, Gil set about straightening the office. Truth be known, he'd rather have Ginger off the ranch before he did anything about finding Lizbeth.

Gil left his office, check in hand for Mrs. Morley, in time to see his ex depart via the front door, carrying a load of expensive luggage. In Ginger's haste, she nearly bowled over a tall slightly stoop-shouldered older man. A stranger, Gil saw before the door slammed. A horse buyer? He waited a moment, although he wasn't feeling very sociable. He heard the murmur of voices, but as the bell didn't ring he decided it was someone Ginger knew. Shrugging, he went to deal with the Morley woman.

"Excuse me, miss." The man on the porch doffed his hat and backed away from the woman with the flame-colored hair. "I'm looking for Gilman Spencer. Could you tell me where I might find him?"

Ginger brushed past him, then stopped. "Why do you want Gilman?"

"It's personal business concerning my daughter," he said politely. "Lizbeth Robbins," he added as the silence stretched.

Ginger cast a quick glance at the tightly closed door. "I'm *Mrs.* Spencer," she said, lowering her voice. "Gilman's wife. Exactly where is Lizbeth? She stole a valuable piece of jewelry from my husband before she left the Lone Spur."

"Stole? A piece of jewelry, you say?"

"A gold spur on a key chain. The spur's inside a horseshoe and studded with diamonds. It's an heirloom, crafted from a solid gold nugget. It has a great deal of sentimental value to the family. We've contacted the authorities. I'm afraid Gilman's quite upset with your daughter. You may want to postpone your visit, Mr....?"

"I...I believe you may be right, Mrs. Spencer. Now is probably not a good time to talk with your husband. I'll drop by some other day."

Ginger watched him hurry down the steps and climb into a waiting car. Just before he shut his door, she called, "Do tell Lizbeth what a pickle she's in, won't you?"

LIZBETH STARED out the kitchen window at the lane leading to the paddocks. Coffee cooled in her cup. She should be helping her mother pack for their upcoming move as Melody was doing, but she lacked the energy for it. She lacked the energy for everything. The barns and fences needed a coat of paint before the old place was turned over to a new owner. The farm, which had always been so pristine, looked shabby. Was this her fault, too? Had her parents spent so much money trying to locate her that they'd neglected the farm's upkeep? And where was her dad? Away on business, her mother said. Lizbeth couldn't ever remember him being gone for more than a day when she was younger. Counting today, he'd been absent three full days.

Her folks had begged Liz and Melody to move with them to the condo they'd leased in town. Did her father's sudden trip concern money? If not, why weren't they buying a place?

Lizbeth felt like she was being sucked down a rabbit hole. If only she could stop thinking about Gil and how much she missed him. How much she missed everything back at the Lone Spur. She pulled out his key chain and cradled it in her palm. Mailing it back would sever her last tie to Gilman Spencer. Perhaps then she'd get out of this uncharacteristic depression.

Toliver Whitley found her in exactly that same spot an hour later, still clutching the gold piece. "What's that you have, Lizbeth?" he queried sharply, letting his garment bag slap against the fridge.

Liz jerked and dropped the spur. "I, uh, nothing," she said as she scooped it up and rose to kiss his cheek. "Something I need to wrap and mail."

"No! Don't do that. Throw it away."

"Father? I know you never approved of wasting money on jewelry. But—"

"Listen to me." He pulled out a chair, tossed his bag over the table and sat across from her. "I know you longed for pretty things growing up. Your mother and I...well, we were brought up strict and we thought it was the right way to raise our only daughter. I never meant to drive you away."

She nodded and patted his hand. "I know that now."

"Well know this. Whatever it takes, your mother and I will defend you against any charges of having stolen that bauble."

Liz jumped up. "What are you talking about? I've never stolen anything in my life."

Sighing, the elder Whitley loosened his tie. "Lizbeth. I...I know you took the key chain from Gilman Spencer. The authorities know, too."

"This? I didn't steal it. Gil gave it to me. For luck, when I went into the tunnel after Dusty. Dad, why would you think I took it, for heaven's sake?"

Pouring a cup of coffee, he sat and let the story flow, beginning with how Melody wanted with all her heart to go back to the Lone Spur—and how she'd begged for his help. How he'd taken it upon himself to visit the Lone Spur.

The longer Liz listened, the angrier she got. Her temper had quite a head on it by the time he finished. "Let me get this straight. You decided I'm moping around because I didn't want to leave Gil. You went to the ranch to smooth things out, met Ginger, and she filled your ear with some preposterous lie. And as a result, you've concluded I had an affair with a married man—and that I walked off with the Spencer family jewels?" She inhaled deeply and waved her arms in a wild gesture. "Well, thanks a lot, Pop."

Mrs. Whitley poked her head into the kitchen to see what all the yelling was about. Her husband reached out and clasped Liz's hand. "Put like that, it sounds silly. Obviously I've been duped."

"Obviously. And me, too. The worm. The snake. For your information, he's not married to that viper. They're divorced. Now I see they're two of a kind. How could I have fallen in love with such a louse? Set the law on me, will he?" Jumping up, she began to pace. "I'll give this back all right. I'll take it to the Lone Spur and stuff it down Gilman Spencer's throat, chain and all. Will you watch Melody for me?"

Her mother looked bewildered. "Toliver. Would someone please tell me what's going on? Oh, Melody, dear." The older woman glanced up in time to see the child fly through the door and into her mother's arms. Melody began to wail.

With all the crying, it was a wonder Mrs. Whitley heard the doorbell. But she did, and made her way through the boxes she'd started to pack. She opened it at last to reveal a lean auburn-haired stranger and two freckle-faced boys, who looked like matched pearls on a string.

"Mrs. Whitley?"

"Yes." Her gaze traveled up a long way, to the man's gold-flecked eyes.

"My name is Gilman Spencer. These are my sons, Russell and Dustin. We're looking for Lizbeth Robbins, ma'am."

"And Melody," one of the boys piped up.

Lizbeth's mother smiled when the second boy gouged the first one with his unbandaged elbow. "They'd be together, bat-brain. Melody ain't goin' nowhere without her mom, you know."

"Boys." Gil tapped them each with his Stetson and offered the woman an apologetic smile. "I'm sorry to bust in on you like this, but I'm desperate to find Lizbeth. Hoot Bell hasn't seen them. She gave me your address once. I...well, this is my last hope. After that, I'm hiring a detective."

Toliver Whitley left the kitchen in time to hear the conversation at the door. "Hire a hundred detectives, young fella. You've wasted a trip. She's not here."

His wife looked agog at her husband as he tried to rudely slam the door.

Disappointed beyond belief, Gil blocked its closing with a palm. "I know things are strained between you and Lizbeth, sir. When I find her—once I do and we get married—all that will change. Our door at the Lone Spur will always be open to Lizbeth's family." Resettling his hat, Gil turned his sons away.

"Wait!" Lizbeth's father opened the screen. "Married? You intend to marry Lizbeth?"

"Yes. I do. We do. Isn't that right, boys?" Gil ruffled both boys' hair. Hair that needed cutting.

"Yep," they said simultaneously. "We want her back."

Mr. Whitley opened the screen wider. Before he could actually invite them in, Melody dashed headlong into the room. She skidded to a stop beside her grandmother. "Hot diggity dog! Rusty and Dusty!" she yelped. "You did it, grandfather! You did it."

The boys rushed to greet her. "We came to get you and your mom," Rusty said. "Dad borrowed Mr. Littlefield's airplane. Flying is cool. You'll see."

Melody slipped her hand into her grandfather's wrinkled one. "Can my grandmother and grandfather come, too? She cooks good. I bet they'd watch us after school. Her and Grandfather need someplace to live."

"Now wait a minute, young lady," Toliver Whitley said with a laugh. "Somehow I don't think Mr. Spencer came to woo an extended family. Call your mother, why don't you? Is she still in the kitchen?"

"What's woo, Dad?" Rusty screwed up his face. "Chinese food?" he asked hopefully.

Gil laughed. "You see?" he said to Lizbeth's father. "This is just part of what Lizbeth and I have had to contend with."

Liz came through the door, saw Gil and stopped dead. "You...you jerk. I can't believe you claimed I stole this." She dug the key ring out of her pocket and smacked it into his hand. "It must be valuable if you came all the way to Kentucky to get it." Her eyes glittered with anger.

So did Gil's. "I don't give a damn about that, Lizbeth. I came to Kentucky to give you this—and ask you to be my wife." He hooked the golden spur over his thumb, dug into his jeans watch pocket and removed the ring with the rare pink diamond. When he held it out, Gil enjoyed watching Lizbeth's eyes widen.

"It's the ring I saw in that jewelry store in Fort Worth. But how did you know I liked it? I never said a word."

He took her left hand and slipped the ring on her third finger. "I'm not sure you want me to say how I knew in front of an audience."

Liz blinked up from the sparkling gem. Her family and his had mysteriously disappeared. "What audience? I think my parents took the kids into the kitchen to bribe them with apple pie."

"Well, in that case..." Gil stepped close and took her into his arms. "I thought you looked at that ring the same way you looked at me the night before, when we made love. I wanted to give you everything I had then— and I still do."

Flustered by the vivid memory, Liz stammered, "But...but what about Dustin? He hates me, Gil. I know he does."

"I don't, neither. I swear." The earnest voice emerged from the shadows.

"He means it," a second excited child promised. "An' he won't pull no more mean tricks on you. 'Cause he said, and we believe him." Rusty and Melody dragged Dustin into the center of the room. All three had apple-pie-filling spread from ear to ear. Dustin tried hard to look humble, but he didn't have the face for it. He happened to be blessed with red hair, freckles and a devilish gap-toothed smile.

"Grandmother and Grandfather said they'd keep us while you go on vacation," Melody announced, hurrying up to Gil.

Dusty jabbed her with his good elbow. "Not vacation, Jell-O-brain. Honeymoon. That's what people do when they get married. Buddy Hodges said they rent a room at some fancy hotel and—"

"That's quite enough, Dustin," Gil broke in. "Lizbeth and I will take pictures of Acapulco so you can show Buddy exactly what the hotel and the beach look like. And stop calling Melody names. She's going to be your sister."

Liz covered her mouth to keep from laughing. "Wait a minute, guys," she said. "Haven't you put the cart before the horse?"

The room got so quiet the occupants could have heard an ash fall. Gil and the twins gazed at Lizbeth. A triple hit of curiosity from matched hazel eyes. Melody's were darker, but also full of questions. Even her parents hovered in the kitchen doorway, exchanging puzzled glances.

"Honeymoons follow weddings, which normally come after acceptance of a proposal—usually preceded by a declaration of love." Liz crossed her arms. "It's a big leap from how I left things at the Lone Spur. A very big leap."

The twins and Gil all began talking at once. Suddenly a piercing whistle rent the air. Everyone in the room turned and gaped at Lizbeth's sweet delicate-looking mother. "Seconds on pie, anyone?" Her suggestion was as innocent as her smile. But that was all it took to clear the room. The kitchen door swung gently closed on Toliver Whitley's heels.

Lizbeth led Gil to the chintz-covered couch. "Suppose you start by telling me why you hired Lex Burnaby to replace me as Lone Spur's farrier."

"Suppose I start by telling you how much I love you, Lizbeth Robbins." And that was exactly what Gil did, which greatly impeded the progress of telling Liz about Ginger's mischief.

They traded stories throughout the afternoon. By evening their tales were interspersed with lengthy kisses. Nightfall brought a resolution. Gil's announcement of their forthcoming marriage sent up a cheer from the pie-logged family members waiting in the wings.

Late that night, when the house was dark and silent, Gil tiptoed into Lizbeth's room. "I'm not big on words," he murmured against her lips, "but I want you to have this as a token of my love forever." He carefully parted the ties of her white cotton nightie and fastened the golden spur around her neck on a slender chain her mother had lent him.

"I love you, Gil. And I'll cherish this forever, because one way or another it would have brought us together."

"Oh? How so?"

An impish smile played at the corners of her mouth. "I was about to march it right back to your ranch and cause more trouble than the Lone Spur's ever seen."

Gil kissed her slowly and thoroughly. "Sweetheart, this kind of trouble I can handle."

EPILOGUE

LIZBETH MADE a beautiful June bride. Nan Littlefield was her only attendant. Unlike her first wedding, this time Toliver Whitley proudly walked her down the aisle. Melody looked sweet and demure as she dropped rose petals from her flower-girl's basket. The only hitch in the wedding came when the twins, who were charged with carrying the pillow bearing matching wedding bands, didn't want to share the duty. Somehow in jerking the pillow back and forth, their dad's ring came undone and flew into the audience.

But what's a best man for, if not to come to the rescue? Morris Littlefield got down on the knees of his new Western suit and crawled between the church pews until he found the ring.

Gil laughed and gave him a big hand for his performance. The chaos seemed so normal that Liz, who'd been extremely nervous, relaxed and enjoyed their most special day.

Acapulco in June exceeded the beauty promised in travel brochures. Walking down the beach holding hands, Gil finally gave up nibbling Lizbeth's ear. "That's your third roll of film," he reminded her around a groan. "Doesn't one sunset look like another?"

"At the reception, didn't you see Buddy Hodges deep in conversation with our kids? I'm going to make that boy a honeymoon scrapbook so he'll quit spreading lies about what men and women do when they fall in love."

"I hope there'll be gaps in this exposé, my love." Chuckling, Gil led Liz back to their room, where he soon divested her of the bikini swimsuit that had been one of Nan's gifts to the bride. Afterward, when they lay naked and entwined in each other's arms, he reminded her that this would be one very large gap in Buddy's album.

Two glorious weeks later Buddy's scrapbook made a big splash all over town.

NINE MONTHS from the day of their wedding, Liz gave birth to twins, a boy and a girl. It blew their image, and the small town buzzed with speculation as to how Mr. and Mrs. Gilman Spencer had *really* spent their honeymoon.

Rafe, Luke and Yancy paid a visit to Liz in the hospital. They brought pink and blue gifts for the babies and stayed to lament the loss of the best darned farrier in the state of Texas.

Ben Jones hobbled in, aided by a cane. "Good thing your folks moved into the cottage," he told Liz. "Tell 'em to get skateboards. Twins keep a body hoppin'."

Dusty, Rusty and Melody had a lively argument over names. Surprisingly Dustin insisted his sister be named Rachel. "Like this girl I know at school," he said shyly. Eventually the three kids settled on Wade as a name for their brother. The book of names Lizbeth had bought suggested someone named Wade was a "cool dude." Oddly enough Wade happened to be the name of Gil's grandfather, so it stuck.

During the first lull in visitors, Gil presented Lizbeth with earrings to match her gold-and-diamond spur necklace. "It's hard to believe, but the first time I laid eyes on you, I said to myself that you spelled trouble for the Lone Spur. I was right. Another set of twins." He grinned.

"Trouble? Me?" First Liz looked annoyed, then she threw back her head and chortled. "I thought you were a hardheaded perfectionist who didn't give second chances." Leaning forward, she kissed him lingeringly on the lips. "This is one time I'm supremely glad to have been proved wrong."

"Could somebody get that on tape?" Gil murmured as he gathered her close to deepen the kiss.

"Ick. Suck face," the three children popped up and shouted in unison. Rolling his eyes, Dustin herded his siblings from the room. "According to Buddy Hodges..."

Gil and Lizbeth ended the kiss and broke up laughing. "I know what the real trouble is at Lone Spur," Liz confided with a wink. "It's Buddy Hodges. What do you suppose that kid'll be if the neighbors ever let him grow up?"

"A marriage counselor," Gil muttered. "Or a doctor. Come to think of it, I may finance his education myself. At least buy him a good anatomy book. It just might save us going gray before our time, Mrs. Spencer."

Weddings by DeWilde

Since the turn of the century the elegant and fashionable
DeWilde stores have helped brides around the world
turn the fantasy of their "Special Day" into reality. But now the
store and three generations of family are torn apart by the
separation of Grace and Jeffrey DeWilde. Family members
face new challenges and loves in this fast-paced, glamorous,
internationally set series. For weddings and romance, glamour
and fun-filled entertainment, enter the world of DeWilde...

Watch for *FAMILY SECRETS,*
by Margaret St. George
Coming to you in December 1996

In an attempt to shed the past and get on with her future,
Grace DeWilde has left her new store and her new life in
San Francisco to return to England. Her trip results in a
devastating discovery about the DeWilde family that has
shocking implications for her children, for Ian Stanley,
whose unrequited love for Grace has been years in the
making, and for Jeffrey DeWilde, the estranged
husband Grace can never stop loving.

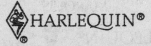

HARLEQUIN®

The collection of the year!
NEW YORK TIMES BESTSELLING AUTHORS

Linda Lael Miller
Wild About Harry

Janet Dailey
Sweet Promise

Elizabeth Lowell
Reckless Love

Penny Jordan
Love's Choices

and featuring
Nora Roberts
The Calhoun Women

This special trade-size edition features four of the wildly
popular titles in the Calhoun miniseries together in
one volume—a true collector's item!

Pick up these great authors and a chance to win
a weekend for two in New York City at the
Marriott Marquis Hotel on Broadway! We'll pay
for your flight, your hotel—even a Broadway show!

Available in December at your favorite retail outlet.

Now's your chance to get the complete

series!

Order any or all 12 of these great titles:

#30116-2	A Practical Marriage by Dallas Schulze	$3.99 U.S./$4.50 CAN. ☐
#30136-7	Marry Sunshine by Anne McAllister	$3.99 U.S./$4.50 CAN. ☐
#30110-3	The Cowboy and the Chauffeur by Elizabeth August	$3.99 U.S./$4.50 CAN. ☐
#30115-4	McConnell's Bride by Naomi Horton	$3.99 U.S./$4.50 CAN. ☐
#30127-8	Married?! by Annette Broadrick	$3.99 U.S./$4.50 CAN. ☐
#30103-0	Designs on Love by Gina Wilkins	$3.99 U.S./$4.50 CAN. ☐
#30126-X	It Happened One Night by Marie Ferrarella	$3.99 U.S./$4.50 CAN. ☐
#30101-4	Lazarus Rising by Anne Stuart	$3.99 U.S./$4.50 CAN. ☐
#30107-3	The Bridal Price by Barbara Boswell	$3.99 U.S./$4.50 CAN. ☐
#30131-6	Annie in the Morning by Curtiss Ann Matlock	$3.99 U.S./$4.50 CAN. ☐
#30112-X	September Morning by Diana Palmer	$3.99 U.S./$4.50 CAN. ☐
#30129-4	Outback Nights by Emilie Richards	$3.99 U.S./$4.50 CAN. ☐

ADDED BONUS! In every edition of *Here Come the Grooms*
you'll find $5.00 worth of coupons good for Harlequin and
Silhouette products.

AMOUNT	$
POSTAGE & HANDLING	$
($1.00 for one book, 50¢ for each additional)	
APPLICABLE TAXES*	$_____
TOTAL PAYABLE	$_____
(check or money order—please do not send cash)	

To order, complete this form and send it, along with a check or money order for the
total above, payable to Harlequin Books, to: **In the U.S.:** 3010 Walden Avenue,
P.O. Box 9047, Buffalo, NY 14269-9047; **In Canada:** P.O. Box 613, Fort Erie, Ontario,
L2A 5X3.

Name: _____

Address: _____ City: _____

State/Prov.: _____ Zip/Postal Code: _____

*New York residents remit applicable sales taxes.
 Canadian residents remit applicable GST and provincial taxes.   HCTG1196

Look us up on-line at: http://www.romance.net

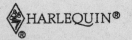

HARLEQUIN®

Scandals

A passionate story of romance, where bold, daring characters set out to defy their world of propriety and strict social codes.

"Scandals—a story that will make your heart race and your pulse pound. Spectacular!"
—Suzanne Forster

"Devon is daring, dangerous and altogether delicious."
—Amanda Quick

Don't miss this wonderful full-length novel from Regency favorite Georgina Devon.

Available in December, wherever Harlequin books are sold.

SCAN

1997
Reader's Engagement Book
A calendar of important dates
and anniversaries for readers to use!

Informative and entertaining—with notable
dates and trivia highlighted throughout the year.

Handy, convenient, pocketbook size to help you
keep track of your own personal important dates.

Added bonus—contains $5.00 worth of coupons
for upcoming Harlequin and Silhouette books.
This calendar more than pays for itself!

 Available beginning in November at
your favorite retail outlet.

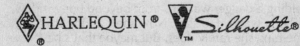